THE

Provence Cure

FOR THE

Brokenhearted

"*The Provence Cure for the Brokenhearted* held me spellbound from the first word to the last, when I put it aside with a sigh of both regret and deepest satisfaction....I madly, madly, madly loved this book!" —BARBARA O'NEAL, author of *How to Bake a Perfect Life*

"Unabashedly romantic...a real charmer about a Provençal house that casts spells over the lovelorn." —*Kirkus Reviews*

"*The Provence Cure for the Brokenhearted* will have you canceling dinner plans, staying up all hours and flat-out ignoring your family, just so you can keep reading. Asher's unflinching portrait of a grieving young widow is tempered by a powerful dose of humor and an unforgettable cast of characters. The result is **an absorbing, beautifully written tale about life, death, love, food, and the magic of new possibilities.**" —J. COURTNEY SULLIVAN, author of *Commencement* and *Maine*

"Love and its sweet secrets bloom gloriously in *The Provence Cure for the Brokenhearted*....A **sumptuous exploration of how grief, love, and joy, when stirred just right, ferry us home to the people and places we most cherish. Asher's novel brims with wisdom and laughter, teaching us anew that hope resides in unexpected places:** a charred box of beloved recipes, a troubled child's earthy wisdom, an ailing house in need of an artful hand, a mother who listens to a silent mountain, and a kiss that unlocks the puzzle of what forever truly means." —CONNIE MAY FOWLER, author of *How Clarissa Burden Learned to Fly* and *Before Women Had Wings*

"I enjoyed *The Provence Cure for the Brokenhearted* so much—it's well written, beautifully characterized, extremely atmospheric, and at times very touching—**an enchanting and compelling tale.**" —ISABEL WOLFF, author of *A Vintage Affair*

ALSO BY BRIDGET ASHER

My Husband's Sweethearts

The Pretend Wife

THE

Provence Cure

FOR THE

Brokenhearted

A NOVEL

BRIDGET ASHER

 BANTAM BOOKS TRADE PAPERBACKS   NEW YORK

A Bantam Books Trade Paperback Original

Published in the United States by Bantam Books,
an imprint of The Random House Publishing Group,
a division of Random House, Inc., New York.

BANTAM BOOKS and the rooster colophon are registered
trademarks of Random House, Inc.
RANDOM HOUSE READER'S CIRCLE and colophon is a
trademark of Random House, Inc.

ISBN 978-0-385-34391-6

Printed in the United States of America

www.randomhousereaderscircle.com

4 6 8 9 7 5 3

Book design by Carol Malcolm Russo

This novel is dedicated to the reader.

For this singular moment, it's just the two of us.

Here is one way to say it: Grief is a love story told backward.

Or maybe that's not it at all. Maybe I should be more scientific. Love and the loss of that love exist in equal measure. Hasn't an equation like this been invented by a romantic physicist somewhere?

Or maybe I should put it this way: Imagine a snow globe. Imagine a tiny snow-struck house inside of it. Imagine there's a woman inside of that tiny house sitting on the edge of her bed, shaking a snow globe, and within *that* snow globe, there is a tiny snow-struck house with a woman inside of it, and this one is standing in the kitchen, shaking another snow globe, and within *that* snow globe . . .

Every good love story has another love hiding within it.

Part One

Part One

E ver since Henry's death, I'd been losing things.

  I lost keys, sunglasses, checkbooks. I lost a spatula and found it in the freezer, along with a bag of grated cheese.

  I lost a note to Abbot's third-grade teacher explaining how I'd lost his homework.

  I lost the caps to toothpaste and jelly jars. I put these things away open-mouthed, lidless, airing. I lost hairbrushes and shoes—not just one of a pair, but both.

  I left jackets behind in restaurants, my pocketbook under my seat at the movies, my keys on the checkout counter of the drugstore—afterward, I sat in my car for a moment, disoriented, trying to place exactly what was wrong and then trudged back into the store, where the checkout girl jingled them for me above her head.

I got calls from people who were kind enough to return things. And when things were gone—just *gone*—I retraced my steps and then got lost myself. Why am I here at this mini mart? Why am I back at the deli counter?

I lost track of friends. They had babies, defended dissertations, had art showings and dinner parties and backyard barbecues . . .

Most of all, I lost track of large swaths of time. Kids at Abbot's bus stop and in the neighborhood and in his class and on his Little League team kept inching taller all around me. Abbot kept growing, too. That was the hardest to take.

I also lost track of small pieces of time—late mornings, evenings. Sometimes I would look up and it was suddenly dark outside, as if someone had flipped a switch. The fact of the matter was, life charged on without me. This realization still caught me off guard even two years later, although by this point it had become a habit, a simple unavoidable fact: The world charged on and I did not.

So it shouldn't have come as a surprise to me that Abbot and I were running late for the bridesmaid bonding on the morning of my sister's wedding. We had spent the morning playing Apples to Apples, interrupted by phone calls from the Cake Shop.

"Jude . . . Jude, slow down. Five *hundred* lemon tarts?" I stood up from the couch where Abbot was eating his third freezer pop of the morning—the kind that come in vivid colors packaged in plastic tubes that you have to snip with scissors and that sometimes make you cough. Even this detail is pained: Abbot and I had been reduced to eating frozen juice in plastic. "No, no, I'm sure," I continued. "I would have written down the order. At least . . . Shit. This is probably my fault. Do you want me to come in?"

Henry hadn't only been my husband; he'd also been my business partner. I'd grown up making delicate pastries, thinking of food as a kind of art, but Henry had convinced me that food is love. We'd met during culinary school, and shortly after Abbot was born we'd embarked on another labor of love: the Cake Shop.

Jude had been with us from the start. She was a single mom—petite, mouthy, with short bleached-out hair and a heart-shaped face—that strange combination of beauty and toughness. She was our first hire and had a natural flair, a great sense of design, and marketing savvy. After Henry's death, she'd stepped up. Henry had been the one to handle the business side of things, and I'd have lost the shop, I'm quite sure, if it weren't for Jude. Jude became the guiding force, my rudder. She kept things going.

I was about to tell Jude that I'd be at the shop in half an hour when Abbot reached up and tugged on my sleeve. He pointed at the watch he wore, its face in the shape of a baseball. Perhaps as a result of my spaciness, Abbot insisted on keeping his own time.

When I realized that it was now after noon, I shouted, "The wedding! I'm so sorry! I've got to go!" then hung up the phone.

Abbot, wide-eyed, said, "Auntie Elysius is going to be so

mad!" He leaned over to scratch a mosquito bite on his ankle. He was wearing his short white sports socks and his ankle looked like it had a golfer's tan, but really it was dirt.

"Not if we hurry!" I said. "And grab some calamine lotion so you don't itch during the ceremony."

We darted around our little three-bedroom bungalow madly. I found one of my heels in the closet and the other in Abbot's bedroom in a big tub of Legos. Abbot was wrestling on his rented tux. He struggled with the tiny cuff buttons, searching for the clip-on tie and cummerbund—he'd chosen red because it was the color that Henry had worn at our wedding. I wasn't sure that was healthy, but didn't want to draw attention to it.

I threw on makeup and slipped the bridesmaid's dress over my head, grateful that the dress wasn't your typical bridesmaid's horror show—my sister had exquisite taste, and this was the most expensive dress I'd ever worn, including my own wedding dress.

When I'd declined the role of Elysius's matron of honor—or was it, to be grimly accurate, *widow* of honor?—my sister had been visibly relieved. She knew that I'd only gum up the works. In a heartbeat, she'd called an old college friend with a marketing degree, and I was happily demoted to bridesmaid. Abbot had been enlisted as the ring bearer, and to be honest, I didn't even feel like I was up for the role of mother-of-the-ring-bearer. I'd made a last-minute excuse to get out of the rehearsal dinner the night before and that day's spa treatment and group hair appointment. When your husband has died, you're allowed to just say, "I can't make it. I'm so sorry." If your husband died in a car accident, like mine, you're allowed to say, "I just can't drive today." You can simply shake your head and whisper, "Sorry." And people excuse you, immediately, as if this is the least they can do for you. And perhaps it is.

This was wearing on my sister, however. She'd made me promise that I would be at her house two hours before the wedding. There was a strict agenda that we had to stick to, and it included drinking mimosas with all of the bridesmaids while each gave an intimate little toast. Elysius likes it when the world finds her as its proper axis. I couldn't judge her for that; I was painfully aware of how selfish my grief was. My eight-year-old son had lost his father. Henry's parents had lost their son. And Henry lost his life. What right did I have to use Henry's death as an excuse—time and again—to check out?

"Can I bring my snorkel stuff?" Abbot called down the hallway.

"Pack an overnight bag and bring the gear," I said, shoving things into a small suitcase of my own. My sister lived only twenty minutes away—a quick ride from Tallahassee to the countryside in Capps—but she wanted family to spend the night. It was an opportunity to capture my mother's attention and mine and hold it for as long as possible—to relive the strong bond the three of us had once had. "You can snorkel in the morning with Pop-pop."

Abbot ran out of his bedroom, sliding down the hall to my doorway, still wearing his sports socks. He was holding the cummerbund in one hand and the clip-on bow tie in the other. "I can't get these to stick on!" he said. His starched collar was sticking up by his cheeks, like the Halloween he dressed as Count Dracula.

"Don't worry about it. Just bring it all." I was fussing with the clasp of a string of pearls my mother had lent me for the occasion. "There will be ladies there with nervous energy and nothing to do. They'll fix you up."

"Where will you be?" he asked with an edge of anxiety in his voice. Since Henry's death, Abbot had become a worrier. He'd started rubbing his hands together, a new tic—a little frenzy, the charade of a vigorous hand-washing. He'd become a germophobe. We'd seen a therapist, but it hadn't helped. He did this when he was anxious and also when he sensed I was brooding. I tried not to brood in front him, but it turned out that I wasn't good at faking chipper, and my fake chipperness made him more nervous than my brooding—a vicious cycle. Now that his father was gone, did he feel more vulnerable in the world? I did.

"I'll be with the other bridesmaids doing mandatory bridesmaidish things," I reassured him. It was at this moment that I remembered that I was supposed to have my toast prepared. I'd written a toast on a napkin in the kitchen and, of course, had since lost it and now couldn't remember anything I'd written. "What nice things should I say about Auntie Elysius? I have to come up with something for a toast."

"She has very white teeth and buys very good presents," Abbot said.

"Beauty and generosity," I said. "I can work with that. This is going to all be fine. We're going to enjoy ourselves!"

He looked at me, checking to see if I was being honest, the way a lawyer might look at his client to see what he's really in for. I was used to this kind of scrutiny. My mother, my sister, my friends, neighbors, even customers at the Cake Shop, asked me how I was while trying to ferret out the real truth in my answer. I knew I should have been moving forward. I should have been working more, eating better, exercising, dating. Whenever I went out, I had to be prepared for an ambush by some do-good acquaintance ready to dispense pity and uplifting sentiments, questions, and advice. I practiced, "No, really, I'm fine. Abbot and I are doing great!"

I hated, too, that I had to do all of this fending off of pity in front of Abbot. I wanted to be honest with him and to protect him at the same time. And, of course, I wasn't being honest. This was the first wedding I'd been to since Henry's death. I'd always been a crier at weddings, even the ones of people I didn't know well, even TV weddings. I was afraid of myself now. If I could bawl at a commercial of a wedding, how would I react to this one?

I couldn't look at Abbot. If I did, he'd know I was faking it. *We're going to enjoy ourselves?* I was hoping merely to survive.

I moved to the full-length mirror that Henry had attached to the back of my closet door. Henry was everywhere, but when a memory appeared—the mirror had tipped when he was trying to install it and nearly broke in half—I tried not to linger. Lingering was a weakness. I knew to fix my attention on something small and manageable. I was now trying—a last-ditch effort—to put the pearl necklace on with the help of my reflection.

"I like it better when you don't wear makeup," Abbot said.

I let the strand slip and curl in my cupped hand. Could he possibly remember having heard his father make a comment like that? Henry said he loved my face *naked;* sometimes he would whisper, *the way I like the rest of you.* I looked so much older than I had two years ago. The word *grief-stricken* came to mind—as if grief could literally strike you and leave an indelible mark. I turned to Abbot. "Come here," I said. "Let's have a look at you."

I set the pearl necklace on the bedside table, folded down his collar, smoothed his hair, and put my hands on his bony shoulders. I looked at my son—his blue eyes, like his father's, with the dark lashes. He had Henry's tan skin and his ruddy cheeks, too, even though he was just a little boy. I loved his knobby chin and his two oversized adult teeth—so strangely set in his still-small mouth. "You look so handsome," I said. "Like a million bucks."

"Like a million-bucks ring bearer?"

"Exactly," I said.

Abbot and I parked at the end of my sister's winding gravel driveway, maneuvering around a multitude of vans—the caterer's, the florist's, the sound engineer's. The driveway continued past the pool and the clay tennis court and faded to grass between the newly constructed studio and the old barn. Elysius was getting married to a sweet and diffident artist of national reputation named Daniel Welding, and even though they'd been living here together for eight years, I was always struck by the grandeur of the place she called home—and now it was even more breathtaking. The wedding itself was going to be held on the sloping lawn, which Abbot and I now marched up as quickly as we could. It was lined with rows of chairs strung together with sweeping tulle, and the exchange of vows was to take place next to the Japanese-inspired fountain where there was a trellis canopy, woven with flowers. They'd installed a temporary parquet dance floor under a large three-pronged white tent.

Abbot had his stuff in a canvas bag he got for free at the local library. I could see the cummerbund and clip-on bow tie shoved in there, among his snorkel gear—the tubing, the mask, and fins, which were gifts from my father. I was trying to pull my little suitcase on wheels. It bumped along behind me like an old obdurate dog.

We hurried to the studio to drop off our bags, but it was locked. Abbot cupped his hands to the glass and peered in. Daniel worked on massive canvases, and his detached studio had high ceilings, as well as a canvas stand that retracted into the floor. This way, he's not teetering on ladders to get to the upper reaches. There was a sofa in the loft that pulled out into a double bed, where he sometimes took a rest midday and where Abbot and I would sleep that night. Daniel's work sold incredibly well, which is why he could afford the house, the two driveways, the sloping lawn, the retractable canvas stand.

"He's in there!" Abbot said.

"He can't be. It's his wedding day."

Abbot knocked, and Daniel appeared behind the glass door, opened it wide. He was broad-shouldered, always tan, his hair tinged silvery gray. He had a regal nose that sat a little arched and bulky on his face—an elegant face. He took off his glasses, tucked his chin to his chest in a way that made his chins fold up like a little accordion, and looked at me, messy but in a lovely dress, and Abbot, in his not-yet-garnished tux. He smiled broadly. "I'm so glad you're here! How's it hangin', Abbot?" He pulled Abbot to him, gave him a bear hug. That's what Abbot needed, bear hugs, affection, from fatherly types. I was good at pecking foreheads, but I could tell how happy he was to be lifted up off his feet by Daniel. Abbot had a silly grin on his face now. Daniel hugged me, too. He smelled of expensive products—hair gels and imported soaps.

"Are you allowed to be here?" I asked. "You're dressed like a wedding-party escapee."

Abbot slipped around Daniel and stepped into the studio as he always did—with an expression of awe. He loved the narrow stairs to the loft, the espresso machine, the exposed beams, and, of course, he loved the huge canvases in various stages of development propped against walls.

"I had a little idea, so I popped in," Daniel said. "It calms me down to take a look."

"Shouldn't you have shoes on?" Abbot said.

"Ah, yes." He pointed to a pair of shoes just a few feet away. "See, if I get paint on the suit, it's one thing, but the shoes are handmade. A cobbler out in the desert had me stand in powder, barefoot, and from that imprint he made a pair of shoes specifically for my feet." These are the kinds of stories that he and Elysius had—a cobbler in the desert measuring bare feet in powder.

Abbot ran to the shoes, but didn't touch them. I knew that he wanted to, but shoes tromp around on the ground and the ground is littered with germs. He would have had to scrub his hands in the bathroom immediately. The gesture of fake hand-washing wouldn't do. "Where's Charlotte?" Abbot asked, returning to the paintings. Charlotte was Daniel's daughter from his first marriage. Daniel had been through a nasty divorce and custody battle over Charlotte, and he swore he'd never marry again—not because he was jaded, but, more accurately, because he was beleaguered. A few months after Henry's death, though, he had a change of heart. There was a natural correlation, of course—what could make you want to cement love more than the reminder of life's fragility?

"She's up at the house," he said; then he turned to me and added, "trying to fly under the radar."

"How's she doing?" I asked. Charlotte was sixteen and going through a punk phase that alarmed Elysius, though *punk* was outdated. They had new terms for everything now.

"She's studying for the SATs, but, I don't know, she seems a little . . . morose. Well, I worry about her. I'm her father. I worry. You know what I mean." He looked at me like a co-conspirator. He meant that I understood parenting from the inside out, in a way that Elysius didn't. It was something he could never admit except in this sly way.

"What's this one supposed to be?" Abbot asked. All of the paintings were abstract, chaotically so, but Abbot had stalled in front of an especially tumultuous one with big heavy lines, desperate and weighted. It was as if there were a bird trapped somewhere in the painting—a bird that wanted out.

Daniel looked at the painting. "A boat far off with full sails," he said. "And loss."

"You've got to cheer up!" I said to Daniel quietly.

He put a hand on my shoulder. "You're one to talk," he whispered. "Are you designing?" I always felt honored that Daniel saw my work as a pastry chef as art. He wasn't rarefied about art. He believed it belonged to all of us, and he always raved about my work. And, at this moment, he was speaking to me as an artist. "You've got to get back to creating. There's no better way to mourn."

I was surprised he put it so bluntly, but relieved, too. I was tired of sympathy. "I haven't started up again, not yet," I said.

He nodded, solemnly.

"Abbot," I called, "we've got to go."

Disappointed, Abbot walked back to me. He said to Daniel, "Your paintings make people feel sad, but you don't know why."

"A great definition of abstract art," Daniel said.

Abbot smiled and rubbed his hands together; then, as if noticing it himself, he shoved them in his pockets. Daniel took no notice, but I did. Abbot was learning to mask his problem. Was this a step backward or forward?

"I'm late for mimosas," I said.

Daniel was looking at an unfinished canvas. He turned to me. "Heidi." He hesitated. "I've had to postpone the honeymoon for a few days to finish up work for a show. Elysius is in an uproar. When you see her, remind her I'm a nice person."

"I will," I said. "Can we leave these here?" I asked, looking down at my suitcase and Abbot's bag.

"Of course," he said.

"Come on, Abbot," I said, disentangling his tie and cummerbund from the snorkeling gear.

Abbot ran to the door.

"It really is good to see you two," Daniel said.

"You, too," I said. "Happy almost wedding!"

Because Elysius and Daniel had been living here together for eight years, the wedding seemed like a strange afterthought. I considered Elysius and Daniel as not only having a marriage but having an enduring one. For my sister, however, the wedding was monumental, and now, walking past the lush lawn, the back-and-forth tracks of a wide riding mower pushing the grass in stripes, I felt guilty for being so removed.

I should have at least agreed to make her wedding cake. Once upon a time, I'd had a growing reputation as a high-end cake designer. People from all over Florida still call the Cake Shop for events a year or more in advance to reserve a spot. Weddings had been a specialty. But shortly after Henry's death, I'd retreated to making the cupcakes and lemon squares in the early morning hours and working the counter. I'd sworn off brides—they were too overbearing, too wrapped up in the event. They struck me as ingrates, taking love for granted. Now I was embarrassed for not having offered to make Elysius and Daniel's cake. It was my gift, the one small thing I had to give.

I looked up at the bank of windows, the kitchen and the dining room lit with a bright, golden hue, and stopped.

"What is it?" Abbot said.

I wanted to turn back and go home. Was I ready for this? It struck me this was how I felt in life now, like someone stalled on a lawn outside of a giant house who looked into beautiful windows where people were living their lives, filling flower vases, brushing their hair while looking in the mirror, laughing in quick flutters that would rise up and disappear. And here was my own sister's life, brimming.

"Nothing," I said to Abbot. I grabbed his hand and gave it a squeeze. He squeezed back and just like that he took a step ahead of me and pulled me toward the house—full of the living.

At that moment, the back door flung wide, and my mother emerged. Her hair was a honeyed confection swooped up in her signature chignon, and her face was glazed in a way that made her look "dewy and young," which she attributed

to a line of expensive lotions. My mother was aging beautifully. She had a long, elegant neck, full lips, arched eyebrows.
It's a strange thing to be raised by someone much more beautiful than you'll ever be. She had a regal beauty, but, set
against this posture of royalty, her vulnerability seemed more
pronounced—a certain weary softness in her expressions.

Her eyes fell on me and Abbot there on the lawn. "I've
just been sent out to find you!"

My sister sent my mother to find me? This was bad.
Very bad.

"How late are we?" I asked.

"You mean, how angry is your sister?"

"Have I missed the mini toasts?" I asked, hoping I had.

My mother didn't answer. She bustled across the deck
and down the small set of stairs. Her toffee-colored dress
swished around her. It was a sleek design that showed off her
collarbones. My mother is half French, and she believes in
elegance.

"I needed to get out of that house!" she said. "And you
were my excuse. Direct orders to find you and get you moving." She looked agitated, maybe even a little teary. Had she
been crying? My mother is a woman of deep emotion, but
not one to cry easily. She's the definition of the term *active
senior*—she puts on a show of busyness meant to imply satisfaction but has always given me the impression of a woman
about to burst. Once upon a time, she did burst and disappeared for the summer, but then she came back to us. Still,
once a mother's taken off without you—even if she was

right to do so—you spend the rest of your life wondering if she may do it again. She turned her attention to Abbot. "Aren't you a beautiful boy?"

He blushed. My mother had this effect on everyone—the mail carrier harried at the holidays, the pilot who steps out to say bye-bye at the end of a flight, even a snotty maitre d'.

"And you?" she said, brushing my hair back over one shoulder. "Where are the pearls?"

"I still need a few finishing touches," I said. "How is Elysius doing?"

"She'll forgive you," my mother said softly. My mother knew that this might be hard for me—one daughter was gaining a husband, one had lost one—and so she was trying to tread carefully.

"I'm so sorry we're late," I said guiltily. "I lost track of time. Abbot and I were . . ."

"Busy writing the speech for Auntie Elysius," Abbot said. "I was helping!" He looked guilty, too—my coconspirator.

My mother shook her head. Her eyes filled with tears. "I'm such a mess!" she said, trying to smooth the ripples from her dress and then laughing strangely. "I don't know why I'm responding like this!" She pinched her nose as if to stop herself from crying.

"Responding to what?" I asked, surprised by her sudden emotion. "The wedding? Weddings are crazy. They bring up a lot of—"

"It's not the wedding," my mother said. "It's the house. *Our* house . . . in Provence—there's been a fire."

My sister and I went to the house in Provence with my mother when we were children—short summer stints every year that my father, a workaholic, was too busy to join. Then one summer my mother went alone, and we never went back. As my mother started to cry, there on my sister's lawn, she wrapped her arms around me, letting me hold her up for a moment, and I remembered the house the way children remember things, from odd angles, a collection of strange details: that there were no screens on the windows, that the small interior doors had persnickety knobs that seemed to latch and unlatch of their own will, that along the garden paths surrounding the house, I thought there were white blooms clustered on the tall weeds, but when I leaned in close, I could see they were tiny snails, their white shells imprinted with delicate swirls.

The house and everything in it seemed virtually timeless, or maybe it would be more accurate to say that it was time-full—time layered upon time. I remembered the kitchen, which housed the dining room table, long and narrow, surrounded by mismatched chairs—each a survivor from a different era. The small, shallow kitchen sink was made of one solid slab of marble, brown and speckled like an egg. It was original to the house, which had been built in the eighteenth century, just past the edge of a small vineyard. In the yard, there was a fountain erected during the 1920s that fluttered with bright orange, bloated koi and was surrounded by wrought-iron lawn chairs, and a small table covered in a white, wind-kicked tablecloth. The house—fifteen minutes from Aix-en-Provence, nestled in the shadow of the long ridged back of Mont Sainte-Victoire—had belonged to my mother since her parents died, when she was in her mid-twenties.

There, my mother fed us stories about the house itself—love stories, mostly, improbable ones that I'd always wanted to believe but was suspicious of even as a child. But still I clung to them. After she told us the stories at night, I would retell them to myself. I whispered them into my cupped hands, feeling the warmth of my breath, as if I could hold the stories there and keep them.

I could still picture the three of us in one of the upstairs bedrooms, my mother sitting on the edge of one of our beds or moving to the window, where she leaned out into the cool night. Elysius and I would let our hair, damp from a bath, create the impressions of wet halos on our white pillows.

The cicadas were always clamoring, always ratcheting up then fading then ratcheting up again.

"In the beginning," my mother would start, because the first story marked the birth of the house itself, as if the family didn't exist before the house was arranged from stone—and she would tell the story of one of our ancestors, a young man who had asked a woman to marry him. He was in love, and it was a great love. But the woman declined. Her family wouldn't allow it; they didn't think he was worthy. So the young man built the house, stone by stone, all alone, night and day, sleepless for one year. He was fevered by love. He couldn't stop. He gave her the house as a gift—and she fell so deeply in love with the house and the man that she disobeyed her family and married him. He was weak and sick from having built the house in such a frenzy of love, and so she tended to him for their first newlywed year, bringing him back to life with bowls of pistou and bread and wine. They lived to a hundred. The husband died and the wife, heartbroken, followed within a week.

The house was built as an act of love. That's what we were supposed to understand. A portentous story, no? It was a little weighty for two girls to take to heart. But there were more like it.

My great-grandparents owned a small shoe shop in Paris and were incapable of having children. My great-grandmother was called back to the house one winter to care for an old-maid auntie. But they were so in love, he couldn't stand to be apart from her. One night he showed up on the doorstep, and he stayed for a week. Every night they heard the ghostly chatter of cicadas—who shouldn't make any noise in winter. They conceived a child there—and went on to have six more.

And so we were told that the house could make love manifest. It was capable of performing miracles.

Their oldest daughter, my grandmother, was a young woman in Paris during the celebrations at the end of World War II. She was stubborn, brash. She met a young American GI in the crowds around Place de l'Opéra. He kissed her passionately, and then the crowds shifted like tides. They got separated. They searched for each other, but they were both lost in the mad swirl. After the war, he made his way back to France, and through a series of more small miracles, found her in this house, far from where they'd met. And they made a vow never to be apart again.

The house had the power to seal two love-struck souls together forever. We loved the stories, even as we were outgrowing them. We passed the stories between us like two girls playing Cat's Cradle, handing off the intricate patterns from one set of hands to the other and back again. When Elysius's interest was fading, I would force her to ruminate on motives, what each person must have looked like. We invented details, elaborated, made the stories longer and more complex.

Leading up to our last trip the summer when I was thirteen, however, Elysius and I started to poke holes in the stories. "What was the series of small miracles?" My mother didn't know. "There are medical reasons why someone can't have a baby for a time and then can again, aren't there?" The answer was yes, but still . . . And of course it's not physically possible for a man to build a house of stone, by hand, alone, forgoing sleep and proper nourishment.

"Yes," my mother said. "But that's what makes it an act of pure love!"

Years later, my sister would be converted. This was the place where Daniel, after eight years together and his solemn vow not to remarry, would propose to her while she was soaking in the bathtub.

And I was almost swayed into believing once. One day during our final trip together, the three of us were in one of the upstairs bedrooms, folding and sorting clothes that had dried on the wooden rack. This was my sister's room and the windows faced the mountain. I don't know who saw it first, but soon the three of us were collected at the window, watching an outdoor wedding on the mountain. The bride was wearing a long white gown, and her veil blew around in the breeze. We had a pair of binoculars for bird-watching. My sister grabbed them off the shelf and we took turns looking at the scene.

Finally, my mother said, "Let's get a closer view."

And so the three of us ran down the narrow stone stairs, through the kitchen, and out the back of the house. The wedding party was fairly high up the mountain so we walked down rows in the vineyard, passing the binoculars back and forth. I remembered adjusting the binoculars each time to fit my small face, and the view through the smeared lens, blurry, surreal, and beautiful. The bride started crying. She cupped her face in her hands, and when she pulled her hands away, she was laughing.

And suddenly my mother, my sister, and I found ourselves in a swarm of butterflies—Bath Whites, to be exact, white with black spotted markings on their wings. Elysius looked them up in a book at a small bookstore in Aix-en-Provence later during our stay. They fluttered around us madly, like a dizzy cloud of white.

I could see only snippets of my mother's bright pink skirt and dark hair. Her white blouse was lost in the white butterflies. And so her voice seemed almost unattached to her body.

"Are butterflies supposed to swarm like this?" I asked.

"No," my mother said, and she told us that it was another enchantment.

We argued with her because we felt it was our role, but I believed in the Bath whites, and I knew, secretly, that Elysius did, too.

That's the summer I've remembered most vividly. I was full of longing in that way that thirteen-year-old girls can long seemingly endlessly because their longing lacks direction. I wanted to be enchanted. I longed for the brothers who lived in the big house next to ours. The older one knew how to balance things on his forehead—sizable things like wooden chairs and rakes—and the younger one would sulk when his brother got attention, and splashed me mercilessly in the pool, which was more green than blue. They had dark hair and eyes. They smiled sheepishly. They were the exotics, the boys I would have dated if my grandmother had kept my grandfather in France, refusing to give up her home, her country, her language. I imagined that they would understand me in a way American boys didn't.

I stole a photo of the two of them—the older boy, Pascal, balancing a pogo stick on his forehead, tall and handsome, already muscled, while the younger brother, Julien, watched disdainfully from a lawn chair. I'd kind of fallen in love with the older boy, the one who'd really been trying to get Elysius's attention. And I kind of hated the one in the lawn chair—the sulker and splasher. I folded the picture up and put it in a zippered pencil pouch in my desk drawer.

In the years that followed, though, I mainly remembered my mother, who was strangely distant on that trip—wistful, quiet—as if she knew, in some way, what might be coming. Maybe her relationship with my father was already fractured—it seemed so to me, and I didn't know anything about marriage.

The next summer, when I was fourteen and Elysius was seventeen, my mother went to the house without us. She disappeared not for a short stint, but for the entire summer—after the discovery of my father's affair, something that my mother was frank about, in a typically French manner. She sent my sister and me letters on tissue-thin airmail stationery, as frail as sewing patterns. I wrote her back, every time, on the pink monogrammed stationery she'd gotten me for Christmas, but never sent the letters. I hid them in my desk. That was the summer of 1989. The last day of August, she called to tell us she was coming home.

Once home, she began making the small pastries she'd fallen in love with while in France—tarte au citron, flan, tiramisu, crème brûlée, pear pinwheels. She never opened a single cookbook. She seemed instead to be working from memory. She'd never been much of a baker before that, but after her trip she seemed to pour herself into the small, delicate desserts. I wanted to be with her, and so I lingered in the kitchen. Maybe this was where I first learned to equate the ephemeral art of baking with abstract things like longing—although, for many years, I'd prefer to call it art, and only until after meeting Henry would I think of it as an act of love. My mother and I sat at the table in the breakfast nook and we tasted cakes—critiquing them quietly in hushed, reverent tones. After a while, she would proclaim that we would never get this one just right. She would claim to give up baking for a day or two, but then she would be back in the kitchen and we would move on to the next dessert.

My mother was quiet and pensive, and a week or so after her return, the last of her letters arrived. It told the story of how the entire mountain had caught fire. The flames came all the way to the back stone steps of the house, but that was where the fire stopped. *A miracle,* she called it. As fond as she was of proclaiming miracles, this one seemed true. But when we asked her to describe the fire, she didn't want to discuss it. "I wrote it down so you can keep the story forever," she told us. It was strange that she wouldn't tell us, but I didn't pester her. We were lucky she was home. She was fragile, and, moreover, she'd proved that she could be run off. I let it be.

One day she stopped baking. She said that we'd tried all the pastries and gotten them all wrong. There was no need for more. After she made the announcement, she seemed less restless, more peaceful, and so I took this as a good thing.

But I kept baking, alone, at first in a clumsy attempt to lure her back into the kitchen to spend time with me, and then simply to be lost in the world I'd found there.

All those years later, I would catch myself pinching dough in a specific way or smelling an exact scent that brought me back to myself as a young woman alone in our kitchen, and I would wonder where the picture of the brothers had gone. Where were my mother's letters now? Where were the letters I wrote back on pink stationery and never sent? Thrown out. Buried away. Lost like everything else.

My mother had led us inside the house and we were now standing in the kitchen. Elysius's kitchen was restaurant grade, stainless steel and marble, with elegant lighting, kept pristine because she barely ever uses it. Her refrigerator was reliably stocked with things like baby carrots, yogurt, and healthy organic sprout salad takeout boxes, alongside exotic things like certain types of fish flown in from far-off islands, edible flowers, and bulbous roots that, I swear, were black market and vaguely illegal. In general, though, the inside of her fridge lacked color and density. It was airy, had a little echo to it, a lot of white staring back at you.

Now the kitchen was bustling with caterers. A woman in a blue cocktail dress was giving orders. She glanced at her BlackBerry and whisked out onto the deck to take a call.

There were tureens with ladles, long trays stacked with frothy appetizers, towers of shrimp, mussels, and clams, cases of wine, rows of stemware.

My mother was trying to explain to Abbot, once again, that no one had been hurt in the fire, that it was very far away in France. "It was only a kitchen fire. We don't know how much damage, but everyone is okay!"

Abbot was rubbing his hands together in unrelenting worry. "How far away was the fire? Where's France?" he asked, and she started explaining all over again.

But I wasn't listening. I felt unmoored. The news of the house fire seemed to have jarred something loose. Suddenly there were the memories of the house from my childhood, and once they flooded in, there was no stopping my brain. I'd taught myself how not to linger on memories of Henry, but Henry was here, and now I couldn't resist. I felt unable to stop the image of him—vivid and real—from appearing in my mind. It was like being pulled under by a great tide. Henry and I had been introduced in a kitchen filled with caterers, after all.

Henry Bartolozzi at twenty-four, standing in a kitchen, just before he met me. He was wearing a pair of nicely creased pants, a sport coat, and Nikes. He had black hair, combed but still curly, and light blue eyes. We were both in culinary school at the same time, and we'd both been invited—through friends of friends—to the house of a prominent chef in town. My mother had warned me not to fall in love with a creative type. By this point, Elysius had been living in New York for a few years as a struggling painter and had dated too many starving artists. My mother was sick of them. "What's wrong with a med student?" she would say at family dinners. "What if someone chokes? I'd like at least one person here to be able to do a solid Heimlich, someone who can fashion a breathing tube from a Bic pen in an emergency. Do you want one of us to fall on a knife and bleed to death?"

I thought the advice was pretty good. I was sick of my sister's boyfriends, too. Plus, I wasn't going to culinary school in order to meet men. I was tired of men. I was pretty sure I'd ruined my share. In fact, at this point, I'd recently ruined someone's career at NASA by talking them into getting stoned, broken up someone else's engagement, and been blamed for a sizable Jet Ski accident—no fatalities. I was afraid of men for the same reason I was afraid of frogs— because I couldn't predict which way they would jump.

In general, I saw love as entering into an agreement that depended on your willingness to compromise. This was rooted in my parents' complicated marriage, of course. The story goes that my father, an attorney for the U.S. Patent Office, saved my mother from the typing pool.

Problematic, on a feminist level, for many reasons, it was made worse because of one of our family secrets: my mother was brilliant. Her father came back from the war and opened a five and dime, which supported the family for years but was struggling by the time she reached college age and, to compound matters, her father's health started to fail, and so college was completely out of the question. As a housewife, my mother watched all of the latest movies, even the foreign films, which she went to alone because my father refused to read subtitles. She referenced films by the names of their directors, a distinctly French trait. She gardened scientifically and read books on physics, history, philosophy, religion, but rarely mentioned these things. She led a quiet, secretive life of the mind. One Christmas, someone gave us the game of Trivial Pursuit. My mother knew all of the answers. We were startled. "How do you know all this stuff?" we kept asking. After the game was over and she won, she put the lid back on the box and never played again. Had my mother needed saving? She accepted the story that, indeed, she had. It was no wonder then that when I met Henry in the kitchen of that party all those years ago, I saw love as compromise, even weakness.

Henry was the first person I met at the party. He was talking to the chef's daughter—a towheaded third grader. He had a smile that hitched up on one side, a smile I immediately loved.

He introduced himself. Henry Bartolozzi. The two names didn't seem to fit together and I said something about it. He explained that Henry was his mother's choice, the namesake of her grandfather, an old Southerner, and his last name was from his father's Italian side.

I told him my last name. "Buckley. A hard name to cart through middle school. I was a walking limerick."

He tapped his chin. "Does *Buckley* rhyme with something?

Funny. I can't think of anything." Then he confessed that Fartolozzi hadn't helped his middle school rep any. Raised in the Italian section of Boston—North End—he had an accent that was New England with a bounce, as if inspired partly by Fenway, partly by opera.

I remembered that night, after the party spilled out onto the lawn, the towhead and her older brother lighting firecrackers that skittered across the pavement. It was dark. It was hard to tell if Henry was glancing at me or not.

Later a lot of people piled into his old, rusty Honda, and when the radio accidentally hit an easy listening station, I started belting out "Brandy." I confessed that I was this kind of unfortunate drunk, an easy listening diva. Despite this, or maybe because of it, Henry asked for my phone number.

The very next night, a new friend of mine from school named Quinn invited me to dinner. I claimed I already had too much work. Quinn said, "Okay, it'll just be me and Henry then." And I said, "Henry Fartolozzi?" I told her I could change my plans.

Henry brought bottles of a great Italian wine—a splurge; none of us had any money. Because I wasn't used to the low futon masquerading as a couch, I kept dousing myself with wine each time I sat down. By the end of the night, I smelled like a winery.

My main mode of transportation was an enormous 1950s-era bicycle—bought at a Goodwill. Henry offered to drive me home—it had gotten chilly. I declined, but he insisted. He stuffed the monstrosity into the trunk of his ancient uninsured Honda, but then the car didn't start. At all. This was a relief. If he was trying to save me, it helped that he was failing.

I said, "I know what's wrong with your car."

His blue eyes lit up. "You know engines?"

I nodded. "The problem's simple. When you turn the key, it doesn't make any noise."

Henry found this charming. I found it charming that he found it charming. "You're right," he said. "It's probably the sound-effects alternator."

Henry walked me home—about six blocks. When we got to my house, I realized I'd left my keys at the dinner party. He walked me back to Quinn's, and then to my place again. At this point it was three o'clock in the morning. We'd walked and talked a good chunk of the night away. Now, back on my front stoop, we lingered.

He said, "So, do you like me?" He tilted his head, his dark lashes framing his blue eyes. He had full lips and the smile appeared again—just a half smile really, just that one side.

"What do you mean?" I asked. "Of course I like you. You're very nice."

"Yes, but by the sixth-grade definition. Do you *like me* like me or do you only like me?"

"I might *like you* like you," I said, looking at my shoes and then back at him. "*Might*. I don't have good luck with men. In fact, I've sworn them off."

"Really?" This is the part I remember so clearly—how close he was, so close I could feel the warmth of his breath. "Can I ask why?"

"Men are work. They think they're going to swoop in and save you, but then they take effort. They need cajoling. They're kind of, by and large, like talking sofas."

"For a talking sofa, I feel like I've got a really strong vocabulary." He whispered this, as if it were a confession. "I did well on standardized tests—when compared to other talking sofas." And then he really stared at me. I was falling in love with his shoulders. I could see his collarbones, the vulnerable dip between them, his beautiful, strong jaw. "I think swearing off men is old-fashioned."

"It's kind of an antiquated notion. I might have been drunk when I said it."

"Maybe you were on a bender?" He smiled his half smile. "Taking a break from belting out 'Brandy'?"

"Probably. And now in the sober light of day, I can see what a bad idea that was—like trying to put on a full-scale production of *West Side Story* in your local 7-Eleven."

He was impossibly close now. "Have you ever tried to put on a full-scale production of *West Side Story* at a 7-Eleven?"

"Twice. It didn't work," I said. "I'm over it now, swearing off men, that is."

"You've officially de-sworn-off men," he said.

"Yes," I said.

"You sure?"

I nodded, but I wasn't sure.

And he kissed me—softly at first, almost just a tug on my mouth, but then I gave in. He held my face in his hands. He pressed his body against mine, against the door. I dropped my keys. We kissed and kissed, a moment that in my memory feels infinite.

The kiss, that was the beginning. Henry and I worked as a couple because he convinced me that I was wrong about love. Love isn't about compromise. *Life* is hard. *Life* demands compromise. But when two people fall in love, they create a sanctuary. My family was fragile. Love was something made of handblown glass. But Henry had been raised so differently. His family was loud, rowdy, bawdy, quick to anger, quick to forgive—with food everywhere—Southern food mixed with Italian set to the mantra of *Mangia! Mangia!*— always frying, bubbling, spattering, the kitchen pumping like a steamy heart.

On one level, I didn't expect to fall in love. I saw this other future version of myself, a tough, independent woman, bullying my way through life. But, honestly, I also felt like Henry was the exact person I'd been waiting for—the *soul* I'd been waiting for—and the package he came in was like unwrapping gift after gift. *And this is what you look like. And this is what your voice sounds like. And this is the set of your childhood memories.* I'd thought I'd been looking but really I'd been just waiting for *him* without knowing that I was waiting, really, without knowing that I'd been missing him before he arrived. I thought he was the answer to the longing I'd felt at thirteen. I thought the ache was a restless lonesomeness, but it was more like homesickness for a place you haven't yet come to.

In my sister's kitchen, I was remembering our first kiss, the feeling of being pressed up against the door, the sound of the keys as they fell from my hand, jangling, and hit the cement stoop. There were so many hours, days, weeks that blurred from one moment to the next and slipped by. I wasn't good at the daily. I was lousy at cherishing the moment. It turned out that my longing was part of who I was. It had subsided, but then—especially the year before Henry's death—it returned. It got in the way of my ability to appreciate the details of my daily life. That's what Henry did so well while I longed. . . . How could I have been so careless? Why didn't I pay closer attention?

I was homesick in my sister's kitchen, on her wedding day. I wanted to go home, but the home I longed for, with Henry, was no longer there.

"Let's get your father and Abbot together. They can keep each other busy until the wedding starts," my mother said loudly over the kitchen noise. She'd managed not to smear her makeup while crying; it was one of her skills.

She pointed to my father, who was wearing a navy suit and sitting in the corner of the breakfast nook, penciling numbers into a book of Sudoku. This was how the ex-workaholic now handled the passage of time. Sudoku was a point of contention between my parents, and my father had to do it on the sly. Sudoku was a putterer's thing to do, and my mother hated puttering. But my father was drawn to detail work, the intricacies that he'd found fulfilling as a patent lawyer. He liked categories within subcategories within subcategories. He talked a good game about his adoration of invention, but truth be told, he enjoyed rejecting claims for "indefinite language." Deep down, I think my father had wanted to be an inventor, but he ended up a legalistic grammarian, a keeper of language.

Abbot looked at me mournfully. He loved his grandfather, but he didn't want to be abandoned in the noisy traffic of the kitchen. Plus, there was something inherently demeaning about being pawned off, and he knew he was being pawned off.

"You two are buddies," I reminded him. "You'll keep each other entertained."

We walked over and my father looked up from his Sudoku. "Well, don't you two shine up nice?" he said. "How do, Abbot?" *How do* was one of Abbot's baby expressions. He'd been a very social baby, asking everyone all day long how they were doing—baggers, bank tellers, librarians. *How do? How do?*

"I'm good!" Abbot said, putting on a happy face.

"Maybe you two can watch a television show in the den," my mother said.

My father glanced at her, gauging her emotion. I assumed he could tell she'd been crying. "Sounds good! Let's get out of the way of all this pomp and circumstance."

"There's a Red Sox game on," I said. Henry had been such

a die-hard Red Sox fan that it was Abbot's legacy, nearly genetic, and now it was my sole responsibility to make sure that
he got hooked. I'd bought him all kinds of paraphernalia—
ball caps, T-shirts, a pennant pinned to his door, curling in
on itself like a dying corsage, as if even the Red Sox pennants
needed New England's chill and this one was wilting in
Tallahassee's humidity.

"There's also a show on whales today," Abbot said.
"Whales have retractable nipples. They're mammals, like us."

"Baseball players are mammals, too!" my dad said.

"But they don't have retractable nipples," Abbot explained, undeterred.

"They don't," I admitted. Abbot is a very smart kid, and
in the world of kid-logic, he'd won this argument. "Whales,"
I said. "Blubber it is!"

"Bring on the blubber!" my father said.

My mother turned away from us. "I hear your sister calling," she said. I could, too, a shrill voice coming from the
upper reaches of the house. She started marching toward the
stairs then called to me over her shoulder. "Don't dawdle!"

My father reached out and touched my arm. He lowered
his voice. "She told you about the fire, no doubt. She's upset.
You know how crazy your mother is about that place." He'd
never been to *that place*, not once. The house had become a
point of contention between my parents—at first because
my father was always too busy to go and later because it represented my mother's abandonment of us after my father's

affair. "It turns out the woman in charge over there fell and broke something."

"She told me, but she didn't mention Véronique," I said. Véronique's house stood about two hundred feet from ours and had also been in the family for generations. Over scattered summers of my mother's childhood, she and Véronique had grown up together. My mother didn't have siblings and Véronique had only brothers, and so they'd said that they were like sisters. A few years after Véronique's divorce and after we'd stopped visiting, she'd renovated her larger house, turning it into a bed and breakfast. In return for minimal upkeep, she used my mother's house for overflow during the summer months. This was the arrangement that had stuck and was still in place. "What did she break? Did it have to do with the fire?"

"I don't know the details," my father said. "Your mother's being emotional. I just warn you. She's more hyped up than usual." *Hyped up*, that was the expression my father used to describe what I saw as my mother's restless longing for something else. For what, I don't know. I knew only my own longing, the kind I'd likely inherited from her. I knew the shape it took now—I longed for Henry, for him to come back to life.

My father's affair didn't strike me as being filled with this kind of longing. I've always assumed that he stumbled into the affair, that it happened the way pilots are taught a plane crash happens. It's never just one thing but a number of contributing factors at once—ice on the wings, coupled with an electrical issue and some clouds. . . . Or maybe it was, more simply, a midlife crisis. He'd saved my mother from the typing pool, and here was his chance to relive that drama. His affair was with a woman at work, though I'm not sure what she did. She was younger, per usual, newly divorced. He had a soft spot for women in need. Did this other woman need him in a way my mother had outgrown?

My mother picked him off immediately. He was a useless liar—part of the plane crash scenario—and, too, his inability to lie proficiently is probably a good trait. At the very least it indicated that he wasn't practiced in it. At six, I broke him down under cross-examination about Santa Claus. I blamed him for his affair but forgave him, too. The affair wrecked him deeply, and my mother's disappearance nearly killed him.

After my father's affair was revealed, my mother fled to Provence, and we weren't sure if she was going to come back. Elysius and I pushed my father on this point, and finally he said, "I guess you should be prepared to make a decision between the two of us. Who knows how this cookie will crumble?" He was fiddling with a handheld can opener at the time and a dented can of soup—baffled by the instrument. In my mind, at that moment, I picked him, but only because he was there and I saw something valiant in that. It's easier for daughters to blame mothers, and mothers to blame daughters—I'm not sure why.

When my mother came home, she forgave my father and

he forgave her for leaving—although we were all just so re-lieved that she was home, there was no need for forgiveness, really. And our upended family life, abruptly and without ceremony, righted itself again. My parents' marriage proved sturdy—but sadly so, like a harshly pruned dogwood.

"Mom will be fine," I told my father now. "She always is."

He nodded. "True," he said. "Very true."

Abbot pulled the satiny cummerbund and bow tie from my hands. "Pop-pop can help me with these things," he said.

"Sure I can," my father said.

I looked around the kitchen one last time, and just as my father and Abbot were about to head off to the den, I paused. "Do you remember my wedding?" I asked my father.

He and Abbot both looked up at me, surprised. I rarely mentioned things so closely tied to Henry like this.

"Yes," my father said, sadness in his voice. "You were beautiful."

"You kept referring to my veil as the wedding hat and the rehearsal as the warm-up drill."

"I've never been good with words," he said.

"They saw each other the morning of the wedding," Abbot said, "which you're not supposed to do, because it's unlucky." Abbot knew all the details of our wedding because instead of bedtime stories I told him Henry stories. The Henry stories were the only time I'd allowed myself to linger over memories, for Abbot's sake. I wanted him to remember his father.

"But they were lucky," my father said, "because they found

each other in the first place. It's a big world full of people."
My father wasn't a wordsmith, but he could get things right.

I felt suddenly teary, so I changed the subject. "How much trouble am I in with my sister?" I asked.

"Moderate to heavy," he said, laying the cummerbund on the table and trying to press it flat. "I'd brace yourself."

E lysius's house had high ceilings fitted with recessed lighting to strike the art that filled the walls. Banks of windows overlooked the surrounding hills, stands of thick oaks, their own well-tended gardens. The furniture was spare and modern. Four of my living rooms could fit in Elysius's living room. As sleek as it all was, I couldn't imagine calling it home—maybe because Henry and I had a definition of home that didn't include the word *sleek*. I always felt a little disoriented and ill at ease in my sister's house. My mother, on the other hand, felt completely at home. She told me once, a little drunk on Dewar's, "I'd have made a wonderful rich person." I told her that everyone would—I meant it politically. She shook her head and raised her finger in the air. She was right. Some are more suited for it than others.

I tapped on the door to the master bedroom and opened it. "Sorry I'm late," I said.

My sister was sitting on the edge of the bed, looking wistful, cradling a half-filled glass of mimosa with an orange slice floating in it. Elysius had creamy skin and my mother's honey-colored hair. It was swept in a loose but stiff swirl at the back of her head. Her ivory gown was long and fitted, with a plunging neckline.

She smiled up at me. "You look pretty," she said, and that's how I knew she was drunk. I didn't look pretty. My hair was still frizzing; my makeup wasn't finished. Normally Elysius would have jumped up from the bed and stridden over to fix me. Elysius was a natural strider—long legged, purposeful. She strode everywhere. She even was striding at Henry's funeral, which I hated her for at the time, but I turned on a lot of people for the smallest of things that day—the way they tilted their heads when they talked to me, too much sympathy. I was angry at my father for coughing into his fist, and then realized I was really just angry that Henry was gone.

"How many mimosas has she had?" I whispered to my mother while glancing around the room counting empty glasses. "And where are the other bridesmaids?" I realized that I wanted them here—an excitable distraction.

"She sent the maid of honor and the other two brides-maids down to the lawn to coordinate with the woman with the BlackBerry," my mother said. "She's so efficient with that little handheld machine!"

"Did you tell her about Nix?" Elysius asked.

"That was your idea," my mother said. "I thought I'd leave it to you."

"Nix?" I said.

"Jack Nixon," Elysius said. "He's coming to the wedding, and I didn't let him bring a date. No plus one."

"Jack Nixon? And he goes by the name Nix?" I said.

"Well, back in college, they called him Crook," Elysius said, smoothing her hair. "I kind of told him that you'd be here, and that maybe you two would hit it off, and, well, it's a blind date without the pressure of a blind date, really."

"Did you fix me up without my permission with a guy named Crook Nixon?" I asked.

"He's a sweetheart and a liberal. He does nonprofit work. Don't get all arch!" my sister said.

"I'm not arguing with his politics one way or the other. I don't like people trying to fix me up without my consent—on principle." My voice was pitched. Did I sound as rattled as I felt? How was it possible that my sister could immediately set me on edge?

"If we don't try to fix you up, you'll never date again. You have to keep in some kind of dating shape. Can I tell you honestly—your natural flirting skills, which were suspect to begin with, are really starting to atrophy."

"How do you know what my flirting skills are like? I don't flirt with you!" I paused. "My natural flirting skills were suspect to begin with? What's that mean?"

Elysius rolled her eyes.

"Nix is very handsome," my mother said. "I saw a picture. And he can't help that his last name is Nixon. You could just talk to him. What harm would that do?"

"I don't want to be a charity case," I said. "That's not too much to ask."

My sister teetered ever so slightly, waggled her face, raised her *V*-for-victory fingers over her head, and said, " 'I am not a crook.' "

"Seriously," I said, "how many mimosas?"

"She's fine!" my mother said.

"I'm fine!"

Flustered, I switched gears. "Dad told me about Véronique. Is she okay? Was it related to the fire?"

Elysius glanced at my mother as if they held a secret.

"Her ankle. I don't think it was related, but I don't know," my mother said. "I tracked down one of her sons. He was sketchy about the details. He hadn't seen her yet but was on his way."

During our last visit, Véronique's younger son dared me to climb up the mountain to a small chapel haunted by a hermit whose ears had been chopped off and who was later beheaded. I remembered the chapel now, as if still feeling the force of memories set loose by the mention of the house fire. The chapel was dark as a cave, the dim echo of our voices. The boy slipped his hand around mine and led me to the altar, where we held our breaths and waited for the hermit to appear as a ghost. Then he confessed that the hermit was a good ghost. "*Écoute*," he kept saying. "Do you hear him whispering your name?" I listened so hard that I thought I did.

"We can talk about it later," my mother said, then smiled at Elysius. "Today's your day."

"It's almost time, isn't it?" Elysius said. She stood up, with the slightest wobble, and looked at herself in the full-length mahogany-framed mirror. She wasn't much of a drinker, I should add—unlike my mother, who could put it away. "I wish Daniel weren't being such a workaholic. He's like Dad, you know. Am I marrying a version of my father?"

"Daniel is a very nice guy," I said, sticking to my promise.

"And you could do worse than a version of your father," my mother said, a little defensively.

"Have you seen Charlotte?" Elysius said. "Where *is* she? I just don't have any patience for her today. Can't she just let me have a day, one single day, without some crapola from her?"

"What happened?" I asked.

"She and I had an argument about communism, of all things," she said. "Her hair has become an indicator of her mood. It is now dyed blue with black tips. She's a walking mood ring."

"And what does blue with black tips mean?" I asked.

"It means *moping*. Her mother couldn't stand her moping around anymore and sent her to live with us for the summer— as if we love moping—at our wedding!" Charlotte's mother wasn't particularly well balanced. She'd tried going back to school for various advanced degrees. She was often going to various retreats when Daniel felt she should be going through some kind of rehab. For what? He didn't really know. In any case, Elysius and Daniel always picked up the slack. Elysius resented it, but she knew that it meant the world to Daniel and so, by and large, tried to keep her mouth shut. She didn't want to have children of her own, but there was something to be gained by the title of motherhood, and she was happy enough to have that common ground to share with other women when the conversations turned—as she complained they inevitably did—to kids.

"Why is she moping?" I asked.

"*A:* She's Charlotte. She mopes."

"She's a good kid," I said. This was my refrain, really— *Charlotte's a good kid. She'll turn out just fine. She'll own all of us one day once she sets her mind to ruling the world.* I didn't know her very well, but I liked her and had confidence in her—a luxury afforded me perhaps by some distance.

"And *B:* Adam Briskowitz," Elysius said. "She's obsessed with him."

"She has a boyfriend?" I asked.

My mother sat down and rubbed her bunion through the leather of her high heels. She refused to wear comfortable shoes, claiming that they made her look orthopedically aged. "She doesn't have a boyfriend. She has a *disaster.* He's going to college next year."

"Heidi, go round her up and make sure she's getting ready. You'll be able to talk her out of showing up in camouflage. Sometimes, I swear she's *trying* to get profiled as a school shooter."

"Okay," I said, picking up a brush and running it through my hair. "I need another coat of makeup, I think."

My mother looked at the clock on the bedside table. "We're supposed to be lining up on the deck so we're in the right order for the procession."

I started for the door.

"Wait," my mother said. "Your private toast for Elysius. The one that you and Abbot worked on?"

"My toast!" my sister said, raising her glass.

"Yes," I said, and then patted my dress as if it had pockets. "I think I lost it!"

My mother looked at me suspiciously—was this a sign that I was backsliding? Henry was the one who'd kept track of everything. If he'd been alive, he would have found the toast, even probably typed it up for me and kept it folded in his pocket until I needed it. He wore a watch so I didn't have to. He kept a real to-do list—for both of us—whereas I would start a to-do list with things I'd already done so that I'd have the pleasure of crossing them out. I was dependent on Henry, even though this made me feel like a child. "I don't need you to herd me around like a lost sheep!" I'd say. Sometimes this started a little argument that he usually won, because I did, in fact, need to be herded. And sometimes it was part of a larger argument between us—maybe both of us were afraid I would drift too far, as my mother once had.

Maybe it would have been better if I had lost the Cake Shop—if I'd hit rock bottom and needed to get back up on my own two feet in order for Abbot and me to survive. I knew, deep down, that Daniel was right—I should have been pouring myself into my work. In the past, I'd done just that when I was trying to mourn a loss. Henry had loved that about me, that I could turn my sadness into something beautiful. He would sometimes confess at the end of the day that he'd watched me from the small window in the door while I was swimming in my work, without any sense of self-consciousness. I lost track of time sometimes then, too, but Henry said I did it in a graceful way, "a thing of beauty." I was afraid to work like that now, afraid to look up at the empty pane of glass.

It was hard to say what this lost toast meant, exactly. Regardless, my mother knew that I was still a mess, that I hadn't really even begun to recover from Henry's death. In all honesty, I wasn't sure that she had fully recovered, either. She loved Henry, deeply. She called him her boy. Daniel was too close in age with her and so clearly a man when she met him. But Henry was her boy. She once whispered to me, "I couldn't have saved him." "Of course not," I'd said. We all shared the mostly unspoken language of guilt. My family and his, too—we passed it among ourselves with quiet absolutions. *There was nothing we could have done. It was an accident, a fluke. We couldn't have stopped it.*

And so, with no reference to Henry except this very associative one—my lost toast wouldn't have been lost if Henry were here—my mother reached out and held my hand and said, "I miss him, but he's here. He really is here with us."

My sister looked at me and then away, as if to give me privacy. I wondered what kind of expression of grief I was wearing.

A toast, I thought. I should give my sister a toast—a real toast. The only thought that came to me was this: *Don't die on each other.* Was that what I'd scribbled down on the note I'd lost? I took a step forward and said, "You have beautiful teeth and you give wonderful presents. And Abbot and I love you."

Elysius tilted her head, her eyes glassy. She walked over to me and cupped my face in her hands. "My sweet sister. My Heidi. That was a bullshit toast," she said, "but it almost made me cry."

I walked down the long hall past one beautiful bedroom and then another beautiful bedroom. But I stopped before I got to Charlotte's door and leaned against the wall for a moment, just to feel something stable hold me up. *Nix?* I thought. I shook my head.

I knocked on Charlotte's door.

There was no answer.

I knocked again, slowly pushing the door open.

There, sitting on the floor, surrounded by books and notebooks, was Charlotte, staring at a window across the room, bopping her head to music coming through earbuds wired to her iPod. I realized that Charlotte had often had that distant look, like someone spellbound by something no one else could see, even when she was little. She was wearing a ruffled dress that puffed around her like a cupcake with overly ornate icing.

Her bedroom was not really hers. It was obviously one of Elysius's creations. There were no posters, no funky chairs, or wild bedspreads. The walls were mauve. There were oil paintings on the walls—real art, probably costly real art—and built-in bookcases, on which was a shelf entirely devoted to classic, probably first-edition, Nancy Drew novels. Elysius had loved them as a kid. Charlotte likely had no use for them whatsoever. All that cardigan-wearing pluck? No, Charlotte would have none of that.

"Charlotte!" I shouted.

She lifted her head and gave the wires of her earbuds a tug. They fell to her lap, the music sounding tinny. Her hair was, in fact, blue with black tips, cut short and a little spiky with a fringe of bangs across her forehead. Charlotte was startlingly beautiful. Beneath the blue, black-tipped hair, the nose ring, and the eyeliner, she was a stunning girl. Her posture was awful, but every once in a while she'd tilt her head, or reach for something, and there was a hidden but undeniable gracefulness. Her eyes were a gray blue like her father's. But she didn't have his thin frame. She was a bit boxier. In fact, the baggy clothes she usually wore—the black concert T-shirts and camo pants with tons of pockets—made me think that she might be a little self-conscious about her body—and who could blame her? Elysius was a workout freak who could live on her fridge contents of yogurt and baby carrots. And, if memory served me well, Charlotte's mother was tall and thin. I'd met Charlotte's mother only once, at one of Charlotte's early birthday parties. Charlotte's mother was not happy. That's what I remembered. She didn't want Charlotte to open the gifts in front of the other kids.

"It's too showy," she said. "No one wants to sit through someone else's happiness."

"Are you doing SAT prep now?" I asked. "You know, we're supposed to be lining up in a few minutes."

"I'm trying to look like I'm studying," she said. "It's the one thing they can't give me shit for."

"You look like you *are* studying," I said, "except for staring out the window."

"I've gotten very convincing at looking like I'm studying. You just crack open a heavy book and uncap a highlighter. You have to make yourself look like you're in charge."

"I'm in charge of making sure you're ready."

"Am I ready?"

"I think so."

She started stacking her books.

"Are all those books just props?" I asked. "Do you set-design little fake study scenarios?"

"Yep," she said, and she stood up. "It looks very believable, though, doesn't it? It's very . . . rapacious."

"Rapacious?"

"It's, you know . . ." She looked at the palm of her hand where she had written some words in red ink. She was wearing black fingernail polish. "Um, it's very redolent and recalcitrant."

"Do you know what those words mean?" I asked.

"I'm supposed to use them in sentences so that I come to understand them. My father told me to."

"I think he meant that you're supposed to use them in sentences, correctly, though—not just to use them."

"Right. That makes sense," she said. "But it's harder." And I was pretty sure she knew that she was being funny, although she didn't smile in the least.

"You look beautiful," I said.

"I look like a dough-fart," she said. Dough-fart? It seemed like the kind of expression that I, as a pastry chef, should know, but I'd never heard of it. "I hate this dress. I'm in the third ring of hell. Weddings are just reminders that love is so pathetic it needs a whole institution to hold it up." Then she looked up at me, wide-eyed, like she'd said the wrong thing. Had bad-mouthing marriage made her think that she'd said something insensitive about my marriage and therefore my dead husband? "I'm sorry," she said. "I forgot. I mean, I didn't forget. It's just that I wasn't thinking."

"Your father's getting married again. My sister's getting married," I said. "This might not be the easiest day for either of us."

"My father is already wrapped up in his own life. He'd marry his work if he could, you know. That's the sad part. He can't marry art."

I'd heard Charlotte make these kinds of comments before. She wanted more from her father, and he was capable of only so much. She seemed to accept it, but the acceptance didn't take the sting out. "I think it's good they're making it official, Elysius and your dad."

"It's a little bureaucratic, but I'm fine with it." She shrugged. "I'm okay, in general, you know. I'm fine!" She seemed to want to get off the subject.

"I'm okay, too, despite the fact that Elysius is trying to fix me up with a guy at the wedding."

"Really? Who?"

"Jack Nixon."

"Huh," Charlotte said. "He came for dinner once. He's nice."

"Well, I'm not ready for that kind of thing. And setups are sneaky."

"True," she said. "Veracity."

"We're supposed to go down and meet people on the deck so we can line up like ducks," I said, and then suddenly felt like I was underwater, sinking. We were going to line up. We were going to a wedding. We were all going to talk about love. I remembered Henry, vividly, his first confession. When he was eleven, he'd witnessed his younger brother almost drown in a swimming pool at a barbecue party. Henry had frozen. He'd taken swimming lessons with CPR training at the Y, but he panicked. "It seemed like hours, like in a bad dream, watching my brother sink, but finally I shouted for my dad, who ran out into the yard and dove in, fully dressed." His father saved him, but the incident had made Henry overly protective. He was the one to remember the suntan lotion, the first-aid kit, the helmets, who, at the beach, waved us in, calling, "Too far! Too far!" I felt like I needed to hear his voice now, calling me in. Too far, I thought, too far.

Still, I kept walking. Charlotte followed me.

At the bottom of the stairs, she said, "Wait, I can get this." I felt a tug on the back of my dress, and with two quick pulls, Charlotte zippered it the rest of the way up. It was a little act of kindness, but, in that moment, I felt like she might be able pull me to shore, if I needed it.

"Thanks," I said.

She shrugged. *"De nada."*

In the kitchen, Abbot was standing in the back of the line with bridesmaids and groomsmen shifting by the French doors that led to the deck. He was all gussied up with his matching red bow tie and cummerbund—a miniature Henry. I felt a hitch in my breath. Luckily, he spotted me, ran up, and quickly said, "I want some coffee."

And I was able to play the role of mother, setting limits. "No," I whispered, almost unable to speak.

"Howdy, Absterizer," Charlotte said, sticking out her hand to shake his. "You look very snazzy."

"Thanks," he said shyly, slipping his hands into his pockets. He didn't want to shake her hand—germs. But, still, he was starstruck by Charlotte. And so he jerked his hand back out of his pocket and shook hers. During scattered holidays throughout the years, they'd talked and played board games and card games and strung popcorn. They were both the only child in their families, and as it is for many only children, the role of the cousin was heightened. But Charlotte was more of an adult each time they met up again. They seemed to always have to start over and, as Charlotte grew up, that became harder each time.

My mother and father were already on the deck, standing stiffly side by side. I could see them through the French doors.

I said to Charlotte, "Your fake study area looks very authentic, genuine. You could say that it has real . . . what's that word? Verisimilitude."

"I don't think that's on my list. Verisimilitude?" She looked up at the ceiling, searching her memory. "No. I don't have to know that word."

"But it's a good word."

"Verisimilitude," Abbott said. "It sounds like a color."

"Like vermilion?" I asked.

He shrugged.

"It can be a great word," Charlotte said. "I don't have anything against it personally. I just don't have to know it."

"But you could," I said, trying to be encouraging.

"It's not on the list."

"Got it," I said.

"This isn't what your wedding to Daddy was like," Abbot said.

Charlotte glanced at me, trying to read my reaction. I didn't mind. She was a curious kid. She wanted to know how the world worked, and not just its pleasantries. She'd suffered plenty, and she was likely looking for options on how to deal with it.

"That's right," I said. "It was nothing like this."

Truth be told, Henry and I had had no real wedding plans in mind, and that was a good thing, since we didn't really have much money to pull off anything. I didn't love the idea of the wedding day being my "big day." I wanted to look forward to bigger days with Henry—maybe quieter, but days that belonged just to us, nonetheless.

Throughout the wedding itself, I'd had the sense Henry and I barely existed. We were already married, in our own way. This was an adaptation of some sort, something that was only loosely based on us. There were the usual problems: battling bridesmaids, a couple of overly drunk groomsmen, the lead singer of the band getting laryngitis, and the beauty shop that gave my sister a satellite-dish hairdo. But I mostly remembered that Henry and I were kept in the church basement right before the wedding in two separate rooms, like holding pens. There was a door between us. I opened it and saw him across the room. He was wearing a rented tuxedo with the red bow tie and cummerbund, like Abbot's now. He was pacing, hands in his pockets. I whispered his name and he looked up.

"Hi," I said.

"Hi."

"I'm getting married," I said.

"Me, too," he said, as if this were the strangest thing—two strangers, a bride and a groom meeting up like this. And it did seem like a giant coincidence. Throughout our marriage, when one of us would say *I love you*, the other would say it back, sometimes adding, "What are the chances?" He didn't walk over to the door. It seemed like we were already breaking the rules just talking like this. "I'm getting married today . . . but I think I'm falling in love with *you.*"

"Should we run away together?" I'd said.

He'd nodded.

Then his father had walked into his room, and I'd given a little wave and quietly shut the door.

The woman in charge of Elysius's wedding, tight-fisting her BlackBerry, shouted, "Where's the ring bearer? We need to get you people in the order of the wedding procession!"

"That's you, Abbot," I said. "Good luck!"

Abbot dodged through the mix of bridesmaids and groomsmen, avoiding elbows, out onto the deck with my parents, leaving Charlotte and me behind in the kitchen. We were standing by a large fabric-matted corkboard situated on the pantry door. It was covered with photos of Daniel and Elysius's friends and their friends' offspring pushpinned to it. There were kids in various poses: kids with stylized hair standing in front of tall beach grass, in bumblebee and mermaid costumes that looked like they were handmade by Broadway costume designers, and more than a few holding violins. I never knew Elysius had so many intense friends with intense kids.

There was a photo of Charlotte, too, an old one, taken before she had started dyeing her hair violent shades and had pierced her nose. She was holding a fish on a dock, presumably on Daniel's family's lakefront property in the Berkshires. This was taken back when she was outwardly thrilled by things like fish. I understood Charlotte's gloominess. She reminded me of my own intensity at that age—all longing with nowhere for it to go. And of course, we both understood what it was like to live in Elysius's perfectly elegant shadow.

"Look at this baby," I said, pointing at a particularly uptight-looking newborn. "That brow is furrowed like a Yale law student's, isn't it? It's like she was born complete with a full head of hair, a pink Binky, and corporate angst."

Charlotte leaned in and said, "I suspect that the Binky was added later."

When Henry died, I was flooded with cards that all suffered from the same wispy, murky sentiments. Charlotte was likely forced to write the one that she sent, but she made it her own. She wrote at the bottom, *He was so anti-corporate. That's one thing that made him so lovable to me.* This was one of Charlotte's highest compliments at the time. *And he taught me how to play air guitar. In fact, he got me an air guitar for Christmas when I was ten. I still have it. It's electric blue.* Henry and I also got her a real present—I insisted on that. It was something that she unwrapped and forgot. But the air guitar stuck, as did the image I had of the two of them wailing on imaginary guitars to Lenny Kravitz. That was my favorite card. I threw out all the cards one night in a fit of anger that I can't explain—except for Charlotte's. Henry would have loved that card.

"Did you fight with Elysius about communism?" I asked.

The woman in the blue dress was pointing at us now, urging us to come forward and get in line.

"Is that what she thought we were fighting about?" Charlotte shook her head.

"What do you think you were fighting about?" I asked.

"Greed, consumerism, and, per usual, we were fighting over my father," Charlotte said. "She doesn't like me."

"She loves you," I said.

"But that doesn't mean she *likes* me."

There was something about Charlotte in that moment. She was so vulnerable, so hurt. I wanted to tell her that the world was going to open up for her. Yes, this time in her life was hard but she would find someone someday, she'd fall in love—she'd be loved and liked by someone who really understood her, someone she could trust.

But could I guarantee these things?

No.

And if I did tell Charlotte that all of these things would come to her, then the unspoken understanding was that it could also all be taken away. No matter how much joy we can even *endure* in life, there's always death. See? This was how it was for me. Death was everywhere. It popped up into the most unsuspecting moments—even just trying to give a little advice. I couldn't think of anything to say to Charlotte about being loved and liked. I was just a sad reminder, after all, of loss.

I can say that Elysius and Daniel's ceremony was beautiful. In fact, I can be fairly objective here because I was feeling objective, removed. I wasn't sure what came over me, but I didn't even have the urge to cry. I knew that if I did, the crying might turn, palpably, into grief. To be in a state of grief at your sister's wedding is unforgivable. But it wasn't so much that I took control of myself as it was that I felt empty. This ceremony was beautiful, yes, but seemed to have nothing to do with love as I knew it. Had I convinced myself that I was watching a play and been pulled up from the audience to act out a certain role? That's how it felt.

I kept my eye on Abbot, who was trying very hard not to rub his hands together. After he handed over the rings, his hands went straight into his pockets and were restless there, sometimes hopping like frogs. I looked for a man who'd been denied his plus one on his wedding invite and who could have possibly carried off the name Crook in college. At a certain point, I concentrated on SAT words—ribald, fastidious, contrived.

I smiled in photographs, noting the golden late afternoon light, the elegance of the guests. At the reception, I skirted the edges of the brilliant conversations, the dance floor, where people danced tastefully, and the bar, where people ordered expensively. Since Henry died, I'd had a gnawing in my stomach, but it wasn't hunger. I ate lightly. I picked at things. I left my crusts behind. I'd become a nibbler, a sipper. And so, at the reception, I nibbled hors d'ouevres—airy and rich—and sipped expensive, dry, subtle wines.

Of course, I was drawn to the wedding cake. I wished I'd had the self-restraint to ignore it, but I couldn't. I found myself circling. It was a modern, five-tiered cake, circular, a little too hatboxy, and white with black piping—which I always tried to talk brides out of. Black piping was, to my mind, too tuxedo-esque, something that would date the cake too quickly, faddish. I assumed that the designers had talked to Elysius, perhaps even walked through her house. There was an echoey sense to the cake itself—as if the cake might actually be hollow. It was the kind of design that Henry and I would have enjoyed critiquing, joyfully.

I knew that some would say our kind of closeness was borderline unhealthy. We lived together and worked together and parented together. But, honestly, when I was with Henry,

I felt like I was more myself. Who had I been before Henry Bartolozzi? I remembered my girlhood self—awkward, shadowed by my beautiful older sister and my parents' tenuous marriage, almost like they sucked up all the air in a room, and I was left feeling oxygen-deprived. But with Henry, I had air again. I could breathe. He thought I was funny, and so I got funnier. He thought I was beautiful, and so I felt more beautiful. He thought I was brilliantly experimental in the kitchen, and so I experimented more brilliantly. We had our problems, yes, but even our problems bound us closer. And now I knew what it was like to be only half of a pair and less of myself.

One night, lying in bed together, about a month before Henry died, my calf seized. I shot up in bed and cried out, "Leg cramp!"

Henry was almost asleep. The room was lit only by the hall light. He said, "Your leg or mine?"

I was flexing my foot, rubbing the knot violently. "What do you mean, your leg or mine? How would *I* know if *you* had a leg cramp?"

Henry was quiet a moment, and then said, "You're right. My legs feel fine."

The truth was that Henry and I had grown so close that sometimes it was hard to know where one of us began and the other ended. We'd been together for so long that most of our memories were the same film, just different camera angles, and from years of playing the memories, even the camera angles were mostly blurred to one by this point.

"Isn't it gorgeous?" A woman beside me nodded toward the cake. She was older and smelled of gardenia perfume.

I nodded and, before I could utter a single critique, I slipped away. I'd missed my chance to design a cake that truly reflected Elysius and Daniel. I would have concentrated on the art in the house. The spare furnishings are supposed to allow someone to fix their attention on the art. I would have spent time in Daniel's studio, taking in his work—the restless birds that seemed to beat just below the surface—and I would have talked to them about why they loved each other. That's where I would have gone. I was this kind of cake designer—my thoughts always churning to the most ambitious interpretation. A cake to reflect abstract art? A cake with the restlessness of wings? A cake about saying yes to marriage after so many years? How would it be done? I felt the smallest inkling of desire—the step before wanting to create, the want to want to create.

As I drifted through the reception thinking this, I caught myself keeping an eye out for Henry. I did this often. It was one of the theories that I had for why I was always losing things. I was looking for Henry. He was lost and my mind was waiting for him to return; my eyes wanted to find him. I still saw him everywhere—his broad back in line at the movies, his hand reaching out to pay ahead of me in line at a drive-through. I'd see Henry walking along with some other family—holding hands with one of the kids or locking arms with the wife. But he would always turn into some other man—his hair too dark or too light, his nose too fine or too knotted—a stranger, no one I knew. For a while, each time this would happen, I'd feel betrayed, tricked. And, just as I'd learned not to linger in memories, I learned when to look away—just before the man glanced back, just before his face appeared in the window—and I learned how to have a peripheral husband—one still alive, when I could time it right.

At an event like this, my subconscious was even more determined to find him. On some level, I was sure that he wouldn't miss an event this big, this important to Elysius and Daniel. Finally, I saw him from behind, talking to a bartender, slapping someone on the back . . . and I looked away.

When I did, I turned abruptly, almost bowling over Jack Nixon—Nix and/or Crook. He'd been poised to say hello, but I'd knocked his bottle of beer up against his chest. It was a full beer and some of it spilled onto his shoes—nice shoes, black leather with some stylish trim, squared off at the toe in a season when squared off at the toe was in.

"I'm Jack," he said, but somehow I already knew this. He was the right age, alone, a little nervous, and he was handsome, by my mother's definition, which is to say he was traditionally handsome. He had all the right features—a nice nose, gentle eyes, a tough jawline, closely cut hair. He wasn't fat or skinny, tall or short.

"Hi," I said. "I'm Heidi." I stuck out my hand, which seemed to make things worse. He smiled and shook my hand, and, in that moment, it hit me that my sister was right—my flirting skills had atrophied. And, to be honest, they never really were that pumped up to begin with. That's one of the reasons I'd fallen for Henry so immediately—it hadn't ever felt like flirting.

"I know that your sister is trying to turn this into a blind date," he said. "I hate blind dates, and I just want you to know that there's no pressure on my end."

"Oh," I said, feeling a little disappointed. Was he trying to get out of it? "No pressure on my end either," I said quickly, maybe too quickly. "I'm just being myself anyway."

"Um, okay then," he said, and he smiled graciously. "We can try to just mingle normally then, telling them that we've done our best. We were good sports."

"I'm a very good sport," I said. "I won sportsmanship awards in lieu of actual sports awards when I was younger. I lack basic eye–hand coordination." I looked down at his shoes. "For example," I said, "sorry about your shoes."

"No," he said, "it's okay. I don't mind being bumped into by a beautiful woman."

I wasn't sure how to respond to this. "A hypothetical beautiful woman," I said, as if correcting him.

"A hypothetical beautiful woman or a real one," he said.

"Well, then," I said, taking a deep breath. "We have established that we're good sports! We'll just try to mingle normally."

"Right," he said.

And I walked away. A beautiful woman? I wasn't sure what to make of that. I hadn't felt beautiful in a very long time. In fact, I'd barely felt like a woman. I was a widow, a single mother. I decided to not think about it and to instead locate Abbot. How long had it been since the last time I spotted him? I stood on my tiptoes and looked through the crowd.

Finally I saw him in a pack of other kids his age. They were scurrying around a table in the back of the tent. The band started up just then, and this seemed to send them into a frenzy. Something about the drums, I thought, made them tribal. A few of the other kids had started to crawl around under people's tables. And so Abbot was standing there, hands in his pockets, bouncing on his toes. He wouldn't have interacted as intimately with the ground as the other kids did. As much as the kids on the ground seemed like unruly beasts, I wished Abbot would join them, or at least feel like he could if he wanted to.

I walked up to him. "Are you having fun?" I said. "You can let loose, you know."

"*You* let loose," he said.

"I'll try if you try."

He asked me to unclip his tie. All the other kids had long since abandoned theirs. I flipped up his collar and unhooked the metal clasp. He shrugged off his jacket and handed it to me. "Okay, I'll try," he said, and scuttled off.

Charlotte and I crisscrossed paths, as if on the same migratory loop. "Keep moving," she said, "and you can avoid the attack of awkward conversation."

"I don't know how long I can last in these shoes," I said.

"If a shark stops swimming, it dies," she said. "Have you seen the clarinet player?" she asked. "He's like a hundred and twenty-eight years old. I figure if he can make it through this wedding, then I can."

I looked over at the wizened, bowed old man playing the clarinet, his cheeks taut with trapped air. "Impressive," I said, and we glided on.

I looked up and saw Jack Nixon dancing with one of the bridesmaids. He looked over and saw me and gave a small wave. I pretended not to see him. I'm not sure why.

It was at events like this where the married women would eventually clump together. I could see such a group congregating around one of the tables in a far corner next to one of the air-conditioning fans. And as much as Elysius felt like conversations among women turn always to children, I had been aware, throughout my marriage and now, of how conversations among women will, inevitably, turn—as if by a will of their own—to husbands.

Disappointing husbands. Emotionally inarticulate husbands. Weary husbands. Crabby husbands. Demanding husbands. Thoughtless husbands. Late husbands. Unfaithful husbands. Messy husbands. Lazy husbands. Workaholic husbands. Cheap husbands. Bad-father husbands.

Not to mention those men who could never man up and become husbands, and their counterparts, ex-husbands.

The truth was, I'd always tried to avoid these groups, even when Henry was alive. Not even my fights with Henry were worth talking about. We would hurt each other from time to time, but what was hardest was when one of us had to tell the other we'd been hurt—we were so sure that it was unintended, and yet it wasn't something we risked keeping quiet.

When we were first married, I tried to tell stories about our fights. My friends' eyes would glaze over.

"Are you serious?" one of my friends said to me once. "Not to belittle your issues with your husband, but you don't really have any. I mean, when you guys fight over where the can opener is, the can opener is just a can opener. It's not some larger issue."

"I'm sorry," I said.

"It's fine," my friend said. "Just so you know, it's a little chafing to others."

Henry and I agreed that, in general, it was the men's faults—by and large. They were clumsy with affection, ill-equipped for conflict; they got angry when they needed to be sorry, lied when they should have opted for full disclosure, disclosed opinions they should have kept to themselves . . . etc., etc., etc.

"Talking sofas," Henry said.

"And look at *my* sofa!" I said. "He learned to walk upright and not bifurcate his emotions!"

"I'm a non-bifurcated upright walking talking sofa. What can I say?"

Most of all, however, we knew we were shit-lucky, because in other environments, with other partners, we'd have said all of the wrong things, done all of the wrong things, made all of the same mistakes.

One time Elysius overheard me say at the end of a phone conversation with Henry, "I like you, too."

And after I hung up, Elysius said, "Don't do that in front of others."

"What?"

"It's one thing that you two love each other. What's so offensive, though, is how much you *like* each other. It's unbearable."

Was it unbearable? I was aware that Henry and I had created one life together. And sometimes, if Henry was a little late or when we kissed each other goodbye before one of us took a trip, a small flash of fear would run through my body—something almost electric. *What if this is the last time I see him? What if he dies? What if I die?* We confessed that we'd each imagined wrecks of various sorts, but that we couldn't see much beyond it. "What would your life be like without me?" I asked him.

And Henry, who usually had an answer for everything, didn't know. He could only shrug. "What about me?" he asked.

"I don't know how I'd survive it," I said.

But then Henry died.

And here I found myself, inexplicably, surviving it.

What was unbearable now? How much I'd taken for granted and the fact that I had only seemed to want more.

I sat far away from the clutch of women, pushed my high heels off, and rubbed my aching feet together under the table. As if sensing that my guard was down, one of my aunties teetered over. Aunt Giselle was my grandmother's youngest sister, now quite elderly. My own grandparents had died when my mother was young—one from cancer, the other a faulty heart. Aunt Giselle wore her hair in a thick gray bob and wore deep red lipstick. She'd come to visit her sister as a young woman and, once here, married an American botanist, who'd died young.

"How are things going with you?" she asked. She'd never lost her accent. It was still thick, her red lips puckering to speak.

"Oh, I'm doing fine. It was a beautiful ceremony."

"Yes," she said, in that bored way the French sometimes have. "Of course."

"I heard that there was a fire," I said.

"I heard this, too. The news has deranged your mother."

"I think it's the lack of information that's upset her. No details."

"Yes, maybe this is true," she said. "But this house, it will not burn completely. The fires on the mountain in 1989, they came to the doorstep, but not a centimeter more."

"I know that story, yes," I said. I thought of how Henry had always loved the lore of the house. I'd told him all of the stories. He especially loved the story of my mother and sister and me getting lost in the swirl of the fluttering wings of Bath whites. He loved that my mother raised us to be French-proud. His father had been the type to wear KISS ME, I'M ITALIAN shirts on the beach and so we had this in common. My mother played Jacques Brel albums, read Babar books to us in French, had us put shoes out for Santa on Christmas Eve. She made us take French lessons with a strange woman who lived down the street and had parrots in cages. The parrots spoke French, too—dirty words that the old woman told us never to repeat. Henry had always wanted to go to his family's hometown in Italy and to the house in Provence, but we either had no time or no money. If Henry was here, would he have insisted that we go and pay our respects?

"This house, it cannot burn," Aunt Giselle told me. "It only desires something. It is being like a child. It wants attention." I'd heard this kind of talk before among my mother's relatives—the house as having a will of its own. The house's mythology was not just my mother's. It was passed down through the generations—how else could it have survived and thrived?—mostly down the line of women. Giselle had used the house herself when she was younger, my mother had told me. After her husband died, she lived there for a few years to "reinvent herself," as my mother put it.

"I guess we all just want some attention now and then," I said lightly.

"I know," she said. "I am sorry about your husband." She then fit her hand over mine. It was bony with thick knuckles, but soft. She had taken good care of her skin. "I suffered a loss young," she told me. "The war took my first, but I went on. Back then, we all had to. We had no choice."

"I didn't know you were married before you came to the States," I said.

She shook her head and smiled at me. "It wasn't a marriage. It was a love. Some people get one and the other. Some people get both at the same time," she said. "You understand."

"I do," I said, and then my throat felt tight; my cheeks flushed. I started coughing. I slipped my shoes back on, stood up, and walked away without excusing myself. *I went on . . . we all had to. We had no choice.* I walked quickly back in to Elysius's house, my heels pushing divots into the earth. I moved through the caterer-clogged kitchen and into the bathroom.

I locked the door and looked in the mirror. I thought of my aunt. I was jealous of her. She was on the other side of it, looking back. I thought that I should have told her, right then, what I'd never told anyone. I'd heard about the traffic accident on the radio after I'd dropped Abbot off at school. I heard about the accident, that there were multiple fatalities, an oil tanker ablaze, and the backed-up traffic on the interstate, and I had one simple thought: I would take an alternate route.

That was it. I would take an alternate route. Worse, I felt lucky—not because I was alive and others were dead, but because I'd caught the update in time to avoid the exit ramp that would have landed me in the thick of it.

Later, after I'd been informed that Henry's car had crashed, after I screamed and cried wildly and they fed me tranquilizers, I woke up in a dark room alone, and I remembered the radio reporter, the sky traffic update, and I thought of that woman I used to be, listening to the radio, passing the exit ramp, and I hated her more than I've ever hated anyone in my life. It was an accident, a fluke, but he could have been saved by another smaller accident and fluke. I could have saved him. I know I could have. What if I'd let him sleep in? What if I'd stepped into the shower with him that morning and delayed him? What if I'd simply called him to tell him that I loved him and he'd pulled over to talk?

And now, holding on to the bathroom sink, I felt that hatred again. Who was I then? Why didn't I save him? Why did I let him go?

The thought of how much I loved him made my chest seize. Aunt Giselle had said, *Some people get one and the other. Some people get both at the same time.* Henry and I had both at the same time, a love and a marriage. I missed him with a deep ache, desperately. I loved his soul—it lit him up from within. And I loved his body—this physical shape that carried his soul, this body I never got to kiss goodbye, that I never saw again. Not even in my dreams about Henry, which were always strangely bureaucratic. He would be stepping out of a squad car being returned to me while some voice-over narration explained that he wasn't really dead. It was simply a clerical error. The dreams always ended before he reached me. He was gone. *Gone.* I used to beg to have him back, pleading God, but here now, I wanted simply to be allowed to touch his skin with the tips of my fingers. If I asked for just this one small thing, did I have more of a chance? Could I be allowed to have just that?

I was crying breathlessly now—quick, sharp sobs.

There was a knock at the door, a loud one, four hard pops

of the knuckles. "It's your mother." She jiggled the knob. "Unlock the door."

I drew in a breath, turned on the faucet. "Wait," I said, but I wasn't sure if I'd whispered it or shouted it.

"Let me in."

I looked at my face in the mirror: dark eye-makeup pooled under my eyes, my lips looking bitten and chapped, my cheeks seemingly fevered.

My mother whispered, "Heidi, listen to me. Let me in."

I touched the knob, then twisted it. The lock popped.

My mother opened the door, slipped in, and shut it behind her. She looked at me and opened her arms. I fell into them and she hugged me. "It's okay," she whispered. "I know. I know. It's okay." She held my hair in her fists.

"Abbot," I whispered. "I have to go check on him."

"He's surrounded by family," my mother said. "Take your time."

I'd left a spot of mascara on the shoulder of her dress. I pointed it out. "Sorry," I said.

"Who cares?" she said. "It's just a dress."

"Why are you here?" I asked, pulling a tissue from the box and wetting it. Had Aunt Giselle told her I was upset?

"I have an idea," she said. "Your sister is upset because Daniel has an important conference call tomorrow morning. I was thinking that we could distract her. The three of us— just us girls—we could have a light brunch, here at the house—you, me, and Elysius. She would like it."

"That's the idea?" I was barely listening. "Brunch?" I was

trying to wipe the makeup off my face but only managed to smear it more. This was how the world persisted. The heaviness of despair—how could it exist in the midst of mascara, zippers, brunches? It marched forward even when I was barely able to stand.

"I've been watching you," my mother said. She leaned against the door and looked weary, older than I'd seen her look in a long time. It had been hard on all of us—not only missing Henry, but facing the idea that your whole world can change, suddenly, irreversibly. We were reminded how flimsy everything is, as frail as the airmail envelopes my mother had sent us the summer she disappeared. This is the life you have and then it's gone. I felt sorry for my mother. I knew what it was like not to be able to help your child, to change the incomprehensible randomness of life, to reverse a loss. But she had a plan. She was being valiant. "Come to brunch," she said. "Let's just talk."

Children. For all of the times that you miss out on things you'd like to do because of them, there are an equal number of excuses they offer to get out of things you'd like to miss.

"Abbot is exhausted," I said to Elysius and Daniel. "I've got to get him to bed before he passes out."

Abbot was revved up on cake, Shirley Temples, and chocolate cubes. He could have gone on indefinitely. I was the one who was exhausted. I was fairly sure that my sister could tell I'd been crying. My makeup had been all but erased, and my eyes were probably still red-rimmed. But she didn't say anything about it, for her own sake, maybe, but also for mine.

It was dark now. There were small white lights strung around the tent like glowing beads and larger spotlights propped at the edges. The guests were still here, talking and laughing, the sign of a good party. Elysius looked tired but happily so, gorgeously so, and Daniel had kicked back at a table littered with purses and waning bouquets.

"Thanks for staying so long," my sister said without any hint of sarcastic subtext. She'd gone soft with all the displays of affection and really was forgiving me.

I accepted it immediately. "I wish I could stay longer. It was a beautiful ceremony and a great party."

The wind was kicking up now, a strong breeze.

"It might rain," Daniel said, looking at the distant sky.

"It's allowed to rain now," my sister said, like a small god. "My work is done."

And so Abbot and I headed back down the sloping lawn toward the studio. If his father were here, I thought, he'd carry him into the studio, up the stairs, and into bed. Did Abbot remember times when Henry had lifted him up from the backseat of the car after a long night? The scratchiness of his coat, the smell of his aftershave? Every child deserves that memory. I had my own: my father walking along the narrow walkway up to our front door, boxed by hedgerows that my shoes brushed against as we made our way, and he would hum a tune I didn't know, the low register of his baritone vibrating from his chest to my cheek.

Abbot was too heavy for me to carry, and so we walked along, hand in hand, and I became painfully aware, as I often did, that I was lucky to have Abbot. I could have been walking down this slope alone. Without the responsibility of Abbot, how would I have managed to go on? But this was something that Henry and I had wondered when we were still together, too. How had we managed to find life meaningful before Abbot?

Abbot was a surprise, or, well, a kind-of surprise. . . . We finished culinary school and were both dizzily working, he in an upscale, high-pressure restaurant, I in a bakery. We both wanted to have a child but knew the timing wasn't right. We had student loans. We wanted to save up to buy a house. We would take turns telling each other that rational people wouldn't have a baby now. It wouldn't make sense. It would be foolhardy, but this struck me as fool-*hearty*. "Fools of the heart," I said. "Fool-hearty."

Henry was the one who finally came out with it. "Why don't we have an accident?"

"You mean you want to knock me up?" I said.

"Accidentally," he said.

"But if I know about it, wouldn't that be on purpose?" I said.

"This isn't a question of logic. Let's be fool-hearty."

Instead of practicing safe sex, we practiced accidents. We got good at it. One week I was expecting my period and it didn't come. I sent Henry to the store for a pregnancy test. I took it and the pregnancy box looked like it had a blurry line.

"Go get another one," I said. "I'll fill up on fluids."

He went to the store and came back with three more but then had to race to work. He didn't have a cell phone, and so, after three pink lines had shown up clearly in three clear windows, I drove to the restaurant around the time he got off work. When I saw him crossing a street to the parking garage, I blew the horn, parked the car at a red light, and got out.

He turned around.

"I am!" I shouted.

He ran across the intersection, wrapped his arms around me, and lifted me off my feet. The guy in the car behind us stuck his head out the window. "And?" he shouted. "So what is it?"

"She's pregnant!" Henry shouted joyfully. "A kind-of accident!"

"In that case, kind-of congratulations!" the guy said. "Can you get in your car and drive now?"

We were ebullient. We called family and friends. Henry boasted about his sperm. We immediately jumped into name books. Henry said, "How about we go with Bantu? It means 'the people.'" I was stuck on cheese—Gorgonzola, Gruyère . . .

But eventually the thought of cheese made me sick, as did all foods. The nausea and exhaustion made me feel bludgeoned, drugged. I shuffled around the house talking about all of the women who came before me, all of the silent suffering. "I feel like I've survived a bomb blast." I looked in the mirror and expected to find myself dusted in char.

Henry rubbed my feet, my lower back. He made me chicken salad with cranberry dressing on croissants—breakfast, lunch, and dinner—for three weeks straight. It was the only thing I would eat.

It turns out that the nausea and exhaustion had a purpose: they were blocking fear. And as soon as they lifted, the anxiety swept in. Now, looking back, it's no wonder that Abbot is borderline obsessive-compulsive. I was terrified of pregnancy. That level of anxiety has to make its way through the placenta.

Henry was calm about this, maybe because Italians have a history of big families. Babies get born, one way or another. One time I woke him in the middle of the night to tell him that childbirth was the number-one way women died through-out history. "Go to any old graveyard and read the tombstones and count how many women are buried with their babies."

He rubbed his face. "What are you talking about?"

"I could take you to a graveyard right now and we could count tombstones of women and their babies."

"Are you asking me out on a date?" He smiled sleepily, seductively, and I slugged him in the arm and then laid my head on his chest.

I read all of the pregnancy books I could get my hands on until Henry told me that he thought I should stop. "Not cold turkey. I don't want you to get the DTs, but you should cut back."

I'd already read them all anyway. "The damage is done," I told him.

I sweated out every test, every ultrasound, every doctor visit. Each one that the baby and I passed only seemed to make it clearer to me that we were bound to fail a bigger one, until, finally, there was only one left: childbirth.

Childbirth began in a textbook fashion: with small cramps and twinges that became more and more uncomfortable.

Henry said, "We should head to the hospital or you'll end up giving birth in the back of a cab."

"That only happens in movies. We're not taking a cab."

"I know, but still . . ." He was standing beside me, somewhat hunched, his arms in front of his chest as if he were expecting the baby to fall out and he wanted to be ready to catch it.

"I'm not supposed to go in until I can't talk through contractions anymore," I said through a contraction.

And so we walked through the neighborhood. Sidewalk, birds, sun, fences, dogs . . . It was a normal neighborhood, completely unaware of what was going on inside of me. And what was going on? Abbot wasn't a baby as much as he felt like entire landscapes shifting, tumbling, cinching, and releasing.

The contractions grew stronger, and I wanted to get out of my own body, to escape. I had the terrifying realization that there was something lodged inside of me. *Lodged.*

I told Henry it was time. I remembered the sky through the car window, phone wires, trees. I said, "If I don't make it out alive, you should tell the baby everything about us, how much we loved each other. You should tell the baby that love is possible—that it's bigger than all of us."

"You're going to live," Henry said. "The baby is going to live, too. It's going to be okay."

I looked at him pityingly, as if he were so naïve.

"Think of all the people who are alive," he said. "They all came from mothers. Mothers who went through this. The world is filled with people!"

This didn't comfort me. So many women, so much pain. How was it possible that everyone was born in this way? How could the world hold all of this suffering?

"There was a woman who had a baby in a tree during the monsoons," Henry explained. "She and the baby were fine! Even the tree was fine! People—and trees—are hardy."

I didn't care about the woman in the tree. I closed my eyes during a contraction and the world disappeared. And then by the time we got to the hospital, I was aware only in small windows of painlessness—crisp, bright windows of nurses and IVs and gurneys and a small room with a rocking chair and Henry—Henry talking to the doctor, Henry holding my hand, Henry rubbing my lips with ice.

The doctor said that he could see the head crowning.

Henry said, "I see it."

See what? I thought. There was only this force of will. There was only a desire, wanting. There was no longer fear. Only breath. Only legs. Only the swell of my stomach and wanting to be above it so that I could bear down on it.

A nurse arranged a mirror so I could see the baby's head, but mirrors were beyond me. The heads of babies were beyond me. They meant nothing.

There was a dense opening in my body, the movement of bones, the bearing down. And then someone said that the head was out, another push, and there was a release, something tumbling. And I never could have imagined what came next. Something squalling and ruddy and bloody. Something hefted up and moving toward me, placed on my chest.

And Henry said, "You did it." His face was flushed. He was crying.

It took a moment for me to realize that this was what had been inside of me—this body with heels and elbows. All of the months of kicking made sense in a new way. I touched the baby's fingers. I watched the flicker of heartbeat on his chest. I ran one finger over the fine, slick hair on his head.

"It's a *baby*," I said to Henry.

"I know," he said. "It's *our* baby."

"And we're both alive."

"Yes," he said. "Just like I told you."

I have a pared-down version of this story that I told Abbot, one of many Henry stories. Abbot liked this story in particular because it was about him as a baby—an Abbot story, really, the making of. He loved his own baby stories. But the truth was it always left me feeling unsettled. The unspoken deal between Henry. At the end of this story about life, Abbot was still alive, and so was I. And Henry was not. This fact—this irreversible fact—loomed at the end of this story in starker relief than all the other stories. The last time I told it, I pushed Abbot's bangs from his face and kissed his forehead. "Goodnight," I whispered, and then felt a catch in my throat. *Don't cry*, I said to myself. *Don't cry.* I turned out Abbot's Red Sox night-light, and the tears were already streaming down my face. I went to bed and cried until I couldn't cry anymore.

I didn't tell anyone that these collapses were still happening almost two years later—not even my mother, who would likely have found something comforting to say. I didn't want comfort. I was afraid to tell someone, because I didn't want to stop—grief was my connection to Henry. I couldn't bear the thought of losing it.

The night of my sister's wedding, I tucked Abbot into the silky sheets on the sofa bed in the loft in Daniel's studio and it struck me that I told Abbot Henry stories the way my mother once told us stories of the house in Provence. A weakness for her, too? Maybe it was a family tradition. Abbot knew all the stories by heart. If I left out a detail, one single small item—like the dollop of white sauce on the lapel of Henry's tux at our wedding—he'd stop me. "Tell it right," he'd say. "Don't skip a thing." I'd always thought that Abbot was my greatest ally, the keeper of the details. He would remember everything even if I slipped. Together, I thought, Abbot and I could keep Henry alive.

I wondered if he was going to ask for a Henry story tonight. But I was now overwhelmed by all of the memories that the day—the announcement of the fire, my sister's beautiful wedding—had drummed up. Maybe Abbot sensed this. *Not tonight*, I urged Abbot in my mind. *Not tonight.*

I was surprised, though, when he reached into his canvas bag and pulled out his dictionary. He then climbed into bed and tucked it next to him, partly under the covers, like a teddy bear. Henry had given it to him on his fifth birthday. Originally, it had been a gift from Henry's father when Henry went off to college, and there was a stiff inscription in his father's scrawl, a quote from Galileo. It was written in Italian and then translated: *All truths are easy to understand once they are discovered: the point is to discover them.* And then he added: *Use your words well.*

Henry had written a note to Abbot on the next page. It read: *Ditto what Papa said. Be curious. Happy 5th Birthday! Love, Daddy*

The dictionary usually sat on Abbot's bedside table. Was it a sign that Abbot was clinging to the past too much?

It was an American Heritage second college edition— and what made it so special to Abbot was that Henry had taped tiny Xeroxed photos of Abbot over the pictures that lined the outermost columns of the pages. He'd taped Abbot's picture over the head of a bison; over the astronaut's head for the definition of *pressure suit;* on top of one of the polo players above the word *polo;* over the face of an immigrant; over the face of a helmsman as well as a statue of Eros. Of course, he also put Abbot's face in the column on the page where *abbot* was defined, but he scribbled in his own second definition: *Abbot (ab'at) n. The world's most wonderful boy. [ME abbod < OE < Llat. Abbas . . .]*

I'd seen Abbot thumbing through the dictionary at night before, but I didn't know he'd become so attached.

"You brought the dictionary," I said.

"It helps me sleep," he said. He smiled and gave a quick jerky shrug of his shoulders. He tapped it with his knuckles, a strange gesture that I couldn't read, and then stared up at the night sky through the skylight.

I opened one of the windows to let in the cool breeze and then hung his tux on a hanger I found in an old wardrobe, its mirror fogged with age.

"Remember when you, me, and Dad went to that aquarium," Abbot asked, "the one with the huge tank of beluga whales?"

"Yep," I said. "We walked through that glass underwater tunnel. I loved the jellyfish." Their pink headdresses, all glow and flounce, seemed like lurid turbans, and their bodies moved like bright ball gowns, pulsing over our heads—puff and glide, puff and glide. Henry had caught me looking a little teary-eyed. I told him that they made me think about Abbot's childhood, how it seemed to be slipping away from us.

"I thought about that today when Pop-pop and I were watching the show on Animal Planet," Abbot said. "Remember how Daddy loved the belugas?"

"Yes," I said.

"He said that the beluga's leg bones looked so real when it kicked its fins. He said it was like a man was trapped in the whale's body. And how they had belly buttons. Whales are just like us."

Could Abbot know that this memory resonated with me so deeply? Children register things, I believe, even though they don't understand a conflicted moment rationally, or maybe because it's not rational, they register it not in the conscious mind but more deeply, and so it gets stuck.

That night after the aquarium, in the hotel in downtown Atlanta, I'd asked Henry if he felt like he was trapped, the way he saw the body of a man inside of the beluga. I worried that it had been symbolic, a metaphor, even a subconscious one. He looked at me, startled, and then said, "I'm not trapped inside of a whale or a life," he said. "Are you?"

I realized that maybe I was projecting my own fears onto him. Did I feel trapped? Was that the reason for the inarticulate longing I sometimes felt? "No," I said, unwilling to admit to anything that awful. I was lucky. We were lucky. But then I whispered, "I just wonder if this is what life is, just this moment and then the next and the next and then it stops. And that's all."

I could tell that I'd hurt him. "We've built this around ourselves together, but we're not trapped. There's a difference."

And now I saw the giant belugas in my mind. Henry was right. You could see their powerful legs beneath their skin, and it was so very human. Did I feel like a woman trapped inside of myself? I couldn't think of any other way to live. Henry and I had built this life—a trap or not, it was what we'd built. And even though I felt lonesome now within it, I didn't want out. All I wanted was our old domestic life back again.

I told Abbot that I remembered what Daddy said, too, the beluga's leg bones, its belly button. "Did you like the wedding?" I asked.

"Yep," he said. "But it wasn't as good as yours and Daddy's wedding."

"Why do you say that?"

"Theirs was too fancy. Yours was just right."

I agreed but didn't reply. Ours was just right—for us, that's all. "Are you sleepy now?"

"Mm-hmm."

"Go to sleep," I said.

He opened his eyes wide and stared at me. "They have a smoke detector in here even though it's just a studio, right? Not a house."

"They have a smoke detector in here," I told him. "We're fine."

"Okay," he said, and then he closed his eyes. I sat there listening to his breathing, which quickly smoothed into an even rhythm. He was exhausted after all. Once I was sure that he was asleep, I lifted the dictionary out of the bed and held it for a moment on my lap. It had sharp edges. I didn't want Abbot to bang into it in the night. I thought of opening it, letting myself indulge in what Henry had left behind. But I didn't. I couldn't. I set it on the end table, and then I looked up and caught myself in the wardrobe's mirror—foggy, ghost-like, someone who used to be but now was almost gone.

From my seat in the dining room, where Elysius, my mother, and I were having brunch, I could see Abbot and my father in Elysius's heated pool. Abbot was already trolling around the surface. My father was wearing swim trunks that I found a bit skimpy. It was quite possible that he purchased these trunks in the seventies. He had nearly hairless pink legs and a paunch. He and Abbot were quite serious this morning. They were going to pretend they were in the Caribbean, and this would take some imaginative effort, especially since neither had ever been.

My mother, Elysius, and I were eating pastries that my mother had picked up at the local bakery, as if there weren't a huge block of uneaten wedding cake. I was eating the pastries while trying not to judge them. But every once in a while, my critical mind would kick in and I'd think, *Pretty enough, but if it's dry, what's the point?*

Elysius had made a pot of coffee with some exotic beans that she claimed had a powerful effect on Daniel's work. "Top grade, high octane."

There was an agenda. I knew that there had to be. Elysius and my mother had talked, and Elysius had written notes, and there was a list of items that we were going to get to, like it or not. I was not given a copy of this agenda, but I knew it existed, and so I proceeded through the conversation with caution.

We talked about the wedding—anecdotes, details, other people's dresses. My mother and I let Elysius complain about Daniel's postponing the honeymoon to work until she came full circle and defended his art. "When you marry an artist, you also marry his work. I know that well enough by now. And I love his work. Not as much as I love him, but I do love it." And, as if love were an appropriate segue, my sister said, "Jack Nixon said that you were charming."

"Charming?" I said, and I could feel myself blush. "I could barely make eye contact."

"I told you," Elysius said, "the art of flirting—use it or lose it."

"Well, it's already lost." Jack Nixon was good looking and nice and he'd called me a beautiful woman, even after I let him off the hook, and now he'd said I was charming. Still, I was scared not only of him, but everything he represented.

"So, did you like him?" Elysius asked. "He was hinting

that he wanted to ask you out on a date. Something casual. He's never been married. He has no kids, no baggage. He's *uncomplicated!* He's perfect!"

Was that a sales pitch for me? I'd been married. I had a kid. I didn't just have baggage; I hauled around steamer trunks! Not that there was anything wrong with Jack Nixon. There wasn't. He seemed perfectly fine, but he wanted to date me? Dating? How could I be expected to date someone? I must have looked slightly stricken, because my mother jumped in. "Now, now," she said, "she'll find love again on her own time."

"Wait," Elysius said. "You were in on this. You thought Jack was a good catch."

"I'm not ready," I said, and then quickly asked where Charlotte was.

"She's still asleep," Elysius said. "She tends to need a full day's sleep to function."

"She's that age," my mother said.

"I was never that age," Elysius said. "I always woke up early."

"You had plenty of other ages, though. Your back talk phase. Your diet of cream cheese and chocolate phase. Your cigarette phase," my mother said gently.

It was quiet for a moment.

"Well," my mother said to fill the space.

"Well?" I said. I was impatient for her to get on with it. What was her idea and how could I remove myself from what it required of me?

"Well . . . ," Elysius said.

"The house," my mother said. "It needs someone to look after it."

"The house?" I said. My house was a little on the messy side, sure, and the back porch needed a coat of paint, and the dishwasher was on its last leg, but it seemed a little extreme to say that I wasn't looking after it.

My mother reached into her pocketbook and placed a stack of photographs on the table and pushed them across to me. "The house in Provence," she said. "How many times do I have to tell people that it caught on fire?"

"Maybe it really was just a little kitchen fire," I said, thinking of the house as my Aunt Giselle had rendered it— a child having a small tantrum.

"We don't know the extent of the damage," my sister said. "But the house has been virtually ignored for decades. I'd go, but Daniel and I have already booked this yacht with its own crew."

"And I can't go. Your father would refuse to go with me, and I can't go without him. That's too . . . loaded," my mother said.

Elysius and my mother were quiet as I started flipping through the pictures, blurry color photographs from the late eighties, the last time the three of us had been there. My mother wearing a fitted skirt, Elysius with her long hair and thick bangs, me wearing a baseball cap. Behind us, Mont Sainte-Victoire was luminous. There were photos of the stone house, the three of us eating dinner in the yard by the fountain, the big house next door, Véronique—square-shouldered, a slight smile on her lips—and her boys, looking sheepish, per usual. One picture of their father wearing black socks and sandals, his mouth open as if he were singing. There were cathedrals, one's architecture blurring into the next, the rows of vineyards, a field of sunflowers, the three of us standing beside them on the roadside.

The next photograph I turned to caught me off guard: my mother wearing a yellow swimsuit, sitting on the edge of our swimming pool, surrounded by a wrought-iron gate and a garden with small paths running through it. She looked elegant and young, so unbearably young, but she had to be at least the age I was now. "I don't remember this swimsuit," I said.

"That picture is from the following summer," she said, without emotion, as if that weren't the summer of her disappearance. In the photo, she was shielding her eyes from the sun, a coquettish salute. I wondered who took this picture. Who was she smiling at?

She must have felt a little uncomfortable about the way I was examining this photo, because she filled in with some idle banter. "No one has done any real updates on the house for, well, nearly a decade. Even if the house isn't a pile of charred stones, there's real work to be done."

"She's right," Elysius chimed in. "Everything is just on the verge of collapse—the kitchen, the bathrooms . . . It was beautiful when Daniel and I were there, but in a decaying way."

I tidied the stack by tapping them on the table like a deck of cards. "I stole a photo from this stack once upon a time."

"Really?" my mother said.

I nodded. "The one where Véronique's older son was showing off for the camera, balancing a pogo stick on his forehead."

"I remember him doing that!" Elysius said.

"Pascal is the older brother," my mother said. "But it was her younger son I talked to about the fire, Julien."

"The one who was always pouting and splashed me all the time in the pool," I said.

"It rings a dim bell," Elysius said.

"Where have these been all this time?" I asked, sliding the pictures back across the table.

"Locked away," my mother said. "There's no need to have them on display. All's well that ends well." She was talking about her marriage, our family. Why put these pictures in albums for my father to see? This was the place she went to and almost never came back from.

"You both know I'm not going," I said. "I have work to do. And Abbot is going to a day camp where they teach juggling. . . ."

"Henry's been gone for nearly two years," my mother said. "You have to keep living in the world."

My fork rattled against my plate. Each time someone told me that it was okay to move on, that I *should* be moving on, the less I felt able. It was as if they were telling me to leave Henry behind, and it felt like a betrayal. In my mother's defense, she'd never made this claim until now.

And that was when my mother delivered the line that she had obviously practiced. She leaned forward and said, "Every woman needs one lost summer in her life. This is yours."

"Is that mandatory?" I asked, an old resentment resurfacing.

"It is."

"You *needed* to disappear that summer when we were kids?" I said.

"I came back," my mother said, defensively. "That summer allowed me to come back."

"This is about what *you* need, Heidi, right now," Elysius said.

"You want me to leave Abbot behind for the summer? Are you two insane?" I said.

"Bring him," Elysius said.

"Maybe you both need a lost summer," my mother acquiesced.

"It's a little elitist," I said.

"I didn't say that every woman *gets to have* a lost summer," my mother said. "I'm just saying that every woman *needs* one—*deserves* one—what with all of the shit we have to put up with from men!" She was momentarily flustered. I couldn't remember the last time I'd heard her curse. "Plus, this isn't just any house. It's like going on a pilgrimage to Our Lady of Lourdes, blind, and then gaining your sight back, but only for us, the women in this family, and only having to do with matters of the heart."

"Like Our Lady of Lourdes? Really?" I said. My mother was never devout, but still sometimes her Catholic upbringing would surface, as if to offset some of her other traits— her frankness about sexuality, her desire to be rich, and her indulgent behavior with chocolate and good wine.

"Yes. Lourdes."

My sister put her elbows on the table and said, flatly, "Eight years, Heidi. Daniel and I have been together *eight years*. He was never going to get married again. Ever. But then I took him to the house in Provence, and he opened up. I can't explain it, but that's what happened! He proposed to me. Just like that."

"Not to mention your grandmother," my mother said. "That is the house where my own parents fell in love." She was invoking the old love stories now. I took this as a sign of desperation.

I shook my head. "Who can afford to have a lost summer?" I said. "I can't. It's that simple."

"You can," my mother said. "You know Jude will take care of the store. She's already taken charge of most everything. And I have an account for the house. I've never tapped it. It would be an investment in the house. Someone needs to go and help oversee that it's properly restored."

"And," Elysius said, lowering her voice. "This trip could really help me. . . ." She glanced at my mother for approval.

"Go on," my mother said. "Tell her."

"It's about Charlotte," Elysius said. "When Mom came to me with her idea, I knew you'd never go without Abbot, never, and I thought about how hard it would be to travel alone with an eight-year-old. And then I thought of Charlotte, and how it might be . . . mutually beneficial."

My mother summarized, "Since you've decided to take Abbot with you, you might want to also bring Charlotte."

"I have not decided to bring Abbot with me or to go at all," I said.

"Charlotte is at that age when she needs to expand her horizons. She needs to learn that there's more to life . . ." My mother didn't finish the sentence but now I knew that this was a reference to Charlotte's needing to learn that there was more to life than her boyfriend, Adam Briskowitz. "And it would get her out of Elysius's hair. Let both of them breathe."

"Charlotte can help you with Abbot," Elysius said. "You know, so you can get out and live a little." This was another way of saying that I needed to move on. "Plus she'll boost her French, maybe skip on to French III, and she'll have time to study for her SATs without distraction." Here, again, the unnamed distraction was Adam Briskowitz.

"You need the house," my mother said. "You don't believe it, but you will."

I remembered the three of us lost in the swarm of beautiful Bath whites. I didn't want to be enchanted. I shook my head. "It's a nice house. That's all. Let's not get carried away," I said. "I went to that house as a kid and I wasn't magically transformed."

"You weren't heartbroken yet," Elysius said. "That's the difference."

I looked out the window to the pool. *And now I am,* I thought. *And now I am heartbroken.* My father was picking through a large bin of water toys. Abbot's snorkeling gear was sitting on the cement. He was in the pool without it, a colorful shadow in the deep end. I watched for him to push himself off the bottom, bob to the surface, and shake his hair. But several moments passed. Was he drowning? I jumped up from the table, letting my napkin fall to the floor, and I ran out of the dining room through the kitchen, already screaming his name.

"Abbot! Abbot!" I shouted, as I ran across the deck, tipping a small potted plant on the railing that cracked with a thud on the grass.

By the time I was running downhill across the lawn, Abbot was holding on to the ladder, shaking the water from his hair.

"What is it?" my father called to me. "Is everything okay?"

I was breathless. My heart was thudding in my chest. I stopped and doubled over, my hands on my knees. Finally, I stood up and waved. "Everything's fine," I called. "Fine." I turned around, and there stood my mother and Elysius on the deck, the door flung wide at their backs, the cracked pot having spilled its dirt on the grass. I knew what I must look like to them: so gripped by fear, imbalanced by sorrow, terrified of living, a widow screaming for her only son who, on a beautiful morning, hasn't drowned, who hasn't even come close.

I shook my head. "I'm sorry," I said. "We're not going. We just can't." I started toward Abbot again. "Time to go!" I called. "Get your stuff!"

There was a Henry story that I told Abbot only in a blur. He knew that I'd had a miscarriage, that there was a baby that didn't make it, but it wasn't a Henry story. How could it have been? It was a story I told myself, and I told it to myself a lot, because the loss of Henry echoed this earlier loss.

Abbot was so perfect—fat, with gummy smiles and purring snores—that Henry and I felt almost guilty wanting another baby, but we did, right away. We didn't give in, though, not immediately, mainly because Abbot made us dizzy with sleeplessness and selflessness—or maybe Abbot, as the manifestation of us, meant that we were dizzy with self-fullness. In any case, we were dizzy with love.

But when Abbot turned four—years that flew at breakneck speed—we were ready, more than ready. Overdue.

Henry and I knew that the world was going to demand that we hand Abbot over at some point. We weren't going to be allowed to keep him with us forever. "The more children we have, the more we have to fear. Is that the way it works?" I asked Henry.

"I think so. But it's more of everything," Henry said.

This time, I handled the morning sickness better. I had no choice. I had Abbot to tend to. And so did Henry. He couldn't simply dote on me. After the nausea subsided, right at week twelve, I noticed that my breasts weren't as engorged, either. At a routine checkup, the Doppler didn't pick up a heartbeat.

"Not to worry," the obstetrician told me, wiping the goo off my stomach. "We'll get you in for an ultrasound tomorrow and just make sure all's well!"

Not to worry, I told Henry on my cell phone while getting dressed. But later, while waiting to check out, I heard one of the technicians calling in an ultrasound. "Stat," she said.

And that's when it hit me—the possibility that there was reason to worry.

My mother came over to babysit Abbot, and Henry came with me to the ultrasound. We were stoic. He kept telling me that the doctor said there was no reason to worry.

I said nothing.

Finally, the technician took us to a small room and started the ultrasound. The tech said nothing. When I was pregnant with Abbot, the technicians talked through every ultrasound. They pointed out his parts like they were tour guides. "Here's the vertebrae. Here's a foot. . . . If you turn your attention this way, you'll see Big Ben. . . ." That's what it was like.

Henry said, "Is that the baby?"

The tech said, "Yes."

"So, how does everything look?" he asked.

The tech said quietly, "Your doctor will want you to come in to talk."

"Oh," Henry said. "Okay."

But I already knew, knew in a way that Henry couldn't, knew in a way in which dread precedes devastating news, the way a phone ringing at the wrong time of night is never good. I turned my face to the wall and cried in a way I hadn't ever cried before—it came from deep within me, something guttural and barbaric.

Henry said, "Heidi, listen to me. Heidi, I'm here. Look at me."

But I was gone, lost inside of myself.

By the time I was dressed, we'd gotten a message from my doctor's office telling us to come straight over. There, we heard the news. The baby no longer had a heartbeat. It had died within me.

Henry had to call my mother. He said, "This baby didn't make it." Henry told me later, in bed, that he felt that he'd failed, that he'd done something wrong, that it had been some genetic deficiency on his side.

I wasn't ready to share the blame. It was a miscarriage, and I was the carriage. I imagined myself rattling over cobblestone, a wobbly thing on wooden wheels. I said flatly, "It wasn't your fault. I can tell you that as easily as you can tell me the same."

Eventually, I was able to whisper that I felt sorry for him. "I got to hold the child inside of me, and you never did." It seemed like a gift to have been able to carry the baby with me, for a short time.

"Good God," he said, and he got out of bed and paced. "You cannot be sorry in any way. I'm only a beggar here." I understood what he meant. He was a beggar. He'd gotten more than his share. We're all beggars, really. He climbed back into bed and put his face next to mine on the pillow. He was so beautiful—his soft blue eyes, his beautiful teeth that were so very slightly crooked.

Then there was the sterile hour that Henry spent alone while I was having the small surgery that often accompanies a miscarriage—as if the emotional loss weren't enough, there was the physicality of it all. Henry read about sports. He told me later that he'd never felt farther away from me. He looked around the waiting room: old men turned inward, women his mother's age knitting some fabric out of idle chatter, the news prattling on in high spirits. He didn't know that what would come next would be a flood of miscarriage stories. It seemed like everyone we knew could tell at least two miscarriage stories: mothers, daughters, children, wives, friends. Henry said, "Miscarriage. It's another secret society, like the secret society of married people, but this one we joined by accident, just by living."

"How many more secret societies are there?" I asked him. "I don't want to know."

I would find out later about the secret society of young widows—the way people would introduce one young widow to another, how they would want you to talk about your losses. How many times did my mother tell me that I should spend time with my Aunt Giselle? "Maybe she'll have something important to say." I already knew the truth, that when it is only you and another widow, there is nothing to say. Nothing at all.

After the operation, there was a leak in the house. Henry tore up the bathroom tiles, went rummaging through the house's piping looking for the source of the leak. Henry wanted desperately to make something right.

And I tore into pastries. My mind was filled with elaborate designs. I created gorgeous wedding cakes. We had the Cake Shop by this point, but we hadn't yet developed more than a small, local following. Henry called in professional photographers. The business began to rev up.

A few months before Henry died, he confessed to me that he still wanted another child. "I don't care about money or stuff. And I don't mind the diapers or the sleeplessness, of course. I am not in it for the pride in that first step or any of that. It's more of you that I want—one more angle, one more topic of conversation, one more knowing glance we give each other in the day before we both fall asleep. That's what children offer, isn't it? Isn't that what Abbot's given us—a lifetime of more conversation, our own common ground? He's given us more of each other. Is that wrong, to want more of that? Is it greedy?" His face was so open, his eyes clear.

"I don't care if it's wrong," I said. "Do you?"

"We could really hone our greediness, really blow past our amateur status, and play on the professional greed tour."

And so we started trying again.

Leading up to his death, we felt new to each other, and because no one else knew that we were trying to get pregnant, our sex life took on a kind of covertness that made it feel secretive, urgent.

"Don't you feel like we're romping?" I said. "I just keep thinking of the word *romp.*"

When Henry died, I was waiting to find out if I was pregnant.

I wasn't.

There was the blood proof. Another loss. Gone.

What would I have done with a new baby to raise without Henry? I didn't care about the details. I didn't care about how hard it might be for me and for Abbot, too. I knew only that I'd had a chance to have more of him—to have life in the face of death—but then only death. One more part of Henry, one more potentiality, lost.

I found myself walking into a dress boutique with my mother, Elysius, and Charlotte a few days later, an event orchestrated by guilt. Normally this would be the kind of thing that I would find any excuse to avoid, and certainly, so close on the heels of our brunch—"You have to keep living in the world," and "Every woman needs one lost summer in her life," and "You weren't heartbroken *yet.*" I was feeling cornered, but guilt was creeping in, and my mother knew how to work with guilt. She was going to keep circling until she got what she wanted. Right now, I wasn't taking Charlotte to the house in Provence. I didn't know if Charlotte would want to go if given the chance, and, furthermore, she had no idea that there was a possibility of an offer, but still I felt I was denying her something. And I felt sorry for my sister, too, what with the honeymoon on hold, and so I was also doing a good deed by helping to orchestrate a distraction.

Elysius and my mother charged into a large, airy, over-priced shop called Bitsy Bette's Boutique, occasionally stopping for a brief moment, like butterflies alighting for two wing flaps, to pinch some fabric and decide whether it was "delicate" or "luscious" or "dreamy." Charlotte and I followed with much sighing and eye-rolling. Charlotte despised the place more than I did, but every time Elysius or my mother remarked on an article of clothing, Charlotte and I would whisper to each other the store's slogan, "Forever elegant."

Elysius turned to Charlotte and said, "I'll buy you anything you want in here. A couple of new summer outfits. Your choice! Anything in the whole store."

Charlotte's eyes widened with fear.

"I'm serious," Elysius said, misreading the fear for excitement. "Anything!"

Charlotte looked pale—paler than usual. A whiter shade of pale, one might say—and I'd never understood that lyric until this moment.

Charlotte pulled on my sleeve. "Make it stop."

"Just pick something and let her buy it," I whispered. "It shouldn't take too long."

"You don't even know," Charlotte said. "Time has no rules in this place. Years can pass and she doesn't even know it."

It wasn't long before all of the sales staff was fawning over Elysius and my mother. The fawning was so thorough that I was pretty sure they worked on commission and that they'd made some money off these two in the past—a lot of money. There was a regal woman a good six inches taller than I was and reed thin named Rosellen, a horsey blonde named Pru, and a man, Phillip, who was bogged down shoving shoes onto an old woman's foot, trying to glom on to the Elysius conversation from afar. They didn't look at either Charlotte or me.

"You should see the silk dupioni bolero!" Rosellen said. "Let me go get it in your size." Elysius's size was obviously common knowledge here.

"Oh, but you know," Pru said, undermining Rosellen, who'd gone off in search of the bolero, "you'd really look better in the pleated georgette cocktail dress."

"Don't forget the tulle with gardenia appliqué," Phillip cried out. "I'll get it when I'm through here." This was a nice way of saying, *Hurry up, old lady. I've got real paying customers on my hands.*

"I'd love to get something for Charlotte," Elysius said.

"Something a little youthful," my mother added. "And something for you, too, Heidi. Something lightweight and cool."

The three salespeople froze, as if they'd just seen Charlotte and me for the first time. She was wearing her baggy camo shorts and a suicidal-smiley-face shirt, and before leaving the house she'd slipped on a pair of authentic knee-high fishing boots. I was wearing jeans and a tank top with a sweater over it, an old, ratty cashmere sweater. I wore that sweater a lot those days. It was soft, familiar.

If Elysius knew Charlotte better, she'd have been aware that Charlotte didn't want to be youthful anymore. She didn't want to wear old-lady Bitsy Bette's Boutique clothes and look "forever elegant" either. She wanted to be grown up, deep, appreciated. She was well aware that the real world is painful and violent and sometimes ugly, and she needed her awareness of this to be evident. She couldn't go fluffing around in youthful Bitsy Bette's Boutique–wear. But Elysius could go on these kicks to help others. She saw it as an act of generosity. I'd been the target of many of these kicks throughout my life. When I was little, she was the one who gave me bangs. In middle school, she gave me my first makeover. She made me wear makeup to the roller rink, where some other kid called me a "clown whore." She tagged along and then commandeered my prom dress shopping. Luckily, she was disdainful of weddings when I got married, not being married herself, and so boycotted it, much to my relief. Her desire to fix me up with Jack Nixon came from this same instinct. Although it seemed like she was trying to help— and I was pretty sure she thought she was—it came across as a criticism, as if she were saying, "You're a mess. Let me take over for a few minutes and make your life better . . . more like mine." Charlotte and I had Elysius's do-good bullying in common. Our suffering was an unspoken understanding between us.

"Do you want to take a peek at the stretch-twill ankle-length pants and/or walking short?" Rosellen asked Charlotte. There were so many things wrong with luxury stretch-twill ankle pants that I wouldn't know where to begin. Stretchy twill? I imagined twill grasping at women's doughy thighs. And then some sadist thought to fashion stretchy twill into ankle pants? Poor Charlotte.

And then Phillip added, "Oh, I know, the authentic crochet-trimmed sweater vests. You can't go wrong."

An *authentic* crochet-trimmed sweater vest? As opposed to an . . . *inauthentic* crochet-trimmed sweater vest? "You couldn't go wrong if you were eighty years old," Charlotte muttered, and then she whispered to me, "Did Bitsy Bette's Boutique have the authentic crochet crocheted on by authentic little old ladies in nursing home sweatshops?"

"Charlotte, what do you think? Would you like to try that on?" Elysius asked.

"Forever elegant!" Charlotte said.

"There's also the belted dress," Pru said, noting the sarcasm. "It's youthful, but elegant."

And here I could no longer stop myself. I blurted, "It looks like a dress on a leash."

The salespeople stiffened.

Charlotte laughed. It was the first time I'd heard her laugh in as long as I could remember.

I imagined telling this story to Henry: "And then I said that it looked like a dress on a leash!" I had a backlog of such stories and nowhere for them to go.

Elysius said, "I think it's very tailored and polished. One day soon, you're going to have to start thinking about outfits for college interviews. This is a good start!"

"And what size are you?" Pru asked Charlotte. This was a painful moment, and I wondered for a brief second if it was an unfair payback for Charlotte's laugh at my dress-on-a-leash line. It had a tone that seemed to indicate that it was. Charlotte is bigger than Elysius. No one has Elysius's obsessive-compulsive workout habits. But because Charlotte was wearing baggy camo shorts and baggy shirts with suicidal smiley faces on them, it was impossible to tell how much bigger she was than her stepmother.

Charlotte shrugged.

The three salespeople were staring at her. (The old woman had been left to buckle her own shoes.)

"Where should we start?" Rosellen said.

"I don't *even* know," Phillip said.

Pru said, "A ten, a twelve?"

"Really?" Elysius said.

"Just try a few sizes," my mother said, trying to intervene gently. "Every store varies so much these days, no one knows what size they are anymore!"

Pru grabbed a few different sizes of the belted dress and led Charlotte to the dressing rooms.

Once she was out of sight, I said, "Let's not go with the belted dress or the ankle pants. It's not her thing."

"But it could be her thing, if she tried," Elysius said. "She needs to look professional every once in a while.

Refined. She's Daniel's daughter and she needs to start acting like it."

"What's that supposed to mean?" I asked.

"We're not some middle class family hanging out in a remodeled basement playing GameCube," she said. "Jesus, have you looked at her? She can barely make eye contact. She lives in her own head, and who knows what it's like in there?"

"She's just going through a phase, dear. Don't you remember some of your artsy phases?" my mother said, the second time she'd mentioned Elysius's phases in just a few days. This was, I assumed, some kind of delicious payback for my mother, who'd suffered Elysius's phases—her moving to New York to be an artist had surely caused a lot of sleepless nights.

Elysius stared at her. She didn't want her days as an aspiring artist to be referred to as a phase. This was dangerous territory.

I diverted. "She's just trying to be taken seriously," I said.

"I am trying to take her seriously. One day, someone will take her to France, and what will the French think of her?" Elysius said.

"I don't really care what the nation of France might think of Charlotte, and neither does the nation of France!" I said.

"She could use some adult touches, some refinement!" Elysius looked me up and down. "You could use some refinement yourself."

"Your way to live isn't the only way to live. Your decor has all the coziness of a morgue. You know that, right?" I regretted it the moment I said it. But I didn't apologize. I just walked away.

"Girls," my mother said.

"Fine," Elysius said. "But I'm trying. I am trying." She *was* trying. I could tell that much. It wasn't my place. Motherhood is hard. Stepmotherhood is a land all its own. Elysius was still saying things, but I'd stopped hearing them. I didn't want to talk about this. Moments like these, a buzzing would rise in my ears and the world went muffled, and I felt like saying, "Henry's dead, so you'll have to speak up."

Charlotte appeared in the belted dress, wearing the fishing boots. The belt was too tight. She looked like she'd been shoved into a tube. Her cheeks were bright pink.

"You look beautiful!" Elysius said, with too much desperation in her voice.

"We could go a size bigger," Phillip said.

"I hate it!" Charlotte said. "It's awful and *corporate.*"

"Look," Elysius said. "I had to work to get where I am today. You have been given *everything.* And you're squandering it." This comment was irrational and everyone knew it. The salespeople suddenly dispersed. They'd seen this argument before.

"To squander," I said to Charlotte, trying to bring back some levity. "It's probably on your SAT vocab list." I hadn't realized how bad things were between Elysius and Charlotte. This was a car wreck.

"I'm not *squandering* anything," she said to Elysius. "You squander our money on all of this stuff that doesn't matter.

Stuff, stuff, stuff. This dress costs one-hundred and sixty-eight dollars and it's just a stupid dress on a leash! But if you want me to wear it, I'll wear it. Let's buy it. Go ahead. Let's *squander.*"

I'd never seen this side of Charlotte, this assertiveness. She stood there in the dress, folded her arms across her chest. She was on the verge of tears but was refusing to cry. Her face was stoic except for an occasional bobble of her chin.

Elysius stared at her and then at me and back to her. Some new customers were buzzing at the entranceway to the store.

"Um, okay," Pru said. "Why don't you go back to the dressing room, and then we'll ring it up."

"I'll wear it now. Thank you," Charlotte said.

"Charlotte," Elysius said. "Just take it off. I won't buy it."

"I'll wear it now. Thank you," Charlotte said.

"I'll go back with her," my mother offered.

"No, thank you," Charlotte said.

It was this moment when I felt my loss lift slightly. Here was Charlotte in pain, and she was showing her pain, not hiding it. Although her pain wasn't the same as mine, it was the same. It was dark and deep. It was beautiful. And what if the world has only so much suffering to offer? If so, Charlotte was shouldering more than her share, and it allowed me to take a breath.

The people at the front of the store were inching back toward us. Elysius glanced over her shoulder. "Damn it, Charlotte," she whispered. It was obvious Elysius knew these people—a perky young woman in a spiky haircut, pushing a stroller, talking to her husband—I could see only the beefy back of the man in a pink polo shirt.

"Okay," Elysius said, fishing out her wallet, "we'll just wear this home, then." She put her card on the counter.

Pru looked at her and then began ringing it up. Rosellen disappeared and then reappeared with a bag of Charlotte's clothes, retrieved from the dressing room. She handed it to Charlotte with more tenderness than I'd have given her credit for. Charlotte still wasn't crying, an incredible act of restraint. She held her chin up high.

My mother took the bag from Charlotte. "I'll hold this for you," she said, trying to be helpful.

Elysius folded up the receipt and said, "Let's go out this other way," pointing in the opposite direction of the woman with the stroller.

The ride home was quiet. I sat next to Charlotte in the backseat.

At one point, I reached over and gave her shoulder a light pinch. "That was one way to cut the trip short."

She gave me a sad half smile and pinched me back. "Forever elegant," she said.

"Forever," I said.

That night when I was putting Abbot to bed—the dictionary back on his bedside table—he asked for a Henry story. It had been a long day and I wasn't up for a long story. I said, "Well . . . when your dad was a kid, his parents would sometimes take them to their friend's house on a lake in New Hampshire in the summer. There was a farm next door that had about six Great Pyrenees, huge white dogs that worked the farm. They dug little pits in the yard. And when he and his brother Jim rode by on their bikes, the dogs would come bounding out, howling, all joyfully. They were so happy to see them, but they were so big, and they skidded on the pavement. They were terrifying with all of their happiness, and your dad said it was like trying to ride a bike through a big-dog avalanche. Can you imagine all those massive white dogs coming at you all at once?"

"I know that story," Abbot said solemnly.

"I already told it?"

"Yes," Abbot said, "and Daddy told me it, too."

"Oh," I said.

He rubbed his hands together and said, "Tomorrow night, tell me a story that I don't already know."

This surprised me, but I paused only for a moment. "Okay," I said, and I brushed back his bangs and kissed his forehead.

"Can I have a new pillowcase?" Abbot asked then.

"Why?"

"This one has germs in it from last night and the night before and the night before that."

"It's fine," I said.

"Are you sure?"

"I'm sure."

He pushed the pillow out from under his head. "I don't need a pillow."

I stood up, turned on his Red Sox night-light, and walked to the playroom. I paced a lap and then another. Abbot wanted a new story? One he hadn't heard before? I wasn't inventing Henry Bartolozzi. I was keeping him *here*, alive with us. I felt a frantic, electric buzz in my chest.

I opened the front door. I wanted some night air. It was one of those late-spring nights when the house gets stuffy but the night air is cool. I was trying to rein in a growing sense of panic.

I looked at the yard, lit by a streetlamp. I thought of my

mother pressing me to change my life. *Every woman deserves a lost summer.* I thought of Elysius saying, *I'm trying. I am trying.* And Charlotte, so brave, standing up to everyone in Bitsy Bette's Boutique in her fishing boots. Then I thought of the beluga whales in the aquarium and Abbot talking about their belly buttons. *They're just like us.* I looked over my shoulder at the lit-up house. It struck me then that my life felt like a museum, a museum of loss, and I had created it. Whether I didn't let myself linger or I was overcome with memory, everything reminded me of a story of Henry; everything deserved a plaque: a framed picture of Henry and me at a Japanese steak house with five-year-old Abbot wedged between us; Henry's old Red Sox cap; his cleats from the over-thirty softball league tucked under a bench. There was a picture of Henry and Abbot standing next to Abbot's half-eaten cake on his fourth birthday. That was the birthday that Abbot wished for a candle and then blew out the candle.

I hadn't boxed up a single thing belonging to Henry—a task that seemed unfathomable.

I stared down at my stoop, as if seeing it the way a stranger might. *Because I am a stranger here,* I thought. There were pots that I had neglected for over a year. I picked one up and dumped the dirt in the bushes beside the house and then dumped another. I was crying by this point, my breaths choppy.

When I picked up the third clay pot, I found a purple plastic Easter egg. I picked it up and held it in my hands, as if it were a real egg, as if a baby bird were about to peck its way out.

The past spring, Abbot had gone on a hunt with friends at the local park, which meant that this egg had been hidden by Henry two years ago.

I popped the egg open—the small release of stale air. Inside were two stiff Gummi bears and a piece of hardened bubble gum.

This simple thing broke something inside of me. I was barely there. I was a little pop of air, then nothing.

That spring, Abbot had been obsessed with why the Easter Bunny left eggs and why we all used fake grass and baskets. What did it all mean? Henry wrote Abbot a letter from the Easter Bunny to go along with his chocolate bunny. In it, the Easter Bunny confessed that he had no idea how it all got started. Henry read the note aloud to me. *I'm just a bunny, you know. There's only so much that I can understand.* "I think that we should be honest when the world doesn't make sense." I agreed. "We're just bunnies," I said. He slipped the note in the basket with the fake grass.

Unsteadily, I walked back in to the house. I placed the egg on the dining room table—its two halves, its Gummi bears, and little wrapped piece of hardened gum.

I missed Henry so keenly. This desire for him would well up in me in an unexpected rush. I missed the whole of him—the reality of him, not the stories. I missed his neck, the smell of aftershave that collected there. I sometimes put on his T-shirts after he took them off, still warm from his body, and slept in them. I missed laying my head on his chest and feeling his heartbeat. And I missed his shoulders, his collarbones, his beautiful hands, the fan of his ribs. His body buoyant in the ocean, red with sun. His body in the tight cocoon of sheets. His body bent over tying Abbot's shoes. I wanted to *adore* him. I missed how his face, in sleep, looked as young as the day I met him. I missed his stomach. He had what I called rapper abs. Of course, I missed having sex with him. I would have given anything to have sex with him again—summer sex, if I were allowed to choose—on the bed stripped of its blanket and top sheet, collapsing at the end, the rapt and dazed panting that came after, like two shipwreck survivors who've just crawled onto shore.

I didn't need to go to Provence to appease my mother and sister, to become enchanted. I could learn the lessons I needed to learn right here. *From now on I will try not to lose or be lost. I will not fix my gaze solely on Abbot. I will relearn to live in the real world. Abbot and I don't need a lost summer to learn to live. We've lost enough. We've been lost enough.* But even as I said this to myself, I knew it was probably a cop-out.

Now that I had the little purple plastic egg, I needed something more—a message from Henry. He would tell me not to go. He would tell me to stay with him, to be bound to this house, to let the fig vine that grew around the door actually weave me and Abbot in. Or would he want me to save Charlotte? I wanted to save her. Maybe I wanted to save her because I had the overwhelming desire to save *someone*, and I couldn't save Abbot or myself.

That was when Abbot's dictionary came to me. I walked

back to Abbot's bedroom. There was the dictionary, lit by the dull glow of the Red Sox night-light. I looked at Abbot, his face softened by sleep. I picked up the dictionary, heavy in my hands, and I felt like a thief. But still, I took it.

I walked to the dining room, set it on the table, and sat down in front of it. I opened to the dedications, Henry's father's dedication to him and Henry's dedication to Abbot. I thought of Henry's father then, a tough guy, a man who played football in college, tight end, and was proud of how flimsy the helmets were back then, but at the same time, a romantic, tenderhearted. At Henry's funeral, he broke down and cried. He grabbed my hand as I was getting into the backseat of some long, dark car, and said simply, "I can't accept this. He's my *boy*. He's my *son*. It's not right. I can't get over it. I won't." It felt like he was making me a promise of some kind. Henry's mother appeared then, over his shoulder. "Let her go, honey," she said in her soft Southern drawl. "The cars need to move on." I couldn't bear to look at him. I nodded and slipped into the backseat next to Abbot. Henry's father closed the door for me and then pressed his hand to the window—and that gesture I understood. *Hold on*, he was telling me. *Just hold on.*

Henry, I thought to myself. I wanted to look up *Henry*. Would the word exist? Had he put a little picture of himself there?

I flipped through, found the right page, and let my finger slide down it. This is what I found.

Hennery, a poultry farm.

Henotheism, the belief in one god without denying the existence of others.

Henpeck, to dominate or harass (one's husband) with persistent nagging.

And then *henry. The unit of inductance in which an induced electromotive force of one volt is produced when the current is varied at the rate of one ampere per second.*

And next?

Hent, to take hold of; seize. Obs. Obsolete.

I'm just a bunny, you know. There's only so much that I can understand.

But I did understand—this poultry farm, this henpecking, that I can believe in one god, but didn't have to deny the existence of others. I understood the electromagnetic force of Henry and that he was saying one thing: *Seize it.*

Go.

Part Two

And so the lost summer was seized.

Or should I say that it seized us? Apparently, this is how you get *hent*—without being prepared, without time to brace.

The three of us had passports—Abbot and I had ours because of Henry's good intentions to get us to Europe one day, and Charlotte from a trip to Canada with the French club at her private school for two weeks when she was in eighth grade. I asked Jude to take over the bakery, completely, which was not a dramatic step. She was already in deep. Still, at first I was sure that I could spare only two weeks. But my mother insisted that two weeks wasn't enough time to get the work of remodeling under way. Six full weeks in Provence was the minimum that would do it. I made the reservations quickly, then, knowing I'd back out if I waited too long. We arranged to fly out within a week.

My mother and I had a remodeling meeting at my dining room table a few days before I left. She'd spoken with Véronique and had a better sense of the fire damage, which seemed contained to the kitchen. I was to remodel the kitchen, update the bathroom, and spruce up the four bedrooms with paint, new fixtures and updated wiring for outlets, and wireless Internet access. The yard was also supposed to be brought back to some former glory—including the pool and the stone fountain.

She'd gone out and accumulated a dozen magazines and, bestowing them on me, said, "Feel free to remodel the house with a more modern interior. The juxtaposition of old and new will give the house life. Maybe we'll keep the bedrooms' crisp whites, like linens." She pulled out some color samples she'd picked out at Sherwin-Williams—creams and ivories, a few soft, buttery tones. When she showed me a magazine wholly devoted to tile, I realized that I was in over my head. My mother had even dog-eared some sleek, environmentally friendly toilets. "Which one do you like the most?" she asked.

I thought about it and finally pointed to the wrong one. I knew it was the wrong one by the way my mother tilted her head.

"Really?" she said.

"I guess," I said, and then I pointed at another one. "Or this?"

"Yes, me, too," she said. Suddenly, she shut all of the magazines and piled them neatly on the table. "Listen to me," she said. "I want a lot of things for the house. But dictator is not my role. In the end, you have to do it as you see fit."

"Really?" I wasn't sure I believed her.

"Really," she said. "I have full confidence in you."

She and my father had worked out a budget, a generous one, and she gave me instructions on drawing money from her account to pay for the remodeling. "You must be patient. There's a good bit of bureaucracy when it comes to things like this in France."

"What kind of bureaucracy?"

"Véronique will explain," she said. "Just go and begin to feel the house. You'll connect and then allow decisions to form."

"So, my job is to feel and connect and then make decisions?"

"*Allow decisions to form*," she said. "It's different altogether. The house will tell you what to do."

We were set to fly in to Paris, so my mother booked a hotel for us, insisting that we enjoy a few days in the city before heading out into the Provençal countryside. In addition to sparing me some logistical concerns—she bought our train tickets, too, and made our rental car deal—she gave me a neatly typed list of restaurants, salons, dress shops, parks, museums, theaters. I dutifully tucked them into my bag. It was a list that would take months to tick off—her dream trip, not mine. There was only so much I could do.

Then came time for the flight. Movies on tiny screens, chicken Alfredo served in small, compartmentalized, plastic-wrapped trays, and thin, navy blue airplane-regulation blankets.

Charlotte slept with her earbuds in. Elysius and Daniel had sat her down to tell her the plan. They were braced for resistance, certain she'd say no. But she blinked and said, "Wait, are you telling me that I'm going to France with Heidi and Abbot? Is that what's with the bad-news faces and all the seriousness?"

They nodded.

"Well, I'm in."

"In where?" her father asked.

"Where do I sign?" she said.

Elysius and Daniel still weren't sure they understood.

"Yes!" she said. "Is that clear enough? Yes! I want to *go!*"

Abbot, on the other hand, had to be talked through it. He wanted to pore over the photos. He got out books from the library and found out about scorpions in the South of France. "You have to shake your shoes out before you put them on because scorpions like to live in shoes," he said. "Do you want to live in a place where there are scorpions in your shoes? You're endangering our lives!"

He was afraid of germs. "They have completely different germs there. French germs. We won't have built-up immunity!" We'd discussed, at length, the upside of germs, and so he was very comfortable with the term *immunity*. In fact, he liked throwing it around. I finally gave in and agreed to buy him a travel-sized bottle of Purell for the trip.

He said, "We won't be able to drink the water. The Powells went to a foreign country and couldn't drink the water."

"They went to Cancún," I said. "That's Mexico. It's different."

"Mexico is a foreign country, and France is a foreign country. I'm not drinking anything."

He wouldn't let go of the fact that there had already been a fire there. This was irrefutable proof that France was dangerous territory.

I found the dictionary packed in Abbot's suitcase under a stack of underwear. I picked it up and looked at him. "I can put it on the table next to my bed in France."

I shook my head. "It should stay here. We'll look forward to seeing it again when we get home."

He came up with more fears and excuses, and I told him time and again, "You can't let your fears stop you from living your life." I was talking to myself, mainly. I knew that.

Still, we went. There was no turning back. His barrage of fears only made it clearer that we needed to go.

In the airport, he was afraid of terrorist plots and kept pointing out suspicious people. He begged me to turn in a kid carrying what looked to be a clarinet case.

As the plane touched down at Charles de Gaulle, I looked at Charlotte. She seemed shut off from the world, wearing her earbuds and staring blankly through the small plane window. I thought of what Elysius had said about her—living in the world in her own head. What was that world like? I wondered if I'd ever have any idea, and it struck me for the first time that this trip could be a disaster. What if Charlotte hated it here? What if she shut down completely? I didn't know anything about teenagers. Elysius and Daniel were rational people, and they were at a loss as to how to handle Charlotte. I hadn't really imagined everything going wrong, but it so easily could. I could get stuck in France with a teenager who'd come unhinged. What then?

Meanwhile Abbot was squeezing my arm with his Purell-slick hands. What if the French germs and the contaminated water and the possible house fires and the threat of scorpions proved too much for him? He could come unhinged, too.

And was I really all that sturdy?

Why were we here? The three of us suddenly seemed like an unlikely trio. This was a time for Charlotte to broaden her horizons, a chance for Abbot to overcome his fears, and me? I was on a pilgrimage for the brokenhearted and was supposed to learn to live again—to be alive. And how was I to go about that, exactly? Wait for some enchantment? Feel, connect, and allow decisions to form? I thought of Henry. I had closed my eyes on the plane and whispered to him, "We're going, after all these years. We're really going." And by we, I didn't mean just Charlotte, Abbot, and me. I meant Henry, too. How could I see Paris and the old house in Provence without seeing it as Henry would? How could I do this without sharing it with him, without seeing the world with my eyes and his?

And, on top of all else, there was a house—a charred one, overstocked with various love stories—that I was supposed to restore?

At this point, though, these were all abstractions, and the screaming brakes of the jet, the tires skidding and bumping along the runway, the French flight attendant welcoming us to Paris, these things were real, very real.

By our internal clock, we landed in Paris in the middle of the night. We were exhausted, bleary, but had a jagged energy. There was customs to go through, that slow, shuffling line, and then the swell of a foreign language. I heard things crisply for the first time in a long time, because I had to. I remembered the Babar books from my childhood, the Jacques Brel albums, the French woman in our neighborhood, and her parrots, screeching French vulgarities.

I was surprised how much French I recalled from my mother, who made us speak to her in French from time to time in between our summer trips, seemingly on a whim. She would make a rule. "If you want something, you better ask in French. I'm no longer taking requests in English." She also taught us French through English. "*Maigre* means 'skinny.' Do you hear the word *meager* in it?" She had us listen for words we knew: *sorcerer* in *sorcier*, *obligatory* in *obligatoire*, *roses* in the color *rose, rouge* in the color *rouge*... But most of all I remembered the scolding. In public, she scolded us in French because she thought it sounded elegant to strangers. But to us it just sounded like being scolded. "Ne touchez pas!" "Écoutez!" "Faites attention!"

As we walked out into the bright sun, these phrases flooded back to me. I didn't touch anything! I was listening! I was paying attention!

Outside the airport we got in a taxi and I gave the address of the hotel. The driver understood, and I was impressed with myself.

"Look at you, trotting out the nice French," Charlotte said.

"Try it," I said.

Charlotte stuffed one of her earbuds back in. "All I know is how to sit in language lab and listen to the tapes with the earphones on," she said, a little loudly. She stuffed the second earbud in—with finality—turned, and stared out the window as the taxi pulled away.

Abbot said, "They have smoke detectors at the hotel, right?"

"Of course," I told him.

At first there was only highway, a stadium, traffic. Abbot pointed out the tiny cars; Charlotte, over her music, the preponderance of scooters and motorcycles. Nothing, however, was strikingly different until we entered the city itself.

In Paris everything was foreign, even if only slightly so, but the effect was cumulative: the phone booths, the grille-work balconies, the little alleyways, the lush, green parks—

and then, rounding a corner, there would be an occasional burst of scenery: bridges spanning the Seine, Notre-Dame rearing up as if from nowhere, the Eiffel Tower piercing the skyline mysteriously. I remembered visiting as a child, and then that last time at thirteen. My mother always flew us in by way of Paris, never Marseille, so that she could shop and get us haircuts. There was an afterimage burnt into my mind: the taste of the air, the energy, the brawn of large, stoic buildings mixed with the sudden delicate ornamentation of a gate barring a private entrance. The language everywhere— how it rolls in the throat and bunches the lips.

La France.

I was the inelegant bastard child who'd lived in the wilds of America—and here I was home again in some deep genetic way. I felt proud. Inexplicably proud. Not only of having come from these beautiful people—exquisitely harried and elegantly leisured—but also of having left, of being an American. Rugged, loud, wide-eyed—I was the product of a war that bound two countries together. I imagined my grandparents swept up in the crowds, celebrating the end of the occupation—that kiss. I felt that knot within me.

It was morning in Paris, and we had to survive until the room that my mother had arranged for us was ready that afternoon. So we parked our luggage in a corner of the small lobby of the hotel, the Pavillon Monceau Palais des Congrès. Abbot pulled on my arm. "Ask about the smoke detectors. Ask!" I told him I'd show him the smoke detectors in the room later.

The hotel was in the seventeenth arrondissement, a neighborhood with lots of families and strollers and kids on scooters. Exhausted, we killed time by dipping in and out of shops, one street almost solely reserved for children—toy stores, a bookstore where we bought Astérix comic books, children's clothing boutiques. We wandered through an open-air market and bought fresh peaches, yogurt, Chinese takeout microwaved in waxy bags on the street, a bottle of Sunny D, and bonbons. All the while, Abbot kept close. He wanted to hook his arm in mine, in lieu of holding germy hands. He dipped around people we passed on the narrow sidewalks on the side streets. I knew he was thinking of French people with their completely foreign set of germs.

I remembered bustling around Paris with my mother and Elysius. We would get our hair cut in a salon and then shop wildly, my mother gathering shopping bags along her arms until they were lined with indentations. We did our Christmas shopping, our birthday shopping. We ate in cafés. My mother would only occasionally let us take pictures with our Instamatics. I still don't know Paris by its greatest monuments or landmarks. Anytime we pulled our cameras from our bags, she sighed, as if we were breaking some kind of unspoken promise—we were *not* tourists. As Abbot and Charlotte and I strolled, I missed my mother and Elysius. It wasn't that I wanted them with me at that very moment. I wanted them in the past. I wanted to have back just one sunny afternoon together—before the affair, before my mother disappeared, just that last summer when I was thirteen. I wanted to have back the threesome that we used to be.

In a little open air market lined with shops on rue de Levis, there was a hat kiosk.

Abbot broke from me and pointed, shouting, "Berets! Berets!"

"Absterizer, look around," Charlotte said. "Real French people don't wear berets. They've gone the way of the sombrero and the feathered headdress."

"But we have to!" Abbot argued. "We're in France! We need berets!"

My mother would never have let us buy something as touristy as berets. Still, I wanted something that would bond us together, something frivolous and spontaneous. "Sure! Why not?" I said. "Berets!"

"I want a black one, like the artists," said Abbot.

Charlotte sighed. "I'll take red. A beret will help me with my accent, I guess." She plucked one from the cart, put it on, and said, smiling, "Forever elegant!"

I chose blue. "I don't know whether to wear mine or throw it in the air like Mary Tyler Moore," I said. Neither of them got the reference. Henry would have. I felt like there was so much to tell him. At every turn, I wanted to fill him in. "Here's the little hotel." "Here's the open-air market." "Here we are in our berets."

We ate in Parc Monceau, which was filled with schoolchildren in uniforms and pale office workers and joggers looping the paths. We had no way of washing the peaches—

if there was a water fountain, we'd missed it—not that Abbot could have handled the water fountain germs anyway. We washed the peaches in Sunny D instead. Abbot was liberal with his Purell and refused to sit on the ground, picnic style. Instead he hovered around us and stared at the schoolchildren. We had no spoons for the yogurt, which ended up being unsweetened. My French was not foolproof.

Charlotte caught people's attention. I told her that in London she'd have blended in. London has enough punk ingrained in the culture that they wouldn't register blue hair with black tips. But in Paris, the style always hinges on beauty, not anything else. Not politics or revolution or youthful disgust. No. Beauty. And maybe that, too, was what confused the Parisians about Charlotte. Under the blue and black-tipped hair and the nose ring and the baggy clothes, there was this startling beauty. It was undeniable.

During the morning, she still seemed to be ducking behind me, trying to exist in my shadow. But by midday it seemed to have dawned on her—and maybe the complete exhaustion helped—that she wasn't going to see anyone she knew. No one was keeping tabs on her. If she embarrassed herself completely, it didn't matter. This is the joy of a foreign country.

Abbot must have felt the liberation, too. Even though he kept his hands to himself, refusing to use his hands to push the turnstile in the Métro and waiting for someone else to open the door to a shop first, he started saying *bonjour* to clerks and *excusez-moi* when he dodged around people on the street, like a wee Frenchman.

As we sat at a café, sipping Cokes, I said, "Doesn't it feel good to be anonymous?" Here, I was no longer part of the secret society of widows.

Abbot looked at me strangely. "That means that you don't sign your name to something you've written."

Charlotte said, "Not in this case, Absterizer. In this case, it means that no one knows us. We're flying under the radar. We could be anyone."

Abbot glanced at me sharply. Maybe he knew, deep down, that I'd been having a crisis of identity ever since Henry's death and that being able to be anyone would terrify me. But just the opposite was true. It was comforting.

I said, "No one here knows anything about us." And I meant that no one knew that Abbot and I were survivors of heartbreak. Here, no one was going to hit us with unwanted sympathy and advice and inspirational pick-me-up phrases.

We were free of all that.

That night, in the hotel, I smelled smoke.

Of course, I knew that we had a smoke detector attached to the ceiling in our room, because I'd pointed out its small flashing light to Abbot. It was silent, still flashing.

We'd kept the windows in our room open for cross ventilation—no screens, just as I remembered from my childhood. There was no need for screens. There were no mosquitoes wafting in—just air, a warm breeze. I thought of summer nights in Tallahassee, how Henry and Abbot would watch the small lizards that trawled our screens for moths drawn to our lights. Sometimes they rooted for the lizards and sometimes the moths. Charlotte, Abbot, and I had fallen asleep early to the sounds of people laughing and shouting, distant horns and strange sirens, and to the smell of people cooking dinner, in one window and out the other.

But during the middle of the night when I woke to the smell of smoke, I could tell it was real smoke, not cigarettes, not dinner frying. Abbot was in bed with me and I had to walk past Charlotte's bed to the door. I grabbed the key and stepped out onto the landing.

The stairwell had an old-world graciousness—wide, with faded red carpet, and at each landing stood tall, heavy, old windows that were kept wide open.

Was the smell of smoke stronger here? It was. Just slightly stronger.

I hurried down the stairs, landing after landing.

Was it stronger here? Could I see smoke in the air? Not in the air, no. But the smoke was there and then gone. There, and then nothing.

When I got to the lobby, I realized that I was braless, naked under my white T-shirt and pajama shorts. I was barefoot. I rang the small bell, knowing that I was likely waking up the night clerk. And what exactly was I going to say and how?

The weary clerk emerged from the back room, where, I supposed, there might have been a cot. He was a young man, tall and lanky, trying not to seem sleepy. He patted his hair and straightened his glasses.

"Fumer," I said—the verb *to smoke*. I knew that the verb *to smell* and the reflexive *to feel*, as in a sentiment, were linked somehow. I tried to tell him that I smelled smoke. But I knew that I might have been telling him that I felt smoked.

Regardless, he understood. He stepped out from behind the desk and asked me where I'd smelled the smoke. The fact that he took me so seriously made me more nervous. Why was I down here? I should have woken Charlotte and forced her out of bed. I should have been holding Abbot in my arms at that very moment. Why wasn't an alarm sounding?

I pointed up the stairs and started walking. He followed. We paused on the first landing. I sniffed the air and held up my finger. I said again, "Fumer?"

He shook his head but walked with me to the next landing. We leaned out the window together. We listened to the noises of the city and smelled the air. I remembered my wedding night. Henry and I skipped out of our own reception early. We drove to an old hotel on the Cape where we had a room. There was an Old Home Day going on—a kind of founder's celebration common in New England towns. This one included fireworks. There was a window in a hallway that led to a tar roof. We climbed out the window and stood there—me in my wedding gown and Henry in his tux. Amid the humming air conditioners, we watched the fireworks as the air clouded with smoke. We were new then, our lives stretched out before us. Our families had let us go. Abbot had yet to find us. For this very short time, it would be just the two of us—just two kids.

Was there no smoke? Was the smell only my memory of Henry? Was it some hallucination?

"Non?" I whispered. "Non fumer?"

"Non," the night clerk said. He put his hand on top of mine and said in English, "The night has no smoke. The air is clear." It wasn't flirtatious. It was tender. He seemed to know that I needed someone to say that it was okay.

"Okay," I said. "Thank you. *Merci.*" My mother had once told my sister and me to listen for the word *mercy* inside of *merci.* I could hear her saying, "*Merci,* mercy. Do you hear it? One language hidden inside of another?"

After that night wandering the hotel in search of smoke, I decided that the role of tourist might be best—to hit some of the things on my mother's list and not slow down to think. I recognized that the real challenge would come once I got to the house, where there would be long stretches of time. For now, though, I would push Charlotte and Abbot through Paris.

First stop: the Eiffel Tower. We took the elevator, even though it felt like cheating.

At the top, Abbot kept his distance from the edge, but

Charlotte leaned on the railing and looked over the city. The wind whipped her hair like she was on a ship. The city was sun-dazzled, laid out before us. I walked up to her. "It's pretty up here."

She sighed restlessly then glared at the other tourists. "Paris is cluttered with lovers," she said. "You begin to wonder whether they're paid by the tourist bureau or something."

I agreed. None of them were doing me any good, either, but I wasn't sure what to say. Should I bring up Adam Briskowitz? Was I allowed to know about him? "They're a bunch of fakers," I said, trying to sound light.

We saw the pyramids outside of the Louvre, but we didn't make it inside because the lines were too long. We hadn't purchased ahead. It was summer, and so the tourists came in packs. It began to feel like a betrayal to be in Paris without Henry. *How could I do this without him?* And yet I saw him in the crowds—a glimpse of sneakers; his face hidden momentarily behind a camera; and, once, a Red Sox ball cap, perfectly faded and frayed. I glanced. I didn't let my eyes linger. I always looked quickly away, and we kept driving through the throngs, Abbot chirping, "Excusez-moi!"

I insisted that we go to Place de l'Opéra, where my grandparents once kissed. I told Charlotte and Abbot my grandparents' love story on the Métro as we made our way there. I set up the end of World War II, the massive crowds, how they kissed then got separated and how, later, after the war, he came back to France, and, through the ever-mysterious series of miracles, found her in the house in Provence. I ended the story the way it always ended: "They vowed never to be apart again." When I said it, I felt a chill run across my skin, just like when I was young.

"That's very romantic," Charlotte said, and for once, she didn't sound jaded.

"The house in Provence has a long history of love," I said. "I've told you the stories, Abbot. Haven't I?"

"No," he said. "I know all the Henry stories, but not any house stories."

"Oh," I said. It crossed my mind that maybe I believed the stories still, after all this time, and I hadn't been telling the stories because I didn't want anyone to poke holes in them, as I once had in my youth. But Charlotte and Abbot needed to know where they were headed. "Well, I can fix that." And that's when their history lessons began, the history of the house in Provence, its long history of love, as I put it, all of its miracles.

And Place de l'Opéra itself? It was stunning. We stood in front of the huge building, standing as broad-shouldered as it had been when my grandparents found each other in the crowd. I saw it as a cake—the tiers of arches then pillars then ornate trim and beading, topped with a beautiful greened-copper dome and brightly shining gold angels.

We bounced through the city from story to story, monument to monument. At Notre-Dame, Abbot was impressed by the stained glass portrayal of the man condemned to hold his decapitated head for eternity and, of course, the gargoyles. Charlotte lit a candle and stuffed money into an offertory. This surprised me. Wasn't she too jaded for this? The three of us took seats in the back of the cathedral in the cool darkness.

Tourists shuffled at the edges, creating a hushed noisiness.

I said, "I could use some buttresses, you know, support. Maybe I have buttress envy."

"You could crouch lower to the ground," Abbot said. "Except it's all dirty."

"I hear buttresses take a long time to build," Charlotte said, and she handed me the brochure, and then seemed to disappear into herself. She could do this in a way I'd never seen before—turn her presence on and off.

But she seemed to be taking everything in, even if she was quiet about it and kept her commentary to a minimum. She was impressed by the crêpe vendors on the street, the quick wisps of their instruments. She said, "I love the way the French shove chocolate into everything. It's, like, the best nervous tic ever." She loved the morning coffee and the cubed sugars. She wanted to stroll through the market and look at the fish and roasted pig. She stopped to read the menus that were posted outside of nice restaurants—the ones translated into English. "You could really just eat your way through this town and understand it just as well as walking around and looking at it."

She reminded me of, well, me at the age when I first started to understand food as more than food. Henry had loved food, for all the right reasons—comfort sometimes, but also artistry. To him food was identity, culture, family, how you define home and love and who you are—all of it at once. If we were someplace for a couple of days, he'd try to hit the local market, try to find the quintessentially local cuisine. "It all tells a story," he said.

Charlotte talked about food the way he had. "The sauce hits the roof of my mouth, almost too bitter or something, but then its aftertaste is sweet. How do they do that? Taste this."

I nibbled. This was when the tourism bustle fell away. Time slowed. But I found myself fighting my own desire to concentrate on the taste. I was willing to register texture, but resisted the rest. If Henry and I had been there together, we would have tasted.

"Do you taste it?" Charlotte asked. "Do you know what I mean?"

"I know what I should be tasting," I said. "You describe it perfectly. I just don't. . . . I'm not there. . . ." I shook my head. I remembered seeing Henry tear up once at the end of a meal in New Orleans. "Are you crying over the pecan pie?" I asked him. "No," he said, pressing tears from his eyes. "It's not just the pie. It's chemistry and physics. It's place and time and history and religion and music. . . ." He was overcome.

For all the distraction of Paris tourism, I felt blurred by his presence, overwhelmed with double vision—the world as I was seeing it and the world as Henry would have.

Charlotte seemed to understand that there was more to it and didn't push me.

As we left the café, we were quiet until Abbot spotted the Place de la Concorde. "Look! They have a giant pencil just like ours in D.C."

"Look the world over," Charlotte said, "and you'll find men erecting erections. That, Absterizer, is a sign of patriarchal oppression."

"What have you been reading lately?" I asked Charlotte.

"No need to read anymore to be able to say stuff like that. That's just banter."

"I didn't banter about patriarchal oppression until college."

"Banter has evolved," she said. "Plus, my boyfriend, well, my ex, he was a good banterer and very anti–patriarchal oppression."

And so there was Adam Briskowitz: not a boyfriend, a disaster. And now her ex. How awful could Adam Briskowitz be, really, if two of his defining characteristics as a young man were to be very anti–patriarchal oppression and a good banterer? I knew there was more to it, and so it was my turn not to push. I would push later.

Near Les Halles, we came across a giant statue of a tilted head resting in an open palm. We took turns posing with it as if we were picking its nose.

We were Americans, after all.

Four days after arriving in Paris, we took the TGV—an incredibly fast train—to Aix-en-Provence, and I was relieved that we wouldn't have to keep up the pace of tourism. It hadn't worked as a foolproof distraction, as I'd hoped. We were going to set up house, create daily rhythms. We weren't going to have to comment on what we saw, photograph it, treat it as a memory in the making. We were just going to live, to be. I'd gotten fairly good at faking this at home. How much harder could it be in Provence?

With much confusion and anxiety, I picked up our rental car near the Aix-en-Provence train station—which is not to be confused with the other Aix-en-Provence train station, as my mother had. This was a sad reminder that my mother hadn't been to Provence in decades. We'd never talked about the details of her return home after her lost summer, but I knew that she and my father had reached some agreement. Had she promised never to return to the house in Provence if my father promised never to stray again? Or was it unspoken? Had my mother simply felt that she had to give up some part of herself in order to keep the marriage intact?

While we loaded our baggage into our rented Renault, I realized what was wrong. It wasn't simply that I was frazzled after demanding a rental car in the wrong place then having to take a taxi across town to the right train station. I was going to have to drive—in France. I remembered my mother navigating these roads, peeling out anxiously into rotaries, pulling over onto shoulders choked with high weeds to avoid oncoming cars. French drivers terrified her. And although I once prided myself on my driving, Henry's crash had shaken me. I would sometimes grip the wheel and imagine its impact on his ribs, his chest. As I asked Charlotte to get the map and directions out of one of the pockets in my bag, I must have sounded nervous.

"Do you want me to drive?" she asked tentatively. "I will, you know, even if it's illegal or something here."

"It's okay," I told her.

"But you know the way," Abbot said from the backseat, where he'd already buckled himself in. "You were here when you were little a lot."

"Things have changed," I said, "but we'll be fine, and eventually I should recognize things. Mountains don't change."

I started up the car and pulled onto the narrow street. Aix-en-Provence was a bustling city, traffic zipping everywhere. We took the highway to lesser roads via rotary after rotary—what is with the French and their love of rotaries? The signs, the tollbooths, the rest stops were all foreign, the strange scenery that tried to lure my eyes from the road—maybe these were good. I couldn't think too much of Henry. I had to focus.

Charlotte called out route numbers and matched them with road signs. She kept me on track. Eventually we found ourselves in the countryside, which was somewhat calmer. The ancient Mont Sainte-Victoire looked like it had only freshly torn itself up from the ground—muscled ridges, pockets of light and shadow from the spotty dark clouds set against a bright, bruised sky.

I thought of the stories from my childhood—this landscape, the promise it held for me then. "In the beginning," I heard myself say, just as my mother had always started the first story of the house—the birth of the house itself, one of my ancestors, who built the house, stone by stone, alone, without stopping, for one year, all to win the heart of a woman. "And she fell in love with the house and the man who'd built it." The car was quiet, and each of us was windblown from the open windows as we drove on past farmland, a fruit and vegetable stand, and beautiful, old Provençal homes.

"The sky is like one of Uncle Daniel's paintings," Abbot said, his voice wistful. "If you tilt your head and squinch your eyes."

"Everything looks like my father's paintings if you squinch your eyes enough," Charlotte said. "In fact, it's best if you close your eyes altogether if you want the full effect of my father's work." Charlotte's resentment of her father's career—or maybe, more accurately, not his career but his singular, passionate focus on it—cropped up in an angry edge to her voice.

"But Abbot's right," I said. "His new work with the thick lines reminds me of the mountains."

Charlotte didn't reply, but leaned forward to turn on the radio. For the next several minutes, she fiddled with the dial, finding only techno-pop and French ballades. Eventually she landed on Pat Benatar singing "Hit Me with Your Best Shot." I started belting it out and she and Abbot joined in. The cicadas were noisy in the tall grass, so noisy, you could even hear them over the noise of the engine and the music and our boisterous singing.

Benatar was followed by a Jacques Brel song. I told Charlotte to leave it on. I remembered it from my mother's albums. I hummed along, following signs to Puyloubier, the small village in walking distance from the house.

The kids had both seen photos of the house—my mother's, and Elysius's most recent album, too, from her trip with Daniel the summer before, when he'd proposed to her. Her photos showed an older, wearier version of the house than in my mother's pictures.

"There will be a small sign and a long shared driveway," I reminded them, "and two houses set way off the road. The smaller one, with blue shutters, is ours. The mountains will be there, pressed up to the backs of the houses, and big trees. On our land there's a fountain with fish in it—fat orange koi—and a pool."

They knew all of this, but they listened quietly. Maybe they wanted to hear it again. On either side of us, there were vineyards—long rows of thick stalks, green leaves, the posts, and thin guide ropes. The whole valley was trilling with cicadas. I remembered describing their sound to Henry, and the way that, in early spring, he would always take Abbot and me out to hear the peepers in the swamps, the frogs' shrill mating calls, a chorus of love songs.

As we pulled onto the route leading directly to Puyloubier, the road narrowed, the tall weeds and fences dotted with small white snail shells I remembered from my childhood. I was sure only one car could manage at a time but soon realized that cars coming in the opposite direction weren't afraid of the tight squeeze. They barreled along at breakneck speeds, their engines roaring by as I bumped off onto the road's edges. I held my breath when they passed— an instinct to suck in my stomach, as if that would help. My heart felt like a battering ram in my chest. I thought of Henry—I imagined the steering wheel in my ribs, an engulfing fire . . .

We didn't see the sign or the shared driveway that led to the house, and so before we realized it, we ended up in the town. "How did I miss it?" I said aloud, jangled.

"It's still back there somewhere," Charlotte said. "I mean, it didn't disappear! We should just get out and walk around."

"I want to see what the town is like!" Abbot shouted.

"Okay, we could take a little walking tour and hit the market for some groceries," I said, trying to calm down.

I parked near a small bus stop in front of a wine shop. Another Renault parked beside us. As we were getting our bearings, the two passengers were stretching their legs, preparing for a hike on one of the nearby trails. Both men wore man capris, and I assumed they were German tourists. By the way they looked at each other, almost furtively, I thought maybe they were lovers.

We walked past a group of boys, shirtless, in long madras and flowered shorts, playing soccer in the square, and old men playing bocce under small trees in a dusty courtyard in front of a large municipal building, painted deep orange with large windows and a Spanish-style roof. A beautiful woman with straight black hair had parked a stroller with a sleeping baby inside of it and was sitting on a bench near the circular fountain surrounded by a cobbled square. She was watching another child ride his bike around the courtyard. "Doucement, Thomas!" she called to him, wanting him to be more careful. "Doucement!" Other than that, the town was quiet, almost empty.

The village was small, the kind to have only one of everything—one store, one café, one church, one school—all nestled amid a grid of only six or so main streets. The streets, steep and winding, were lined with tall, narrow row houses, interrupted occasionally by alleys of stone stairs. Built into the base of the mountain, it was a sturdy village, as if hunkered against stone. We wandered to a scenic overlook on a hillside covered in lilacs. Beneath us was an expanse of farmland, rich earth, well tended.

"Do you smell that?" Charlotte asked. "It's like I finally understand what all those scented candles want to be."

Abbot had to pee, and so he found a hidden spot among the lilacs. He discovered the snails. "They're everywhere! Look."

We examined them closely—their long-stemmed eyes, the fragile swirls of their shells.

"*Escargot*," Charlotte said. "I know that one."

We strolled up a side street, past the schoolyard and the church with its bell tower and row houses with steep front steps and colorful shutters, washed-out blues and greens. We passed a small fountain with a statue of a cherub holding a water jug. An old woman was scrubbing a marble bench.

And then we were heading downhill. We passed a sign that read LES SARMENTS. Up an alleyway of stone steps, there was the promise of a restaurant, hidden away somewhere. *Sarments*—I didn't know what the word meant. I'd have to look it up.

We turned left, passing Café Sainte-Victoire. There were a few locals standing at the bar, a television mounted in the corner playing a French music video that had to have been produced in the eighties. Charlotte and Abbot dipped into the ice cream cooler and pulled out ice cream cones wrapped in thick paper. I ordered a coffee. We lingered by the tables in front of the shop as the waitress shuttled back and forth, handling the customers who sat on the raised, shaded deck, eating late lunches. I remembered the bustle of this little hub not far from the square. The air was what felt most familiar—crisp and clear. I felt like my lungs were learning to breathe in a new way.

Next door was the Cocci market, a tight grocery store with a wall of produce and a half dozen rows of essentials. Abbot was obsessed with the Haribo candy stand, with its small pictures affixed to the flip-out windows. He wanted to pull all of the knobs and peer inside. But knobs? Touched by hundreds if not thousands of grimy kid hands before him?

He stood there with his hands in the pockets of his shorts. He'd stopped wearing his gym shorts a few weeks earlier, opting for shorts with pockets only. He glanced at me, but I pretended not to notice his dilemma and instead told him that I'd buy him one packet. "But that's it, so choose wisely."

Charlotte waltzed by. "Get the Gummi Fizzy Colas."

He looked at Charlotte then at me. "I just had ice cream," he said. "I'm not hungry."

"You don't eat candy because you're hungry," Charlotte said. "That's a very basic rule of childhood. Are you an alien?"

She didn't say it with any malice, but still Abbot looked at his shoes and shook his head. I knew that he felt like an alien sometimes.

"We'll be back," I said.

We bought simple necessities: bottled water, milk, Brie, crackers, strawberries, shampoo.

And that was it. That was the town. Simple. Lit up with afternoon light. As we walked back to the car, we noticed a few gloomy clouds collecting overhead, a light, whipping wind. Still, the air was so clear and light, it felt otherworldly, as if some of the rules of gravity might not apply here.

As we piled back into the car, Charlotte said, "So, let's give this another shot."

"I'll call Véronique," I said, "to let her know we're coming and maybe ask for a landmark or two."

"Or six," Abbot said.

I started the car and reached for my phone in the side pocket of the door. It was gone. "Where's my phone?" I asked, then turned to Charlotte. "Maybe it's in the camera bag or in with the laptop."

Charlotte looked in the footwell and then twisted around to check out the backseat. "Where's my camera bag?"

"Abbot," I said. "Do you see the laptop bag?"

"No!" Abbot said anxiously.

We'd been robbed. The realization washed over me slowly. I popped the trunk and jumped out of the car, cursing vividly. Abbot's suitcase and mine were gone. Charlotte had carried an Army-issue duffel bag that had been sitting in the backseat—gone, too. Plus all of our electronics—camera, laptop, Charlotte's iPod.

"Wait," Charlotte whispered, "my music!"

I thought of the two guys in the other Renault, stretching in their man capris, the two gay German tourists who probably weren't gay or German or tourists, but ordinary thieves who'd followed our rental car off the highway. Their car was gone.

"It's only stuff," I said, trying to be calm. "They only stole things. It's okay."

But Abbot looked stricken—pale and stunned. "The dictionary," he said. "The dictionary!"

"No," I said, "we didn't pack it, remember? It's on your bedside table."

He started crying uncontrollably. "I hate robbers," he said. "I hate them! I hate them!"

"Yes," I said. "But it's okay. We're all fine."

Charlotte was furious. "I can't believe it!"

"How did they get in the car? Did I not lock it? Is that possible?" It was possible, I realized in a sickening flash. I'd been so on guard in Paris, on the train, but here, in this little idyllic village, I'd let my guard down.

I looked around for witnesses. The old men playing bocce were too far away. The mother with the stroller and the boy on the bike were gone. But at a nearby bus stop, there was the group of shirtless boys who'd been scuffling around with a soccer ball earlier. They were staring at us, still scuffling.

I decided to start with them. Maybe they'd seen something.

Abbot was out of the car now, too, clinging to me, his arms wrapped around my waist. He was crying. "I packed important stuff," he was saying. "Really important."

Charlotte stepped out of the car, too. "It's okay, Absterizer," she said, but she looked shaken herself.

It had started raining, only lightly, but the kind of rain that could build into a fleeting summer storm.

I glanced at the group of boys again, not one of them older than thirteen. "I'm going to ask them if they saw anything."

Just then, a boy, a little taller than the rest in filthy sneakers and flowered shorts, lifted a gun over his head and very slowly and methodically lowered it so that it was pointing right at us.

"Get in the car," I said in a low, urgent voice. "Now."

"What? It's only rain," Charlotte said, getting into the passenger's seat and looking around.

I picked Abbot up by his armpits and threw him into the backseat, slamming the door. "Heads down!" I shouted as I jumped into the driver's seat. My heart was hammering in my chest.

Charlotte and Abbot crouched low in their seats.

"What is it?" Abbot screamed.

"Nothing. Just keep your heads down." I threw the car into reverse, peeled out, and then jammed the car into drive and drove off.

Charlotte and Abbot shrank down farther into the footwells.

Charlotte said, "I saw it. I saw it, too."

"Saw what?" Abbot cried.

"I can't die," Charlotte whispered. "I can't. Not yet."

I was thinking now only of how to get away, how to push the car as fast as it could go, how to put as much distance as possible between the gun and us. The robbery was nothing now. My hands gripped the wheel. I leaned into the windshield and gunned the gas. The rain had picked up and was now drumming down on the car's roof. My head was full of noise. I drove the cramped roads, the wipers beating back and forth. I could barely see through the windshield. It had been raining on the morning Henry died; fog had rolled onto the highway. I turned on the headlights. The road was a blur.

"I've got my phone!" Charlotte said triumphantly, pulling out her cell phone from one of her many pockets and handing it to me.

I glanced at it—forty-one missed calls. Forty-one? I flipped it open and dialed 911. It was the only thing I could think of. It started ringing. I felt relieved. "It's 911! It works!" I slowed down a little.

And then an officer answered in French. Well, of course. Had I been expecting English? I suppose I had.

"Bonjour!" I said, reverting to primary French. I told the officer, in short, declarative French sentences, that I was in Puyloubier, that we'd been . . . *violated*, then I said, no, not violated. *Robbed.* The two words are similar in French, but one means "raped," the other "robbed." The car was robbed, I told him. And then I said, "Je suis Américaine." I don't know why this seemed crucial. Did I expect someone to call the American embassy? I told him that there was a boy with a gun.

"Non, non." He laughed and then corrected me. The words for *gun* and *rocket* are also similar.

"Oui! Correct!" I said that it was a boy with a gun. Not a rocket.

An oncoming car came at me down the narrow road and

I swerved. The Renault stalled out on a shoulder of high weeds.

The officer said he would put me through to someone at the station in Trets, someone who spoke English.

The rain was so loud now that I could barely hear the officer's voice. I was losing reception. I got out of the car, pacing in one direction and then another. I hunched over, trying to keep the phone dry.

And then a man's voice came on the line and spoke to me in English. "Yes. Can I help you?"

The phone beeped that it was running low on batteries. It was going to die. Charlotte's charger had been in the computer bag. The computer bag that was now gone.

I explained what had happened, as quickly as I could.

The officer was very calm—*tranquil*, as the French would say. "The gun probably wasn't real. They're illegal here. Children have fake guns. It was probably, how do you say? A joke."

"Where I come from, guns aren't funny," I said, near hysteria.

"Well, no," the officer said. "Where you come from, the people shoot each other."

I wasn't sure how to take this, but I was insulted—although it was true. "We're staying in the house next to Véronique Dumonteil's bed and breakfast. My family owns this house."

"Yes. I know the house you're telling me. Listen, the thieves sometimes leave the non-valuables by the road. I will send someone to look. You must make a report at the station in Trets." Trets was the closest good-sized town. I knew it well. We'd gone there sometimes as kids for the attraction of the larger grocery store. The village of Puyloubier was too small to have its own police station.

"Today?" I asked.

"No, no," he said. "Tomorrow is fine. Rest. Be calm."

I got back in the car, soaking wet, humbled. "The gun was a fake," I said. "That's what the cop said." This was no comfort. My head felt like it was filled with air. My chest felt swollen and my breaths became shallow.

"What gun?" Abbot said.

"The fake one," Charlotte said. "They were just kids in flowered shorts with a fake gun."

"They could have been in a gang," I said.

"It's absolutely possible that gang members in the South of France wear flowered shorts," Charlotte said.

I turned the key in the ignition. The engine sputtered then died. I slammed my fist on the steering wheel and tried it again. The engine coughed then nothing. I imagined Henry, standing on the shore while calling to Abbot and me in the ocean, *Too far, too far!* This was when I started to cry.

"What if we're stuck here and the robbers find us and want to shoot us?" Abbot, still shaken and sniffling, said from the footwell in the backseat.

"I can't breathe," I said. "Roll down the windows."

"It's still pouring," Charlotte said.

"It's a rental!" I shouted. "Get up off the floor, Abbot! It was a fake gun!"

"We don't have to panic," Charlotte said, calmly now.

Abbot kneeled on his seat, his forehead pressed against the window, trying to see out. "We're in a car in the South of France. The robbers are gone. No one is coming after us. It was a fake gun! Everything is fine!"

I squeezed my eyes shut. Henry would have known what to do. Henry would have saved us. But he was gone. All of our things were gone. "What am I doing here?" I said. "What in the hell am I doing here?"

"Call Véronique," Charlotte said. "That's what you were going to do before."

I looked at Charlotte. Her eyes were clear and bright. She was focused. She was good in an emergency. Charlotte! "Right," I said. I dug the phone number scribbled onto a lit-tle piece of paper out of my pocket. I dialed. The phone rang. I was expecting Véronique, but it wasn't her voice. Did I have the wrong number? "Allô?" I muttered.

Charlotte took the phone. "We're looking for Véronique Dumonteil," she said, then listened. She cupped her hand over the receiver. "Yes, yes. Thank you." Charlotte explained that the car had died, where we were, and then said, "Mm-hmm, okay, blue. Thank you." She shut the phone. "Some-one's coming," she said, rolling up the window.

"Why blue?" I asked.

"What?"

"You told them blue. Why?"

"The color of the car," she said. "It sounded like a party was going on in the background."

"A party?" I said. "We just got robbed!"

"I don't think the party's for us," she said. "No correlation. Are you going to be okay?" she asked me.

"No," I said. "Probably not."

The rain kept pounding the car. We sat there in silence, except that Abbot was still crying a little, and the car filled with steam that fogged the windows.

Eventually, a sporty convertible came racing toward us in the rain. The top was down. A man was behind the wheel. He pulled off the road and headed right at us. He stopped just short of hitting us and parked the cars nose to nose. "Jesus!" I said.

Since the convertible lid was down, he put his hand on the top of the windshield, the wipers still batting back and forth, and pulled himself up to sit on the top of the seat, then rubbed the rain back into his dark hair with his free hand. He waved.

Charlotte waved back. "That must be the someone who's coming."

I recognized him immediately. I knew his boyish face even though he was all grown up. "That's the other brother," I muttered.

"Brother other than what brother?" Charlotte said.

"The sulky boy from the lawn chair," I said. "The one without the pogo stick."

Stay here," I said to Charlotte and Abbot. "Let me check things out."

"Are you sure?" Charlotte asked.

I nodded, but I wasn't sure. I felt panic stricken, irrationally suspicious, and hostile. I climbed out into the pouring rain and walked to the convertible with no idea where to begin.

"The roof of the car is broken," Julien said in a French accent, *the* sounding more like *zee*, and the *rs* in *roof* and *broken* making a little buzz in his throat. He was wearing an expensive suit, tailored, with a thin gold tie—completely soaked. If he hadn't been in a convertible in the driving rain, he would have looked like the kind of man you'd see in an advertisement for expensive shoes—a man on a speedboat. "Usually, I only drive in the sun."

"What about when it rains unexpectedly?" I asked. This was not important now, of course. But it was all I could think to say.

He spread his arms wide. "I become wet," he said, and he smiled, his lips shiny from the rain. Then he leaned over the dashboard, wiped the rain from his dark lashes. He was beautiful. He had a broad chest. I could see the muscles through the thin, drenched white shirt. He was tan, as if he'd spent a good bit of time on Mediterranean beaches. As kids, our families had gone on a few beach trips together. We brought pails and caught small crabs in them. He and his brother, Pascal, wore little tiny French swim trunks that my sister and I made fun of behind their backs. It was as if he was remembering me in his childhood, too. He said, "You came here when you were a girl with your sister and your mother. You would arrive, stay for a little while, and then go. I haven't forgotten you. You have the same face."

"You used to splash me in the pool," I said.

"Me?" He seemed to consider this for a moment—had he been the kind of kid to splash American girls in a pool? He decided that he wasn't. "No," he said. "Not me."

"We've been robbed. All of our stuff was stolen from the car while we were out walking around town," I said flatly. I was trying very hard to breathe normally. "I'm having a panic attack."

"Really?" he said. "You don't seem like it."

"I don't seem robbed, or like I'm having a panic attack?" I said.

He tilted his head and gazed at me. "You were a strange little girl," he said. "You were always very courageous. You wore a barrette right here," he said, pointing to one side of his head. "The barrette had a flower. Is that how you are now?"

I was having a panic attack. That was how I was now. I said, "After we were robbed, some kid aimed a gun at us, in the parking area." I pointed down the road. "Just a few minutes ago."

"Ah," he said, folding his wet arms across his wet chest. "It was probably a fake gun."

I was already a little tired of having this pointed out to me. "I think it's best to go through life assuming that guns are real."

He looked at me as if he were about to say something smart-assed but then changed his mind. He'd been a smart-ass kid. I remembered that his brother was the one everyone loved. And Julien was the one who shrugged a lot and kept things to himself and muttered funny things under his breath and sometimes cheated at the card games we played.

"Are you drunk?" It dawned on me now that he might be—a man in a suit driving in a top-down convertible in the rain. Charlotte had said that it sounded like a party was going on in the background.

"A little," he said, shrugging. "It's a party."

"What's the party for?"

He paused a moment. "No occasion," he said, and he slid down in the seat, turned off the car, and pulled the keys from the ignition. "Maybe you should drive?" He threw the keys up in the air to me. I made no attempt to catch them. They landed at my feet.

"I can't drive," I shrieked. "I'm having a panic attack!"

We stared at each other; then he tilted his face up to the sky. "We are unlucky at this moment," he said loudly, above the din of the rain. And then he squinted toward our rental.

"The girl?" he said. "She can drive, no?"

"I don't think kids learn to drive stick shift anymore."

"What is stick shift?"

I pretended to shift gears. "Manual," I said.

"Ah," he said. "Stick shift." He gestured for her to roll down her window.

"What is it?" she called out.

"Can you drive?" he shouted. "It is a manual stick shift."

"Manual stick shift?" she said.

"Can you drive a stick?" I shouted.

"Oh, yeah, stick," she said. "I learned in a mall parking lot at night." I imagined her out in a mall parking lot driving in the dark with Adam Briskowitz. Maybe the disaster, as my mother called him, had come in handy.

"Excellent," Julien said, and then he shook his hair out the way Abbot does when he comes up from under water. It struck me as a very boyish thing to do. Had he grown up at all? "It is normal for an American to assume all guns are real, isn't it? You cannot fault yourself. Americans have guns the way Brits have bulldogs."

"Are you calling me a typical American?" I asked.

"Do typical Americans have long conversations in the rain?"

"I prefer the other brother—the one with the pogo stick," I said.

"Yes," he said. "You are not all alone in that."

The car had died less than a mile from the house, which struck me as a real defeat—like the stories of people in the desert who collapse inches from a watering hole. Hydration wasn't our problem, however. We were drenched. And the rain was still coming down hard. We must have looked strange, the four of us packed in the sports car, driving along with the top down in the rain. Charlotte was doing well behind the wheel, Julien giving gentle directions, his elbow propped on the passenger's-seat window, which was rolled down—with the top down, what was the point of rolled-up windows? He seemed oddly happy to get out of that house with a nice buzz going, to have an excuse to drive out in the rain in his father's old sports car, with its busted lid. There was something else about him—a deep restlessness, a nervous energy, something riding underneath.

The seats were drenched. But the sharpness of the rain on my arms and the cool air was good for me, as if bringing me back to my body.

"Gently," Julien said, as Charlotte ground through the gears. Once she got it puttering along in third gear, Julien leaned out the window, the way a dog would on a sunny day.

All the while, Abbot rattled off the story of what we'd just endured—the robbery, the fake gun, the rain, calling 911. Julien was surprised that 911 worked. Sometimes Abbot did this when he was nervous, "the word barrage," Henry used to call it. Abbot was rubbing his hands wildly, like someone desperate to get warm. I kept an eye on him. We were sitting side by side in the backseat with our groceries on our laps. Buying groceries seemed like it had happened in a different lifetime, another era, back in the good old days when people could walk the streets safely without the fear of being robbed and taken aim at, albeit with fake guns. Abbot finished his account, ending with, "My grandma would say that when things go wrong, it's a Buddhist gift." I was surprised that my mother had shared this insight with Abbot. Her far-reaching knowledge was something she kept to herself. But, of course, she knew about world religions

and had once confided in me that she liked Buddhism because "it was the kind of religion that didn't begrudge you a
BMW." My mother is a complicated woman.

"Are you a Buddhist?" Julien asked Abbot.

He shrugged. "Kind of. But I miss my stuff. We had good
stuff."

"I used to have good stuff," he said, and he pulled at his
thin necktie. "Just up ahead," he said. "See the sign?"

There it was: a white sign with small black lettering dug
into the roadside. "No wonder we missed it before," Abbot
said.

"No one has stayed in your house since the fire," he said,
"except this one Parisian couple when we had no rooms.
They were desperate. But then they had a fight while playing
croquet and left."

"Someone stayed there?" I asked. "It must be livable then."

"It is," he said. "The bedrooms were not touched by the
fire. But the house needs help. I think the Parisian couple saw
the destruction as symbolism. This is the French."

"Romantic," I said.

"Like we are trapped in an old French film," he said. "An
American film, well, that is different. You can have a happy
ending sometimes. But a French film? No, but here we are."
He held out both hands, proof of his existence. He was lean
and muscular, that lithe European body type that lent itself
to the development of soccer players.

"I never realized the heavy responsibilities that come with
being French," I said.

"It is a burden," he said.

We drove up the long shared driveway, vineyards on either side, tires clipping along through a few fresh puddles. On the left was their large stone house, and on the right was our smaller one. Our house looked disheveled, embattled. The shutters were askew, as if the house had been beaten by too many mistrals, the cold violent winds that whip through the region most bitterly in winter and spring. The yard was newly mowed but not tended beyond that. Weeds had taken over the flower beds, bullied up higher than the lip of the old fountain, barely visible from afar.

"It's still standing," I said quietly.

"It's not only the fire," Julien said. "My mother's fatigued. She has let things fall. She wants to talk to you." He looked at me for a moment, his dark lashes still wet. "Yes," he said as if answering a question I hadn't asked. "I studied in America one summer in university. I expected to run into you."

"Oh," I said. "Were you in Florida?"

"No," he said. "Boston. I didn't realize how big the country is. I never found you."

"You should have gotten your mother in touch with mine, given me a call."

"No, I wanted to run into you. It's different. But here you are now." He glanced at me, smiled. Was he confessing that he'd had a crush on me all these years? He changed the subject. "The rains here are rare and brief." And he was right. The rain was already letting up. On the distant ridge of the mountain, there was late afternoon sun, clear and bright.

Julien told Charlotte to park in a garage that sat between the two houses—both in the shadow of Mont Sainte-Victoire.

We all climbed out of the car. The rain was ticking in the tall trees overhead. Our view of the mountain was its long, ridged back. It went on for miles, ending at the far left in a steep cliff that plummeted down to the villages outside Aix-en-Provence. Massive and hulking, Mont Sainte-Victoire, one of the earth's ancient monuments. I remembered walking on the mountain as a child. The mountain's terrain was rough—dusty, with large rocks for handholds and footholds, but small stones that made your sneakers slip. It was easy to fall, skin a knee. But it was worth the effort—the idea that you could pull yourself up, at least partially, to afford a view high enough to make the houses look like dollhouses, to make you feel mighty.

The Dumonteil property stretched all the way to the base of the mountain, but the large backyard was delineated by tall trees, and within the space, there was a long table, covered by a tablecloth, slack with water. There were a few drenched candles and abandoned wineglasses, filled now with rain.

"You're welcome to join us," Julien said. "I have old friends of the family and many archaeologists, wild archaeologists." He sighed as if wearied by wild archaeologists.

"*Wild* archaeologists?" Charlotte said, indicating that *wild* didn't go with her definition of *archaeologist*.

"There has been . . . an infestation of archaeologists here. They have lived in both houses. One archaeologist started the fire, in fact. They work here during the day and some-times take meals but are now living in Aix. Less dangerous."

"Why are they here?" I asked.

"A man found something while digging for the pipes. It was a tomb. They have been pulling things from the earth." He gestured vaguely beyond the trees.

"Bones?" Abbot said.

"Yes, a Gallo-Roman tomb, ancient," he said. "My mother is very, how do you say, nostalgic about old tombs."

"I see." I didn't see. I'd never formed an opinion about old tombs.

"Come in?" he asked. "The food is excellent, the real Provençal." It seemed like he didn't want to go in himself. He was lingering. A round of laughter rose up from the house, and the back door opened.

Véronique emerged. She was wearing a small cast on her leg, taking the back stairs one at a time—and then she said, "Our Americans!" I walked to her, and Charlotte and Abbot followed. She smiled at us, embraced me, kissing each of my cheeks. "You became a woman. You're beautiful." I didn't feel beautiful in the least, especially not in this moment. "Always a surprise!"

I was always a surprise? Or my family was a surprise? Or all Americans were a surprise? Maybe this was a vague his-torical reference to D-Day? "Didn't my mother tell you that we were coming?" I asked. "I'm so sorry if there was some misunderstanding. . . ."

She raised her hand and shook her head. "No, I heard

from your mother. She is always a surprise. That is how you learned it."

Learned what? I thought. *How to be surprising?* Maybe she knew that my mother's running off to the house was a surprise—a woman running away from her life. Véronique now kissed Charlotte's and Abbot's cheeks. He braced himself for the kisses' germs, squeezing his eyes shut and scrunching his nose, even though I'd warned him.

Three men walked out of the house at that moment, holding glasses of wine, then onto the yard. I felt like a strange spectacle. *Look, some Americans have landed on the lawn! Hurry before they fly away!*

"Thieves broke into their car and took all of their things," Julien told his mother.

"All of your things were taken?" Véronique said. "It is necessary to tell the mayor."

"The mayor?" I asked, looking at Julien.

He nodded. "Yes, the mayor of Puyloubier. He will want to know this."

Abbot piped up. "The house has a smoke detector, doesn't it?"

"Yes, of course," Véronique said, maybe a little insulted.

"He's a little nervous," I said. "That's all."

A gorgeous young woman appeared on the steps. She was wearing a tank top and a faded jean skirt, barefoot. "Julien!" she called to him, pouting. "Viens! Je t'attends!"

"J'arrive, Cami!" he called back, and then he smiled. It struck me that Julien, the splasher, the sulker, the boy who'd led me up to the mountain chapel haunted by a decapitated hermit, had become a playboy. "Coming in?" he said to me.

"Please!" Véronique added.

"Another time," I said. "We're still recovering. You know, the robbery, the gun . . ."

"Tomorrow," Véronique said, shooing everyone back inside. "Breakfast!"

"Yes, thanks," I said. "We'll be there."

"Do you have your papers for the rental car?" Julien said. "I can take care of that for you. Calling, explaining, arranging . . ."

I dug in my purse and handed him the rental agreement. "I have to make a police report in Trets," I told him.

"If the car is not here, then I will take you. With luck, it's not raining."

"Thanks," I said. "For everything." Abbot and Charlotte were talking about bedrooms, who would get the biggest one, which one would be left empty. I walked toward them but turned back to say, "Maybe I'll run into you!"

"Maybe," he said, and then his eyes flitted over my body, my wet clothes. I wondered if it was all see-through. He seemed embarrassed, and he quickly said, "There are, what do you call them, coats for leaving the bath? They are in the closets. You can wear them while your clothes dry." And then he turned and loped off into the house.

"Clothes," I said to myself. We would need all new clothes.

"Clothes," Charlotte said. "Where am I going to find clothes that aren't all . . . French?"

"They make the boys wear very small bathing suits here," Abbot said. "I saw pictures of them in my word books." My mother always bought him French word books. He looked a little terrified at the prospect of having to wear a tiny *maillot de bain*.

"We'll survive this," I said, and then I added, "Forever elegant, right?"

"Right," Charlotte said. "Forever elegant."

The Dumonteils' house and our house stood about two hundred feet apart, separated by a long gravel driveway that split in two and curved behind each house. The vineyards on either side of the driveway ended abruptly at the grassy edges of the two front yards, ours with its stone fountain, larger and twice as high as a plastic kiddie pool. Behind the Dumonteils' house stood the garage, and behind our house, slightly off to one side, was a gated pool. From there, vineyards stretched to the base of the mountain, which took about fifteen minutes to reach on foot. I knew that the Dumonteils owned the land behind their house, renting it out to farmers. Ours had been parceled and sold by our ancestors so that little of it was actually ours. Who could blame them? The land was worth a lot of money. Still, we had the view.

But crossing the driveway to our house, I could see an area cleared out of the vineyards behind the Dumonteils' house. And within the clearing there was what seemed to be a maze dug into the ground. It was about one to two feet down into the earth. An excavation. I knew that Abbot would love this. It had to do with death. Abbot's relationship with death was, for good reason, intense.

But there would be plenty of time to explore later. I led him away from the dig, for now, toward our house, holding his hand.

"It doesn't look like the pictures," Abbot said. He broke from my grip and ran to the gated pool and tipped forward. "It's empty."

I walked to the stone fountain in the front yard, ringed with tall weeds. I saw a white snail shell, holding a bead of rain. The fountain was now filled with old rainwater, no fish.

"It's a jungle," Charlotte said.

I looked up at the two-story house and saw a swallow dip out of an open upstairs window. "We don't have to update this house. We have to *reclaim* it," I said.

The back door was open, its stone step worn to a smooth dip. We carried in the grocery sacks. That's all we had aside from my pocketbook, which luckily was home to all of our passports. We stepped into the kitchen, which smelled like stale smoke. The oven was a blackened hull, a dark, empty mouth, completely destroyed. Its door was off its hinges and propped against it. The kitchen used to have a fireplace and hearth. The chimney was made of stone—put into place, as the family mythology had it, by my ancestor, the lovesick young man who built the house. It had subsequently been repurposed as the exhaust for a contemporary oven. The stones were blackened, but they'd withstood the fire. The wood cabinets on either side of the oven were destroyed, but the tile backsplash on either side of the stone chimney was still intact. The walls and the ceiling were also blackened—darker and thicker the closer to the oven. The kitchen was charred, but the house itself was sturdy and strong.

"It's like those pictures of smoker's lungs they showed us at school," Abbot said, "just in case any of us were thinking of being smokers, so we wouldn't."

There was a tiny refrigerator, still operating, and a washing machine tucked under the counter. The washing machine had a cracked face. I wasn't sure it would hold water. The sink, though elegant speckled marble, was impractical. I was used to my double sink, deep enough to wash a toddler in. This sink would overflow in a matter of seconds if the drain were blocked by a few pieces of chopped lettuce. One circulating fan was propped beside the long kitchen table. Abbot turned it on and it started rotating noisily, a slow, back-and-forth buzz, nodding to a stop at either side, as if it, too, were checking out the house and finding it, well, disappointing.

"I've never wanted to scrub a floor before in my life, but this one . . . ," Charlotte said. She bent down and touched the tile work. It was beautiful, but the stains looked entrenched.

"I don't know that you'd get much satisfaction out of this floor," I said.

There was a tall, empty drinking glass on the table with a clutch of ashen lilacs propped within it. I pointed it out.

"Left by the French couple trapped in the French film?" Charlotte said.

"I guess so."

I toured the small sitting room, ran my hand over book bindings without reading them. I looked at the small bathroom, its tight shower. I walked up the steep, narrow stone steps. I toured the four bedrooms. The walls were a bit dingy. I thought of my mother's plan to make them look clean and crisp, like white linens. *This one for Abbot. This one for Charlotte. This one for me.*

I turned on the light beside the bed, a double bed with white linens and a thin comforter, and opened the empty wardrobe and dresser drawers. I had nothing to fill them. Charlotte and Abbot had found a radio and turned it up— an old French song with a creaky accordion. They were pretending to sing along in French. *Boshswacheeee Savaasweee ponshadooo . . .*

The shutters were cracked, the window partly raised. I opened the shutters wide, cranked the handle to open the window. I looked out at the mountain, a misty gold in the last bits of hovering sun. The air was already drying out. A wind dipped in and out. I felt like I had landed, touched down in a place that was both very strange—the taste of the air, the slant and bounce of light—and also familiar, as if I'd always known that this was the way that air and light should be. I felt like I'd known this feeling before—in the kitchen with Henry Bartolozzi amid the caterers, and then on my stoop falling in love with him that night of the dinner party and the lost keys and the kiss—that sense of being homesick for the place you've never been and then arriving somewhere new, unknown, and sensing home.

I missed Henry deeply. Here, I would have had some new angle on him. What would Henry the foreigner in a foreign land have been like? There were endless versions of him to mourn—he was my lover, my confidant, my business partner, my son's father. He was one man's son, another man's brother, his mother's boy. Everyone I met had some other version of Henry—my mother and father, Elysius and Daniel, Jude, all of our neighbors, relatives, friends, his old college buddies, his friends from childhood. After he died, they offered me their memories, *their* Henry, and it only added to the loss. I wanted to say, "He's gone, too? How many Henrys can we lose?"

Abbot ran in and dived onto the bed, spread eagle. "What are these pillows made of?" he asked, squeezing them.

"Feathers," I said, turning from the window.

"Mom," he said in a quiet voice, squeezing the pillow in his arms.

"What is it?"

His eyes filled with tears. He squeezed them shut. "I packed the dictionary."

"Oh, Abbot," I said, rushing to him, wrapping my arms around him.

He started sobbing. "I didn't listen. I packed it down deep under all of this other stuff. I wanted Daddy to come with us."

"It's okay," I said. "Hush. It's okay."

"But it's not okay. It's gone. The robbers have it and they don't even know what it is."

"Abbot," I said, and I lifted his chin to look me in the eyes. "It's a dictionary. It's not your father. That dictionary isn't Henry Bartolozzi. Daddy is in here," I said, tapping on his narrow chest. "He's with us all the time."

Abbot grabbed me around the ribs. "I didn't mean for it to get stolen."

"Of course you didn't," I said. "It's okay. It's better this way, in fact. Now you'll know that it isn't your father in the dictionary. You'll know that he's always with you."

He looked up at me and nodded.

Just then Charlotte walked down the hall, peered in, and leaned in the doorjamb, looking happy.

"What are you smiling about?" I asked.

"I just realized something," she said.

"What's that?"

"The thieves stole my SAT prep books," she said. "It's almost like feeling *unfettered*!"

"SAT word?" I said.

"Ironically, yes."

When I woke up the next morning, I was in a bed far away from my own bed. For a moment, I didn't know what bed I was in. I'd slept in only a white bathrobe, the windows open, the night air breezing in and out. The room was empty. Empty. My things gone. For a moment, I didn't feel like I'd been robbed; I felt like I'd been released.

I felt a pang only when I thought of the dictionary, but even then, I knew that the dictionary had already, magically, done its work. It had gotten us here. And it was better for Abbot not to think of his father as a spirit in a book that could be stolen from us.

Maybe Abbot had been right to quote my mother. Maybe the robbery was a Buddhist gift. If we'd had all of our things—clothes, toiletries, and, most of all, technology—not to mention a working kitchen and a healthy rental car, we could have been independent, holed up here in the house. But that was the mistake that Abbot and I were making at home. Today, we would have to head out into the world.

We'd hung our clothes on a rickety wooden drying rack in Charlotte's room. The air was so dry that the clothes dried stiff. The fabric felt strange against my skin. I remembered the feeling from my childhood—the scratchiness of the towels that dried as stiff and rough as loofahs.

While Abbot shook out our shoes—his sneakers, Charlotte's Converses, and my clunky sandals—just to be sure there were no scorpions, I jotted a list of all the things we'd need. The list was long. We needed everything—including, most important, a charger for Charlotte's phone.

I looked up as I wrote this down. "Forty-one missed messages?" I said to Charlotte. "Did I read that right?"

"Briskowitz," she said. "I think he gets on there and just starts reading *The Iliad* or something. Who knows."

"You don't listen to his messages?"

"Nope," she said, and then changed the subject, rolling her shoulders around in her shirt. "Does your shirt feel freshly starched, Absterizer?"

"It's like wearing an exoskeleton," Abbot said.

As we stepped out the back door to walk to the Dumonteils' house for breakfast, we saw the mountain in full morning sun. It took on a bright azure, its shadows orange, looking luminous, rippling like a gown from the sky to the earth. This seemed like the best way to step out of any house into the world.

"It's bigger today than it was yesterday," Abbot said.

"Seems like it, doesn't it?" I said.

"It's kind of humbling," Charlotte said. In the clear light of day, I saw how different she looked without makeup and hair products that stiffened her hair. She was softer, more vulnerable, even more beautiful. I imagined all of the love stories of this place: the man who built the house, stone by stone; the couple who miraculously conceived a baby here during the mistral; my grandmother and grandfather after World War II; the flurry of Bath whites that enveloped my sister, my mother, and me one summer afternoon. And what of my mother's lost summer?

Elysius had been proposed to here. No wonder. Was it the mountain that had worked its magic on Daniel? Perhaps. I still held on to the impact of Henry's death, how everything had become suddenly fragile for us all. Henry proposed to me at a Red Roof Inn off of I-95, where we'd decided impulsively to have sex, midday. This was astonishing to us in retrospect only in that we'd been so damn poor, still in culinary school and broke. Sex at a Red Roof Inn was a huge luxury. It was there, perhaps inspired by the grandeur, lounging naked under the orange comforter, that Henry told me that he wanted to spill his guts.

"Okay," I said, propping myself on my elbow.

Henry took a moment and then finally said, "I really like you."

Now, this didn't strike me as spilled guts. We'd been inseparable since the night of our first kiss. He'd just taken me to a family reunion on his mother's side in North Carolina. And I'd phone-introduced him to my parents and Elysius. We'd pretty much covered the liking, even the *really* liking. I said, "I don't think that constitutes having spilled your guts."

"How about this?" He paused and then said, "I'm in love with you and I want to spend the rest of my life with you."

Now this, *this* was spilled guts. It was completely courageous and elegant, especially amid the Red Roof Inn decor, paintings bolted to the walls. I took this as a real proposal. I said, "Yes," as in *I accept,* as in *I do.* "I love you, too."

This was the moment that we always came back to. The wedding that followed, with all of its foofaraw, was nothing in light of this essential moment that we considered to be the start of our marriage. We'd talked about how embedded in every marriage there was a true moment when your hearts sign on for good. It didn't necessarily happen when the guy mows WILL YOU MARRY ME into your lawn or trains a puppy to bring you a velvet box. It doesn't necessarily happen in the white hoop gown or because some exhausted justice of the peace says so. It usually happens in some quiet moment, one that often goes unregistered. It can happen while you're brushing your teeth together or sitting in a broken-down car with an engine that just won't budge. Some unplanned, unscripted moment. And this was ours. This beginning was finalized by the two of us, unceremoniously, stealing mini hotel soaps and shampoo bottles from a Red Roof Inn.

I wasn't jealous of Elysius and Daniel's proposal—though, granted, it made a much better story. But I was jealous that they'd gotten to be here together to create a love story. Henry and I wouldn't have that chance, and I was a little pissed at us for not making the time and/or blowing the money. We should have, but we were taking time for granted.

Abbot, Charlotte, and I made our way down a small path worn in the grass from our back door to the Dumonteils' back door. We walked up the steps and gave a knock.

"Entrez-vous!" a woman's voice called out.

We stepped into the cool, dark foyer at the back of the house. There was a richly ruby-colored Persian runner on the floor, orangey and pink, that stretched down the length of the hall all the way to the front door, which stood with brightly lit panes at the other end.

Véronique appeared from the doorway on the right—the kitchen—wielding a cane and hobbling around on her cast. I still wasn't sure what had happened to her. She clapped flour from her hands—small bursts of white clouds. Again, we did the ritual cheek kisses. There were pleasantries.

"Look at this boy!" she said about Abbot. "He has a little of you. A little!"

This made Abbot proud because it meant he had a lot of his father.

Julien walked down a set of pantry stairs and dipped

under the low doorframe into the room. I didn't remember his being so tall, though he was slouching, a little beaten from the night before. His eyes looked bleary; his hair was a mess of curls, a bit matted down on one side. He was unshaven, wearing white pants, a white shirt without a collar, and he was barefoot.

Evidently, he hadn't expected to run into anyone. "I was coming down to steal breakfast." I noticed that his nose had a French buckle on the bridge, and he had beautiful teeth that flashed when he spoke and one dimple that was slightly girlish. I remembered his face when he was a child, this time on Bastille Day, lit up by the celebratory paper globes that swayed on the ends of sticks. He gave a small shrug and then did the polite thing. He bounded across the kitchen and gave all of us kisses on either cheek.

"What happened to your foot?" Abbot asked Véronique.

"I fell in mounting the stairs," she said, "like an old woman. It is broken. The month past, I asked a girl from the village to help me, but she had legs like a colt—big knees, no balance. She was too young and tired to comprehend work. So now Julien is helping me, but I don't need it." She wagged her finger at him. "Julien, show them the dining room. I will arrive in an instant," she said.

Julien led us down the hall. "Did you sleep well?" he asked.

"Did you?" I asked.

He smiled that old sheepish smile from our childhood. "Fine," he said, rubbing his head with his knuckles.

"No scorpions were in our shoes this morning," Abbot said.

"The scorpions are rare. Probably you will not see one," he said.

"Probably?" Abbot muttered.

"Where's Cami this morning?" I asked, knowing that I was prying.

"At home," he said, not really supplying any information.

He walked into the dining room. There were two hung-over archaeologists at the far end of the table, and they lifted their heads. One gave a shout. "Bonne anniversaire!"—happy birthday.

Julien smiled. "Merci!" he said, with a quick smile and a nod.

"You didn't tell us it was your birthday," I said.

"It's not my birthday. There's a confusion."

"I lied about my birthday once," Charlotte said, "to get a free dessert at Olive Garden."

"They think that the party last night was for my birthday."

"And what was it for?" I asked.

"Just for living," he said.

Aside from the two hungover archaeologists, the dining room was elegant. The walls were covered in portraits, oil paintings of ancestors, I assumed. A lowboy was covered with trays—pastries, coffee, sugar cubes, cream, a loaf of bread, a bowl of berries, butter, jelly—as well as gorgeous pots, glazed in brilliant blues and reds. We sat in regal, tall-backed chairs at the far end of the table, giving the suffering archaeologists space. They drank a lot of coffee—bowls of it, actually, dipping in their crusts of bread with butter and jam. They mumbled to each other in French.

While we were eating, I asked Abbot if he remembered when he was little and I tried to teach him French.

"No," Abbot said. "Was Dad there, helping teach me French?"

"He took French in high school, so he helped some," I said. "You would get so mad. You'd clamp your hands over your ears and scream. Once you told me that you hated it because French had a different word for everything."

"A wise child," Charlotte said.

Abbot laughed and shoved butter into a hole he'd scooped out of his bread. The archaeologists shuffled off, looking bleary and already dusty.

Julien leaned on the table and said, "My mother and I have a plan. I can take you to the police station in Trets and to the supermarket there. I am happy to drive you. Meanwhile, the children can help my mother. And this afternoon, you will walk the land with my mother, Heidi. You will talk with her alone."

"Will the supermarket have clothes?" I asked. "Is it that kind of superstore?"

"It will have everything."

"I don't think they're going to have stores that sell the kinds of clothes I wear," Charlotte said. "My clothes are kind of ironic. Does France do ironic?"

"No one you know will see you here," I said. "You can get away with some unironic clothes for a while."

"I could also take the family to the cathedral in Saint Maximin later today," Julien offered.

Abbot let out a sad sigh. He'd had his fill of cathedrals.

"This cathedral has a crypt," Julien said, in response to the sigh. "I could also throw in some . . . what do you call them? Pigs with big teeth?"

"Pigs with big teeth?" Charlotte said.

"This type of big teeth," Julien said, gesturing tusks.

"Warthogs!" Abbot said.

"Yes, maybe warthogs," Julien said.

"How many warthogs?" Abbot asked.

"About thirty, maybe more. Do you want to come?"

Abbot thought about it and nodded.

J ulien and I rolled out of the driveway and onto the main road. My rental car was no longer on the roadside. Julien told me that they would be sending me a new car. They would deliver it to the house. "So," he said, "I am your chauffeur now!"

We drove through Puyloubier, past the patisserie and boulangerie, and the petite église with its silent bell, and then the road widened, spreading into the vineyards on the slopes of Mont Sainte-Victoire. Julien shifted out of the village-paced second and third gears, taking it up to highway speed on the D12, still a country round, then up to fourth and fifth so that the vineyards clipped by on either side. He was the kind of French driver I'd already come to fear.

I loved the order of the vineyards. The thick trunk of the vine, the neat rows, the way leaves and fruit were supported by the guidelines. But there was also chaos in those vineyards. Every once in a while, an empty spot. One vine that didn't make it, got an infestation of some exotic beetle, or didn't quite get enough water from the irrigation cannon. The leaves and the gnarled vines and the lurid green grapes grew up wildly from their ordered rows. It was green against dusty rouge, chartreuse against chocolate.

The drive from Puyloubier to Trets would become one of my favorites. Not that there was anything spectacular in Trets, other than the Monoprix supermarket and the Laundromat and, for the purposes of this trip, the police station, but the drive itself across the vineyards in the arid basin between the two mountain ranges was stunning.

"I waited a long time for you to come back," Julien said, his shirt billowing in the gusty convertible. He was sexy in a way that most American men didn't allow themselves to be. American men seemed stiff, as if trying to be masculine by its bulkiest definition. American men aren't really allowed to be sexy, in a way; that's the domain of American women. But European men are supposed to be sexy. They're comfortable with the idea of it, and so, oddly enough, they're sexy without even trying to be sexy—or at least Julien was. He wore cologne, something earthy and rich. His clothes cost good money, but he wore them loosely and confidently. His white linen shirt was unbuttoned one button lower than an American man would have worn it—maybe two, depending on the American man—but this was elegant.

"What do you mean, you waited for me?"

"You and your sister and your mother were strangers who took over our lives," he said. "My brother and I waited for news from you when you were not here. Sometimes there were pictures at Christmas. Not much. And then some summers you would appear, magic, and then, just as quick, you were gone."

"I never really thought of it from your perspective," I said.

"And then, when you were becoming interesting, you stopped coming."

"Interesting?" I said. "I thought you said I was courageous and strange."

"You were."

"Huh. I think of myself as terrified, actually," I said. "Was I brave?"

"Very," he said.

"Why did you splash me?"

"You terrified me."

"Me? With my little flowered barrette?"

"Absolutely." He glanced at me.

I wondered if he was flirting with me. I guided the conversation to safe terrain. "So, you're here helping your mother?"

"I'm trying. She's stubborn. But it's good for me to help her now. A good distraction." I looked over at him—one arm out the window pressing against the current, the other stiff-armed against the wheel, his hair blustering all around his face. He had the same quick, dark eyes he'd had as a child. "I am running away, back to my childhood. Back to my mother, in fact," he said, staring at the road ahead. "That is what little boys do. They run away."

"Are you a little boy?"

"This is what I have heard." He turned to me. "And you? Are you running away?" he asked.

"I'm not sure."

It was quiet a moment. I tried to practice appreciating this moment in this place, but everything was screaming, *Past, past, past.* The stone farmhouses with their faded shutters and ancient equipment retired to rust in the Provence sun, waiting for the winter's mistral to wind-whip them, to punish them for these gorgeous summer days. The very thickness of the vines showed their age, their maturity, their ability to bear fruit that years later would be the wine on a table with a simple meal of pistou and crusty bread. "So who calls you a little boy?"

"My wife," he said.

"You're married?"

"I am so new to divorced that I can count the number of times I have called myself that word on one hand. This is the fourth. She has the house, and I am staying here when I'm not traveling for business. My mother needs the help now, and so the timing is good for this. But I'm miserable, actually."

"You have a strange way of showing it."

"The more miserable you are, the harder you have to work at joy."

"So last night was work?" I asked.

"Of course," he said. "They say that a divorce is harder to recover from than a death."

"Well, they're wrong," I said with an anger that surprised both of us.

"I'm so sorry," he said, painfully embarrassed, but more than that. He was truly sorry. "My mother told me, and I don't know why I would say something like that. It was in a book. It struck me. But it's stupid, of course. Death is death. I'm so sorry that you lost him."

"It's okay," I said. "It's stupid to compare misery anyway— death or divorce. Everyone has a right to their own suffering. That's the parting gift. It's a shitty parting gift, but there it is."

"Exactly," he said, and I could tell now that he felt so terrible that he would agree with anything I had to say at this point.

"Let's do it," I said, trying to break him out of it. "Let's compare our misery. Find out which of us has it worse."

"No, no," he said.

"You're only afraid you'll lose. You're afraid that I'm more miserable and that would reduce your misery and make you feel more miserable for feeling miserable when really there are those more miserable, including me and people who are starving in war-torn countries."

"Are you trying to forgive me?" he said.

"I've already forgiven you, whether you accept or not," I said. "Let's play."

"Fine," he said. "But I should tell you, I am *very* miserable."

"Fine," I said. "I'll go first."

"Good, because I don't know how you play this game."

I thought for a moment. "Okay," I said. "Sometimes I pace instead of sleep, and I still sometimes cry so hard, I can barely breathe."

"I cannot sleep to begin."

"Well, I can't really eat. And when I do I barely taste it."

"I eat and eat and eat, but never feel satisfaction."

"I think I see my husband everywhere," I said, "in little glimpses."

He looked over at me, startled. "I do this. I see the back of her head, her hair, her shoulders in a dress, and then she turns and it's not her—another woman has taken her body."

"You don't time it right," I said softly.

"What's that?"

"Nothing," I said. Henry, for a moment, flashed so viscerally in my mind—his arms, his chest, the sheets of our bed. "I lose everything all the time."

"I have lost fifty percent of everything," he said, "including my daughter."

I had all of Abbot, every bit of him. I closed my eyes for a moment very slowly and just let the sun warm my face. Julien's confession resonated with my own grief. "What's her name?"

"Frieda. She is four years old. She's with her mother for the summer," he said. "I needed to save my marriage—but I couldn't. If I had been a better type of me, then I could have. But not me." I remembered that feeling of recognition when I watched him from the backseat of the convertible in the rain just after we'd met—a deep restlessness. Now I knew what was familiar about it: the restlessness of guilt.

"My husband's death was an accident," I said. "I was fifteen miles away. But still I feel like I should have been able to save him."

We'd turned onto a busier road now and were passing a motorbike course. Four-wheelers buzzed around a small dirt loop. A lonely horse was looking on from a lean-to.

"I'm not the first person to say it wasn't your fault," Julien said. "People have told me the same, but, for me, they're wrong, or at least half wrong. What does it matter? Because you can't apply logic to something that's illogical and have the expectation that it will become logical."

I leaned back in my seat. "I don't want to get over it," I said. "That would be a real ending. I don't want an ending."

Julien stopped at a rotary, waiting his turn. "I want to get over it," he said, "but I'm afraid I never will."

"Who's more miserable, then?" I asked, one hand over my eyes to cut the glare of the sun. "You or me?"

With the car idling, he jiggled the stick shift. "The people starving in war-torn countries," he said.

"Ah," I said. "They always win."

We arrived at the Trets police station, at a strange three-way intersection. There was a parking lot for all the police cars in the back, but only two spaces for the public in front. I took this as a lesson from the French police—an intimidation tactic. *We've got you outnumbered*, or, perhaps, *We're so good, we don't even have to leave the station.*

And maybe they were, because one of the two spots was open.

"My French is rusty," I said as Julien and I got out of the car. "By that I mean encased in a decade or more of rust."

"They speak English," he said. "You'll be fine, and I'll be with you, if you need me."

We walked up to an iron gate around the entrance to the gendarmerie. Next to the button there were instructions that I couldn't really understand. I looked over my shoulder at Julien. He gestured the pressing of the button, and so I did.

Someone responded in that international intercom voice, and I was flustered and quickly answered, "Je suis l'Américaine qui était..."—I'm the American who was...I didn't want to say *violated* again. And I couldn't think of the word robbed so I said, "qui était *robbed*, hier."

Oddly enough, this worked. The gate buzzed, and I pushed it open.

"What's with the gate?" I asked Julien. "Is Trets a hot spot of terrorism, of violence against the police?"

"They are like the movies of the American police, always eating pastries. The French take their pastries seriously. They're protecting them."

"Doughnuts," I said, smiling. "American cops are world famous for their doughnuts. That's nice."

"Doughnuts," he said. "Yes, with the holes."

The long counter was unattended. A row of empty chairs was off to the right.

"Is there a bell to ring? Should we take a number?"

Julien shrugged. "We wait. It's summer in Provence."

We sat there listening to men bantering in a back room, laughing. I should mention that Julien seemed to be a popular guy. He didn't have his cell phone on ring or vibe, but it made a little noise much like a ticket being punched by a train conductor every time someone left a message. I wondered who was calling him. He always glanced at the incoming caller ID but never walked out to call that someone back.

"What do you do for a living?" I asked.

"I'm a graphic designer, also with a background in business. My main client is in London, and so it is fine that I'm staying here now, working. It's flexible. I will have to go to London some this summer and fall."

"Are people from work trying to reach you?" I said. "It's okay if you need to call people back."

"No," he said, "it isn't work."

Was it more women? I wondered. Was it Cami, for example?

Finally, an officer strode up to the counter. He was right out of French stereotype, the type of old French guy that Norman Rockwell would have painted if he painted old French guys. Long, crooked nose. Dark mouth with cigarette-stained teeth. Oily hair and a two-day beard. Bad posture. Shabby, police-issued sweater vest that looked to be about twenty years old.

"Bonjour," he said, and then he rattled off some pat phrase that ended in a question.

Julien looked at me to respond, but I had no idea what the man had said. The lack of response from me made it clear to the officer who I was. "Ah, l'Américaine. Venez ici. *This way*," he said, gesturing around the counter to the left.

I stood up, and Julien paused, not sure whether he should follow.

"Ton mari aussi," the officer said. Your husband, too.

I quickly explained that this was not my husband.

The officer looked at us as if he thought we were lying. "Mais oui, c'est évident," he said, meaning that it was obvious that Julien was, indeed, my husband.

Julien now explained that he was not my husband.

The officer seemed offended that we would lie to him so boldy, and I was immediately resentful. I felt bullied. Was this some kind of tactic—to immediately treat people as liars—to put people on the defensive?

We followed him back to an office with four World

War II–era desks. Off to the left were two more private offices, with posters of French soccer stars.

I guess I was expecting something different from the station in general, something more French—something, I'm embarrassed to admit, like the French Foreign Legion from old black-and-white movies—but this was just a village police station, and the man in front of me was a cop, and the walls were painted an almost nauseating pale green, industrial, unsettling, and completely familiar.

As we walked into a small anteroom, we were joined by another officer. This one had a fat mustache. He handed me a form and told me to fill it out. I listed all of the things that had been stolen, including the dictionary. That was what I really wanted back. Even though I'd told Abbot that there was something good for us to learn in having had it taken from us, something important, I still wanted it back more than anything else. I put a star next to the word *dictionary*. I'd explain to them how important this was to my family, personally—not that they'd care, really, but I felt I needed to.

The officers asked me to describe what happened. I told them as well as I could in French. I explained the two men were *habillés comme les touristes d'Allemagne*—dressed like tourists from Germany. They asked me if I'd locked the car. I wasn't sure. They wanted me to describe the thieves' car. I remembered that the car had no hubcaps but didn't know the word for hubcaps. Julien did and so he jumped in. They asked about damage, what was stolen.

The one in the sweater vest asked what I meant by *habillés comme des touristes allemands*.

I explained tight shirts, sandals with socks, and acted out capri pants and then realized that *capri* was probably a French word. I looked at Julien for a little help, but he seemed to be enjoying the pantomime. "Go on," he said. "You're doing well!"

The officer with the mustache asked me why I thought German tourists wore capri pants.

I couldn't answer this question. I had no idea. It was a resolute notion I had about German tourists and capri pants on men. I shrugged.

Julien translated the question.

"I know what he's saying," I said. "I just don't have a good rationale to share with him at the moment!"

They had a transcript of my phone call and, referring to it, the one in the sweater vest asked skeptically if the thieves were armed. "Les voleurs ont eu un pistolet?"

"Non," I said, and explained that boys in flowered shorts—*les shorts avec les fleurs*—had the gun. To avoid the embarrassing confusion between the words *gun* and *rocket*, I stuck with the term *pistolet*. "Les voleurs n'ont pas eu un *pistolet*."

"Le pistolet était un jouet!" the officer in the sweater vest explained with amusement. The gun was a toy.

Julien looked at me with his head tilted and gave a shrug. "See?" he said. "It's like this."

"I know," I said. "I get it. The fake guns."

Finally the officer in the sweater vest asked about the star next to the mention of the dictionary.

I explained in French that the book was very important to my family, that it was the book of someone who is now dead, someone we love.

"Qui?" the officer with the mustache asked.

"Mon mari," I said. My husband.

"C'est une veuve?" the officer in the sweater vest asked Julien. She's a widow? His eyes were glassy with tears. I wondered if he had lost his wife.

"Oui," he said.

"Si jeune," the officer in the sweater vest said, shaking his head. *So young.*

They leaned back in their chairs and told me they would search for our stolen goods. One officer leaned in close to the other and they had a quick, hushed conversation. Then the officer in the sweater vest leaned across the table and motioned for Julien to come closer. He asked him something in a quiet voice.

Julien looked at him quizzically then shrugged and said to me, "They want to know if you know any well-known Americans."

"Famous people?" It was too hot to wear a sweater vest. "Celebrities?"

"Yes!" the officer in the mustache said in a heavy French accent. "Des stars!"

The officer in the sweater vest added, "Do you know

Daryl Hannah?" He pronounced *Daryl Hannah* with such thick *r*s and a silent *h* that I couldn't recognize the name.

"Who?" I asked.

"You know!" the sweater-vest officer said, annoyed with me. "Darrrrrr-elle Anna! From the film *Splash,* wif Tum Anks."

"Daryl Hannah," Julien said.

"Oh, Daryl Hannah," I said.

The officer rolled his eyes as if Julien and I were mocking him and he hated us a little for it.

"I know *of* her," I said. "The way I know *of* Sophie Marceau and Edith Piaf."

"Edith Piaf is dead," the officer with the mustache informed me.

"That's true," Julien said, though he was having a hard time keeping a straight face now.

"I assumed as much," I said.

"But Sophie Marceau, she is very good. Even in bad films, she is good. She is French."

Julien looked like he was going to burst into laughter.

"You disagree?" the officer with the mustache said to him defensively.

"She's good," Julien said. "She's very good."

"Like Julia Roberts!" the officer in the sweater vest said. *Roberts* was pronounced *Rrrrro-bearrr.*

"I know," I said.

"Anyone else?" the officer in the sweater vest asked. "Well known?" The two men looked at me expectantly.

"I once saw Al Pacino," I said. He was walking in to a premiere in New York, wearing a black linen suit. Henry and I had been there for a friend's wedding. It was a fluke.

"Pacino," they said, with reverence, narrowing their eyes, nodding.

"And I heard Bill Clinton give a speech once," I said.

The officers laughed at this, and asked Julien something very quickly in French. I heard the word *embrasse* very clearly.

Julien shook his head, lifting both his hands in surrender. "Gentlemen," he said. "*Non.*"

The officer in the mustache glared at him for his disobedience. "We want to know . . . Did you embrace him?"

"Like the woman . . . ," the officer in the sweater vest asked.

"Monica Lewinsky?" I shook my head. "No, I did not embrace Bill Clinton like Monica Lewinsky."

"Monica Lewinsky," they said, laughing. "She is well known. . . ."

"Okay, okay," Julien said. "Enough."

"We can go now, right?" I asked.

Julien stood up. "We're going."

"Absolument," the officer in the mustache said. And with that, they both reverted back to French, handing me my police report, telling me to file it with my insurance just in case.

The one in the sweater vest walked me to the door and said, in French, with a French shrug and a French pout of his mouth, "Maybe we'll find your things. Maybe you'll step in shit with your left foot!"

"He's wishing you good luck," Julien said.

"Thank you," I said to the officer.

The officer put his hands on his hips and smiled, a posture of grand benevolence.

As I waved goodbye, I whispered to Julien through my smile, "I can kiss our stuff goodbye. It's gone forever, right?"

"Yes," Julien said. "Gone forever."

Moments later, Julien witnessed what could only be described as a buying frenzy. I'd promised Charlotte real shopping at the little shops in Aix and convinced her that this was just to tide us over until we could get there. So she'd given me some sizes and set me loose. "When in doubt, go with black," she said, giving me a pat on the shoulder.

At the Monoprix, I bought everything from little-boy underwear, bras, shoes, and a few stretchy dresses that would fit various sizes, to toothbrushes, hairbrushes, and vitamins. I bought foods that didn't need to be cooked, as we had only the blackened hull of what used to be an oven, including a monster vat of Nutella, which Abbot had fallen in love with, and a bizarre pâté, just because it was a sale item that the French seemed to be buying in bulk. I bought a camera, adapters, and a universal phone charger. I couldn't stomach buying another cell phone. The idea of bullying through the details of a French plan was too daunting. We would make do with Charlotte's phone.

"I feel so American," I said on the drive back, the car

packed with thick, reusable bags—each of which I had to pay for—rattling in the wind.

"An invasion," he said.

"*Storming the beaches of Normandy.*"

"You stormed."

"But I had to," I said.

"Churchill is proud of you."

"In my defense, I didn't enjoy it," I said, and I hadn't. Except for the pâté, it had been a chore. I felt American in part because the Monoprix felt so American—a big, airy, fluorescent supermarket.

"To make you feel more French, we will go to the patisserie—you can buy French bread and feel better."

Julien drove us back up through the tight, winding streets of Puyloubier. He turned down one of the side streets, stopping in front of a small bakery.

A bakery.

I realized now, quite suddenly, that I didn't want to step into a bakery. I hadn't been in a bakery, aside from the Cake Shop, since Henry's death, and I'd avoided the Cake Shop as much as possible. Wasn't I here to get away from the things that weighed on me? Wasn't I allowed some small measure of relief?

I thought about telling Julien that this was what I did for a living, but I couldn't. He might ask questions—just ordinary, polite questions—but these would force me to recount the details. There was no way to separate my life's work from my life's love. I wanted only to tell the stories that I wanted to tell, and questions could catch me off guard. I was afraid of the whimsical nature of memory.

I was unsettled. My hands were shaky. I rubbed them together to try to get rid of the feeling. I convinced myself that it was easier just to go inside, to get it over with. I could turn on my critical eye, as I had with Elysius and Daniel's wedding cake, which would allow me some objectivity, distance, and I hoped that it would see me through.

We stepped out of the car and into the small patisserie-boulangerie, a stone building with a green awning, which sat at the end of a row of houses with their big wooden shutters. A bell on the door alerted the baker, who was a lean man in his mid-sixties. He stood behind the domed display cases, wearing a crisp white shirt and a fine chain with a delicate silver medal, plain and circular, with an inscription too small to read. He spread his broad hand on the counter and leaned on it, bantering with Julien, the medal glinting now and then.

I gazed at the glass-encased flans topped with berries, the croissants spotted with chocolate, the miniature glazed cakes.

"We came here as kids," I said. I remembered Véronique and my mother bickering over who would pay for what.

"Yes," Julien said, "we had your birthday party."

Once—it was that last visit, when I was thirteen—we'd arrived in France early enough in June to hit my birthday and had a small party. This was where we'd bought the goodies for it. I remembered thinking I was too old for a party with little cakes.

But still, I remembered this shop exactly. And now I knew what all of the cakes were. I knew some of them quite intimately. Suddenly I wanted to hear the words in French. I pointed at one of the beautiful, exquisitely detailed desserts. "Qu'est-ce que c'est?" I asked. What is it?

"Américaine?" the baker asked.

"Oui," I said.

The baker grew serious then. He looked at me and then at Julien. He seemed to want to ask a question—something about Daryl Hannah?—but he didn't. Instead he described the framboise, a raspberry mousse with pistachios and two layers of genoise soaked in a raspberry syrup.

I pointed to the next and asked again.

He described, patiently and reverently, the tarte citron, a lemon curd in a sugar pie crust.

I asked about the next and the next—the tiramisu, where the almond jacond was soaked in coffee syrup; a pear pinwheel, poached in white wine; a hazelnut meringue with buttercream and chocolate ganache; a white circular mango-topped cake that involved rum, sautéed mango, and toasted coconut; truffles with spongy layered centers and bitter, dark-chocolate ganache; and tarts, one with chocolate, nut, and marzipan.

I repeated the words in a quiet voice, almost mouthed them. I loved the feel of the words themselves: *framboise, mousse, pistaches, citron, coco* . . .

I remembered working in the kitchen with my mother, after her lost summer when she'd come home, her hands dusted in confectioners' sugar as she rolled out fondant, whipped cream, separated yolks with the delicate back-and-forth between cracked shells. My mother worked frenetically and I dipped around her elbows. Elysius disappeared with her friends, but I stayed with my mother in the steamy kitchen as much as possible, dizzy from the scents of the cocoa, caramelized sugar, and cakes, all of it billowing around the kitchen in gusts.

There was a bakery not far from the house I grew up in, the white cardboard cake boxes tied with string, curved, clear display cases, and little glass figurines that you could buy to put on top of a birthday cake, women in white uniforms who took our orders and wrote our names on the cakes in swirling letters right in front of us. And eventually, when my mother's obsession with baking came to its end, we went there only for birthday and graduation cakes. But I always had the desire—so strong and fixed on each beautiful cake, my hand pressed to the chilled glass—to be back in the kitchen with my mother, to witness what must have been part of some kind of healing process, to witness a woman who'd come home, yes, but who was then returning slowly to herself.

I wasn't sure what had come over me here in this little French bakery. I felt light-headed and hungry—but in a way I hadn't felt in a very long time—a hunger as restless as my guilt. I nodded along with the baker and found myself saying, "*Une* of those. *Trois* of those. *Deux* of those. *Non, non, quatre.*"

The baker kept glancing at Julien as if asking if I really

had permission, if I was sane. Julien kept nodding, *Yes, yes, do as she says.*

I felt absurd driving home. With the backseat filled with bags from the Monoprix, I had to stack the boxes of pastries on my lap. They were so high, they blocked my vision. I wedged loaves of bread between the door and the passenger's seat. "It's part of our French education," I said.

"No need for a rationale," Julien said. "But that was . . ."

"What?" I said. "It's just my contribution."

"Exactly," he said. "I understand. But that was . . ."

"Joyful," I said. "It was very joyful. I'm working on joy, right? That's what people are supposed to do, according to you, when they're miserable."

"It was . . ."

"What?" I said. "What was it?"

"Erotic."

I raised my eyebrows. "Don't be so French about it," I said, smiling a little.

"I'm not being French. That was the international language. It was erotic."

I sighed. "I was overcome."

"Yes," he said. "That's what it was. It's a start."

"A start of what? Am I living a little?"

"Yes," he said, "just a little, but a start."

Julien helped me unload all of the bags from the Monoprix into my house, but we carried the patisserie boxes and loaves of French bread to the Dumonteils' house. Through the open windows, I heard a strange, atonal moan, one sad note and then another. Music? Some awful, sad goose?

We found Charlotte, Abbot, and Véronique in the kitchen, all working with rapt intensity. Véronique was sitting on a stool pulled to the counter, checking on something in a Dutch oven.

Charlotte looked up from a chopping block, teary-eyed. Was she the one who'd been moaning? A nervous alarm shot through me. Had something awful happened? Had someone called with bad news?

But then she said with a smile, "I've never cut an onion before."

"How is that possible?" I asked.

"No one I know cooks real food," she said.

"It's a chemical reaction," Abbot said. "The onions have tiny cells and you break them open." This sounded like something Henry would have taught him. Henry was a cook who talked about the chemistry of food. How did Abbot hold these things in his head still?

Abbot was sitting in front of a row of wineglasses filled with various levels of water. He dipped his finger into one of the glasses and rubbed its delicate lip. That was the noise I'd mistaken for moaning. It *was* music. "I already dissected a sardine," he said. The intensity in the room was studious, not sorrowful. Was I not able to make these kinds of distinctions anymore?

"See," I said to Julien, shaking off my alarm, "their French educations have begun."

"They are brilliant children," Véronique said. Although she seemed completely relaxed and serene, it was clear that she'd orchestrated the children into this state of wonder and curiosity.

We set the boxes down on the kitchen table.

Véronique turned and gasped. "What is this?"

"I had a kind of attack in the patisserie," I said.

"Open them!" Abbot cried.

And so we did—popping open lids, revealing the bright confections, swirls, glazes.

"Why so much? We will keep these for dessert," Véronique said, shutting the boxes—perhaps uncomfortable with the abundance.

"What did the police say?" Abbot asked. "Will they find everything for us?"

"Probably not," I said.

He looked down at the row of glasses in front of him.

"I promised a cathedral and warthogs this afternoon!" Julien said.

"But first!" Véronique said, and I thought for a moment of Hercule Poirot from the movies made of old Agatha Christie novels that I loved as a child. I was expecting her to say, *I would like to tell all of you why I have asked you here today,* and then to go on to discuss our various ties to a murder. "Before going, I want to walk the land with Heidi," she said, a silent *h,* which made my name sound like *ID*—as if walking the land required us to take proper identification. I was a little afraid of Véronique and in awe of her, too. She seemed like a powerful force, running this bed-and-breakfast on her own, having been divorced for so long. She kept an eye on me, as if she were trying to see inside of me. I wondered what she was looking for. "It will take a moment to prepare," she said.

"I was going to do some unpacking in the house," I said. "Why don't you come over when you're ready?"

"Okay," she said.

"And then we'll go see cathedrals and warthogs," I said. "I don't want to miss them."

Charlotte and Abbot began helping Julien prepare sack lunches that we would eat on our outing, and I went back to our house to put away the things from the Monoprix and to organize.

During the short walk between the two houses, the mountain surprised me again. It appeared so suddenly and was so massive that it could stop me in my tracks. The fact that this was what a backyard could look out onto still seemed unnatural—not to mention the dig, archaeologists in the distance arguing next to the pattern they'd cut into the earth.

I walked into the house, and it was strange to be there alone, the quiet settling around me. I moved quickly, divvying our new clothes into piles, putting food into the cupboards, the mini fridge. If, thousands of years from now, the house was dug up, our things unearthed, it would be quite a stack, I decided. How would these things define us? What would it mean—our wrappers, our plastic, rubbery toothbrushes, our chunky adapters? I thought of the archaeologists, what it's like to unearth the past, to dust it off and try to re-create some semblance of what lives had once been lived. It wasn't really possible. If they dug this up, they would find no trace of Henry. Yet, Henry still had the greatest presence of all.

I dug to the bottom of one bag and found the charger. Charlotte's phone was where she'd left it, on the kitchen table. I plugged it in with the adapter. It gave a hearty beep and blinked to life. There were now fifty-seven missed calls.

Adam Briskowitz, I thought to myself. Poor kid. Was he pining away? I imagined John Cusack in *Say Anything*, the boom box raised over his head—that failed serenade.

I went upstairs to my room and changed into a skirt and a T-shirt, some of the casual clothes bought at the Monoprix, and flip-flops.

As I walked back down the steep, narrow stone steps, I heard the buzz of Charlotte's phone as it rattled against the kitchen table.

I picked up the phone. The caller ID read BRISKY.

I sighed. "Brisky," I said to myself, and flipped open the phone. "Hello?"

"Hello?" he said, astonished. "Hello? Charlotte? Hello?"

"It's Charlotte's aunt," I said. "Heidi."

"Is Charlotte there? Can I talk to her? This is urgent. I've been trying to reach her, and it's really very urgent."

"She isn't here right now," I said.

"Where is she?"

"She's here with me, in France."

"She flew to France?"

"Yes," I said. "I don't think she wants to talk to you, but I can take a message since I don't think she's listening to the ones you leave."

"It was really irresponsible of her to fly to France," Adam said, more to himself than to me.

"Irresponsible?"

"Yes," he said. "She really shouldn't have done that. At least, I don't think she should have. Do you?"

"Is that the message you'd like me to give her?" I asked. "That she's irresponsible because she's traveling this summer?"

"No," he said, the edge of his voice softening. "No, please. Please tell her that I love her. And that I didn't mean for her to get Briskowitzed."

"Okay," I said. "I'm not familiar with that term, but I'll tell her."

"And I know she doesn't want to see me," he said, "but maybe I could write her a letter? An old-fashioned letter?"

"That might be better," I said. "We haven't yet gotten on-line here."

"What's the address?" I could hear him scrambling for pen and paper.

I walked over to the fridge, and I read the address that was posted there.

He repeated it back to me and I confirmed.

"Great," he said. "Thank you so much. You can forget my message. Don't even tell her I called. I'll send a letter out today, explaining everything. So, we have a deal?"

"We do."

"Yes, yes, okay, thank you so much. Excellent," he said. "I'll never forget this. Thank you."

"You're welcome," I said. "Bye."

"*Au revoir!*" he said then, in a lousy accent. "*Merci and au revoir!*"

C ézanne regarded Mont Sainte-Victoire from the front. We see the mountain from the side. *La longueur.* A wider canvas," Véronique said. We had walked out of the back door of her house, past the gravel driveway, toward the vineyards and the archaeological dig, now abandoned in the heat of the day. She had a cane with her, a cane with a marble handle. She didn't use it to walk as much as to point things out. It was such a natural accessory I wondered how she'd ever done without it. "The mountain changes color through the day, if you have patience. Your mother watched this mountain for a long time that final summer she visited us."

I wasn't sure how to take this bit of information. I had the impression that Véronique wanted me to ask a question but I wasn't sure what it should be. I only remembered our lives without her—my father in the kitchen, fumbling with the can opener. *I guess you should be prepared to make a decision between the two of us. Who knows how this cookie will crumble?* The cookie didn't crumble. She came home. I tried not to dwell on what her lost summer meant to her or to me. It was lost.

She was found and returned to us. But now that I was here, I couldn't help but wonder what had happened to her. What had she learned that allowed her to come back?

"The mountain's beautiful," I said simply.

She paused, waiting for something more. "Yes," she said. "It is." She pointed to a tree some distance between our two houses. "That is where your land commences. The line goes all the way to that tree, more or less." This divided our properties as if the driveway between the two continued as a boundary. "That is yours. We will walk the perimeter."

"But your foot," I said.

"I have to keep moving. The circulation," she said, "it moves and it is good for the bones." We walked for a bit. "Your mother is a very strong woman," she said.

"I think she had a lot on her mind the last time she was here. I guess she had to decide whether or not to come home, if we were worth it or if she should chuck it all for life in Provence." I meant this as a joke, kind of, but the lightness didn't translate.

"Her children were always *worth it.* The question was her husband," she said. "He was—a cheat? That's what you call them?"

I nodded, uncomfortable with my father being called a cheat, even though he had been one. He was still my father, and after all of these years devoted to salvaging their marriage, I'd restored him to some higher position.

"My ex-husband was an imperialist. He was a cheat. He left. When your mother was here that summer with her marriage breaking, my marriage was breaking, too." I hadn't known this. It was something more that my mother and Véronique shared.

"Where is your husband now?"

"He is dead. He left us during a winter. Not a word. He took another family and lived in Arles. The boys did not have a father, not in reality." She sighed. "And I prefer this. Without a man."

"See, it's possible to be a woman on her own terms and to be happy," I said. "I can appreciate that."

She stopped and dug her cane into the dirt. "No," she said. "I closed the doors of my heart and they were locked. Your mother could not do this. She has a heart with open doors. She has left the doors open. One woman closes and locks her heart. Another leaves the doors open. Who is strong? Who is weak? Maybe both are only stubborn?"

"I don't know," I said.

"When she was here, my marriage ended. We lived together, but I knew that he would leave one day. After he was gone, I had lovers but did not fall in love. I closed the doors because of fear. That is not a good life. But I made my rules and now I'm content."

"I think that making your own rules, making your own happiness is good," I said.

She glanced at me and I felt immediately transparent. Had I closed the doors to my heart out of fear, and were they locked? She started walking again. "So, after so many years, was your father worth it? Is she happy?"

I nodded. "I think she's happy. They have a strong marriage." This was my attempt at telling her that my father hadn't cheated again. It had been a one-time thing.

"I see," she said, without a hint of emotion.

I wanted to edge away from my mother's life. It frightened me now. I could see how powerful it must have been for her to be here, on this solid ground with this mountain's gravity, and, from here, how very small and frail her family must have seemed, so far away. Did she try to imagine Elysius and me in our swimming lessons, singing at day camp, trying to fall asleep at night? Did she wonder if we had wandered into poison ivy, had sunburn, had gone hiking without our hats and now had a tick crawling through our hair? These were the things she was supposed to take care of. My father knew nothing about any of these things. Elysius and I took care of each other that summer. I got my period for the first time, and Elysius was the one who showed me the box of pads hidden in the linen closet, and who taught me to use cold water and salt to scrub a spot of blood from my sheets. Did my mother know that we were going through the motions and waiting, holding our collective breath, for her to return to us? I said to Véronique, "My mother told me that you'd have information for me about renovating the house, about the . . . *bureaucracy*? Maybe you have some people to recommend? I'd like to get things under way, you know, really have the construction going before I leave. Then I can check in and see if we're on track."

"You are here for how much time?"

"Six weeks," I said.

She started laughing.

"What's funny?"

She laughed so hard now that she had to stop and try to catch her breath.

"Seriously," I said, a little offended now. "What's so funny?"

"Your mother," she said, shaking her head, regaining composure. "She is a very funny woman."

"What do you mean?"

"This is France!" she said with a wave of her arm. "You will wait one to two months to obtain the *permis de construire* and to obtain the *devis* from the workers, *le cahier des charges.*"

"*Permis de construire*, you mean construction permits?"

She nodded. "From the government."

"The *devis* is the *cahier des charges?* The quote?"

"The *devis* is, how do you say it, when you ask the worker for his price? *Le cahier des charges* is a very long document here with very specific details. And you want these with *les tiroirs.*"

"With drawers?"

"Of course," she said as if this explained what drawers had to do with a bid. "And it is difficult to make the workers arrive and make this document. You have to call them and ask them many times and you must tell them that you have heard spoken wonderful things about their work, *bouche-à-oreille,* 'mouth to ear.' If they're quick to arrive, do you really want them?"

She talked a bit more, but all I understood was that some things about construction were universal. Everything would take longer than they predicted. Everything would cost more money than they predicted. And one thing that was predictable was that something unpredictable would happen in the course of something seemingly small and predictable. Then she looked at me very seriously. "It may be that no one will touch a thing for months."

"I won't be here months from now!"

"This is good. Because when they begin to break the walls, you will be living in dust. You will breathe the house into your lungs and taste it in everything. It is better to not be here."

"And you think that my mother knew this all along?"

"She wanted you here. She pulled you here."

"Was the fire faked?"

She shook her head and made a *tsk, tsk* noise as the French do. "The fire was real, but she used it to bring you here."

I looked up at the mountains, the ground, then at the house itself. "But she also showed me magazines completely devoted to tile! She gave me paint samples! She lectured me about bringing in a modern touch. She told me to feel and connect to the house and allow decisions to form!"

"Ah!" Véronique raised her finger in the air, smiling. "*Et voilà!* All of these things you *can* do!"

By this point we were standing by the gate around the empty pool filled with dead leaves. *Months? It would take the French months of bureaucracy? I would have to kiss up to the workers just to get them to give me a quote?*

"The pool is not broken, but it has a crack," Véronique said.

"How many months will *that* take?" My tone was surely pissy.

"I can arrange this. I know someone who will come for the pool," she said.

"I'd like to get it filled with water."

"Water is possible."

"Can I get the fountain going again? Maybe put in some koi?"

"Koi?"

"Fish."

"The pump," she said, "is broken. That we can fix without permits. We can put in water, but finally you will want to work on the stone."

"I'd like koi," I said, aware that I was sounding petulant. "At the very least."

She looked out toward the excavation and pointed at the mounds of dirt with her cane. "These are the real workers. They found a tomb," she said.

"That's what Julien told us," I said, trying to shake off my frustrations with my mother, what now felt like a fake mission.

"Bones," Véronique said. "We are all eventually bones."

"That's true," I said. "Well, not always *eventually*. Some die before they get to *eventually*. *Eventually* is a gift."

"Your mother told me about your husband," she said.

"I'm sorry, but I promise to you I will not force sympathy on you. I have always hated sympathy." She smiled.

"Me, too," I said.

"I have something of your mother's. Something that was found after the fire."

"What is it?" I couldn't imagine what this could be. My wily mother. I thought of the yellow swimsuit in the picture of her by the pool. I never saw her in that swimsuit at home. Had she bought it here and left it behind? This thought made no sense. Of course Véronique wouldn't have held on to a swimsuit all these years.

"I will give it to you before you go. It is small. But I think it will be important to her. Only a small box of things." The wind rippled her shirt. And before I could ask her to tell me what it was, she said, "You know that your mother is a thief." She said this without anger, just stating a fact.

"A thief?" I said. No one ever said anything bad about my mother, not ever. On the other hand, she wasn't the kind of person people gushed about. No. People didn't stop me in town to tell me that my mother had brought over a casserole at their darkest hour or that she'd done a wonderful job raising money for charity. But no one ever said anything bad about her. "My mother? Did she take something from you?"

"A little thief. A heart thief."

"What does that mean, a heart thief?"

Véronique shook her head. She wasn't going to talk about it. It dawned on me now that there must be some misunderstanding. A heart thief sounded like a nice term for adulterer, mistress, home wrecker. Was my mother a home wrecker? Had she somehow played a part in the departure of Véronique's husband? I thought of a story my mother had told me once about a friend of hers who was treated badly by her relatives in a foreign country for years after the death of an aunt. One of the relatives finally explained that she'd never given them the ring she'd promised. "What ring?" my mother's friend said. They explained, "You told us you would give us a ring, and it never arrived." My mother's friend had to explain the expression—give you a ring, a call. There was no actual ring. Maybe this is the kind of thing that had happened here. I decided that it was a simple misunderstanding that we could unravel and then laugh about later.

Véronique hooked the cane on her elbow and crossed her arms. "I am worried about the house and the land. What will happen when I'm gone."

This took me by surprise, the confession as well as the fact that she'd chosen me to tell. I was a little afraid of her, but also drawn to her. This conversation was loaded and vexing and hard to follow, but it was strangely exhilarating. I had no idea where it might go next.

"I'm old," she said.

"Would Julien want the house?"

"The boys would fight. They have problems, as you know." I didn't know anything about the boys' problems. She shook her head. "The children want money these days. They will sell the house."

"Have you asked them?"

"No," she said. "When they sell, this will be a good time to sell your house, too. Someone may want both of the houses and the land."

"It's not mine to sell," I said.

"I see."

"What about Pascal?" I asked.

She shook her head and clucked her tongue.

"Look," I said. "I think you should tell the boys that you're worried. They might love the chance to make it their own. They might surprise you."

"Voilà," she said, touching my arm. "I hear it so clearly. Your voice, you are like your mother, no?"

"Not really," I said. "Elysius is the one who . . ."

"No. Your sister has your mother's face, but you," she said, "you have your mother in you." She tapped her chest. "The way you look at the mountain. Your sister never looked at the mountain like that. She is . . ." Véronique snapped her fingers in the air around her head, her eyes darting from one snap to the next.

"Distracted?"

"Distracted," she said. "Yes. But you." She shook her head and really looked at me for what felt like the first time. I wasn't sure what she was seeing. "Have you asked yourself why your mother never returned here?"

I knew there were many very complicated reasons. My mother loved this place, always wanted to return, but it was a sore spot between my parents. Even I had come to associate this place with her abandonment of us. "It's far," I said. "It's expensive to get here. . . ."

"No," she said. "It's not that. Ask your mother. She has lessons." She faced the wind and let it blow her hair back. I pictured Véronique as a little girl. She and my mother had known each other during their childhood summers. I imagined them doing something idyllic, running through the vineyards, row after row. Véronique said, "You know the Provençal summers are dry, which makes the earth and the air perfect for a fire, like the one that your mother saw before leaving. The fires burned the trees, cleared the earth, and that is why it's possible for the archaeologists to dig." She tapped her cane on the grass. "It is interesting, no? A tragedy, the fire, but it makes it possible to dig into the past."

"Yes," I said. This was a metaphor, of course. Was the tragedy my mother's, the near loss of her marriage that summer, her heartache? Or perhaps Véronique's own failed marriage? Or was she talking about my own tragedy, Henry's death? Was it now time to dig?

Regardless of how I was supposed to read the metaphor, it was a conclusion. The tour was over. Véronique started to walk back to her house. Her hobbled gait was so quick and strong that it seemed her limp was propelling her forward, not holding her back. She called out, "In the end, your mother, that thief may surprise you."

She already had.

In the gusty wind of the convertible, Julien explained that we shouldn't mistake Saint-Maximin-la-Sainte-Baume for Saint Maximin, another cathedral not too far away, in Arles. "The main difference is that this one has the body of Mary Magdelene and that one doesn't." We were on our promised outing of a cathedral and warthogs—cathedral first, as warthogs were the reward for enduring a cathedral.

"Wasn't Mary Magdalene hanging out in the Middle East with Jesus?" Charlotte said.

"She was," Julien said. "But then!" He lifted his finger in the air. "She got on a fragile little boat without a sail, without a rudder, along with Maximin, before he became a saint. And there were others—and they found themselves in Marseille. A miracle."

"It sounds miraculous," Charlotte said, "in a touristy way."

"I think *pilgrim* is the old word for 'tourist,'" Julien said.

"Well, then, it's very pilgrimy."

"How did she die?" Abbot asked. He was sitting in the backseat with his arms folded and propped on the door, the air pushing his hair straight up off his face. His brow was furrowed, his eyes narrowed to keep from tearing up in the wind.

"She converted the people of Marseille, and then when she was old she was living in a cave in the Sainte-Baume mountains."

"But how did she die?" he asked.

"I think she was very old," I said. "She died peacefully because she was old. The way most people die." I knew that Abbot was afraid of dying before his time, like his father. Death must have felt like a legacy. I couldn't imagine such a weight. I tried to explain to him at every chance that death was usually a very natural process at the end of a long life. I worried that I hadn't talked about death with him enough, and I worried I'd talked about it too much.

Abbot lifted his raw hands, letting the wind stream through his fingers. Did he think he was getting rid of germs this way, like the heat of a hand blower in a restaurant bathroom? "Where is her body?" he asked. "In the church?"

"In a crypt in the church," Julien said. "And they have the best graffiti. Really. It is very old."

"Antique graffiti," Charlotte said. "Interesting."

I wondered if I should tell Charlotte that Adam Briskowitz was going to write her a letter explaining everything.

She'd seemed much lighter since we'd arrived, freer, funnier, less...doomed. I didn't want a surprise letter to break the spell. But she could choose to ignore it when it arrived, like the messages. She obviously had that kind of willpower. I decided to wait.

There was a square in front of the cathedral with a stone slab bench and a kind of trough fed by a single water spigot. We ate our sack lunches there in the sun, sandwiches of ham and butter, bottles of Orangina, and water. We watched a woman let her dog drink from the trough, and later a man drank from it himself. Abbot finished quickly and ran around the square. Like most open areas that we'd come across in France, there were lots of cigarette butts and hardened, sun-dried dog poops. Abbot pointed out all of the poops as if on patrol. This was the kind of thing that was unique about traveling with children. They had a different worldview— sometimes because of their innocence and sometimes simply because they are positioned lower to the ground.

The cathedral was made of uneven gray stone with massive, dark, wooden doors. Inside, it was narrow, dim, and tall. There was a small pulpit to one side with a short, curved staircase. Hidden near it, Abbot uncovered a sound system with lights and knobs, which I told him not to touch. It was unseemly. The voice of a man of God should reverberate naturally, or so it seemed to me.

Charlotte drifted again to the nooks of the cathedral, just as she had at Notre-Dame. The nave was lined on either side by sixteen chapels. She worked her way down the row of chapels, pausing at each one, taking in the art, and then she stopped at one to pray. Her father and Elysius were atheists. I tried to remember if her mother was religious. She struck me as New Agey, but I couldn't say. I didn't really know her. But Charlotte, with her blue, black-tipped hair and her nose ring, looked oddly as if she'd found the right place to be. She looked at ease, head bowed, hands clasped. I envied this. I'd been one to pray at night before bed as a kind of meditation. But when Henry died, I felt shut off. I couldn't remember what I'd once prayed for or how. It was as if prayer were a foreign language that I'd once known but could no longer remember even in the most pidgin way. I remembered the idea of prayer, the feeling of calm that I'd had even as a child, but it seemed very distant now.

Julien walked up. "Abbot wants to search for the crypt."

"Huh," I said. I worried for a moment about this morbid fascination—the crypt here, the archaeological dig near the house. Was it odd that Abbot wasn't afraid of their germs? I doubted he really remembered his father's funeral. We'd never really talked about his death—I always concentrated on the living Henry. Perhaps Abbot's interest in death was because I'd blotted it out—or wasn't it the normal fascination of any child?

"Is that *sacrilegious?*" Julien asked. He said *sacrilegious* in a French accent and then asked, "Is it the same word in English?"

"It is," I said, choosing to let go a little. "And it's fine. He can search for the crypt."

"Okay." Julien walked down the aisle to Abbot, gave him a pat on the back, and said, "Come to us when you find it."

I sat in one of the pews. Julien walked back to me and took a seat beside me. His knee brushed mine as he sat down, and I noticed how long his legs were—or was it that the pews were made generations ago, for smaller people?

"Do you remember my mother when she was here that summer of the big fire?" I whispered.

He nodded. "I was only a kid," he said, "in my own world, but yes. I remember her."

"What was she like?"

"She was quieter. And she took lessons. She worked in the garden. I saw her in the window of your house, looking at the mountain. She was lovesick. I knew that. And you weren't here with your sister. Things were wrong."

"Your mother called her a heart thief," I said.

"What is a heart thief?"

"I thought you'd know."

"I don't."

"She said that the doors to my mother's heart were open and hers were closed."

"This is an expression of my mother. She talks about people's hearts this way, as rooms—sometimes locked rooms."

"I think my mother had an affair here," I said.

"People fall in love," he said, looking up at the tall pipes of the organ encased in dark wood.

"She was here because my father had an affair. She kind

of disappeared. We didn't know if she was coming back. Maybe she thought about not coming back."

"My father left and didn't come back. You have good luck. She came home."

I nodded. Véronique had been goading me, hadn't she? She wanted me to ask my mother. She'd said that my mother had lessons, something to pass down. But my mother's lost summer was her own. If she'd wanted to tell me about it, she would have. Perhaps that was an important thing about lost summers: they should stay lost.

Abbot ran up to us now, breathless. "I found this place that has steps going down and I think it's in there. I think that's the crypt."

"Show us," Julien said.

Charlotte wandered over, and the three of us followed Abbot to a set of stone steps leading down into a darkened room.

"Look at this," Charlotte said, and she ran her hand on the engraved graffiti. "It's from 1765. And here, this one is from 1691. Who was the wisecracker in 1691?"

I said, "There are wisecrackers throughout history, I guess."

"There's graffiti in here that's older than our entire country," Charlotte said. "If this were our graffiti, we'd have a museum just for it in D.C., on the mall. We're ancient-deprived."

"But we invented the cowboy hat," I said. "Or at least I'm pretty sure we invented the cowboy hat."

We walked down the dim, narrow stairs, Abbot first. He stopped at the bottom of the steps. We all looked to the other end of the small, empty crypt, with its low, domed ceiling. There, in a halo of light, was what looked to be a golden helmet. A sarcophagus. The remains of Sainte Marie-Madeleine—Mary Magdalene.

"There!" Abbot said, and he started running toward it.

"Wait," Julien said.

But it was too late. Abbot didn't see the reflection of light off the Plexiglas protecting the sarcophagus, and he went flying into it, like a bird into a window. He fell backward onto the floor, hitting it so hard that the back of his head rapped off the stone with a sickening thunk.

"Abbot!" I cried out and knelt next to him. "Are you okay, baby?" I fit my hand on the back of his head, searching for blood. His head was dry, but there was already a red welt on his forehead. I thought of concussions and hospitals. I imagined French doctors like the French police, lazing around in their sweater vests wanting to talk to me about Daryl Hannah. A small flare of anger rose in my chest. Why was I angry? Because I was alone. Henry had left me here, alone. He wasn't on the shore this time, calling to us in the ocean, telling us that we'd paddled out *too far, too far.*

Abbot slowly lifted his head. His eyes filled with tears, and then he blinked two tears that rolled down his cheeks. He looked at his palms, held them open in front of his face. Already raw from washing, they were scuffed with dirt, thinly scratched, a little bloody. But he didn't rub them together. He looked at me, smiling. "I found her," he said. "She's shining!"

Before getting back in the car after the cathedral, I washed Abbot's hands with the leftover water from my bottle. I waited for him to tell me that I'd drunk out of the bottle and therefore my germs could get into his cut. But he didn't. He was quiet, distracted. The red welt had popped up into a small, blue knot on his forehead, and there was a matching knot on the back of his head from whacking it on the stone. I made him look up at me so I could test for a concussion. He was facing the sun, and I made sure his pupils were dilating in unison. I was relieved to see that they were. Julien found a little pottery shop in the square that was open and, in the back, the potter had a small fridge with ice. I was now applying napkin-wrapped ice to both the front and back of Abbot's head.

"We could go home and relax," I said. "Eat little glazed cakes."

"I think he has had a miracle," Julien said. "Do you eat cake after a miracle?"

"What kind of miracle was it?" Abbot asked.

"I don't know," Julien said. "We have to wait to see what happens to you. Were you blind and now you can see?"

"I've never been blind," Abbot said.

"We should go home," I said. "It's always appropriate to eat little glazed cakes."

"Absterizer?" Charlotte said. "What do you want to do, warthogs or cake?"

"Warthogs," Abbot said. He was determined. I looked at him with the small, blue egg in the center of his forehead and thought of the word *blessure*—French for an "injury." But this was an English word, too—to be blessed on the head was to be struck. Abbot had a blessure. He was blessed.

I insisted on sitting in the backseat next to Abbot, though he edged up close to the door, wringing out the soaked napkins and staring out at the passing landscape, vineyards upon vineyards. Charlotte sat up front, and, music-deprived since the loss of her iPod, she fiddled with the radio. Bad Euro techno-pop song after bad Euro techno-pop song, she finally lighted on ABBA and we were all weirdly relieved when she let the song play out.

Julien followed signs for the Legion Etrangere down a dusty dirt road. "This is where some of the real legionnaires are," Julien said to me. "The ones from the black-and-white movies. There are little houses out here for the elderly veterans and some who need special care, rehabilitation."

"Warthog rehab?" Charlotte said.

"I don't know why a person decided to bring warthogs here," Julien said. "But they're here."

"*C'est comme ça,*" I said.

"What's that mean?" Abbot asked.

"It means 'it's like that.' It's a French expression," I said.

"Because sometimes things just are like that. That's all. It's just—like that," Julien said.

"That's true," Charlotte said. "Things are like that."

We parked and walked up the long road to the pens. We smelled the warthogs before we could see them—a dank, beastly smell. The warthogs were massive, coming up as high as Abbot's waist. They had broad barrel ribs; wide, mud-caked rumps with skinny tails; sparse, wiry fur; tusks that curved up from their rubbery snouts. Their hooves were comparatively dainty, as were their back legs, which seemed to buckle, making them look knock-kneed from behind. They blended in with the dusty pen, pitted with mud holes and hollow logs. Some of them trotted away when we arrived. Others bumped up angrily against the metal fence, deep, growling grunts in their throats. A few were fixed by the water trough and food—seeds and grains piled on a cement pad near a row of little cavelike huts that the warthogs could retreat into. Only one seemed to want to nuzzle a hand. Abbot was gazing at this one eye-to-eye through the fence.

"He's dirty," Abbot said.

"Really dirty," I said, for once relieved that my child was phobic and wouldn't be shoving his hand through the fence to touch them.

"Very dirty," Julien said, leaning on the fence.

"Look," Charlotte said. "There're little ones." She pointed to a back corner of the pen where, between their hefty mothers, there were some young warthogs, whose legs seemed longer and more proportioned to their not-yet-wide bodies. "The little ones look just like the big ones, only smaller."

"But without tusks," Julien said.

"It would be rude to have to birth something that had tusks," I said.

"It's hot," Charlotte said. "Let's go back to the car. Big pigs in a pen. I get it." The sudden shift in mood surprised me only in that I hadn't seen more of it. It's what Elysius had warned me to expect.

"Warthogs are natives in West Africa," Julien said.

"I'm done," Charlotte said, and with that, she started walking back to the car.

I kept my attention fixed on the wart hogs. I was impressed with how the warthogs were *of the earth*—that was the expression that kept coming to me. They were of the earth—not off in their heads, not always living in their minds. They weren't, from what I could tell, obsessed with the past.

Abbot said, "They live in all that dirt and their own poop."

"And they're completely fine," Julien said, "except they're in exile, in a little foreign prison." I thought of Julien's divorce and how much he must have been missing his four-year-old daughter, Frieda. I wondered if she looked like him—his dark eyes, his quick smile.

"But at least it's a real prison," I said. "Not a metaphor, like the Parisian couple who thought the burnt house was a symbol of their life together."

He smiled at me. "Very true!"

"They're really of the earth," I said. "Look at them. They

blend in with the dirt and the log. They root around and they wallow."

"In dirt and poop," Abbot said.

"You can touch them," Julien said. "They live in dirt and poop, but they are happy with it."

Abbot looked at me. The shiny blue welt on the middle of his head reminded me of the small candy-coated robin-sized eggs that showed up on shelves just before Easter. *I'm just a bunny, you know. There's only so much that I can understand.* I stared at the warthogs. I wondered what Henry would think of us here—Abbot's head doubly blessed, standing by the filth of warthogs. I imagined that if Henry were here, he'd be worried—not a lot, just that small stitch of worry in his brow, the leftover guilt from his brother's near drowning still tugging on him in ways he couldn't control. We would both convince the other that Abbot was fine. We'd tell each other that it obviously wasn't a concussion, that he was going to be okay. Abbot was our only child, and so there was no one to diffuse our parental anxiety, but we were also a good team, balancing out worry with reason. "Pet a warthog," one of us would have said. "Live a little!" the other would have chimed in.

But Henry wasn't here to help strike that balance. I had to make up for his absence and worry for two. What would happen if Abbot did touch them and then later regretted it? Would he melt down? Was this a breakthrough, or was he not himself really yet, still dazed by the knocks to his head?

If I had to worry for two, didn't I also have to encourage for two as well? I felt paralyzed. Finally, I just blurted, "Do it, Abbot! You're a kid. Do what kids do!"

Abbot stared up at me, baffled, as if he had no idea what kids do.

"They will not bite you," Julien said gently. "They feel like rubber." Julien reached out and pushed his hand to the fence near a warthog's nose. The warthog shoved its snout into Julien's hand, its tusks scraping against the fence. "They are ugly but very tender."

Abbot looked up at Julien, and then he pulled his hands out of his pockets. He lifted one hand and then flattened it, just as Julien had, against one of the holes in the fencing. Another warthog wobbled up on his little hooves and pressed against the fence, then nuzzled Abbot's palm, probably rooting for food.

Abbot turned around but kept his hand pressed to the warthog's grunting mouth. I thought for a second, *Is this the miracle? Is he enchanted?* Because there was Abbot, biting his bottom lip with his two oversized front teeth, smiling, and then laughing. "It's a real snout!" he shouted. "A real live snout!"

When you've felt shut down and then begin to open back up, what comes alive first? You think of all the usual suspects: the senses, the heart, the mind, the soul. But then maybe all of these things are so interconnected that you can't differentiate a stirring of the heart from a scent, the rustling of the soul from a breeze across your skin, a thought from a feeling, a feeling from a prayer.

If I were pressed now to pinpoint a moment when I began to open up again, I don't know that I could. Maybe it was the jolt of being terrified in the rain after the robbery. Maybe it was the gravity and expanse of the mountain. Maybe it was in the bakery, amid the heavy scent of bread in the oven and carmelized sugar and cocoa. Or was it watching my son, doubly blessed on his head, holding his hand up to the rubbery snout of a warthog?

Or was it, quite simply, while eating?

That night, we ate a Provençal feast at the long table in the dining room, dimly lit by the late-day sun. The chairs were uncomfortable. The seats were lumpy. They put you at the wrong height and tipped you forward. But I was so tired, so hungry, I allowed the seat to seat me at the angle it wanted.

There were no guests, no spare archaeologists, and so it was just the three of us with Véronique and Julien. Charlotte set out the bread I'd bought at the bakery with a grainy, dark spread made of crushed olives to put on the slices.

Julien walked Abbot through the syrups that sat on one of the lowboys in a metal tray, the kind that milk may have been delivered in once upon a time, with a metal handle. But these were bottles of thick syrups—blueberry, mint, raspberry . . . He taught Abbot and Charlotte how to mix the syrups with water to make sugary-sweet non-carbonated drinks, the syrups swirling and thinning to just the right shade of blue or green or deep purple.

Véronique then limped into the room, placed the Crock-Pot on the center trivet. When she pulled away the lid, a breath escaped, and the room filled, and my mind emptied.

I could see the pale gold chicken resting in its deep sauce of tomatoes, garlic, peppers. I could smell the garlic, wine, and fennel. Véronique served and the juices ran sparkling to the edges of my plate, carrying a hint of citrus. And the smell bloomed.

"Lemon?" I asked.

"No, orange," she said. "This is chicken. It is common." Véronique put the serving spoon back in the Crock-Pot and seemed to wave the contents away as she sat. "There's more, if you like." She seemed disdainful of the meal, which also included beautiful russet potatoes and a brimming salad. It was as if this was what she cooked when she didn't really feel like cooking.

I began to eat, and it was like eating for the first time since Henry's death. Why now? Was it because I was someplace else? Was it because my senses had already begun to give in? Was this what it was to feel enchanted?

The first bite was almost too much for me, so much flavor, and I was so hungry. Julien offered a bottle of rosé from a local vineyard. I said, "Yes, please." He poured me a glass, and I took a long drink and let it all wash down. I usually avoid rosé, tending to think of it as too girly, too sweet. But the Provence rosés were complicated, the cool bringing out the fruit, but not allowing it to topple into sugary sweet.

I couldn't remember anything, not the day, not the night. I was entirely focused on what was in front of me. With the next bite the sweetness of the onions and peppers swelled quickly with the lightly salted, melting chicken. The orange and fennel came later but finished the mouthful sweetly.

I looked over at Abbot, who was head-down and shoveling. This was its own type of compliment. *Abbot is fine,* I thought to myself. *Look at him. He's fine.* He'd washed his hands before eating, per usual, but he didn't scrub them. *He's fine.*

Julien said, "This is a meal of genius."

"No," Véronique said. "It is simple."

"It's so good," Charlotte said. "I won't even be able to ever explain it!"

I, myself, was speechless.

And then the cakes. Véronique set them out, one little cake after the next, a long seemingly endless row that ran the length of the table. I picked up the citron tart and tasted it. It was almost how I remembered my mother's tarts tasting that fall when she came home from Provence, and I followed her around the kitchen. "My mother made French desserts after she came back . . . and we almost got it right. We were close," I said to the air.

Véronique looked at me and then Julien. She raised her fork in the air. "She started baking when she came home?" she asked.

"Yes." I nodded. "It's when I first started baking myself."

"Yes," she said. "Your mother told me that you have a bakery."

"I don't do much baking anymore, but I'm a pastry chef, by trade."

Véronique nodded. "So that is what stays. How funny, these things."

"What things?"

"No things," she said. "Eat. Enjoy."

I caught Charlotte staring at me from the other side of the table. "So you're really tasting this, right?" she said. "I'd hate to have to describe it all to you later."

"Yes," I said. "I'm here." And I thought of the verb "to

be," *être*. I thought of being. I thought, *Here I am. In the present. I am.*

"Are you okay?" Julien asked.

I probably looked a little crazed. Glassy-eyed, I imagined. Exhausted and enthralled.

Without thinking, I said, "I am. I'm amming."

He looked at Charlotte for a translation. She shrugged. "Is that an expression?" he asked.

"It's not even a word," Charlotte said. "Am I right?"

"Yep," I said. "It's just how I feel."

"I'm amming," Julien said, trying it out.

"I'm amming, too!" Abbot said.

"I'm definitely amming," Charlotte said, slipping more chicken into her mouth.

"Are you amming?" Julien asked his mother.

"Amming?" she said.

"Are you living in the present?" Charlotte said.

"The present? What is the present?" she said. "I am *le passé*. I am the past."

That night as I was walking across the Dumonteils' yard to our house, feeling full, my chest warm with wine, Julien called out from the back door, "We didn't eat all the cakes. Come and have them for breakfast."

The air was clear, the night cool. The mountain was a deep, velvety purple. Abbot and Charlotte weren't too far away. They'd fought through some weeds, clearing spots to sit down on the edge of our broken fountain. Abbot had his hands cupped to his ears, fluttering them to modulate the sounds of cicadas. Charlotte was staring up at the night sky.

"We will and thanks," I said to Julien. "For everything. For today, really. It was great. Abbot touched a warthog! Maybe it was a miracle."

"Maybe," he said.

"He's a little high strung," I said, "like his mother."

"High strings?" Julien said. "Abbot has good strings, like his mother."

"Thanks," I said. "I'll take that as a compliment."

"It *is* a compliment," he said.

"You're a very nice little boy," I said.

"I thought I splashed you too much," he said.

"You've outgrown the splashing," I said.

"And you've outgrown the flower barrette."

"Are you flirting with me, Monsieur Dumonteil?"

"Me?" he said. "Of course not. I'm too miserable." And he smiled, dipped back into the doorway, and disappeared.

When I woke up the next morning, I called my mother. It had been too late yesterday, what with the time difference, but nine in the morning our time would be three in the afternoon in Florida.

She picked up and I started in directly. "So, two to three months for permits and just to get quotes? Is that the bureaucracy you were talking about?"

"Heidi, what are you talking about?"

"I'm not going to get anything rolling here. I'll be lucky to nudge this renovation in six weeks' time."

"Ah," she said. "Yes, but—"

"But nothing!" I said. "You made me come here under false pretenses. Feeling and connecting and allowing decisions to form! Listen to the house?"

"And I stand by it. I want you to do all of those things."

The line was silent. Of course, the renovation was only the surface issue. I had told myself that I didn't want to know about her lost summer, but I couldn't help myself. It seemed only fair that I should know what was going on. I was here, after all, feeling haunted by her lost summer. I hit her with this question. "So, do you mind if I ask you a question?"

"Anything," she said.

"What did you steal?"

"Steal? What are you talking about?"

"It seems you have a reputation in the South of France as a thief."

"I do not."

"Well, maybe not the entire region, but certainly right in these parts here."

"Who told you I stole something?"

"Véronique."

The line went quiet.

"I don't know what she's talking about."

"Huh," I said.

"What do you mean, *huh?*"

"You're blushing or something."

"I'm in America. How would you know whether I'm blushing or not?"

"I can tell by the sound of your voice."

"Okay, then." She cleared her throat. "I did not steal anything to my knowledge from Véronique."

"I didn't say that she said you stole something from her."

"Yes, you did." She was flustered.

"No, I didn't."

"Actually, she says that she also has something for you. Something you left behind. It was found after the fire."

"In the kitchen?"

"She didn't say. But the fire was mostly in the kitchen." I remembered how rattled my mother was the day of Elysius's wedding. She'd started crying. She said she didn't know why she was reacting that way, but now I thought I might. "Is this why you were so upset by the house fire?" I said.

"No. I just didn't want anyone to have been hurt or the house to be ruined," she said.

"But you knew no one was hurt and you knew it was a kitchen fire," I said. "What was in the kitchen that you left behind?"

"Did Véronique say what was found?"

"You didn't answer my question."

"I didn't answer your question on purpose. I don't know what she found in the kitchen. How could I?"

"You left something behind in the kitchen, something found because of the fire. So it must have been hidden and the fire exposed it somehow." I thought of what Véronique had told me about the air in Provence in the summer: because it was so dry, it made the mountain ripe for fires, and that the fires of 1989 were what made it possible for the archaeologists to dig. Maybe it wasn't a metaphor, as I'd thought it was. Maybe it was a fact. Maybe she was speaking of what had been unearthed in our own kitchen. "Were you afraid that the fire had destroyed it?"

"I really don't know what she's found. I don't know what *it* is!"

But I knew that she had a very good idea of what it was. "Véronique said it was nothing, really, but that it would be important to you. What is it? Take a wild guess."

"Well, I'm sure it's nothing important or I would have asked to have it returned a long time ago. Right? How is my Abbot? How is Charlotte doing away from that Adam Briskowitz?" She was now diverting attention. I let her. What more was there to say? I was convinced that she was a thief, and she had hidden something in the kitchen, something that she likely knew she'd never find again but couldn't give up.

Julien had gone to London to do some work for his main client. He hadn't said goodbye. That morning when I went to the Dumonteils' for breakfast, he simply wasn't there. His mother said, "It was an emergency. Work. He told me to say that he will be back in a week or so."

"A week or so?"

She looked at me a little startled. Had I said it like I was disappointed that he'd be gone so long?

Was I disappointed? I pushed the thought aside.

I realized that there was no way that I would be able to navigate the complexities—cultural and bureaucratic—of renovating the house. I asked Véronique for the equivalent of a contractor—a project manager or, as the French say, an *entrepreneur.* It would cost an additional 10 to 15 percent, but what alternative did I have?

"I know a man who is very good and honest and well known," she told me. "And the economy isn't perfect, so maybe you will not wait."

"Thank you," I said. "I really appreciate this."

She nodded. "Not a problem."

In the meanwhile, I was bent on doing everything that we could do ourselves. I made a list of things that didn't require *permis de construire* and *devis*: weeding, planting, painting, removing ash from tile and stone.

As those first few days progressed, we learned quickly not to sleep in. The morning hours were cool, best for working outdoors, not to be wasted.

Every morning, Abbot shook out our shoes, still on the lookout for scorpions, but now, oddly enough, he seemed frustrated that he didn't find them. "Where are the scorpions?" he said one morning. "I mean, the book said there would be scorpions!"

"I was here a lot as a kid," I broke it to him, "and I never saw a scorpion."

Abbot, Charlotte, and I worked the yard, uprooting weeds, clipping vines. We planted, too. Charlotte asked Véronique what was best to put in this time of year. She produced a list of annuals—marigolds, cosmos, petunias—and the flowers that would bloom in the fall after we were gone—chrysanthemums, asters, colchicums.

I worked in the kitchen without the kids, wearing one of

Véronique's handkerchiefs over my nose and mouth. I jettisoned the braided rug, demolished the burnt cabinets. Véronique gave me free use of all the tools in the garage. She called in a few locals to pull out the oven and take it away in the bed of a truck. I scrubbed the stone with a wire brush and a hot, sudsy mixture that Véronique conjured up for me in a large bucket. I wiped down the tiled backsplash, the tiled floors. It felt good to strip the kitchen down. It felt personal and cleansing. It was a transformation that was gratifying because it was so visual.

I kept tabs on the Cake Shop from afar. Véronique let us use the computer that she kept in a quiet corner off the kitchen, and I checked emails sporadically. Jude kept me posted on all things to do with the Cake Shop, including sales of a popular ice coffee she'd invented called the Cooliocino. Abbot even checked in on his own email, but Charlotte had no interest. She refused to even peek.

The rental car agency brought us a new Renault, and I drove into Aix often, so that I could begin to get a *feel* for what might be out there, begin to *connect*—like new tiles for the bathroom and kitchen backsplash—without *making* decisions. While we waited for a proper oven to be installed—a process that, with all of the damage, would take time—I bought a hot plate, a microwave, and a Crock-Pot so that we could survive. Still, Véronique often insisted that we eat our meals with her.

My favorite errand was to the patisserie. I visited every

couple of days for fresh pastries. The baker was always pleased to see me because, I assumed, I always bought so very much and always wanted to try anything new. He spoke to me only in French and told me once that he remembered me from when I was little and came in with my mother. He remembered that it was my sister who looked like my mother back then.

But he told me now that I was like my mother. *Your quick eyes and your gestures.*

I told him, as I had Véronique, that it was my sister who looked more like her, really.

But he raised his finger and shook his head. *I'm right,* he assured me. *I'm right, absolutely.*

I didn't disagree. Maybe there was something the same about a mother and a daughter at a certain time in their lives when they're both lost—something that shines from within and is undeniable.

Once he asked how my mother was doing these days, and it made me think of Julien, the way he'd waited for news from us as kids. I imagined all of the shopkeepers in the tiny village getting used to us one summer and then, like migratory birds, we would reappear the next year or maybe not until the one after that.

But despite my visits to the patisserie, I still had no desire to bake. I had no desire to make the cakes that I found so beautiful, so perfect. Normally I would have been inspired, especially since these desserts touched something deep inside

of me, the memory of my mother in the kitchen when I finally had her back again. But, no. I only wanted to eat them,
to delight in each bite, to be fed.

Sometimes Charlotte and Abbot came with me on er-
rands, but usually they wanted to stay behind. Abbot liked to
watch the archaeologists squatting in the dig with their small
delicate tools and brushes. Sometimes they became animated
and shouted to each other. Their work was painstaking. They
dug only a quarter of an inch at a time and then documented. At first Charlotte and I stood out there with him,
but I became comfortable allowing Abbot to go out on his
own, and the archaeologists got used to his dogged shadow
and let him linger at the edges under an umbrella that he'd
found in a large cupboard under the stairs.

The dig was the footprint of a Gallo-Roman villa, and,
not far from it, a tomb. The dig was about a five-minute walk
from the back door, but the ground was flat, the mountain
rising up beyond them, and so we could see Abbot's small
figure amid the larger ones.

I could tell why Abbot was fascinated. They'd unearthed
an ancient fountain, a system of aqueducts, a tiling pattern
of small crosses, a hearth, one room after the next. And all
of it had been lying there under the brush stripped by the
fires of 1989, and then hidden by only about a foot of earth.

Eventually, they showed Abbot the tools: trowels,
brushes, dental picks, tape measures, line levels, screens for
sifting. They talked to him about what they found, how

things had been made, why the people had settled here, and why perhaps they'd left.

The archaeologists were very serious workers. One was a thin, fair-haired but suntanned Brit who was lithe and spry, seemingly the one in charge of things. When they let loose at night, they were wild, as Julien had said. Day in and day out, though, they were reserved, digging away, awaiting something to celebrate, it seemed. They had a limited amount of time in the field. Most had to return to universities to teach in the fall, and they worked long hours. In the evenings, Abbot described how the archaeologists thought the people who'd lived in the villa cooked their food and took care of their babies.

"They were real people," he said.

I wondered if it gave him perspective. If there was something about the fact that people live and die and leave things behind and centuries pass that was helping him with his father's death and with the idea of life and death in general— or did it make life seem too fleeting? I wasn't sure, but it seemed important to him, and so I let him spend time out there, perhaps figuring something out, something important. In any case, it seemed like it would do no good keeping him from it.

Each time I took a break from painting the bedrooms, I kept an eye on him from my favorite spot in the lawn chair, absorbing the view of the mountain.

And Charlotte kept an eye out for him from the wide

window in Véronique's kitchen. It turned out that Charlotte was quite good in the kitchen, better than the French teenager with legs like a colt, as Véronique had described her. Charlotte was efficient, patient, well organized. She followed Véronique's curt instructions. It reminded me of being with my mother after she returned. I wondered if Charlotte, too, was drawn to Véronique and the moist steam of the kitchen because of some deep desire for an attentive, sure-handed mother. Véronique quietly praised Charlotte in my presence. "She asks the right questions," she said. "She has smart hands that know what to do, when."

I didn't ask Véronique anything more about my mother, the thief. I didn't mention the box that had been found after the fire, the one she wanted me to return to my mother. How important could it be really, after all of these years? What difference would it make?

Elysius and Daniel were on a yacht and hard to reach. I sent them short email updates, little things about the house renovations and expenditures. Charlotte checked in with her mom from time to time. She never brought up Adam Briskowitz to me, so I didn't, either.

By midafternoon, Charlotte, Abbot, and I were tired, and we often found each other again in the cool pockets of the house. We read the books that the bookshelves had to offer, a strange collection left behind by other visitors. They included things like a Hachette guide to Italy from 1956, published by the Touring Club Italiano, frail pages with small glued-in, brightly colored maps. It was an updated version of the first Hachette guide to Italy, from 1855, and it lured in new readers with this promise: "A certain number of modifications making the use of the guide more easy and adapting it to present-day conditions of travel have been introduced!" I loved the book, oddly enough—the antiquated language, the way it transported me through place and time.

Abbot became interested in a field guide to birds called simply *Les Oiseaux.* It had no copyright date, but it was very old. It offered four pictures of birds per page, and occasionally a page was torn tidily in half as if a previous reader had ripped out a certain bird to paste into a scrapbook of his own sightings. This annoyed Abbot. "How am I supposed to know the birds that I don't know I'm looking for?"

I bought Abbot a notebook without any lines on it, and he would take it out with him to the archaeological dig and keep an eye out for birds. He told me that he wanted to find all the birds that weren't in the book, the ones torn out.

In the evenings, the swallows went mad, and for an hour or more they dashed wildly through the dusk, eating all of the insects they could. Abbot and I made a habit of watching the dizzy, mad spiraling and swooping together. The birds were noisy and shrill. We tried to count them. Abbot drew pictures of them in his book. Sometimes he would draw a picture of Henry, too, smack in the middle of the swallows as if he were here with us. It seemed more like realism to me than anything else—one brand of the truth.

Later, we ate sumptuous meals that Charlotte helped Véronique prepare, sometimes joined by the archaeologists before they bustled back to Aix, or other guests, and some-times not. The meals were as wild, dizzying, and mad as the swallows. I would often close my eyes while eating because I wanted to make sure that I wasn't distracted, that I could taste it all.

I tasted it all. But the physical labor of the yard work and the ambitious decision to put a fresh coat of paint in all of the bedrooms was keeping me fit. Did I go with my mother's desire for clean white walls—her creams and ivories? No. What can I say? The house spoke to me, and I listened. I was going with deep blues, a ruby, a vibrant green. Was it a form of payback? Maybe a little. I decided to keep one bedroom white—only one.

In the evenings, I told and sometimes retold Abbot and Charlotte the rest of the house stories. I told them about the Bath whites and about the massive fire that swept the mountain, scorching everything, but how the fires stopped just at the door the summer my mother came here alone.

"Why did she come here alone?" Charlotte asked.

"It's a long story," I said. It wasn't mine to tell. "But she believes that the house performed a miracle for her."

"Like Auntie Elysius," Abbot said. "The miracle that Uncle Daniel proposed."

"That's a little overly dramatic," Charlotte said. "Don't you think?"

"I don't know," I said. "The stories are what you make of them."

Later, after Abbot was in bed and Charlotte was listening

to the radio that she'd moved from the parlor into her bedroom, I would sit in a lawn chair in the dark yard with only the light from the kitchen spilling from the windows and watch the mountain change its final colors of the day.

And sometimes I thought about Julien. He was gone a week and counting. I wondered if he was going to come back at all.

I missed him in a way that surprised me. I worried that I had a crush on him, and, if I did, what did that mean? This pretty simple possibility terrified me. I told myself it was natural. He was handsome. He had no trouble attracting women. I was a human being, after all. What was a crush? Nothing. It didn't have to mean anything at all.

What would Henry think of my having a crush? He would think it was normal, too. I wondered what he thought of me here in the lawn chair, drinking wine, staring at a mountain. Did he have some larger worldview now, the kind afforded the dead?

At night I got into the crisp white sheets on the stiff bed. One wall of the bedroom was blue, the others still the dingy white. The drop cloth and ladder borrowed from Véronique sat in one corner of the room. I fanned my body out like a star, my muscles stiff and sore. I remembered when I was a little girl and how, after my mother told us the stories of the house and all of the miracles, I would tell the stories to myself, whispering them into my cupped hands. I lifted my hands to my mouth, but all I could whisper now was "I'm here. I am. I'm here, now." It felt suddenly like a prayer. I thought of Charlotte in the cathedrals, Notre-Dame and Saint-Maximin-la-Sainte-Baume. Maybe it was the only kind of prayer I could offer, and I did feel calmed by it, so much so that I curled up and drifted off.

And I dreamed of Henry. These were unlike my dreams at home, where I always realized that his death was some kind of bureaucratic mistake, a clerical mix-up. Here, he was standing by a window, his hands lightly caked with dirt from gardening. He was wearing an old long-sleeved shirt. He unbuttoned the buttons at the wrists, one-handed. Just this small, delicate, intimate gesture—that was all that the dream allowed.

And then the bedroom filled with light, and it was morning again. And I missed him—an ache that I carried through the day.

Do you see Abbot in the fields? I would find myself asking him in my mind.

Can you believe this clear air?

I wish I could slip this into your mouth so you could taste it.

The days gathered a quiet rhythm.

In fact, I had a chorus running through my head—*C'est comme ça*—which was to say not only "It's like this" but also, in my mind, I believed *It's like this and this is the way it is and will be* . . . except I was wrong.

How was I wrong? There were things I didn't know, and they would collide.

1. I didn't really know Adam Briskowitz or the definition of the phrase *to get Briskowitzed.*
2. Véronique had the box that belonged to my mother. She had it on her bedside table and was waiting for the right moment to give it to me. I didn't know what it contained or how the contents would affect me.
3. Abbot was going to find an injured swallow and that bird—perhaps more than anything else—would change our lives.

This is how it began.

A few days later, a little more than halfway through our six-week stay, Julien reappeared.

One evening, as the golden light was taking hold of the cool dry air, Abbot and I were beside the vineyard near the archaeological dig, watching the swallows in their nightly feeding frenzy. Abbot had his sketchpad out and was drawing swirling flight patterns. In this picture, his father was trying to flap his arms like the swallows. It was a funny picture and Abbot had worked very hard on it, even remembering a small scar on Henry's knee, an old baseball scar where Henry had been cleated in college. I noticed the injured swallow hopping near the grapevines, but I didn't want to draw attention to it. I wasn't looking for life lessons by way of injured swallows. Abbot had had enough life lessons for a child his age. Why not lessons in the flight patterns of birds, or, better yet, artistic impressions of the flight patterns of birds?

But, of course, Abbot saw the bird himself. "Look," he said, squatting down and waddling toward it.

The bird was hobbled, its left wing buckled.

"We have to take care of it," Abbot said.

"No," I said. "It's a bird. Its instincts will kick in and it will know how to take care of itself."

Abbot ignored me. "We need a box," he said. "There's one in the cupboard under the stairs. I'll go get it. You watch the bird."

"I'll go get it," I said, and I marched off.

When I came back, carrying the box, Julien had driven

up, turned off the car, and gotten down on one knee next to Abbot, studying the bird intensely. He was wearing a white shirt without a tie and gray suit pants. The suit jacket was lying over the front seat of the convertible.

"How is it that the car doesn't become a swimming pool?" I asked.

"I take the train," he said, standing up, "and park the car in a friend's garage in Aix. You love this car, don't you?"

"I might," I said.

He negotiated around the box and kissed both of my cheeks. "Hello," he said. His lips were soft and quick. He smelled sweet and strong—some kind of wonderful aftershave.

"I'll never get used to that," I said.

"To what?"

"The cheek kissing," I said.

"Oh," he said, and then he held out his hand. "You prefer this?"

I shook his hand, which was strong and warm. "No," I said. "The cheek kissing is fine. It just always surprises me."

"We have a plan!" Abbot said.

"You do?" I said.

"Julien says you can't just set a swallow loose. They can't fly up. You have to get it back to health and then pitch it off someplace high, like a roof," Abbot explained.

"Really?" I said. This seemed like a recipe for disaster. "You throw the injured bird off some kind of precipice?"

Julien nodded. "If it flies, it flies."

"And if it doesn't fly?"

"Then it doesn't."

"Great!" I said, and then lowered my voice. "So a boy gets to watch the bird he's nurtured plummet to its death?"

It must have dawned on him that this might not be the best thing for a little boy with a dead father. He looked a little shaken. "Ah," Julien said. "This is what we have always done for injured birds. Sometimes they fly."

"Great."

"We can at least try to help it!" Abbot said. "I mean, if we don't, it'll just die or get eaten by a cat or something." Abbot looked back and forth between Julien and me.

I sighed. "Fine," I said, putting the box on the ground. "Who's going to pick up the bird and put it in the box?"

"I will," Julien said. "I used to do this when I was a child sometimes." He walked up to the bird very calmly, leaned over it, and then in one quick motion, he folded his hands around it, the wings pressed to the body, and set it in the box.

We all stared at the bird in the box. It shuffled around, its claws scratching the cardboard.

"We'll have to feed it dead flies," Abbot said. "And get a little bowl of water."

"No," Julien said. "We have to just give it a few hours to rest, and then we have to get it to the air."

"But it needs to be taken care of first. It's not ready," Abbot said. "Look at it. We have to take care of it."

"Let him take care of it," I said to Julien.

"Okay," Julien said, taking a step back.

The sight of the three of us standing over the box drew the attention of Charlotte and Véronique, who must have seen us from the kitchen window. They emerged from the house.

"What is it?" Véronique called, limping toward us.

"A swallow!" Abbot yelled. "An injured swallow!"

"The swallows," Véronique said. She and Charlotte walked over and peered into the box. "How many injured swallows did you have as a boy?"

Julien shrugged. "I wanted to be a doctor."

"Did they all live?" Abbot asked.

"Some lived and some didn't."

"This is life," Véronique said. "We accept it."

I had no tolerance for this kind of easy talk about the acceptance of death. Abbot was on his knees, his face looming too close to the bird. "Sit back, Abbot," I said. "That bird will peck your eyes out."

We were all locked together in this frozen moment. No one spoke.

What broke our attention was a taxi, rumbling down the long driveway. It stopped fifty feet from us. We could see through the windshield the commotion of someone paying the driver over the front seat. The trunk popped open.

"A guest," Véronique said. "This person has not made a reservation."

The driver stepped out and pulled a suitcase from the trunk—a very old-fashioned suitcase, tartan plaid with a zipper and no wheels. And then a young man climbed out from the back door. He was short and thin, tan. He was wearing dark jeans, faded at the hips, and a black band T-shirt too far away to read and slightly hemmed in by a suit jacket. His hair was massive—curly and frizzy—and it would have given the impression of a wolf man except that it seemed purposefully wild and all of his other details, including a pair of oversized glasses with thick black frames and clip-on shades, the kind my father used to wear, were self-consciously artsy. And wolf men are so rarely self-consciously artsy. He must have tipped the cabbie pretty handsomely, because the man looked down at the cash and gave him a hug that knocked him off balance for a moment.

"That's no guest," Charlotte said with some disgust but also a hint of admiration. "That's Adam Briskowitz."

Brisky?" I said. "I thought he was only going to write a letter."

"You gave him our address?" Charlotte said accusatorially. "You?"

"I really thought he was only writing a letter, a lovelorn apology," I said. "You know, like he was being old fashioned and romantic."

"Arriving from America in person is old fashioned and romantic," Julien said with a pretty clear understanding of the situation. "It would be better only if he'd taken a ship."

"Is he staying the night?" Véronique asked.

As the taxi drove off, Adam Briskowitz walked up and

stood there in front of us, holding his plaid suitcase by its plastic handle. Now he was close enough for me to read the T-shirt—vintage Otis Redding, of all things. He was wearing Top-Siders, tan leather with white laces, a little dusty from the road, no socks. He smiled at all of us and then pointed at Abbot, who was sitting cross-legged on the ground next to the box. The bird rustled. Adam flipped up the plastic shades attached to his glasses and said, "What have you got in there, scout?"

"Injured swallow," Abbot said. "We're going to nurse it back to health and then throw it off of a roof or some other place high."

"Interesting plan," Adam said, and then he turned to Charlotte and said, "Is that what you're going to do with me?"

"Why are you here?" Charlotte asked, over-enunciating each syllable as if talking to someone who's slow-witted.

He dropped his suitcase to the gravel and said, "You know why I'm here. Everyone knows why I'm here."

"No," she said. "We really don't."

He turned and stared at all of us then, mystified. "Look, I'm not some snob. I'm not an elitist, if that's what you're thinking. I dropped out of Phillips Exeter in the ninth grade, for shit's sake, because I wanted to embrace the proletariat. I'm . . . I am . . ." He was at a loss for words. He took off his suit jacket in a kind of angry protest. "I'm one of the good guys."

Charlotte closed her eyes and sighed. "Why do you talk like that?"

"Like what?"

"Like you're giving a speech and everyone knows who you are?"

"But don't they know who I am?" Adam said.

"Not really," she said. "You're just some guy who's shown up proclaiming his desire to embrace the proletariat."

"Is he going to stay for the night?" Véronique asked.

"Yes," Adam said.

"No," Charlotte said.

"I *am* going to stay the night," he said to Charlotte.

She stormed off toward our house. "Do what you want to, Briskowitz! No one here gives a living shit!" She marched up the back steps to our house and slammed the door.

Adam spun around and kicked the end of his suitcase with one of his Top-Siders.

"Will you want to eat your meals here, too?" Véronique asked. "We offer breakfast and dinner."

"Yes, please," he said. "That would be very nice. Thank you."

"I'm Abbot Bartolozzi," Abbot said, standing up.

"I'm Adam Briskowitz," he said, offering his hand.

Abbot stared at it a moment and then looked at me and then Julien, who gave a nod, and then Abbot grabbed Adam's hand quickly and shook it.

"You all know why I'm here, right? I mean, with Charlotte being pregnant and all."

"What?" I said.

"Oh," Julien said. He put his hands in his pockets and

took a small step backward. "Abbot," he said. "We will look for the flies to give to the bird."

Abbot looked up at me. "Charlotte's pregnant?"

"We'll look for flies," Julien said.

"Go on with Julien," I said. "I'll figure it out and talk to you later."

Julien picked up the box with the bird and they walked off toward the vineyards.

"I knew," Véronique said.

"You knew?" I said.

"I'm glad she told someone!" Adam said. "I mean, it's not healthy to keep secrets. It really isn't. It gums up your breathing, your blood flow."

"She didn't tell me. I saw that she becomes tired suddenly," Véronique said. "Sometimes she puts her head on the table, and she walks heavy, like her center has moved. It's evident." Then she turned and walked back to the house. "Bring your suitcase. I will show you your room."

Adam Briskowitz, I thought to myself. *Briskowitzed.* Is that what he meant? *I didn't mean for her to get Briskowitzed?* "Adam," I said, "are you sure?"

"It's why I'm here," he said. "I'm going to get a job or something. I think people quit school and sell cars, right? I was going to be a philosophy major, so what's one less philosophy major? I'll ask her to marry me and she'll say no. That's how it's going to go, I think."

"I don't think there is just one way that people do this anymore," I said. "There's no blueprint."

He looked at me with genuine surprise.

"Come!" Véronique said.

"Coming!" he said, and he flipped his sunglasses back down over his glasses, picked up his suitcase, and followed Véronique across the lawn toward the back door.

I looked at our house. In the upper window, I saw Charlotte. She looked down at me. Her face was full of light from the golden hour of dusk, her head tilted, her expression oddly serene, resigned, and I knew it was true.

C harlotte?" I knocked softly on her bedroom door. I could hear the soft chatter of the radio. "Charlotte? Can I come in?"

The radio went silent. The doorknob turned, and I heard the latch release. If Henry were here, we'd have had a talk about this, and he'd have coached me. He'd have told me that there were things I was supposed to say. What were they? Henry would have known. He was good at these kinds of things. He knew instinctively how to be loving and open. This was my one opportunity to say the right thing. I was, most likely, never going to have a daughter—much less a pregnant teenage daughter. But I was, once upon a time, a teenager myself. What would I have wanted someone to say to me? Maybe I should start there.

I opened the door slowly.

Charlotte stood before me in Monoprix shorts and a T-shirt, and I remembered what she looked like in the shop with Elysius and my mother in that dress on a leash and her fishing boots. She was so strong, so incredibly tough. "He told you," she said.

"Charlotte, I don't know what to say."

"I haven't told anyone," she said. "It's a huge relief, more than anything."

"How long have you known?"

"Since before the wedding," she said.

"That's a long time to carry a secret like this," I said. "Charlotte, you could have told me."

I walked over and hugged her. It took her a moment, but she hugged me back. She hid her eyes in the crook of my neck and started crying, and I thought not so much about the pregnancy and all that was to come, but really about Charlotte holding this heavy secret inside of her for all this time. I'd never told anyone that I'd thought I might be pregnant when Henry died, that there was a small hope, but only because I didn't want to hand that hopefulness over to anyone else. But this was too much to ask of someone so young. She'd known during the wedding, in the boutique in that awful dress, throughout Paris and the robbery. I felt for her and started crying, too. We stood there until it grew dark outside, listening to the swallows twittering amid the noise of cicadas.

Charlotte was breathing steadily now. We sat down on the bed.

"I came here so I wouldn't have to tell my parents," she said, pulling a tissue from a box on her bedside table and wiping her nose. "They would want me to look at all of my options. I just wanted to get to the second trimester."

"Why?"

She didn't answer.

"So you could keep it?"

She nodded.

"They would have supported any decision you made," I said.

She shook her head. "Nope," she said. "They would flip. All of them. But that's not even it. It's not them," she said. "I knew I'd want to have an abortion if I stayed. I'd see school coming, and at my school, well, it would have been worse than death. I'm *privileged*," she said, disgusted by the word. "Getting pregnant is like shitting on privilege."

"Charlotte, this happens. It always has and it always will. Do you think that getting pregnant makes you some kind of ingrate?"

She laughed. "Getting pregnant makes me a *dipshit*. The kinds of friends I have come apart at the seams because of early decisions for Harvard."

"How far along are you?"

"Eight weeks, medically speaking."

"And how are you feeling?"

"A little tired, but weirdly like I'm on calm drugs or something. No morning sickness, and I'm not at all bitchy. It's totally ironic, but I think pregnancy agrees with me. I mean, I've never been all that maternal. I gave my dolls bad haircuts, but I want to have the baby and do this right."

"You're so . . . *sure*," I said.

"It's weird. But ever since I got here, it's been completely clear."

"Really?"

"Really."

"And Briskowitz? Do you think he'll make a good father?"

"Briskowitz makes a good *Briskowitz*. He'll be a lousy philosophy major, frankly. He talks a good game, but he's way too scattered. As for fatherhood?" She thought about it. "He at least has a good one to model off of. Bert Briskowitz. He's a well-mannered orthopedics man who doesn't force Brisky to play golf. What more could you ask for in today's fractured society?"

"You can ask for a lot more," I said.

She looked at me skeptically and then down at her hands.

I thought of Henry after the miscarriage. When he was looking for that leak in the pipes, he had popped off an access panel and then took out the handles of the tub, leaving three holes in the wall. One night, I'd left the light on in what was going to be the baby's nursery. And so, when I walked into the bathroom, the holes in the tiled wall were lit up. I stepped into the tub, fully dressed, sat down, and looked through the holes into the nursery. I was looking in on what my life could have been. It looked perfect and unattainable from there—like someone else's life. Abbot's old crib was back up with new brightly colored bedding. I'd bought a fuzzy, woolly white throw rug. I knew then what I would have said if Henry had been there. I'd have told Charlotte that Henry and I would help her raise the baby. I'd have told her that she could move in with us. She could go to school, and Henry and I would manage the baby for her. We would create a new kind of family. We would make it work. But I couldn't make this offer. What kind of a mother would I be to an infant and a sixteen-year-old in addition to Abbot? I was barely managing as it was. Instead, I said something very rational. "You have to tell your parents."

"Look," she said. "I just need time. My mother is kind of off her rocker. She's not stable. She believes in gemstones, and then she can go hysterical like Alanis Morissette tripping on acid. It's not pretty. And my dad's great, but he and Elysius aren't kid-friendly. I mean, they like kids in the abstract. They love Abbot, of course. But they're not parents by nature. Seriously, the whole time they've been raising me it's been painful to watch—like people playing racquetball left-handed in high heels. None of it came to them naturally."

"You can't do this without them." I wondered if they really would flip. It was hard to say.

"I think I can," she said.

"You don't know how hard it is. And you can't ever really know what the sacrifices will be. It was hard enough for me when Henry was by my side and we were ready. You just can't imagine how hard it's going to be on you and Adam."

"I don't want to talk about it." She flopped onto the bed. "This is why I didn't tell anyone."

"I'm sorry," I said. I didn't want to push her. "We don't have to have all the answers right now."

I stood up and walked to the window. Julien and Abbot were sitting on the back step of the Dumonteils' house, the box at their feet. Maybe they were feeding the bird or helping to make it a nest for the night or planning where to keep it so no feral cats could get to it. And, looking down at Abbot, there was this feeling I couldn't deny. Charlotte was pregnant, and there was a stirring of joy. I couldn't help it. "A baby!" I whispered.

"I know," Charlotte said. "That's the intense part. I'm pregnant with *a baby*."

"Is this what you were praying about in Notre-Dame and Saint Maximin?"

She shrugged. "I don't know anything about praying. All three of my parents are agnostics," she said. "I just kneel down and say the same thing over and over."

"And what was that?"

"I kind of pretend that I'm one of the Flying Wallendas."

"The circus performers?"

"I don't know why, except I read about them when I was a kid, and they made an impression. They did these pyramids up on high wires."

"And so what do you pray for while pretending to be a Flying Wallenda?"

"I'm the kind of Flying Wallenda who prays for a good net. That's it," she said. "Just a good net."

That night, we all ate dinner together, sharing the dining room with a British family with two children who wanted fried potatoes, and three older Australian women who cornered Véronique about where they could find the best Mediterranean beaches.

Julien was there, too. He helped his mother serve and took the two British children out into the yard to look at the fireflies so that their parents could eat in peace. When I looked out the wide windows, I saw the two children running in the grass barefoot, but Julien was watching me. And who was I now? A woman surrounded by a pregnant sixteen-year-old and her strange young boyfriend with his wild head of hair and my eight-year-old son who had to be talked out of bringing the bird in its box into the dining room with him? Everything seemed to have shifted. The fact was that

Charlotte was pregnant the day before, when I'd been think-ing that this was the way it was and the way it was going to be. But now all of that was gone. This was new terrain. We were all interconnected now, locked together by this secret. It wouldn't last, of course. Charlotte would have to tell her parents—Briskowitz too—but for now, I wondered if Julien was thinking what I was thinking: *What a strange family.*

Charlotte described the meal: eggplants stuffed with a mix of prosciutto, anchovies, salt pork, and mushrooms, sea-soned with garlic, onion, salt, and pepper, topped with bread-crumbs, butter, and lemon.

"You helped make this?" Adam asked Charlotte. "I thought you considered stirring fruit-on-the-bottom yogurt cooking."

"That was then and this is now! I know the difference be-tween pressed and chopped garlic. I prefer pressed."

"Huh," Adam said.

"She can cook like crazy," Abbot said.

We were quiet for a while.

"This is a nice place," Adam said. He was wearing a Velvet Underground T-shirt now and had his suit jacket back on.

"Heidi used to come here as a kid," Charlotte said.

"I was a bad little kid," Adam said. "My parents didn't believe in discipline. I once hit my brother during the movie *Gandhi.*"

"Huh," I said.

"I learned that nonviolence is hard, which is one of the lessons of the film. But, in general, because my parents were softies, I've had to learn things the hard way."

"And what way is that?" I asked.

"I got beat up a couple of times for being snotty," he said. "And I went to a do-good liberal school that made us interact with and serve the poor. That stuff is pretty artificial, but it does sink in."

Charlotte couldn't even look at him. He'd come all this way. I felt sorry for him, but I wasn't so sure that I should. Charlotte would have good reason to be cold.

Abbot was the one to bring up the pregnancy. I'd told him before we came in that Charlotte was indeed pregnant. That she was too young, really, and that would make it hard on her. But we can be happy for her. That was about all I had time to cover.

Now Abbot said, "I know that just because you're pregnant doesn't mean you're married. Like Jill and Marcy." This was a lesbian couple, friends of ours, one of whom had twins through in vitro.

"Actually, Jill and Marcy are pretty much married," I said. "They've been together for ten years or more."

"Oh," Abbot said. "Are you a lesbian?" he asked Charlotte.

"Nope," she said. "Unfortunately, that's not my calling."

"Oh, so you'd prefer to be a lesbian right now?" Adam said. "Very nice."

"I was just saying that if I were a lesbian, I wouldn't be in this situation."

Adam looked at Abbot. "I'm going to ask Charlotte to marry me."

"And Charlotte is going to say no," Charlotte said.

"See?" he said to me. "I told you she was going to say no."

"I'm going to say no because it's a bad idea. What are you, from the 1950s all of a sudden?" she said.

"I'm trying to do the right thing," he said. "And last I checked, getting married was the right thing."

"Last I checked, you thought that marriage was the institutionalization of patriarchal dominance. You thought that marriage was just condescending tax code."

"I was probably high," he said, and then he looked at Abbot and then said to me, "No offense. I don't smoke weed anymore."

"None taken," I said.

"It's seriously been, like, two months."

"Okay," I said, not sure that this was really cause for celebration.

"Why aren't you going to say yes to getting married?" Abbot asked Charlotte.

"I'm not getting married, because it just doesn't apply to sixteen-year-olds, Absterizer. Parental units or not," Charlotte said.

"Gotcha," Adam said. "And so this has nothing to do with the fact that you don't *love* me enough?"

"You want to get married because I'm pregnant. What's that got to do with loving *me* enough?"

This was said a little loudly, garnering the attention of the British and the Australians alike.

"Do your parents know?" I asked Adam quietly.

"Not exactly," he said.

"What's that mean?" Charlotte asked.

"They know I'm here," he said. "They just happen to think that I'm here on a tour of famous French painters." He looked at me. "My mother is the one in charge of educational expenditures, and she's a little disconnected."

"Okay," I said. "Listen, you both need to tell your parents. I'll give you a couple days—three, tops—to get some kind of plan, or at least talking points, and then you've got to call them."

They looked at each other.

"My mother is either going to want to throw down or join an ashram. It's hard to say," Charlotte said to Adam. "Elysius and Daniel will go ballistic. It won't be pretty."

"What's an ashram?" Abbot asked.

"Another word for 'community.' It's kind of for hippie freaks," Adam explained quickly, and then he straightened up and said, "Well, I predict Bert and Peg will take this well. I'm the youngest. They've been through the fire. They may make me go to a shrink, and they'll certainly have to up Peg's dosages. But I don't think this will be a total nervous breakdown or anything."

"If you don't tell them, then I have to," I said.

"Well, I guess I don't have a choice," Charlotte said.

Adam smiled. "We can come up with some talking points together. We can manage that much."

Charlotte nodded. "Okay," she said.

"Are you taking vitamins?" Adam asked. It was a question I should have thought of.

"Of course," Charlotte said. "Horse pills. I got them at the co-op health food store."

"They're prenatal?" Adam asked.

"Yes, they're prenatal," Charlotte said. "Do you want me to get out the packaging?"

"Actually, I wouldn't mind," he said. "There's a lot of research on folic acid. Do they have enough folic acid in them?"

And this is the moment I kind of fell for Adam Briskowitz. He'd been doing research. He'd brought baby books with him on the plane. He went on to ask Charlotte about any morning sickness, any spotting, any light-headedness. As far as Charlotte and the baby's health was concerned, there was nothing the least bit scattered or philosophical about him.

Later, I tucked Abbot into bed. The injured swallow had settled down for the night in the box on the floor. He and Julien had made a small nest for it, some sticks, grass, and a dish towel, tucked in one corner of the box. It seemed to me that this joint mission—saving this swallow—held great weight for both of them. What would happen if the bird died? I felt trapped by the two options. I couldn't suggest giving up on the bird, and yet every moment Julien and Abbot invested in it seemed to up the ante on an unwinnable bet.

Abbot's notebook of drawings was next to him in the bed, and he was holding his flashlight, the one he liked to shine out his window some nights, "just to see what's out there," he said, but I also figured he used the flashlight after lights-out so that he could stay up and draw under his covers. He was flipping it off and on.

"Tell me a Henry story," he whispered.

I didn't tell Henry stories at home every night, far from it, but still, there had been no Henry stories since we'd arrived. There had been no Henry stories since the night Abbot asked for a *new* Henry story, the night I ended up on the front stoop and found the purple plastic egg and decided to come to France. I hadn't wondered why before, but now I did. Abbot surely had intuited that I was coming here, in part, to try to free us from some of the grief surrounding Henry. But I wasn't here to free us from the memory of him. I was looking for a new relationship with Henry, in a way. Our house at home was filled with mementos. I had memories of Henry built into every street corner, every park and playground, Elysius and Daniel's house, the neighbors' yards, the Cake Shop, the downtown, Abbot's school. Here, Henry wasn't so much thrown at me as I was allowed to simply carry him with me. For the first time since I arrived, I realized that my relationship with Henry had changed. It was quieter, more peaceful.

"A Henry story," I said. I thought of Adam Briskowitz. Henry would have adored the kid. I thought of a story then, one I'd never told Abbot. "When your father was sixteen, he was a baseball player. They won the state tournament that year. He knocked in the tying run. But he also once confessed that he bought a pipe and a smoking jacket. Your dad could be kind of funny like that."

"What's a smoking jacket?"

"It's something fancy that British people used to wear when smoking pipes," I said. "I asked him where he got the smoking jacket and he confessed that it was really just a robe."

"Why did he want to wear a smoking jacket and smoke a pipe?"

"I think he wanted to be sophisticated," I said. "He didn't want to be just a baseball player. But he didn't really know what sophisticated looked like."

"Did he smoke the pipe?"

"I don't know."

"But he was just a kid, like, Charlotte's age?"

"Yes, just a kid but trying to be an old man."

"But he'll never be an old man," Abbot said.

"Nope."

"So it's good he tried it out when he was sixteen."

"I guess so."

"Tell me another house story," he said. "Maybe one about you."

"The Bath whites, I told you that story."

"Tell another one."

I thought a moment. "This story takes place just a little bit away from the house, up the mountain."

"Okay," Abbot said.

"Julien and I knew each other as kids. And one time, he goaded me into climbing the mountain to get to this little chapel that's built into the rock of the mountain itself. It's the chapel of Saint Ser, home of a hermit who, Julien told me, had his ears chopped off and then his head."

"An earless, headless hermit?" Abbot said.

"Yes, and Julien said he was a phantom, a ghost, but then he told me that he was a good phantom, because he watched over all the souls of the people who died on the mountain."

"Did he hold his own head like that picture in Notre-Dame?"

"I never saw him. But once, I thought I heard him whisper my name."

"A good phantom," Abbot said, "who protected souls."

"Yes, in this little chapel up on the mountain. It's still there. Maybe we'll go one day."

He thought about this a moment and then said, "Julien says we have to throw the swallow tomorrow. We shouldn't have waited. But I think it's got to have time for its wing to get better." Abbot shifted under his sheets. "Do you think the swallow will fly?"

"I don't know," I said. "But you're just doing your best for it. That's more than most kids would do. Most people, for that matter. Regular people would probably just walk on by the bird and go on with their lives. But you stopped to help it. That's remarkable."

He smiled. "Today was weird."

"It was."

"Charlotte is really pregnant?"

"Yes."

"Is she going to get in trouble for it?"

"That's hard to say. Parents can freak about things like this."

"Would you freak if she was your daughter?"

"I don't think so."

"I like babies. Everybody likes babies."

"You were a great baby."

"Remarkable," he said. "I was a *remarkable* baby."

I kissed him on the forehead. "Go to sleep, remarkable baby." I stood up.

"Check on the swallow. Is it asleep?"

I looked down into the box. The bird was standing there, its wing still rumpled. It looked up at me. "No," I said. "But let's turn off the light. That'll help."

"Okay," he said. "Goodnight."

"Goodnight."

Charlotte was already in her room, listening to the radio. She and Adam had gone for a short walk after dinner but came home taking different paths. He'd come back striding through the gardens and she'd walked down a row in the vineyard—both flushed with anger. I wondered if three days was enough time for them to establish a united front—or, perhaps, decide not to have one.

I walked down to the kitchen and poured myself a glass

of red wine. I stared at the place where the oven and cabinets had been. *This kitchen will never be remodeled. It will never be finished*, I thought. I sat down at the table, set the glass of wine in front of me, and rested my head in my hands. I thought of my mother in this very kitchen the summer she disappeared. Had she learned to listen to the house? What had it told her?

I closed my eyes and, as foolish as I felt, I tried to listen. What else could I do at a moment like this?

The house didn't say a word, of course, but it did seem to swell around me. It felt fuller now, knowing that Charlotte was pregnant. I thought of the minute fetus moving inside of her and then, oddly, the swallow rustling in the cardboard box. I wondered what was going to happen next. What would our lives look like a year from now? Where would Charlotte and her baby be? With Elysius and Daniel in their giant house? With her mother, consulting her gemstones? Would she be looking at universities, prepping for interviews? Would Adam Briskowitz be home from college for the summer? Would he be a philosophy major after all? In that case, who would be watching the baby?

The house was quiet. I'd asked too much. I'd started rifling off questions and had stopped listening.

There was a knock at the door and it inched open.

I realized in this split second that I wanted it to be Julien. "Come in."

"*C'est moi*," Julien said. He stepped in and looked around the kitchen. "It looks nice in here. Very nice work."

"Thanks," I said. "It's coming."

"I wanted to tell you something."

"You're not pregnant, are you?"

He laughed. "I don't think so."

"It's been a long day."

"I know," he said. "I think she is doing well. She's healthy and she has been happy here, no?"

I thought about how miserable she'd been at home, and Julien was right. She'd been enjoying the kitchen and drawing birds with Abbot. "She has been happy. The happiest I've seen her in a long time."

"Maybe this will be good, in the end," he said. "The boy, Adam, is . . . interesting."

I nodded. "I like him, actually."

"He's eccentric." Julien seemed restless. I wondered if he was stalling. "Do you want to sit outside?" he said, picking the bottle up off the table. "It's a warm night."

We took wineglasses and the bottle and sat in the lawn chairs by the fountain with its broken pump.

"What did you want to tell me?" I asked.

"It's the bird," he said.

"The swallow?"

"Yes," he said, and he shook his head. "The bird is probably going to die."

"Do they usually die?"

"Sometimes they live. But as soon as you told me about nurturing the bird and then throwing it, I thought of your husband, Abbot's father. Now, after today, and the boy Adam arrives and Charlotte is pregnant, and I'm thinking maybe this is a bad idea. Abbot will throw the bird and what if it cannot fly and it hits the ground and dies. I'm sorry I had the idea. It was from when I was a boy. But your family, now, is . . . delicate."

He took a drink of wine. I lifted the bottle and poured him more. I sighed.

"I know what it's like to lose a father. We were a delicate family. A different type of delicate family. But I know what it is like, in one way. The father is there and then he's not."

This surprised me. It was different—death versus abandonment—but I realized that Julien understood Abbot in a way that I couldn't. My mother disappeared, yes, but only for a summer. She came home. But for Abbot and Julien, their fathers left and didn't come back.

Julien rested his elbows on his knees. "I think that maybe I can take the box and say that I was feeding the bird in the morning and that it was a miracle but the bird flew away."

"No," I said.

"What should we do?"

"I think we should let Abbot throw the bird."

"You do?" he said. "But what if . . ."

"We have to live a little," I said. "We have to work at joy. That's what you told me once, right? That entails taking risks."

"Yes," he said, cradling his glass of wine in his palm. "You're right."

"It's just so hard," I said. "Henry would know what to do. He'd say the right thing. I miss him." My face felt warm and my throat cinched. I knew I was going to cry. It had been building all day. The tears slipped quickly down my cheeks. "I'm sorry," I said, wiping them away. "It still catches me off guard."

"What was he like?" Julien asked.

"Do you really want to know?"

"Yes."

I started talking, haltingly at first, but then I found that it was a strange liberation to describe Henry to someone who'd never met him. I explained not only Henry and the Cake Shop and our lives together, but also his tough father, Tony Bartolozzi, and his doting mother, and his younger brother, the one who almost drowned in the pool at the barbecue when he was little, whom everyone called Jimbo. When I told him the story of how Henry and I met, Julien asked me to sing "Brandy."

"No," I said. "I can't sing. I'm awful."

"But you were awful then, too."

"I was drunk."

"Drink and then sing it!"

I was already a little tipsy by now, but I shook my head. I told him the story of how Abbot was conceived, a kind-of accident, and he confessed that his daughter, Frieda, was planned, that there were ovulation kits, and then doctors who prescribed pills for his wife, and he loved the idea of an accident even if it wasn't an accident.

I told him the story of the miscarriage, Henry busting up tiles in the house. I told him the story of the dry tub, the part I'd never told anyone before—how Henry found me there in the tub, looking in through the holes at the nursery. "I had a fever, unrelated to the miscarriage, but he was worried. He picked me up and carried me back to bed."

Julien was quiet, and then he said, "He loved you."

"He did," I said.

"No," he said, shaking his head. "Not everyone knows love like he did. He *loved* you. Everyone thinks that it is a gift to have someone love you, but they're wrong. The best gift is that you can love someone—like he loved you. To know that kind of love."

"Maybe you're right," I said. "I got to love him like that, too."

We were quiet for a moment, and I remembered what it had been like to fall in love with Henry, that he'd been the exact soul I'd been waiting for, how getting to know him was like opening gift after gift. But right now, I felt aware of handing over gifts, that each story was something for Julien to unwrap. Once upon a time, I'd thought I'd been looking for Henry, but really I'd been just waiting for him, without knowing that I was waiting, and now it seemed like I'd been waiting for myself in some way, without knowing that I was waiting. In telling Julien some of the stories of my life, I was aware that I'd been missing myself, perhaps. And here I was, appearing, one unwrapped story at a time.

I asked him about his ex-wife, Patricia. He took a deep breath, and I realized that he was beautiful not just because of his face or the set of his shoulders but the way he had lis-

tened, his bemused expression when I'd reverted to pantomime to explain something he'd never heard of, the way
he'd shaken his head when he laughed, like he didn't want to
but couldn't help it. And he now was beautiful because of the
things that he told me about his failed marriage and his wife.
Her mother was an opera singer—very harsh and exacting.
Her father was an old softie who cried at commercials. And
he missed his ex-wife in acute detail. She sneezed when she
walked into the sun—four times, always four times. She was
superstitious, even though she denied it and had worn the
same charm bracelet since she was seventeen, having replaced
the chain many times. She talked to herself when she was
cooking. And when they broke up, he tried to disappear. He
went to live with his friend Gerard, a bachelor, who lived in
Marseille. "Gerard is a flirt. He loves women and detests
marriage. I thought it would be fun to be a bachelor again.
But, really, most nights I went to Notre-Dame de la Garde,
the cathedral on the hill near the sea. I didn't go in. There's a
wall outside. And I just looked at the sea, like I was waiting
for a ship to come back home. It didn't. And slowly I
stopped expecting it."

Maybe that was what was wrong with me. I hadn't fully
stopped expecting Henry to come back. "Why didn't it work
out between you two?" I asked.

"I could say many things. I wasn't what she wanted. I
wasn't the man she wanted her friends to adore. I was funny
when she wanted me to be serious. I was not good enough.
And I was tired of trying to be good enough." He smiled

sadly. "She married the wrong one. In the end, it is that simple." He waved the conversation off. "Why are you here?" he asked. "Not the answer about the house. Why are you here, now?"

I told him about that one night I found the purple plastic egg and then looked up *Henry* in the dictionary and found the word *hent*, "to seize."

"And that is why you are here?" he asked. "That one word?"

I nodded.

He sat back and stared at the stones near the fountain left behind by the mason, a hefty man with jowls and the most beautifully scarred hands. "I think it's more," he said.

"What do you mean?"

"My wife, she wore her charm bracelet since she was seventeen, but she doesn't really understand."

"Understand what?"

"It's not the bracelet," he said. "It's because she *believes* in the bracelet."

"Are you asking me what I believe in?"

"Yes."

"I told Abbot the story of Saint Ser tonight, the protector of souls. I believed in him some, you know, when I was little and you made me trudge up that mountain."

He stood up.

"What is it?" I asked.

"That is a good example. There was no ghost. I invented the ghost because I wanted you to be afraid. But then I was afraid myself, and so I said he was a good phantom, a protector. When we rang the bell and called the ghost, and we waited by the altar, you heard him whisper your name."

"I was a kid."

"A kid who believed in a ghost."

I stiffened. "Are you calling Henry a ghost?"

"No, Henry is real. Patricia is real," he said. "Right now, the problem is that you and I, we are the ghosts."

I thought of my ghostly reflection in the fogged wardrobe mirror in Daniel's studio loft. But Julien in this moment was real to me, beautiful and real.

"I should head in," I said. "It's late."

"You didn't sing."

I stood up and slipped on my flip-flops. "The song is about Brandy," I said. "She's a fine girl, but the sailor can't commit to her because he's married to the sea."

"That isn't singing," he said.

"I'll see you tomorrow," I said.

"And tomorrow you'll sing?"

I walked to the door. "I don't think so!" I said.

"But maybe yes?"

"But maybe no."

Over the course of the next three days, Abbot managed to put off throwing the bird. He opened the kitchen windows and let the flies buzz in. And then he hunted them, with quiet intensity and pretty good marksmanship with a swatter, then fed them to the swallow. He always seemed to have his trusty notebook tucked under one arm.

This was bad, of course. Julien whispered to me, "He is attaching to the bird. It's going to more difficult if . . ."

"I know," I whispered. "I get it."

"A miracle?" he said. "In the middle of the night? It flies away?"

I shook my head. "He'll know."

Adam Briskowitz and Charlotte had loud, heated fights. Sometimes I'd see Charlotte walking calmly while Adam

lapped around her like she was a maypole. Each time I overheard one of their arguments, it was never about motherhood, fatherhood, their parents' potential for freak-outs, or a
baby. It was always something abstract: Middle East politics,
talent versus a strong work ethic, corporate greed, the religious upbringing of Michael Moore, and once I could have
sworn I heard the word *Reaganomics*. I couldn't help but think,
What is it with kids these days?

Meanwhile, was I listening to the house? Was I feeling
and connecting and allowing decisions to form? I was trying to.

Véronique's project manager was named Maurice. He
was broad and tan, her age but more weathered, and hunky
by any standard. In fact, when he arrived to talk with me and
Véronique, who was supposed to jump if translation issues
arose, I could have sworn the two were flirting with each
other. Plus, we needed no translation help. His English was
impeccable. He'd lived in California for a time and knew how
to surf. He seemed dumbfounded by the fact that I'd never
surfed. "Really? But you have such waves!" I apologized for
my obvious lack of appreciation for my homeland.

We walked the grounds and around the house. We talked
about my mother's ideas, and Maurice took notes. We sat at
the kitchen table and discussed structural changes, appli-
ances, fixtures, lighting, plumbing, tile, color, and money. He
offered me more catalogs.

"Timing?" I asked. "Is it really going to take two to three
months before we get started?"

He smiled. "The ox is slow, but the earth patient."

"Is that a French saying? Do you all have a lot of oxen?"

He and Véronique smiled. No, not much oxen in France.

I called my mother and told her that I'd decided on Maurice as the project manager and recounted the conversation.

She said, "I can't sleep at night."

"Because of the house renovation?" I asked, trying to make a connection.

"No," she said. "It's not that."

"What's wrong?" I was hanging a load of our wet clothes on the rickety wooden rack in Charlotte's room.

"I don't know. I'm restless. I feel like things are coming apart at the seams."

I wanted to tell her that she was right, that she was prescient, that all hell was about to break loose, but of course, I couldn't. It would put her in an impossible situation. How could she not call Elysius and tell her? And if she knew, even if it was only a day away from Charlotte's telling her parents herself, it could damage the trust between Elysius and my mother. "What are you worrying about when you can't sleep?"

"I can't help but imagine you there with Abbot and Charlotte, and as soon as I do, I remember the last time I was there. It was a hard time for me. You know that."

"I do," I said. "Of course I do."

"What else has Véronique said to you?"

"I told you what she said. She called you a thief, though she didn't say it maliciously."

"I know," she said, "but has she mentioned anything else?"

"She said that you had lessons for me."

"Oh, please!" she said. "I don't have any lessons!"

"Tell me what happened that summer."

The line was quiet.

"Tell me," I said.

"I was lost," she whispered.

"Did someone find you?"

My mother was quiet. Finally, she said, "It's ancient history."

"Ancient history that keeps you up at night."

"Your father doesn't know anything about any of this," she said. "I want to keep it that way."

"If you're telling me not to tell my father, you're overestimating what I know. What would I tell him? I don't have any idea what happened. Did you have an affair?"

"It was worse than an affair," she said. "I fell in love."

I couldn't process this fully. My breath caught in my throat. "Why did you fall in love?"

"I didn't mean to!" she said, almost childishly.

"But you came back, so how did it end?"

"Maybe it didn't really end," she said. "You're the one who asked me why I can't sleep at night!"

"You still think about him now?"

"It's not that I think about him. . . ." She was quiet a moment. "It's that I think about this other life that didn't get lived. . . ."

This made me think of Henry, of course. I would always now have a life without him, a life that wouldn't get lived. It would be a hole that I would carry with me forever. Was this one of the lessons that my mother had to teach me? "But you didn't stay. How did it end?" I asked.

"There were fires," she said. "Huge fires. You can't imagine—an entire mountain on fire. That was a sign, wasn't it? I didn't need a bigger sign than that."

"A sign that told you what?"

"To come home."

The next day—the day Adam and Charlotte were supposed to call their respective parents—happened to fall on Bastille Day. I had vague memories of my mother's celebrations in the backyard, which amounted to a replay of the Fourth of July—getting red, white, and blue bunting at post-holiday sale bins, minus the American flags. And we'd also celebrated Bastille Day here a few times. I remembered taking a promenade with Elysius, Julien and his older brother, and other children from the village through the streets at dusk with paper lanterns suspended from short sticks. That morning, I saw Julien in the yard and asked, "Do they still parade through the streets with the paper lanterns?" I was wearing my painting jeans. I'd finished my blue room and Abbot's ruby-colored room. Now I was working on Charlotte's, so there was a new layer of green flecks.

"I don't know," he said. "But I'll find the answer. Do you want to go to the celebration in the village?"

"I'd like to pretend we fit in," I said, and, too, I wanted to know if it was like my memory of it, the image of the globes bobbing again in my mind after all of those years. I thought of my mother, how strange it must have been for her to have so many memories like these that turned in her mind, and how it must have been to wonder if she would ever return to this place. Would my memories of Henry be the same—drifting and gliding, losing detail, becoming more imagistic? The idea of it made my chest ache.

Charlotte and Adam found me by the fountain talking to the plumber, someone whom Véronique had called in to fix the pump. He was a young man wearing thick, industrial-looking boots and, as was often the case with him, a very loose tank top. He was there on the holiday only to pick up his check. The fountain was now filled with clear water, the pump pumping. The water was burbling nicely. I was planning on buying the koi that week.

Julien and Abbot were in the newly fixed swimming pool, taking an inaugural swim in celebration. It was a vacation day for everyone, and so they were supposed to relax. I could hear Julien teaching Abbot the French national anthem. The swallow was in its box under a shade tree—always nearby, Abbot made sure of it. His notebook was probably propped beside it.

"Merci," the plumber said, and he took his check, folded

it with one hand, and pocketed it. He smiled at Charlotte as he passed, which Adam picked up on, and it made him stand up tall, arch his back some, take a step in closer to Charlotte. I took this as a good sign. I didn't quite get why an incoming college freshman would be heated about Reaganomics, but I got this—a little jealousy.

"We're ready for fish," I said.

"They had fountains in this region during the Gallo-Roman era," Adam said.

"Yep," I said. "Actually, the dig out there has uncovered a good bit of a villa. Fountain included."

"Really?" he said. "That's very interesting."

"It's day three," Charlotte said, getting to the point.

"And?" I asked. "How do things stand?"

"We have talking points," Adam said.

"Have you sorted out global politics?" I asked.

"No," Charlotte said.

"Kind of," Adam said. "We might be as close as we can get."

"Are you a united front?" I asked, rubbing green paint from my palms.

They looked at each other warily, but both nodded.

"We're still different nations," Adam said. "But we're part of the UN, and we plan to invite other countries to the table for talks."

"Do you know what you would like the day-to-day to look like, in a perfect world?"

Adam was going to say something, but Charlotte reached

out and put her hand on his chest. "No," she said. "We don't. We have to see what everyone else says, where they stand."

"Bert and Peg are going to be very laid back," Adam said. "They were almost like hippies. I've seen both of them stoned."

"You go first then," Charlotte said.

"You want me to call right here in front of all of you?"

"However you want to do it," I said.

"I'll just take a little walk," he said. He pulled his phone out of his pocket, stared at it for a moment as if he'd forgotten how the instrument worked. Then he flipped it open, glanced back at Charlotte, dialed, held the phone to his ear, and started walking. I could hear Julien singing a bit of the French national anthem, "*Aux armes, citoyens, formez vos bataillons,*" and Abbot's faint, high voice repeating after him.

"How is it really going?" I asked Charlotte.

"Terribly," she said. "I love him."

"Oh," I said. This wasn't what I expected.

"I know you don't believe me. I wouldn't. I don't believe sixteen-year-olds fall in love, not really. But I don't know how else to put it."

"I believe you. We're wired to fall in love."

"Wired," she said. "That makes us sound like animals, like we have no choice."

"We are mammals," I said, thinking of the beluga whales and their belly buttons.

"My mom is incapable of real love. She just can't handle it. And with Elysius and Daniel it's complicated. It's something like love, but it's not love, or it's not the kind of love I want. It's something else—like a lifetime arrangement to take care of each other. But you and Henry," she said softly, "it was love from the beginning, right?"

"But you can't dismiss these other kinds of love. I mean, maybe your mother is capable of real love, but isn't good at showing it. And Daniel and Elysius have something that will endure, I think. It's already endured eight years. Maybe . . ."

"I know, I know," Charlotte said. "But I want to know, honestly, was it love from the beginning with Henry? I mean, it wasn't something . . . else?"

I didn't want to push my own definition of love. It was narrow, and I knew it. It was all I really understood, though, and I also had to tell the truth. "It was love from the beginning."

"And it lasted," she said.

"It is lasting," I said.

She nodded. "That's what I want, whether it ends up being with Adam or not."

"Yes," I said, "that's what I want for you. The problem is, being in love with Adam Briskowitz is almost a separate issue right now."

"I know, I know. Will he make a good father? Can I trust him to be there for me?"

"Yes," I said. "How involved do you want him to be?"

"Is it up to me, really?"

"You should know what you want."

She sighed and looked up at the mountain, the sky. Adam

was standing in the distance, staring at the dirt, with one hand on his hip. "I think about all the stories you told me about this place. All the love stories, all of the enchantments. But maybe it's only enchanted for all of you—the women in your family, the direct line. What do you think?"

"I don't know that I believe them."

"Huh," she said. "I didn't at first, but now I might. But they don't apply to me."

"You don't know that," I said. "You never can tell . . ."

Adam, still off in the distance, spun around. He was shouting, but we couldn't hear what he was saying. "I don't think it's going as well as he thought it would," Charlotte said.

"He strikes me as a strange kind of optimist."

"He thinks his mother will want to take care of the baby. He's actually said that we could move in together and live in the guesthouse by the pool. That's insane! I'm sixteen. I can't live in a guesthouse by the Briskowitzes' pool, hand my baby off to Peg in the mornings, and then run to first period."

"Does he love you?"

She nodded. "I think he does, but he's scared shitless, really. That's what he's not saying. He's scared shitless."

Adam kicked the dirt. A small cloud lifted into the air. He yelled something, then raised the phone over his head and snapped it shut, as if this were the formal ending of a flamenco dance.

"He's funny," I said.

"He's not trying to be funny," she said. "But he's funny."

Adam strode toward us now, head down. "Plan A," he shouted, "is not going to work out! Peg and Bert have really burnt their bridges!"

"What happened?" Charlotte called out.

"They're demanding I come home directly." He walked up to us and put his hands on his knees, breathing hard. "Peg is fixating on the fact that I lied to her about taking a course on famous French painters."

"Did you tell her that you are, at this very moment, standing in the shadow of Cézanne's Mont Sainte-Victoire?" Charlotte asked.

"I did make this clear. She was unimpressed."

"And the pregnancy?" I asked.

"Now, that made an impression!" he said, straightening up.

"What was her response?" I asked.

"They suggested that I come home and be grounded."

"Grounded?" I said, rubbing my forehead. Bert and Peg Briskowitz. I imagined them at this very moment sitting like two stuffed-doll versions of themselves propped on their sofa stunned, completely stunned. One might say to the other, *Did we try to ground him? Was that what we said?* And maybe the other wouldn't even respond. Just numb silence. "It's a little late for grounded. They need some time. That's all. You've caught them off guard."

"This is very bad," Charlotte said. "If that's how the *hippies* who've *been through the fire* handle their *fourth* child, I'm screwed!" She threw her hands up. "Completely screwed!"

"No," Adam said, "screw them. I'm glad I've seen their dark side. We'll just move on to plan B. No guesthouse by the pool. You weren't completely cool with that, anyway. We'll just move on to plan B."

"What's plan B?" I asked.

"We move in to an apartment in town together. Just the two of us. I commute to UF, taking only night classes, and Charlotte finishes high school, maybe online. And our parents pay no more than they'd normally pay for our current existences, but we both take on small jobs just to cover the additional costs of diapers and wipes and things like that. . . ." He was really talking only to himself now, pacing in small circles.

"Wait," I said. "Let's slow down."

Now Julien and Abbot were singing full bore. "*Marchons! Marchons! Qu'un sang impur abreuve nos sillons!*"

I fixed my attention on Charlotte. "Listen," I said, "can you call? Are you ready for it?"

She didn't look at me. "I want to get it over with," she said. "We need to have some definites."

"Okay," I said, "do you want me here or . . . ?"

She'd already opened the phone, hit speed dial, and was waiting for a voice on the other end of the line.

Adam and I waited together, sitting side by side on the edge of the fountain.

He said, "What am I supposed to be doing?"

"You need to remain flexible."

"Flexible," he said. "Remain flexible."

"The thing is that it's not about you. You're orbiting. She and the baby will be the sun. You simply need to remain flexible. Keep orbiting. Be ready when called."

"I'm just a planet."

"Yes."

"But the baby is half of my genetic makeup."

"That's kind of immaterial now," I said.

"Oh."

"Trust me," I said. "You're getting off light in this whole deal."

"I know," he said. "Respectfully speaking, I've never been so relieved to have been born male—even with all of the socio-economic privilege and societal bullshit, I'm just happy to be a boy on pure anatomy alone."

"And you should be."

"And I am!"

I turned to him. "How did you two let this happen? How? Can I ask that?"

"Of course you can ask," he said. "That's only fair. A good question." He coughed into his fist. "Well, there was this one time that, after, you know, and we weren't maniacs or anything, it wasn't like we were going nuts all the time...."

"I get it. Go on."

"It was gone after. Just *poof!* We couldn't find it."

"The condom?"

"Bingo," he said. "It was just..."

"Poof."

"MIA," he said. "Later, you know, she found it. But, well, the timing of that event must have been pretty, um, serendipitous."

"Serendipitous."

"That's right," he said. "What I want people to know, for the record, is that we were trying to be safe. And maybe I didn't put it on well enough, maybe there was sloppiness in my execution of that . . . point . . . issue . . . but, well, there you have it. It's not something Bert and Peg asked, but I can see a future conversation in which it comes up."

"If I could offer a suggestion," I said.

"Of course."

"I wouldn't use the word *serendipitous*. I'd try to tell the story simply, honestly."

"Okay," he said.

"And so in the spirit of simplicity and honesty," I said, "do you love Charlotte?"

"I do love Charlotte," he said, without hesitation. "I don't know what to do about it, but I love her."

We sat there quietly until Charlotte returned. She'd been crying.

Adam got up and walked to her. He wrapped his arms around her and she put her head on his shoulder. When she lifted her head, he asked, "How was it? What did they say?"

She looked at me and smiled. "Elysius was Elysius. At first, she wasn't really as surprised as I'd have wanted her to be. She's always expected something like this from me, I guess.

And then my dad . . ." She laughed a little. "He said that being pregnant at my age would stunt my growth. I informed him that I haven't grown a millimeter since seventh grade. This was news to him. Then he started to get upset, really upset. But Elysius kicked in. She was great. She calmed him down, and by the end, he was saying all the right things."

"What are the right things to say?" Adam asked.

"He was saying that my health and the health of the baby were the most important things right now." She sat down beside me on the fountain. "He said it was his instinct to get on a plane." Her voice caught in her throat. "He can't, of course. He's already taken off ten days for the honeymoon, and he needs to work."

I put my arm around her shoulder. "I'm so sorry," I said.

"Well, on the upside, he's going to tell my mother for me, and"—she took a deep breath—"he's sending Elysius."

"Why?" I asked.

"To bring me home."

"Do you want to go home?" I asked.

"I could take you home," Adam said.

"Aren't you grounded?" Charlotte said.

"That's not even funny," Adam said.

"Do you want to go home?" I asked again.

Charlotte looked around. "I love it here. I love the mountain. I love that I can breathe a little and no one's making me shove my nose in a book so that I can go off and get good test scores and be some robot who gets into a good college. I'm learning to cook, and Abbot needs me and people seem to like me. And I feel *sure* of myself here. We have about three more weeks. So, no," she said. "I don't want to go. They can't force me to." She looked at me. I didn't know what to say. She shook her head and rubbed tears from her eyes. "Except that they can force me to go home. I know," she whispered. "I know."

I decided to wait for my family to call me. I knew that they would. I expected that Elysius would be first. Maybe she would put Daniel on the line with me. They would want to know how Charlotte was really holding up, the story from my perspective. They'd want to know how long I knew—if I had been in on it in some way—and they'd pump me for information about Briskowitz, whom I was sure they would view as a problem that needed solving.

I assumed my mother would call next, as Elysius would rope her in immediately. The news of Charlotte's pregnancy would snap my mother out of her reveries, perhaps. She would kick in to high gear. She'd be prepared, in an instant, to be there for Charlotte and Elysius, and she would commence, without delay, mentally rearranging lives.

What I didn't expect was a call from my father. I was on a ladder in Charlotte's bedroom, doing the trim work, when Charlotte's phone rang on her bedside table. My father wasn't one for talking on the phone. He still had some old-world notion of the phone as a kind of tool to be used in emergencies. "Phones aren't walkie-talkies," my mother would tell him. "You don't have to just state your coordinates." I assume that his distaste for phones and the idle conversations that took place on them had something to do with his definition of masculinity. He did own a cell phone, but only perhaps because they seemed more like walkie-talkies. But the number that appeared on the caller ID of Charlotte's phone was their landline, so I answered it expecting my mother.

I climbed down the ladder. "Hey, so you heard."

"I did," he said, his voice startling me.

"Oh, Dad," I said, and I was immediately alarmed. "Are you okay?"

"Your mother is coming over, too."

"With Elysius? Here?"

"Correct."

"Why?" I asked. I was afraid I knew why: It had to do with her sleeplessness, what it meant for her to think of herself as a thief. But, too, I knew that my father knew none of this, so asking why was pointless. He wouldn't know the real reason. I steadied myself with one hand on a rung of the ladder.

He said, "She's been an awful wreck, Heidi. An awful wreck. She's pretending to be fine, but she isn't. Not at all. And . . ." His voice was shaky. I wondered if he was going to be able to go on. "And she needs to put it to rest."

"Put what to rest?"

"I've put my past to rest," he said. "I did it ages ago, but now she needs to."

"What past?"

"Her affair," he said. "She had an affair that summer she left us."

"Who did she have an affair with?" I asked, trying desperately to sound appropriately shocked, as if this was the first I'd heard of it.

"She came back," he said. "That was all that ever mattered to me. But I was wrong. She needs to find out if she should have come back. I'd like her to know that. I think it would be better."

"Who did she have an affair with?" I asked again.

"You're asking the wrong question," he said. "C'mon."

"I think it's a perfectly good question."

"It's a question young people ask."

"Why are you telling me this? What do you want me to do?"

"I want you to tell her that she has to figure this out. She has to get to the root of it. She has to find out what her life would have been like." The line was quiet. I didn't know what to say. "Will you do that for me?" he asked.

"I will," I said.

"Okay," he said. "Take care of Charlotte. She'll need you most of all."

"Really?" I said. "But Elysius and Mom are coming, and Adam is here, and—"

"She's already chosen you, honey."

"Oh," I said, unsure whether I was surprised by the insight or that it had come from him. Insights weren't his forte, but he'd just proved that he'd had more insight into my mother than I'd ever given him credit for. I thought of Charlotte's comment on love—that she wanted love from the beginning like it was with Henry. Was that one of the reasons she'd chosen me?

"Okay, I don't want to hog the line," he said, in his typical fashion, his let's-wrap-this-up-quickly phone voice. "Talk to you later."

"Yes," I said, knowing how desperate he was to hang up. "I love you."

There was a hitch in his breath, and I was surprised that he paused, hogging the line, as he would say, but he did. He took a moment, and then, in a voice rough and choked, said, "I love you, too."

Before the celebrations of Bastille Day began, we ate a picnic in the front yard of the Dumonteils' house. It was a sumptuous meal. First there was the moules à la marinière—mussels marinated in white wine, butter, onions, pepper, and lemon with plenty of parsley—then a bouillabaisse that included eel and green crabs. Charlotte explained the derivation of bouillabaisse, *bout et abaisse,* meaning "boil and press." Next there was a salad with warmed goat cheese, and finally an assortment of desserts I'd picked up at the patisserie.

Julien, I noticed, seemed anxious. He was keeping an eye on the long driveway. More than once he got up from his place and walked to the edge of the yard where it becomes brambles, as if he'd seen a car turn down the drive.

"Who's coming?" I asked Véronique, who was sitting next to me at one of the small tables.

"His wife," she said. "More papers to sign. The bureaucracy has no end. I don't know why he walks like that. She is always punctual. Absolutely on time. Like the Swiss."

Patricia. I was surprised by my reaction—curiosity, yes, but also a small hive of jealousy abuzz in my chest. The questions in my head began innocently enough: Would she sneeze four times in the sun? Would I see her charm bracelet for myself? But then I felt myself turn snarky: Would she look like the daughter of an opera singer? And what would that look like, exactly? Someone with excellent posture, ready to belt it out? Someone wearing a Viking helmet with horns?

I had to prepare for the fact that she would likely be elegant, perhaps even beautiful, and in that elegant beauty that the French wear with such ease. The French didn't doll up. They never looked like they'd sprayed their hair stiff or coated their face in a tan base, leaving their necks pale. They looked, more often than not, like they used expensive night creams but truly believed in hydration. I quickly decided Patricia would be overbearingly naturally beautiful.

And would she bring Frieda? I hoped not. That would only be a form of torture for Julien. I could tell that the end of marriage was one thing, but the rupture of the family was another, deeper wound. It would be painful either way.

We'd all been talking, probably at the same time, about socialism, the erosion of the maximum thirty-five-hour workweek set by the French government, when a car slowly pulled

up the driveway. Véronique told us that the town was supported by government funds. How else could the shops afford to compete with the massive expanse and bulk rates of
the Monoprix? This explained the odd hours, the feeling I
got that they didn't need to make money—they didn't. There
was a loud discussion about free markets, capitalism—all of
those things Americans should argue about, for or against,
while in Europe.

"Excuse me," Julien said, and he quietly slipped away.

I watched him jog across the broad yard. The door to the
backseat popped open first, and a little girl jumped out. She
was beautiful and quick. He picked her up and lifted her
onto his back. She wrapped her arms around his neck and
they pressed their heads together. Frieda. She had delicate
features, a little pout of a mouth. She was stunning, her hair
bouncing blond and halo-esque around her head.

The passenger door opened next and Patricia stepped
out. She wore walking shorts, cuffed at the knee, pleated, and
elegant strappy heels. Her black shirt was sleeveless with a
deep V-neck. Her arms were long and tan. She wore oversized sunglasses, and her hair had been highlighted a golden
blond.

They exchanged polite kisses on their cheeks. She was
holding a folder. They talked solemnly at the hood of the
car, Frieda still clinging to Julien's shoulders, piggyback.

And then, much to my surprise, the driver's door opened
and a man stepped out. He was just a bit taller than Julien,
thicker, too. He had dark hair and eyes, just as Julien did, and

a quick smile. I nearly recognized him, but before I could, Véronique stood up and said, "Pascal."

And there are certain moments in your life when something becomes clear, and other things in the past—things that your mind, unbeknownst to you, had earmarked because they didn't quite add up—suddenly all click into place, like small gears in a watch.

In this moment, I remembered all of the little things that could have prepared me for this shock. Hadn't Véronique herself told me that the boys had problems getting along these days? She said it as if I knew the history between them, and I had assumed that she meant the typical rivalries between brothers—not this. Julien himself had told me that Patricia had picked the wrong one. I'd thought it was a strange translation but nothing more. Now I could see by the way Pascal walked over and stood next to Patricia, slipping his hand around her waist, that Julien had meant this quite literally. He'd been the wrong choice—the wrong brother—and she'd corrected her mistake.

Worst of all, I remembered when I first talked to Julien at the beginning of this trip, in the convertible in the rain. I'd told him that I preferred the other brother, the one with the pogo stick, and he'd told me that I was not alone.

Véronique waved and limped to them. Pascal broke from Patricia and kissed his mother's cheeks. Patricia handed Julien the folder and a pen. He started signing the forms on the hood of the car. Véronique was cooing over her granddaughter. She was talking to Patricia, obviously inviting her to join us, to stay. Patricia glanced in our direction, and I picked up my wine and took a sip. I made a blanket statement about feeling patriotic here in France. "In America when someone asks me my nationality, I can't just say American. I have to go back generations, elaborate on where in Europe my ancestors were from. But here," I said, "I can just say it, *Je suis Américaine.* It feels good."

"Except when it doesn't," Adam said.

"That's true," I said. "We've had some shameful moments under shameful presidents."

I watched Pascal climb back into the driver's seat. Patricia was holding Frieda now. The girl was crying, her face red and shiny with tears. She was rubbing a fistful of her mother's hair between her fingers. Her mother hefted her into the backseat, where she helped buckle her in.

Julien stood in the yard. As his ex-wife walked to the passenger's door, he pressed his hand to the dark window of the backseat. He held it there until the car slowly pulled away.

We gathered in the town center at dusk with the other villagers. Red, white, and blue pennants were strung across the face of the government building and draped through the trees. Julien was explaining to Abbot the storming of the Bastille, the French Revolution, the French Republic. He linked it up nicely with American history, Independence Day, how the two ideologies were knotted together in many ways.

Charlotte and Adam were quiet. They looked a little shell shocked. It was perhaps unnoticeable to the casual observer, but they held hands tightly as they walked, lifting their arms over a darting child instead of simply letting go. Charlotte had said that Adam was scared shitless. They both were, but it was good that they had each other. As much as I wanted to help, there was nothing quite like Adam holding Charlotte's hand, that kind of quiet, childlike reassurance.

Véronique had stayed at home. "I've seen enough children with lights," she said. "I will protect this bird." And so Abbot lifted the box with the bird inside of it and handed it to her, very gently, and gave her instructions on how the bird would best fall asleep. She'd nodded along patiently.

A woman with shiny dark hair called for all of the children. Abbot stepped up with the others. I looked around and realized that I recognized faces from town now. There were the people who worked at the Cocci, the Café Sainte Victoire, the old woman who scrubbed the marble bench. I recognized the mason with his wife, an ample woman with ruddy cheeks, and the baker, who was with a little girl who seemed to be his granddaughter, a three-year-old or so, with floaty dark curls. I glanced through the crowd—the older men who played bocce ball in the afternoons, the others who had a miniature track and raced small motorized cars in the basement of the municipal building. Was the man my mother had an affair with still living in town? Was one of these men the one? I was reminded again of Hercule Poirot, that stout Belgian detective, this time playing the whodunit of my mother's affair.

Julien said, "The mayor. He's here. Do you want to meet him?" He pointed to a very handsome man who looked, for all intents, to be a Hollywood actor. He was tan and lean, in his early fifties. He had black hair and wore dark jeans and a black T-shirt with a logo on it that, from what I could translate, was about a liberation movement for the cicadas of Provence. "Why does he want to free the cicadas?" I asked.

"I think he's being funny," Julien said. "Come on, it will make my mother happy. He'll want to meet you."

"No," I said. "I want to tell you something."

"Are you angry with me for teaching Abbot the French national anthem?" he asked, jokingly. "He's part French, so he should know a little about his mother country."

"Yeah, I heard you two belting it out in the pool together."

"Belting it out? We were professionals. We were very good. Not like you and your song 'Brandy.' We really sing."

"I heard you. I think people in Ireland heard you."

He smiled at me. "He is an amazing child. He told me the stories of the house. The enchantments and miracles, the love stories."

"Did he?"

"I'd heard of this before, these stories. My mother told me when I was young. Not all of them, but some of them were familiar. He believes in the stories."

I was sure that Julien was asking if I believed in them, too. "He's deep, that Abbot, and sensitive. He feels everything."

"He reminds me of Frieda in certain ways. The doors of their hearts are wide open, as my mother says." There was Abbot buzzing around with the other kids, trying to talk to one in some strange English-French mix, no doubt. He'd brought his notebook on this occasion but was much too distracted to draw anything.

"I'm sorry," I said. "I'm sorry about Patricia. I didn't know it was your brother. . . ."

"I didn't tell you," he said.

"But you could have. This really boosts your miserableness quotient."

"Do I win now?"

"No, the prize still goes to those in war-torn countries."

"I'd let her go easily if it meant that I could always be a father. Not half the time. A real father."

"But you are a real father," I said. "I saw you with Frieda for five minutes and I knew that I was watching a father, a real father with his child. You get only half the time, but you get to be a father all the time."

He looked at Abbot, who was being handed a paper lantern on a stick by the woman with the shiny dark hair. "Elysius and your mother are coming," he said.

"Yes," I said. "And I still don't know the truth."

"Your mother didn't tell you?"

"I know that she had an affair. My father knows, too. She's a heart thief. I get it. But what did she really do? How bad was it?"

"We're French," he said. "We forgive people who fall in

love even when they feel they shouldn't." He looked at me for a moment, and my heart started pounding in my chest. Then lightly, he raised his hand and let his fingers run down my arm to my hand. I wondered for a moment if he was going to kiss me and then he did—a soft kiss, his lips on mine, tender and sweet. It lingered. I closed my eyes. The world fell away around me. For a moment I felt like the kiss was the only thing holding me there, keeping me grounded. As if without him, I'd billow away like a loose paper lantern. It felt good to rely on someone else like this, to feel tethered. We weren't ghosts in this moment. We were real. And then I opened my eyes and took a small step back. He slipped his hand in mine. His hand was big and warm and strong.

He nodded at the paper lanterns that the children were holding. "Do you remember this?"

"I do," I said, barely breathing.

"It's like they have caught glowing fish," Julien said.

"It is," I said, and I saw Abbot's face now lit up in the golden glow of his lantern. He smiled at us and waved wildly. I quickly pulled my hand from Julien's and waved back. Had Abbot seen us holding hands? Julien waved to Abbot, too. But Abbot stopped waving, gripped the stick of his lantern with both hands, and seemed to stare at us. His expression was hard to read.

I couldn't say another word, and Julien didn't seem to expect me to. Charlotte and Adam were sitting on a bench by the bocce pit, their heads tilted together under the dim streetlight. There was a breeze that flitted between us. Abbot fell in line with the other children, and they started winding up the narrow street, the lanterns swaying and bobbing in the dark.

Elysius and my mother both called, together, taking turns with one cell phone. They were in emergency mode. They'd made their travel arrangements already. They were coming in late the next day from Jacksonville to Marseille. I jotted flight numbers and times.

"Do you want me to come and pick you up at the airport?"

"No," my mother said. "Don't leave Charlotte there alone."

"She wouldn't be alone," I said. "In fact, she could come."

"No need to have her on the road," my mother said. "We'll take a cab."

"It's a long ride. It'll be expensive."

Now it was my sister on the line. "It's only euros," she said, as if euros didn't count as anything more than Monopoly money.

In fact, the more money Elysius and Daniel could spend on Charlotte, the more they could prove that they were still good parents. And they *were* good parents. They had their deficits, of course. We all do. But now they doubted themselves on the most basic level. They were shaken. Toward the end of the conversation, Elysius said, "Where did we go wrong?"

"You can't see this as a personal failure," I said. "That's not what this is about."

"Easy for you to say," she said, which felt condescending. "We'll be there tomorrow night. At least Mom and I get a trip to the South of France out of it all!"

"Right," I said. This again wasn't a bad thing to say. It just wasn't the right thing.

"We'll be there tomorrow night. Around eight or so, the way I figure it."

"Wait, one more thing." I wanted to ask her this while my mother wasn't there, but at least I had my sister's ear, even if briefly. "How does Mom seem to you these days?"

"How is *anyone* doing these days?" she said, exasperated. "She's fine, considering. She's a rock, per usual, I guess." She leaned away from the phone. "Mom," she said loudly, "how are you doing with all of this?"

"Fine!" she said. "We're all doing fine!"

I wasn't doing fine. That night as I lay down in bed and tried to be calm and still, my heart felt concussive. I would see Julien in my mind's eye, and he would turn to me again. I would feel his lips on mine, his fingers run down the length of my arm, the warmth of his hand around mine. I would see the glowing paper lanterns in the background and then Abbot's strange gaze. Was I falling for Julien? Why him? Why now? Unlike Jack Nixon, he was complicated and therefore not perfect. Put us together and the baggage, our emotional steamer trunks, multiplied exponentially. He was the wrong choice, wasn't he?

If I was falling for Julien—beyond logic and reason and sensible thought—could Abbot sense it? I'd told Charlotte that this was how we were wired. Was Julien right when we drank wine near the fountain and talked that night? Were we ghosts and, in the moment of that kiss, were we real? If Abbot had seen us, what had he thought of it? Julien meant a lot to him, and I was pretty sure that Abbot meant a lot to Julien. He was teaching Abbot how to play soccer, to nurture a bird, to sing the French national anthem. Abbot had looked to him to see if it was safe to shake Adam's hand. And, most of all, they had their lost fathers in common.

But was Julien truly interested in me? He'd had a very bad day. He'd seen his ex-wife with his brother. He'd seen his daughter for a brief moment, and then she was taken away. Was he really interested in me or did he simply desire distraction?

I pulled the crisp white sheet to my chest and rolled over, staring out the open window. I loved Henry. I always would love Henry. Was it fair then to show affection for someone else, knowing that I would never be able to give all of my love to them, that it would always be only a portion?

Then I would see Julien piggybacking his daughter, her cheek pressed to his back, the way he looked at her over his shoulder. I would see Julien's face in my mind, the lanterns all around, and he would say, "We're French. We forgive people who fall in love even when they feel they shouldn't."

The next day, I busied myself getting ready for Elysius and my mother's arrival. Elysius and my mother would share the fourth bedroom, the only one not yet painted, where there were two single beds. I changed the linens, cleaned the kitchen as well as I could—it still had the feel of a charred hull—and put fresh flowers in vases. I took a jaunt to the Cocci, the patisserie-boulangerie, the vegetable stand off the highway. I went in to Trets, stopped at a pet shop, and bought three fat koi. They sat in the backseat in large, shiny plastic bags, fluttering their wings.

Once I was back home, I picked up the heavy bags and set them next to the fountain and then I found Charlotte making crepes with Adam and Abbot on the hot plate set up on the kitchen table. She'd also made whipped crème fraîche and mixed it with local peaches and sugar, freezing it all into ice cream. Abbot was in heaven.

When everyone had finished their crepes and peach ice cream, we went out into the front yard. Abbot brought the bird in the box and set it in the shade beside the house. He had his notebook, too, and sat it on the stone lip of the fountain. Adam helped me lift each of three large bags with the koi inside of them and, one by one, we set them loose, with a gush of water, into the fountain. Abbot ran his hands across the surface of the water, making ripples. The fish pulsed their fins, flicked their tails.

"They're happy in here," Abbot said.

"Contented," Charlotte said.

"It's not a bad place to end up," Adam said.

"I'd live in this fish pond if it were an option," Charlotte said.

"Me, too," I said.

Abbot had found an abandoned soccer ball in the Dumonteils' house and Julien had told him he could keep it. He'd kicked it in a bush and was digging it out now. That's when Abbot announced that he wanted to set the swallow free.

"Why now?" Adam asked. "If you don't mind my probing."

"The fish like the fountain. They get to swim around. It's better than the pet store, and yesterday, everybody was talking about the Bastilles, which were prisons," Abbot said, "and I think of the box as a hospital, but it could be a prison, if you look at it like a bird." He pulled the ball out of the bushes and stood up with it propped under his arm.

"Like I used to be claustrophobic. You know, scared of closets and tight spaces," Charlotte said. "But now I'm the closet and the baby is the one in the tight space. And I'd never really asked myself before what claustrophobia is like from the closet's perspective."

"Or agoraphobia from the wide open field's perspective," I said.

"Or hydrophobia from the water's perspective," Adam said.

"Or parenthood-a-phobia from the parents' perspective," Charlotte said.

"The question is, Abbot, are you ready?" Adam asked.

He put down the ball, looked at his notebook sitting beside the fountain, and then at the box with the bird shifting in it by the house. "I guess so."

"Sometimes it isn't a question," Charlotte said. "Sometimes you just have to be ready, and that's that."

"You're lucky you get to ask yourself if you *are* ready," Adam said.

"Is this really about you being pregnant and all?" Abbot said.

Adam nodded. "Right now, everything's about being pregnant. Where are you going to let the bird go from?"

Abbot and I took a walk after lunch to find the highest, most accessible spot in the area—the perfect locale for pitching a swallow. Abbot decided that it was the roof of the Dumonteils' house.

"You're not clambering around on a roof," I said.

"But it's perfect," he said, fiddling with the spiral of his notebook, which he had with him, as usual. "We could wear safety gear."

"Like parachutes?" I said. "No, it's not happening."

"What about up there?" Abbot asked, pointing to a balcony off of one of the Dumonteils' second-floor bed-rooms.

I didn't want to ask Véronique for access to one of her balconies so that we could pitch a hobbled sparrow off it. I didn't want to walk up to the Dumonteils' house at all. I realized that I was ducking Julien. In hopes of what? That Ely-sius and my mother would arrive, and their noise and urgent energy would distract me for long enough that I'd be able to have the right amount of distance? I wanted distance from Julien, urgent energy, and lots of noise. These were things that my mother and sister could provide. I'd never seen it as a positive before. "Well," I said, "I think that room probably belongs to a guest, and so we really can't—"

"It's Véronique's room," Abbot said. "Charlotte and I once played hide-and-seek and I went upstairs and hid under the bed."

I was startled by this confession. It wasn't that I thought what Abbot had done was so terrible; it was more that I'd had no idea he'd done it. He could have gone anywhere. What if he'd decided to hide in an old refrigerator? What if he'd decided to hide in a washer-dryer? What if he'd wandered into some twisted pervert's room? Where had I been during this game of hide-and-seek? "Abbot," I said. "You should pay better attention to the rules." But as soon as I said it, I realized that I hadn't set any rules. I was really scolding myself. I should have been paying better attention.

"It was fine," he said. "Charlotte found me right away. I sing when I'm alone, because I can't whistle, and so I'm always really easy to find."

"Why do you sing when you're alone?"

"So I don't feel like I'm alone," he said. "Dad taught me that."

"Oh," I said.

"I want everyone to be there when I throw the swallow," he said.

This alarmed me. I imagined the public spectacle, everyone watching as Abbot threw the bird and it plummeted, wings fluttering awkwardly. "No," I said. "Let's just do this privately. Just me and you."

"But that wouldn't be fair!" he said. "Everyone helped."

"Yes, but still, I think it's better if we just do it together," I said.

"I don't want anyone to miss it, though!" His expression was grave. He was attached to the bird. He'd been tending to it all this time. I didn't want to be dismissive of the importance of this for him.

"Okay," I said. "Maybe when everyone is already gathering together for dinner?" I asked.

"Okay," he said. "That's good because he'll see the other birds flying and he'll remember by watching them."

"You know, Abbot, that there's a good chance that no matter how well you've taken care of the swallow, he might not ever be able to fly again."

"Yes."

"But you also know it's best for him to try to fly. It's no life for a bird in a box."

"I know," Abbot said. "He's a *migratory* bird. He's got to *migrate.*"

"Right," I said, really realizing this for the first time. "And when you pitch him off the roof, he might not fly. He might simply fall to the ground. He might die."

"Yes," he said. "I know that." He stared up into my face, squinting into the sun. "I don't have any other choice. It's like this. That's what the French say. *C'est comme ça!*" And his accent was startlingly good. Impeccable, really.

"Right," I said. "C'est comme ça."

I hoped that the bird would cause distractions, too. This was awful, but it was the truth. I knew I'd have to see Julien, but maybe amid the confusion of the bird's flying or falling to its death, we'd both forget that he'd kissed me. Suddenly, I wondered if I'd just imagined it all. Was the moment already evaporating? I hoped it was, and I was holding on to it at the same time.

I walked into the Dumonteils' house warily. "Véronique?" I called softly.

The kitchen was empty.

I walked back to the hall, down the long runner. The dining room was empty, too. I turned and dipped into the parlor.

There was Julien, standing by a wide window, one hand pressed to the sunny pane, just as he'd had his hand on the window of the car before his brother pulled out of the driveway with his wife and daughter. He'd abandoned his laptop. It sat on the coffee table, its screen staring out blankly into the room. I was struck by the back of his neck, the curve of his jaw, his sunlit hand. My chest ached. It had been a long time since I'd felt an ache other than grief. But I didn't know what to call this ache. I refused to call it love, but it was something exquisite and exquisitely tinged with regret. Longing? That feeling my mother knew so well? I wanted to hear Henry's voice, calling me in to shore. *Too far, too far.* Julien must have sensed me there. He turned around.

"Abbot wants to pitch the swallow today," I said, fiddling the hem of my T-shirt. "He's ready. He wants to throw it from the balcony off your mother's bedroom."

Julien cocked his head. "Yes," he said as if coming out of a dream. "The swallow. Abbot wants to throw it from my mother's balony?"

I nodded. "Look," I said, lowering my voice, stepping into the sunlit room filled with golden drifting dust motes. It seemed as if they were suspended like small lost planets. I, too, felt like I'd lost my orbit. That had been my advice to Briskowitz: Keep orbiting. "Yesterday was a hard day for you. I know it was."

"Yes?" he whispered back, walking to me.

"And so if, you know, you didn't mean to . . ."

He walked up closer. "We're whispering?" he said. I could smell his aftershave. "Someone might hear us? *Chuchote*," he said. "Whisper." He bent his head down, almost touching his forehead to mine.

"I was saying," I said.

"You were *whispering*," he whispered, his lips brushing my ear.

"Yes," I whispered, "I was whispering that I know you might not really be feeling like yourself, and I'm not, either, here, you know. Not really because I'm far away from all of the burdens of my life." I was thinking of all the things that held me in place, that created my sense of gravity, my orbit. Where was I? "And, well, I still have real responsibilities and—" I really had no idea where I was going with this. I wanted to say that it was too complicated, that I was just a bunny, after all.

He lifted his head and looked at me, surprised. Then he lowered his head again and whispered into my ear, "I don't want to go back."

"Back?"

"You want to go back, to return to the moment before I kissed you, before I held your hand?"

This made it real. He had kissed me. He'd held my hand. He'd done it on purpose and he was standing by it. I paused there for a moment, frozen. I didn't want to move. I couldn't move. I closed my eyes, slowly. I thought he might disappear. *This is what it's like to be close,* I thought to myself. *This is what it's like to almost lean on someone else.* I knew that I could have tilted forward. I could have rested my head on his chest. I could have listened to his heart, and he would have let me. He'd have held me up.

"I want to go back," I whispered. I opened my eyes. I felt breathless and stepped away from him and turned to the hall quickly, almost recklessly. I stopped at the doorway and looked at him over my shoulder. "Do you think it would be okay for Abbot to pitch the swallow off your mother's balcony?"

He looked at me, wounded, and then nodded. "Yes," he said. "I think that would be fine with her."

"But will you ask her?"

"I will."

"Okay," I said. "Good. How about the next time we gather together? You know, around dinner. Abbot wants everyone to be there."

He looked out the window again. "Is that a good idea? Everyone there?"

"He's insisting because everyone helped."

"I'll be there," he said.

"Good," I said. "I'll be there, too."

. . .

A dam and Charlotte stood on the ground below the balcony. Julien, Véronique, and I were in Véronique's bedroom with Abbot. The room struck me as more modern— with sleek lines and a lack of clutter—than French country- side. Abbot was holding the box, which smelled sour and sharp, the bottom of it splotched with droppings. I was try- ing to concentrate on these things—décor and droppings— instead of being aware of Julien's presence, but I was—every move, every gesture, every glance and word.

"Are you ready?" Julien asked Abbot.

"Yep," he said, and then peered down into the box and asked the swallow, "Are you ready?"

The swallow had dark, wet, darting eyes and stared up at us with its head cocked, nervously, wondering what we might do—were we going to off the bird, put it in a stew, or maybe—just maybe—let it go?

The three of us waited.

"He's ready," Abbot said.

Véronique opened the door to the balcony, and, one by one, we stepped out onto it. The other swallows were feeding off in the distance. Their bodies blurred in the late after- noon sun. I walked to the railing, holding on to it with one hand. In the other, I was carrying Abbot's notebook. I looked down at Charlotte and Adam.

"You look like Madonna in that movie about Eva Perón," Charlotte said.

"Don't cry for me, Argentina," Adam said flatly.

Abbot put the box down at his feet. "Is the hermit's chapel up there on the mountain? Can we see it from here?"

"Saint Ser?" Julien said. "You can't see his chapel from here, but it's up there."

"Over there," Véronique said, pointing to a middle point of the mountain, slightly off to one side.

"If the swallow dies, he can go live with the hermit at the Saint Ser chapel and be a protected soul," Abbot said.

"Yes," I said, "that's right."

"Do you want me to do it?" Julien offered. He was somber, his voice steady and deep and calm. We all knew what might be coming.

"No," Abbot said. "I can do it." He reached in and cupped the bird's fine ribs.

"You're like a veterinarian," Véronique said. "You are so good."

Abbot walked to the edge of the balcony. The railing fit under his arms. He whispered something to the bird and then said, "One, two, three!" And in one swift upward motion, he threw the bird into the air.

The swallow was stunned. Wings still tucked to its body, it rose with the trajectory of Abbot's throw, its eyes beady and wide, and then began to fall. I reached out, instinctively, and grabbed Julien's shirtsleeve, gripping tight. Julien turned and looked at me, his face, for a split second, bright and golden in the dying light. I let go.

Abbot gripped the railing. "Fly!" he shouted. "Fly! Fly!"

The swallow's wings popped open, but they flapped awkwardly at the sides of its body, like wild oars.

And then, as the bird fell with skittering wings, it gave one solid thrum. This slowed its descent, momentarily. It gave another thrum, and another, and then, as if its body remembered what it was supposed to do, the bird began to beat its wings rhythmically. The muscle memory was still within it. It was still losing ground, but it was flapping, at least.

I drew in my breath and held it.

"Yes!" Abbot was crying. "Yes!"

The bird batted the air.

"Up," Julien urged the bird, *"Monte, monte!"*

Abbot repeated after Julien. I supposed it had dawned on him that the bird spoke French. *"Monte! Monte!"*

As if it were listening, the bird began to hold its own, and then its wings powered it upward. Its flight pattern had hitches, but it was making it. It was flying toward the other swallows.

Adam and Charlotte clapped and cheered from below. Charlotte whistled through her teeth like a sailor.

"He flies," Véronique said, astonished.

"He flies!" Abbot said.

"He flies," Julien said, looking at me. "A miracle bird! An enchantment."

"It's another house story!" Abbot said, his face lit up with joy. "A real one!"

"I can't believe he flies," I said. "But he does fly."

"You did it, Abbot," Julien said.

"Yep," Abbot said, but he still seemed anxious. I thought that maybe he was simply charged by the miraculous bird, but in retrospect, I wonder if he was feeling a little undone by it all, that this wasn't over. He turned back to the railing, folded his arms on it, and then rested his chin on his hands.

"Dinner!" Véronique said.

"And not chicken or fowl. Nothing with wings," Charlotte said.

"Let's go eat," I said to Abbot.

He shook his head without looking at me. "I'm going to stay here for a while," he said. "Leave the notebook, okay?"

"Okay," I said. I set it down near the box. I put my hand on the crown of his head. "Are you happy?"

He nodded.

"Come down when you're ready," I said.

He nodded again.

We stepped into the bedroom. Véronique asked Julien to go downstairs and help Charlotte and Adam begin setting the tables. "I want to talk to Heidi," she said.

He looked at his mother and then me. "Do you think Abbot is okay?" he asked.

"The swallow flew!" I said. "We were practicing joy, living a little, and it worked!" I could still feel Julien's shirt in my fist. I'd grabbed ahold of him to steady myself. Maybe I needed steadying. Maybe I shouldn't have cut things off. And, too, I was wondering if this was a second miracle for Abbot.

Was it a clumsy miracle that he ran into the Plexiglas guard-
ing the alleged remains of Mary Magdalene and then touched
the warthogs and had since stopped compulsively washing
his hands? What would this second small miracle lead to?

Julien nodded but still looked worried. I was getting used
to this expression on his face. There was something deeply
tender about it. He was a father, after all, and a good one, I
was sure. He walked out of the room, closing the door
gently, leaving me and Véronique, with a view of Abbot
through the balcony doorway. Abbot—the bird flew! I was
still ecstatic, awash in relief.

Véronique sat on her bed and nodded to the bedside
table. There sat a wooden box. "For your mother," she said.
"She's coming, and so *you* can give it to her."

"This is the thing that she left behind?"

Véronique nodded. "She will open the box and understand what is there."

I picked up the box. It was slightly charred on one end. I
held it in my hands. "And what is there?" It was light. When
it transferred from her hands to mine, there was no shift—as
there would be if it were jewelry.

"The proof," she said. "Proof of her love for you."

"Does he still live here, the man she fell in love with?"

She shook her head. "He moved to Paris after she left.
He dedicated himself to his work. He became well known in
his business. You would like him. He was handsome. He had
a great presence and a beautiful voice."

"He sang?"

"Beautifully."

"It just seems so strange. I can see why she didn't tell me, but still . . ."

"I saw him not too many years ago. I was in Paris and found him. He asked me if I talked to her. He wanted to know everything. I told him all I could."

"Do you think he's a good person?" I asked. I wasn't sure why this was important, but I had to ask.

"Yes," she said. "And he loved her deeply, as she loved him. It was one of those types of loves."

I nodded.

"She told me her secrets. I told her mine."

"One of those loves," I said.

"You have a heart like your mother."

"No, the doors are shut," I said.

"Yes, but the doors do not have locks." Did she know about Julien? I assumed that she did. She seemed to know everything.

"I didn't know that Patricia was with Pascal now," I said. "Julien didn't tell me."

"Pascal," she sighed. "He didn't know how to build it himself. He stole his brother's life. That is a real thief. I love Pascal, but this will not continue."

"His relationship with Patricia?"

She nodded. "It will end."

"Then what?"

"Then nothing. We live in the ruins."

The box—was it filled with papers? "Are these love letters?" I asked.

She thought about this for a moment and then nodded. "Yes," she said. "Love letters, in a way."

In what way? I wondered. They were love letters or they weren't. "She can barely talk about that summer and what happened," I said. "She refuses to hand down her lessons."

"But she is coming here," Véronique said. "Things will change when she is here again. It's necessary to have hope."

"*J'espére*," I said, *I hope*—and in the word I heard *despair, air* . . . I heard *I'm air.*

I couldn't go to dinner. I excused myself quickly and walked to our house. I stood in the kitchen with the box in my hands.

I looked at the charred stonework where the new stove would soon be installed. Was that where she'd hidden the box? And why? What was in it? I set it on the kitchen table. I wanted to open the box, of course. But it wasn't mine to open. *It was one of those types of loves*, I thought to myself. The type that I'd had with Henry. Was that what she had sacrificed for me and my sister? If she did, well, it was too much to ask for and too much to give, I decided.

I was unable to be still. I paced the kitchen. My father wanted me to help my mother get to the root of this. How? I was in no shape for that kind of role. I was trying not to fall for Julien. This took all of my effort. Was I going to hide some memory of this summer in this kitchen somewhere? Was that to be my future? Was I going to allow Elysius and my mother to swoop in and take over, packing up Charlotte and hauling her back home? And then would Abbot and I stay on without her until our six weeks were over, and then we'd pack up, too? Abbot and I would go home, pretending that it never really happened at all?

I decided that I couldn't stare at the box. I had to get on with my life. Abbot had probably gotten hungry and come down for dinner. I should eat, too, I thought, even though I wasn't hungry.

I let the box sit there and walked back to the Dumonteils' house. I walked past the kitchen, where I saw Julien's back, his shirt stretching from shoulder to shoulder. He was washing the dishes. Véronique was talking to a lone guest, a French woman wearing a floaty dress and sandals. Charlotte and Adam were in the front yard, in serious discussion, in the dim evening light. They were likely gearing up for Elysius and my mother, who would be arriving before long.

I walked up the stairs, down the hall, and opened the door to Véronique's bedroom. "Abbot?" I called. "Time to come down for dinner." I could see immediately that he wasn't on the balcony. There was only the empty cardboard box and his notebook, which was splayed open in the corner of the balcony as if it had been thrown there. It was open to a page where Abbot had drawn his father wearing a Red Sox hat. This time his father wasn't connected to the earth at all. He was darting around with the birds. He had his human face but giant wings and a swallow's forked tail.

I stood up and looked down to the ground below the balcony, out across the backyard, the vineyards, the distant archaeological dig. It was hard to see. It was getting dark. "Abbot?" I shouted. "Abbot?"

I turned and raced down the stairs. "Where's Abbot?" I shouted to Julien in the kitchen.

"He is upstairs?"

"He's not there!" I shouted.

I ran past Véronique in the dining room. The French woman, a guest, looked up at me, shocked. I ran to the front yard. "Abbot's gone!" I shouted at Charlotte and Adam.

"I'm sure he's fine," Charlotte said, knowing that I had a history of panicking over Abbot for no good reason.

"Start looking!" I said.

Adam looked stricken. "What? Where is he?"

"I don't know!" I shouted at him.

Charlotte started calling for him in the front yard, and Adam followed behind her, dazed.

Véronique searched the house. Even the French woman, a complete stranger, took to looking for places a boy would hide.

"Listen for him!" I heard Charlotte shouting to everyone. "He sings when he's alone." She was right. I'd been too panic-stricken to think of that.

I ran out the back door into the yard.

Julien was already ahead of me. He was searching to the left of the dig. I could hear him calling Abbot's name, and I could see the flash of his white shirt.

I took to the vineyards. I ran up one row and down another. "Abbot!" I called, and I could hear the echo of all of the other voices calling for him, too. "Where are you? Dammit, Abbot!" I said. "Don't do this! Where are you?"

Was this a delayed reaction to seeing Julien hold my hand at the Bastille Day celebration? Had that frightened him? Or was it something about the bird and his father? I couldn't shake his drawing of his father among the swallows. I ran until I couldn't run anymore. I wished I were in better shape. I needed to be able to run forever. What kind of mother was I? I dropped to my knees in the soft dirt, breathless. It was almost completely dark now. "Abbot!" I shouted again.

What if he was dead? What if he was already gone?

I couldn't breathe. I curled on the ground, my head pressed to my knees. I couldn't break down. There was no time for it. I lifted my head and shouted his name again from deep within me.

And then I heard Julien's voice. "Heidi!" he called. "Heidi!"

"Here!" I shouted. "I'm right here!" I got up and ran to his voice and he ran to mine. "Julien!"

He was holding a flashlight and the light swept across me.

What if he went for a swim, struck his head, and drowned? "The pool!" I shouted. I sprinted to him and grabbed his arm to steady myself.

"I looked. He isn't there. My mother is calling the police," he said. "They will arrive soon, but I have this thought."

"What is it?" I said breathlessly.

"Saint Ser," he said. "On the balcony with the bird, he wanted to know where the chapel was. My mother pointed to it. The hermit was the good phantom. The protector of souls. Abbot believes the stories of the house, the miracles and enchantments. He is a boy who believes."

"But the bird flew!" I said. "It's alive. He said that the bird's soul would go to the chapel if it died. But it didn't die."

"Maybe that's not the soul he is looking for," Julien said.

The climb up Mont Sainte-Victoire was difficult in the daylight, and, at night, harrowing. The shadows shifted on the narrow path, turning every stone into a huddled boy. I was breathless, shaking with adrenaline. The path was steep, mostly graveled but also rocky. Julien and I were calling Abbot's name. The brush beside the path was dense and dark. What if Abbot had fallen? What if he was unconscious? Our flashlights barely penetrated the undergrowth. Was it possible that we'd missed him? Each second, each empty shout, each time Abbot did not answer our call, was torturous. I couldn't lose him. I'd lost too much already. I was furious in the way that terror can quickly give way to fury. Henry had abandoned me. How did he expect me to do all of this myself? It made no rational sense, but I blamed myself and felt Henry blaming me, too, so I blamed him back, and then my mind cast around wildly through my memories of the last few days, trying to piece together what had gone wrong and why. My chest felt like it might heave and contract into sobs at any moment. I tried to keep my breathing calm. *It isn't Henry's fault*, I told myself. Finally, all of my anger and blame came back to me, but not me alone. This was Julien's fault, too.

"Abbot saw us," I told Julien while heaving myself forward. "He saw us holding hands at the Bastille Day celebration. He may have even seen us kiss. I should be at home. I should be simplifying my life—if anything. I should be at home right now dating Crook Nixon!"

"You want to date Nixon?"

"No!" I shouted. "You're too complicated! You were trying to be Abbot's father."

"His father?" he said, shining the flashlight at me. "I don't know what you mean."

I kept climbing, my body trembling. "You can't be the father to your own kid, so you were trying to play father to mine." This made perfect sense to me as I said it. I slipped, scraping my knee against a rock. I winced but regained my footing. "He has a father. You're just a distraction. If you hadn't been here, I could have stopped him."

"I wasn't trying to be Henry, not for him or for you," Julien said.

"Don't say his name!" I shouted, my hands gripping a rock. I was filled with fury. My head felt like a hive. My eyes stung from trying to see into the darkness. I was as angry as I'd allowed myself to be since Henry's death—fueled by desperation. "Don't even say his name!"

He stopped and stared at me. The beam of light pointed at my feet. "We'll find him, Heidi. We're going to find him."

I could see the dim features of his face, the watery glint of his eyes. This was what I needed to believe, and his voice was calm, hopeful and tender, but it wasn't enough. I bowed my head, took a steadying breath. *We're going to find him. Yes,* I wanted to say. *And then I will go back to my life—my safe life—and I'll leave all of this behind me.* I thought of my mother hiding a box in the kitchen and returning to her life, pretending her lost summer hadn't happened. Why not? I was my mother's daughter after all. That's all I wanted now: to turn back to how things were before, holed up in the house with Abbot, unaware of the passage of time. Charlotte? How could I help her?

I nodded, but the nod wasn't for Julien. I was agreeing to a new promise. If we found Abbot safe and sound, I would give up on this lost summer, this pilgrimage for the brokenhearted, this house of supposed miracles. Abbot and I would go home and return to our safe lives before we were seized and bent. *Home,* I promised myself, *home.*

It was this promise that kept me climbing. I didn't look at Julien. We both were calling for Abbot. Our throats now sounded rough. My own was raw, and my hands and knees were scraped.

Julien trained the flashlight up the mountain, sweeping it from side to side, and then, finally, he stopped. "I think I see something," he said.

"What, what is it?" I said, my eyes skittering wildly.

He pointed the flashlight at the ground. "There's a light."

And then I could see it, too. A small, bobbling light up ahead, near what looked like a white wall, switching on and off at a slow pace.

Julien started climbing as quickly as he could. He was faster and more agile on the mountain. "Abbot!" he called. "We're coming. Don't move."

"Abbot, keep the light on!" I shouted. "We're here."

I wanted to reach him first, but Julien was there, kneeling beside him. He shone the light on his face. I could see a quick glimpse of Abbot's cheeks, his clenched eyes as he winced away from the brightness. I felt a wave of relief that made my knees buckle.

"He's okay!" Julien called to me, running the flashlight down Abbot's skinny legs, bruised and bloody. "He's fallen. But he's okay!"

Julien was whispering to Abbot when I scrambled to Abbot's side. I knelt on the rocks. "I'm here now," I said to Julien, still angry at him. He stood up, giving us room. "Abbot," I said. "Where does it hurt?"

"My ankle," Abbot said, his voice strained.

Julien lit Abbot's knees again, which were skinned. Blood smeared down his shins, and then his ankle, which was visibly swollen even through his short sports sock.

"It might be broken," I said.

"Maybe. I don't know," Julien said.

Abbot lifted his hands, which were red, scratched up.

"Abbot," I said, my voice choked with emotion. "Why did you run off?"

"I wanted to see the chapel," he whispered softly, his chin quivering, and then he shut his eyes—so much like his father's eyes—and turned his head away from me.

"He came very close," Julien said. "Look." He pointed his flashlight just a bit farther up the mountain, and there was the humble entrance to the chapel. Several rounded steps, like a tiered cake, led to a dark door—more a portal, because there was no actual door to the chapel, just a door-shaped entryway. Two stone buttresses held up the right side, and it looked like the mountain itself was the left and back side of the chapel.

"Let's take him in and lay him down," Julien said. He flipped open his cell phone, probably checking for bars, then shut it. "I'll make calls. The police for the mountain are young and strong and know the mountain very well. They have lamps and can light up the path. They can carry him down the mountain gently, safely. Okay?"

"Yes, yes." I picked up Abbot's flashlight, and he gripped Julien's flashlight. Julien lifted him and held him closely to his chest while Abbot trained the bobbing light on the path. "A little higher," Julien instructed. "Good."

The mountain was steep, the gravel shifting underfoot. Julien carried Abbot up the last switchback, then up the steps and into the mouth of the chapel, and I followed. I could see Abbot's fist gripping the back of Julien's shirt, and for some reason, this was what broke me. Tears started streaming down my face. I wiped them away.

I set my flashlight on the floor pointing up into the cool, dry air; it barely lit the small space. Julien lay Abbot down on the stone floor. I sat next to Abbot, cross-legged. I put my scraped hand on his forehead. The chapel was small and still, very much like a cave, not some high holy place like the cathedrals we'd visited, but maybe even holier in its simplicity.

Julien picked up his flashlight. "I'm going to find a place where the phone will transmit. I will be fast."

"Thank you," I said quietly. I was embarrassed now that I'd turned on him. "Thank you for everything. Be careful."

"It was nothing," he said. "Anyone would help." This wasn't true. Not just anyone. He walked out of the chapel, his cell phone open and glowing. The crunch of his footfalls quickly disappeared and the hollow quiet of the chapel surrounded Abbot and me.

"Abbot," I said. He looked up at me, his eyes teary. "Why did you run away? I was so scared. You can't do that! I thought you were gone. Do you understand me?"

He wrapped his arms over his face.

This wasn't the time to teach him a lesson. I tried to calm myself down. I took a deep breath. "Were you upset about the bird?" He didn't respond. "But you saved him. He can fly."

Abbot shook his head. No, it wasn't about the bird. I

wasn't sure I could handle the deeper sadness right now—the picture of his father as a bird. Was that what all of this was really about? Or was it also about Julien and me? I wasn't sure I could bear this blame, either. It wasn't just Julien's to shoulder, and I knew it.

"Why did you do it? Please, tell me."

He rolled away from me and shook his head more violently.

I looked at the altar rail farther back in the chapel and the walls cluttered with graffiti. I had to know. I couldn't allow him to keep this bottled up. It was too dangerous. "Okay," I said. "How about a multiple choice test, like Charlotte's SATs? You pick *A, B, C,* or *D.*"

He peeked at me with one eye. His face was streaked with dirt.

"Okay?"

He nodded.

"Roll over and I'll wipe your face."

He rolled over. I brushed some dirt and pushed back his hair. "*A.* Does it have to do with the swallow? *B.* Does it have to do with Daddy somehow because you miss him? *C.* Does it have to do with Julien and me? Or *D.* All of the above." My voice warbled with emotion.

He stared at the ceiling. "*D.* All of the above."

I didn't say anything for a moment. I stared around at the small chapel, this holy place. I placed my hand on his head and whispered, "I saw your picture of Daddy as a swallow. It was beautiful."

"The swallow flew away," Abbot said. "It didn't die, but I took care of it and it flew away. It left anyway and didn't come back."

"Why were you climbing to the chapel? Why here?" I asked quietly. "Were you looking for Daddy's soul?"

"Daddy's soul can't be here. He didn't die on the mountain. He died in America."

"Yes, so why were you climbing here?"

"Maybe I would see the phantom," he said. "If he's a protector of souls, maybe he might know something."

"About where Daddy's soul might be?"

He was embarrassed. He nodded quickly and looked away.

"Daddy's soul is everywhere," I said. "He's with us all the time."

Abbot clenched his fists and pounded on the stone floor. "I hate that bird. I got it all better so that it could fly, and it just left. You can't trust birds!"

"But you can trust me. I'm never going to fly away."

"You could die."

"But the chance of that is so remote, Abbot. Daddy was in an accident, a bizarre accident. It didn't make sense." I remembered Henry saying, *I think we should be honest when the world doesn't make sense.* I was trying to be honest. "I'm probably going to live a very long time. You'll have to wheel me around in an old-lady wheelchair."

Abbot was quiet. I looked at the altar, where I'd once stood as a kid, Julien holding my hand, asking me if I heard the phantom. The altar looked gray in the dim light, more like a fence than an altar.

"You know Daddy used to tell me stories about you. I guess they were Heidi stories."

"What stories did he tell you?" I asked.

"He told me that when you were little your mom came here and left you guys there, and your dad said that you might have to choose between your parents. It was a sad story."

"How did that come up?"

"One day, you were mad at me at dinner. I thought you weren't being fair. And he was telling me that you'd been a kid once, like me. But that everyone has different kinds of being a kid and yours wasn't always good."

"Well," I said, "it's true. That's what I thought for a while one summer, that I'd have to choose between my mom and my dad, which one I'd want to live with."

Abbot pressed his eyes shut with his fingers. Tears slid along the sides of his face. His cheeks grew flushed.

"What is it?" I said softly. "Abbot, tell me."

He took a sharp breath and then said, "I would have picked Daddy."

This confession surprised me. I was stung by it for a moment, but there was Abbot. How long had he been suffering, holding on to what he thought was a dark secret? "Abbot, it's okay to tell me that," I said. "Have you felt guilty about it? You shouldn't. It's okay."

He said, "But then I thought that maybe you would have

picked Daddy, too. That's what I thought tonight. If you had a choice . . . you would have picked him, not me." He curled away from me and started sobbing.

"No, Abbot, no," I said, and I lay down on the cool floor next to him, wrapping my arms around his small ribs. "First of all, the world doesn't make us pick, and second of all, Abbot, I would have picked you. Daddy would have picked you. It's an instinct in parents. Once the baby is born, you both know that you'd give up your life for that baby. That's the truth. And I'm not going anywhere. I'm not flying away from you," I said. I wrapped him in my arms and rocked him back and forth on the cold stone. "I'm not flying away."

Three rangers arrived on the scene like miners, lights slashing the darkness from their headlamps on their helmets. They were young and strong and knew the mountain extremely well, just as Julien had said. They arrived with a stretcher, checked out Abbot's ankle, cleaned up his knees and hands. They decided it was only a sprain, a nasty one, but nothing was broken. Julien spoke to them in French, explaining the situation, and I was relieved. I was too exhausted to rehash things. I was still reeling. Abbot had run away. He'd almost been lost. I needed to focus on him and nothing else. Not Julien. Not even Charlotte and Adam. Elysius and my mother would take over. I'd made a promise to go home. I was sticking to it. I spoke to Henry in my head—*Abbot is alive, safe. His heart beating. I'm taking us home, Henry. We're going back home.* Two of the rangers fastened safety straps over a thick blanket, immobilizing Abbot's leg, and tucked a rolled blanket under his head. Abbot stared up at the cloudless night sky, calm, peaceful. The two stretcher-bearers counted *un, deux, trois,* and hoisted Abbot to hip level, and they were off, chattering away to each other in chipper French that I was too tired to translate. I trusted them. They were experts, after all. The third ranger held my arm, helped to keep me steady. I was thinking about swallows and the voice of a ghost in the chapel and my son, not lost, not gone, whole and safe. I kept saying to myself, *Home, home, home.*

When we got to the bottom of the mountain, in the light thrown from the house, I saw everyone collected in the yard—Charlotte, Adam, Véronique, the guest who'd jumped in to help. Julien had already phoned ahead, telling them that Abbot's ankle was fine—only bumps, bruises, a sprain. Oddly, Adam Briskowitz looked the most upset of all. He was sitting on the ground, knees up, head in his hands.

Véronique opened her arms and hugged me. "It's okay," she whispered. "He is home. He is good." I wanted to tell her that she was wrong. *This is not home.*

She released me. "Thanks, everyone," I said, and then to the rangers especially, "*Merci. Merci pour tout.*"

The rangers unhooked a sleepy Abbot from the stretcher.

"Do you want me to carry him to his bed?" Julien asked.

I shook my head. "I can do it," I said. I was still blaming Julien even though I knew it wasn't fair. I lifted Abbot, and he wrapped his arms and legs around me. I'd have thought he was too big for me to carry like this, or just about, but maybe

I'd gotten stronger that summer, hauling paint up and down ladders, ripping weeds from the ground. Abbot held tight, and we headed for the house. I heard Julien saying some final words to the rangers. Charlotte jogged ahead of me and opened the back door.

I walked into the brightness of the kitchen. "Charlotte," I said, "will you get a bowl of warm water and a washcloth?"

"Yep," she said, and she darted off.

I carried Abbot up the steep stairs then into his room. I felt the pain of my own bruised knees, the palms of my hands burning. I set Abbot gently on his bed. The bed had two pillows, so I used one to prop up his swollen ankle, then covered him with the sheet.

"We're home," he said.

"Not really, not *home* home," I said. "In fact, while I was searching for you, I promised myself that if you were safe and sound, we would pack up and go back home, to the way everything was before, immediately. I think we can be home in a matter of days." Elysius and my mother would be arriving any time now. They would take over with Charlotte. Abbot and I would retreat. I thought he'd be relieved.

But he stared at me, wide-eyed, as if suddenly afraid. "No," he said. "That's all wrong. I want you to be happy!"

"I *am* happy!" I said. "We found you, Abbot! You're safe!"

He rolled his head back and forth on the pillow. "The swallow wasn't happy in the box. The box stunk, and it didn't want to eat dead flies. The swallow wanted to fly away."

"Abbot," I whispered, and lay down, put my head on the

pillow. "I already told you that I'm not flying away from you. Remember? And I promise you that I won't."

Abbot and I were nose to nose. "I want you to fly away a little," he said.

"You want me to fly away a little?"

He nodded.

"You want me to fly away a little and then circle back?"

He nodded again. "Julien is good," he said. "He's a good guy."

I was completely startled. "You want me to fly away with Julien and circle back?"

He nodded again and then pushed his nose into my nose and said, "Bing bong."

I wasn't sure what to do. He was just a child. I was the mother. I was the one who had to keep him safe. I couldn't do that with Julien around. I'd proved that I wasn't capable of handling that kind of distraction. The world was too dangerous. It wanted to take people from me. We were going home. We had to. In fact, all I wanted to do was start packing. Normally, I'd push my nose into his and say, "Bing bong." But I couldn't. "We have to go home, Abbot," I said. "I'm sorry. We just do."

He closed his eyes, shutting me out.

Charlotte walked into the bedroom with the soapy water and the washcloth. She helped me get Abbot cleaned up. We worked together in almost complete silence. We undressed him to his underwear, wiped down his face, arms, and legs, going gently over the scrapes on his hands and knees. He winced but didn't whine much. He was too exhausted to whine. By the time we were done, he was nodding off to sleep.

"He's doing pretty well, considering," Charlotte said, holding the bowl, its water now clouded with dirt. "I tried to run away once and only made it as far as behind a sofa. He's a bold kid."

"My heart's still in my throat. I can't shake the feeling that I almost lost him," I said.

"Don't forget to take care of yourself," she said, pointing to my bruised knees, one of which was caked with blood and dirt.

"I will." I dropped the washcloth in the bowl and held out my hands. "I'll take it downstairs."

Charlotte handed me the bowl, and I started for the steps.

"Wait," she said.

I stopped and turned to face her. "What is it?"

"They're coming, Elysius and Grandma, and I lied when I said that I didn't have a vision of the day-to-day in a perfect world."

"What does it look like?"

"I want to stay with you and Abbot."

"I'm a disaster area, Charlotte. A complete mess!" This was the wrong time to ask anything of me.

"You need me, in a way, I think. Don't you?" Her face was

serene and hopeful. Hadn't she proved that I needed her already? Charlotte was steady. She was calm in an emergency. She was patient and strong and, most of all, sure of herself. "And I need you. I only want to be with someone who'll see it as fair. A give and take."

"But what about Adam?"

"We're not ready to play dress-up at marriage. I mean, it's an institution and all. We'd like to date. Have at least one kind of normal thing." She paused. "He's all shaken up. I don't know what it is. Something about Abbot running away made him freak."

I looked at Charlotte's wide eyes, her dimpled chin. She was a kid, really, only sixteen, but she was already smarter than I was in some ways. Charlotte had said that she had felt sure of things here from the very start. I wanted to feel sure. My own vision of returning to the past was already deeply shaken—by Abbot and now by Charlotte. My father had said that she'd already chosen me, and he was right. If Henry were here to help me, I'd have said yes. I'd have hugged her and whispered, "Anything, anything you need at all. We're here for you completely." But I was alone, barely hanging on. I looked down at the bowl, the sudsy, dirty water shifting within it. "I can't say yes, Charlotte. There are too many moving pieces. I think I'm packing up tomorrow and looking into flights. Abbot and I need to go home. We can't prolong this, this . . ."

"Don't leave me here with them! You can't! You need my help and I need yours." She was the one to hug me, the water from the bowl sloshing over its sides, and for a moment, I felt warm and safe—still gutted, still lost and shaken, but for a moment, safe. "Think about the whole idea," she whispered. "Will you?"

I nodded.

"Goodnight," she said, and headed off to bed.

I was frozen there. Charlotte was so sure of herself. Why wasn't I? I heard myself saying, *Here I am, Henry, trying to do the right thing, and I'm pretty sure I'm doing it all wrong.*

I walked down the stairs and there in the kitchen, standing by the sink, was Julien, waiting for me. His face was streaked with dirt, his shirt muddied from Abbot's hands, one leg of his pants ripped at the knee. He folded his arms on his chest and sighed. "Your mother called my mother. She and your sister were delayed in Marseille. They've had dinner and are getting a hotel for the night. They're tired."

He was beautiful dirty like this—dirty from having searched the wilds for my son. He was so beautiful that I wasn't sure what he was saying. I loved his full lips, his teeth, the slight upturn at the corners of his eyes. I wanted to walk up to him and rest my head on his chest, and if I had done what my mother told me to do—to feel, connect, allow decisions to form—I would have done just that. But I knew that it wasn't possible. I had Abbot's permission, but that wasn't what I'd been waiting for. I couldn't afford the weakness that falling in love demanded. I was tired of losing and being lost. I must have looked dirty myself—and dazed, too. "My mother and Elysius are what?"

"They're staying in a hotel in Marseille tonight. They'll arrive in the morning."

"Yes," I said. I walked past him to the sink, where I dumped out the bowl of water and wrung the washcloth and started cleaning my scraped knee. It stung, but it felt good to clean it out, to feel like I was fixing something.

"Are you okay?"

"Fine," I said.

Julien was quiet.

"Did she tell them about Abbot?" I asked.

"No," he said. "I didn't want them to worry. Is he asleep?"

"Yes," I said, and I straightened up, setting the washcloth on the edge of the sink. "And I'm sorry. Really. I shouldn't have said what I did. I was terrified. I didn't mean it." I refused to look at him. Instead I cast my eyes on the charred box sitting on the table that I was to give to my mother. At this moment, the box seemed like an important reminder— of what? My mother's longing—I'd inherited it after all—or was it her ability to pack up the past and go home?

"I understand," he said. "I just wanted to tell you about your mother and make sure that you are okay."

"I'm going home," I said. "I made a promise to myself. Abbot needs me. My life is too complicated. And I think going home is best. The sooner the better."

"But you have more time. Three weeks?"

"Yes, but we've seen what we need to see. It's time." I

paused a moment. "And I want to thank you for everything." Awkwardly, I held out my hand to shake his. I don't know what I was expecting—that I would be saved by a sudden formality?

He was surprised by the gesture. He took my hand— gritty with dirt, like his—but he didn't shake it. He simply held it. "I wasn't trying to be his father," he said. "Or your husband."

"I know." I slipped my hand from his and looked at him.

He smiled—a weary smile—and shook his head. "I guess I'll go home, too. I was only staying here for you."

"I thought you were helping your mother," I said.

"But she doesn't need my help. I can call the girl from the village to help her with cleaning, but that is all. My mother is the strongest person I know."

I nodded nervously. "That's right." He'd stayed here for me? I was trying to take this in.

He reached out and touched my hair, gently, a wisp that had swept forward on my cheek. "I miss the flower barrette," he said. "I will continue to miss it."

I wanted to tell him that I would miss the sulky boy in the lawn chair, the one without the pogo stick, the one driving the convertible in the rain. But I could barely breathe. I wanted to go home, to go back, but what was home? How could I take Abbot back and start a new life when he called this place home? Nothing would ever be the same. Julien existed here in this kitchen. This moment alone meant that everything had shifted. I was silent.

He rubbed his collarbone as if it was an old ache, or maybe it was a sign of the restlessness that I first saw in him. "Listen," he said. "I understand. Have a good night. Have good dreams." And he turned and walked out of the house.

I stood there, stalled in the kitchen with its burnt walls and stonework. I remembered the kitchen of my childhood, hovering around my mother after she'd returned home—the sweet fragrance of all of our failed desserts. I'd met Henry in a kitchen swirling madly with caterers—Henry in a borrowed jacket, looking so young, so handsome, alive. And now I was here again in this kitchen in the house in Provence, with my son who'd run away now fast asleep overhead, in this kitchen where I let Julien go.

I slept fitfully and woke up wondering if I'd slept at all. The night before came back to me in crisp, stark flashes: the miracle of the injured swallow, my breathless sprint through the house calling for Abbot, the weak, bobbling light on the mountain, Charlotte's hug in the doorway of Abbot's bedroom, the way Julien touched my hair in the kitchen. Abbot was alive. I couldn't really be Charlotte's mother. I let Julien go. Did I have a vision of the future? Not really. I knew only that I had to be vigilant. I had to be strong.

Once Elysius and my mother were here and they were in charge of Charlotte, I would call the airlines and start packing. But when I heard Abbot clattering around in his room, I decided it would be better to hold off on packing. I wouldn't do it in front of him, at least. "Abbot?" I called, getting out of bed and padding quickly down the hall.

He was putting on his shoes.

"Did you shake them first?"

"No scorpions," he said. "I guess we won't ever see a scorpion now that we're going to leave."

I didn't want to get into a discussion about heading home. It was final, and talking about it might make it seem negotiable. I wanted to stand firm. "Are you feeling better?" He was wearing a new outfit. His hair was wet. "Did you take a shower?" His scraped hands and knees were still raw. "How's your ankle?"

He'd knotted one sneaker and was moving to the next. "It's still puffy. It hurts. I have a limp like Véronique!" He said this with that strange pride kids have when they get glasses, braces, and casts.

"Auntie Elysius and Grandma stayed the night in Marseille. They'll be here at some point today," I said. "Will you help me with the flowers? Would that be too hard on your ankle?" I wanted him close.

"Julien said he was going to teach me soccer tricks, but I guess I can't with my ankle."

His name had come up more quickly than I'd hoped. I felt a pang. It was worse to hear it coming from Abbot. "Julien might be leaving," I said, and I wanted to add, *This is for your own good. It's best for both of us.*

"Where's he going?"

"Work," I said. "He has a job, you know. Like I do. We can't give up everything and live in a dream."

Abbot glanced at me. "It's not a dream," he said defensively.

"We have to be practical."

Abbot sat on the bed and looked at me. "Wait," he said. "Are Grandma and Elysius going to take Charlotte home?"

"I don't know," I said.

I helped Abbot hobble down the stairs to the kitchen. I got him set up with some cereal and croissants with butter and apricot jelly.

My mother's box sat there, with its charred edge, on the table. I picked it up and put it in the cupboard. But then I stopped. The box belonged out in the open. The fire had come along, and this is what had become exposed. I wanted my mother to have the charred box. It was hers. I didn't want to keep it in the kitchen, where she could pass it by, ignoring it, ignoring the past. What if she continued to ignore it, refusing to get at the root of it once and for all?

I said, "I'll be right back, okay?"

I lifted the box and quickly jogged up the stairs. My mother and Elysius would stay in the spare bedroom at the end of the hall. I opened the door and stepped into the room. There were two single beds. My mother always read at night to fall asleep and always put her glasses on the bedside table, resting on top of her book. I put the box there, where she would have to see it and deal with it, and where she could do so more privately. This, I reasoned, would allow me to feel like I was doing what my father asked me to do without having to do much at all. It was a relief in some small measure to have delivered the box, to have it out of my hands, and I was proud of myself for not having peeked.

Abbot and I finished our breakfasts and headed out to the patch of flowers we'd planted. I taught him how to rub his thumb along the wilted cosmos to feel for the sharp teeth of mature seeds. We gathered about fifteen seeds each, a few of which were still a little green. We made rows near the other, taller cosmos and planted the seeds, covering them with loose dirt and watering them and the rest of the garden. Abbot took breaks, propping his foot in the wrought-iron chairs.

We saw Charlotte through the Dumonteils' kitchen window. She was already talking with Véronique, most likely about the plans for the day's meals. Charlotte needed to focus like this today, and Véronique must have known it. They were up working in the kitchen much earlier than usual.

There was no sign of Adam Briskowitz. I was starting to get a little nervous. Had he really freaked, as Charlotte put it, about Abbot's running away? Was he terrified of Elysius and my mother—perhaps rightfully so? I was a little terrified of them, personally.

And no sign of Julien. I assumed he was in his mother's house, maybe packing his own bags to go. It was impossible for me not to notice that the garage doors were closed. I couldn't see if his father's old convertible was still there or not. I wanted to see him again, just once more, but I was afraid of the possibility, too. What would we say that we hadn't already?

Aside from everything that I knew was about to unfold, the morning took on an ordinariness. If I hadn't been so anxious, it would have been lovely in its ordinariness. I let the sun warm my back as my hands wheedled through the flowers. Abbot was quiet, though I could hear him humming the French national anthem from time to time. I thought to myself, *I won't forget this. I won't ever forget this.* I wanted to pretend that my longing would subside as soon as I got home, and I would be able to appreciate these moments. Hadn't I learned something here? My Henry stories—I thought of how desperately I'd been holding on to each and every one of them, because I believed that if details from one slipped away, it meant Henry was slipping away. But maybe instead it meant that the details were burrowing deeper within me, becoming a different kind of memory, not crystal clear, but more imagistic and just as full—Cézanne's portraits of the mountain, Daniel's canvases of loss, my memories of Henry . . .

Of course, I knew that the ordinariness of this day would not last, and it didn't. When Abbot and I were inside having lunch, I heard voices in the yard—my mother and Elysius, chattering to the taxi driver. The engine was growling in the driveway. Car doors and the trunk were slamming.

I walked to the back door and saw the driver, a stout man with bowed legs, carrying the bags that couldn't roll on the gravel. My mother and Elysius appeared, holding their pocketbooks. My mother paused momentarily to gaze at the mountain. She sighed and then looked up at the back door where I stood.

"You made it!" I said.

"Finally," she said.

Elysius was paying the cabbie, practicing a little French.

Abbot popped past me, hobbled out the door, hopped down the steps, and I followed.

"What's wrong with you, young man? Why the hobbled gait?" my mother asked.

Abbot glanced at me and then back at his grandmother and Elysius. "I let go a swallow and it flew, and then, on the mountain, I slipped some and my ankle is sprained."

They seemed to accept this answer, and I was glad, not wanting to get into it. Luckily, Abbot often rambled like this. There were hugs all around. I ushered them inside. "Are you hungry? Tired?"

"We're fine," my mother said, looking around the kitchen. Was she disapproving? It didn't seem so. Instead, she looked like she wasn't seeing what was there but was overwhelmed with memory, as if with each glance she was running through things that had happened here over the years. The house was charged for her, deeply.

"I feel steamy," Elysius said, plucking at her blouse. "It's hotter than I remember." She plopped down in a kitchen chair.

But my mother was lit up. She hugged me again for no reason. I loved the smell of her perfume and her high-gloss hairspray. She then took hold of my hand. "Remember all of the stories I've told you all of these years?" she said. "And the butterflies? Remember when we went off with binoculars to see the wedding on the mountain and the butterflies were everywhere?"

"The Bath whites," I said. "Of course I remember."

"I know that story!" Abbot said.

"And you didn't believe me, after all of those years and all of the stories I've told you." She stared at me. "But something's changed. Things have happened. I can see it in your face. What is it?"

"Lots of things have happened," I said flatly. I wanted to tell her that I was going home, that this was over. I'd failed. I'd gone on the pilgrimage and maybe there had even been a miracle or two, but none for me.

"No, something in particular." She stared at me. "Elysius, look at her. She's different. Isn't she?"

Elysius shrugged. "She's gotten some sun, thank god. You were so pale at the wedding."

"Did something go wrong?" my mother asked. What was she seeing on my face? Melancholy? Homesickness? Or, worse, did she see longing?

"Well, yesterday was awful," I said, patting my cheeks. "But I'm fine! We're fine!"

"I ran away," Abbot said contritely.

"You did what?" my mother said.

"Why did you run away, Abbot?" Elysius asked.

"There were a lot of factors," I said. "But, aside from the ankle, he's fine." I gave Abbot's shoulders a squeeze, meaning, *Let's not get into it now.*

"Where's Charlotte?" Elysius asked. "Is she okay?"

"Yes," I said. "She's been a huge help. She's at Véronique's. They cook together like crazy." Where was Adam? Maybe Elysius was wondering that, too. I walked toward the stairs.

"You do have a plan with this house, right?" Elysius asked, looking around at the kitchen.

"I've been trying to listen to the house," I said. "But I think the house could use a new listener."

"Oh, no you don't," my mother said. "You can't weasel your way out of the job."

I wanted to tell her that I was weaseling my way out of more than the job. I was going to weasel my way all the way back home.

"I'd go crazy living with it like this!" Elysius said.

"I hear that the ox is slow," I said, "but the earth is patient."

Elysius cocked her head and stared at me and then changed the subject. "We have to have a meeting," she said. "You, me, Charlotte, and Mom. And then Adam. We'll talk to him after..." I knew without a doubt that Elysius had written down an agenda. Just like the brunch where this entire trip was first proposed, they'd first talked and designed a strategy. Once again, I didn't know what the agenda entailed. But I knew it would be compelling and hard to get out of. Charlotte and I hadn't even been able to joke our way out of a dress shop with them. What would we be able to do in the face of a defining family moment?

"I want to see Véronique first," my mother said. "I need to."

"Can we reconvene in one hour?" Elysius said.

"Yes, yes, of course," my mother said. Would she see Julien at Véronique's house? Would she read his face as well and see something there? Or did Véronique already know and would she simply tell her about Julien and me? For some reason, I didn't want her to know—or anyone. My mother put her hand on her heart and said, "We're here again, the three of us." She looked at Abbot. "Anything can happen now. Did you know that?"

Abbot nodded. "The house stories," he said. "I've heard them all."

"Not all of them," I said to my mother.

She looked at me sharply. "One hour," she said. "And then we'll talk." My mother walked out of the house. She was gripping her pocketbook like it was a canteen and she was heading off on some kind of mission. I moved to the window and watched her march to the Dumonteils' house. "She's a woman with secrets," I said to no one in particular.

My mother knocked on the back door, a formality we'd abandoned some time ago, and Véronique opened it. She and my mother hugged each other, swaying back and forth. It was a strange reunion—two people bound together by shared secrets that I would never really understand. This is what sisters are, I thought to myself. Elysius and I were girls who grew up together and knew what no one else could know about our existence. No matter how much I ever told Henry about my childhood, he would never know it like Elysius, from within it. My mother and Véronique shared this kind of bond—not of a fractured childhood, but of fracture nonetheless.

• • •

An hour or so later, my mother walked out of Véronique's house into the sun just as Elysius emerged from our house, freshly showered. I was watching Abbot feeding the koi in the little fountain, wobbling on one foot, and trying to pet them. He missed the swallow.

"Where's Charlotte?" my sister asked.

"She's coming," my mother said.

"Have either of you seen Adam?" I asked.

"He's coming, too," my mother said, taking a seat in one of the wrought-iron chairs. "Véronique was supposed to tell you that Julien is sorry he didn't get to say goodbye."

I felt a jolt. "What did you say?"

"Julien?" My mother over-enunciated his name. Now I was sure that Véronique had told her something. "I think you know who I'm talking about."

"Julien was here?" Elysius asked, sitting in a chair next to my mother.

Julien had left. He was gone already. Where? I was stunned. He'd left so quickly. That was it. "When did he leave?" I asked.

"This morning." My mother glanced at me quickly and then she called to Abbot. He looked up from the fountain. "Véronique needs someone to garnish something for her. Would you help?"

Abbot looked at me for permission.

I nodded. "Sure. Just don't leave the house."

Abbot started limping toward the house as Charlotte was coming out of it and walking across the yard. She was wearing a loose black tank top and a long skirt, coming toward us with her head down, her hands knit together at her chest, like a monk who prays while walking.

"Where's Adam Briskowitz?" my mother asked.

And just then the back door of the Dumonteils' house opened. Adam's old-man's suitcase nudged out first and then he followed. He looked as he did the first time I met him, wearing his jeans, his Otis Redding T-shirt, Top-Siders, and his oversized glasses with the clip-on shades flipped up. I now took this to be Briskowitz's traveling attire.

Charlotte stood in front of us now. She was nervous, glancing around quickly at everyone's faces, trying to predict what might come her way. She reminded me of the swallow in the box before Abbot pitched it off the balcony.

"Where's Adam going?" I asked.

"Home," Charlotte said. "He's grounded."

Adam and Abbot met in the yard. "I'll see you later, Abbot." He pretended to shoot him with an arrow.

Abbot grabbed his shoulder, wounded, and let out a groan, staggered around, and then croaked. I didn't like him even playing dead and was relieved when he popped up, gave a big wave, and quickly limped to the house.

Adam looked like he might cry. He flipped his shades down. He walked to us. "Sorry about the timing, but my cab is on its way. I'm going to meet it at the end of the driveway so it doesn't miss the sign. It's a very small sign."

"It would be better if you stayed just for a little bit," my mother said.

"So we can all talk," Elysius added.

"I'm sorry, but I just can't," he said. "I've got to catch a train and then a flight. It's all been worked out by my parents."

"But Adam," I said.

"I know, I know. You don't think I know?" he said. I wasn't sure what this meant. "I need time to get my head together. I can't even form whole sentences. I want to be a great father. I can do it, but I just can't do this." He waved his hand in a circle, indicating . . . the conversation, our family, France? "Not yet."

"You seem to be forming sentences just fine," my mother said angrily.

"Why are you leaving now?" Elysius asked.

"Seriously," I said. "Tell us what's going on."

He put his suitcase down. "Abbot was lost and I couldn't find him. Shit. This is a nightmare. I heard of this couple who left their kid sleeping in a car seat under a restaurant table. A very nice, smart couple. Ivy Leaguers. They just forgot and got up and left. That's me. What if I can't do this? I'm going to college in a few weeks as a philosophy major. Who can raise a kid as a philosophy major? I have to go home. I have to talk to my family."

"He's lost it," Charlotte said to me. "He's totally Briskowitzing himself."

I was furious. As calmly as I could, I stood and grabbed Adam by the elbow and pulled him a little bit away from the others. "We'll be just one minute," I said.

"What is it?" Adam said.

"Look at me," I said.

He paused and then lifted up the shades while still look-ing at the ground. I waited. He slowly raised his chin and met my eyes.

"You'll get it together," I said. "You'll learn to be a better man because you'll have to."

He started crying and was embarrassed by it. My mother and Elysius were sitting behind me. I imagined their faces—perhaps tired, most of all. Here were all the women together, expected to fix this, to make it right. Adam glanced at Char-lotte and whispered her name.

She shook her head. She couldn't help him.

He cleared his throat. "I've got to go," he said. He reached down and picked up his suitcase. "The cab might miss the turn," he said.

"Adam," Charlotte said. "Brisky."

No one moved.

Finally, he turned and walked down the driveway.

Charlotte took a seat in one of the wrought-iron chairs, too. Instinctively we pulled our chairs in to make a tighter circle.

"I'm so sorry he left," I said. "He needs time."

Charlotte was silent, her face expressionless and therefore beyond sadness. She shrugged. "Maybe we could go after him." She wasn't really suggesting it, more just pointing out the fact that life didn't work that way.

"He's really just a boy," my mother said.

"And Charlotte's young, too," Elysius said. "Regardless of the situation, we can't forget that." This seemed to come from Daniel. Charlotte was his little girl, and I suspected that he'd urged Elysius to make sure everyone kept this in mind.

"Age is relative," Charlotte said.

"In this case, your age has some very serious practical concerns," Elysius said. "And those have to be addressed."

"And I suppose you're going to tell me how to address them?" Charlotte said defensively.

"I can't do this if you're going to be hostile," Elysius said.

"She's not being hostile," I said. "She's sixteen and pregnant and the father just walked out and she loves him."

"Oh, please," Elysius said. "Love! For shit's sake."

"Who's being hostile now?" Charlotte said.

My mother stood up. "Listen to me. Elysius has offered to build an apartment onto the current structure of her house—a place where Charlotte can feel like she has independence. And Elysius and Daniel will pay for a baby nurse and then a nanny. Charlotte can still go to school. Daniel will still produce art. I'll certainly help with the baby as much as possible, as I'm sure you will, too, Heidi. It will be a group effort."

"And in the process, we won't forsake all normalcy," Elysius said. "Our lives will be able to go on. Charlotte will get her degree. She'll segue to Florida State, which is close by, maybe even full-time." Elysius smiled, proud of her plan.

"And we'll make it possible for Charlotte's mother to visit her instead of having to uproot the baby."

"This sounds expensive," Charlotte said.

"Money is no cure-all, but it does help," Elysius said.

"Well, it's a very nice offer, but I'll pass," Charlotte said.

Elysius arched her back. "Excuse me?"

"I'll pass. But really, thank you so much. It was really thoughtful and generous."

"Do you have an alternate plan?" my mother said.

I sat back and held my breath.

"I want to live with Heidi and Abbot."

Elysius glared at me, and before she opened her mouth to say a word, I knew that she would launch into the same old argument—Charlotte as ingrate, and I would be her conspirator. My mother reached out to pat Elysius's leg to calm her, but Elysius was on her feet. "I just offered to build you your own apartment! Your own place! And you're saying no to that? Do you know how hard this is on your father and me? Do you have any idea?"

"I said thank you. It was thoughtful and generous." Charlotte's face had gone blank. She seemed to be reciting definitions from her SAT prep book.

Elysius turned to me. "I can't believe you put this in her head. A new baby and you get to play the savior—that's the idea, right? It won't bring back the dead, you know!"

It felt like a slap. In fact, my cheeks burned. I felt hot deep in my chest. I couldn't say a word.

"Heidi didn't even say yes to it," Charlotte said. "No one put anything in my head. It was my idea. All mine."

My sister was wrong. This wasn't about trying to bring Henry back. But maybe much else in my life was, making my sister as right as she was wrong. Undeniably so. I could pack up. I could go home. But I couldn't go back. Nothing could bring back the dead. Still, what followed wasn't an attempt to punish my sister. Maybe I was listening. Maybe I was feeling and connecting and the decision simply formed. "I'm willing to try," I said to Charlotte.

"That's all I'm asking," Charlotte said.

Elysius walked to the stone fountain and sat down. She looked broken. She stared out across the vineyards, her face slack, her eyes drifting.

"Heidi," my mother said, "are you sure?"

"Yes," I said. "I want to help Charlotte however she needs it."

My mother raised her hands in the air and said to all of us, "Get your chairs. Pick them up. Follow me."

"What are you talking about?" I asked.

"Come with me," she said. "Up, up!"

"Come where?" my sister asked.

"We're going to watch the mountain," she said, and she began dragging her chair out of the shadow of the house across the gravel driveway into the grass, where the mountain was in full view.

Charlotte grabbed her chair, and I grabbed mine. We

pulled them through the gravel and set them next to my mother's.

"Are you all crazy?" Elysius said.

"No," my mother said. "This is how we'll come to our answers and how we'll find our resolve to stick to them." I remembered Véronique's explanation of the mountain, the wide canvas, as she put it, and how she said that my mother used to stare at the mountain that lost summer when she first arrived.

"Staring at a mountain?" Elysius said.

"What do you think the mountain is for?" my mother said.

"It changes colors all throughout the day," I said.

Charlotte said, "There are people who go on tours and spend a lot of money to pay a guru to take them to the mountain so that they can get answers by watching it change colors." I was fairly sure this was a lie but one that would grab Elysius and pull her in, and that made me a little proud of Charlotte for coming up with it on the fly like that.

"There are?" Elysius said. "Gurus?"

"Come on, Elysius," my mother said. "Line up."

Elysius picked up her chair and put it next to mine.

"We won't talk about anything, not until sunset at least. And then we can talk as much as we need to, but for now, quiet," my mother said. "We'll sit here all day and the answers will come."

And so we sat down, in silence, and started watching the mountain, waiting for answers.

The mountain was a force. I'd been feeling its pull since I arrived. It had given my mother answers in the past. She'd gazed at it when she first arrived, and maybe it told her that it was okay to fall in love, to be a heart thief, and, in the end, when it was on fire, it told her to go home.

I didn't expect anything that dramatic. Maybe this gazing would simply allow us all a little time to think—to measure our words, at the very least. And so this was where I found myself, and I was more than willing to give in. We needed something beyond ourselves. Why not this? Why not attempt to find a few answers and some resolve?

The day went on. Abbot resurfaced. He played waiter and brought us drinks, jambon sandwiches, olives, and more of Charlotte's homemade peach ice cream. Charlotte got out of the chair and sat on the ground. Abbot brought out a blanket and pillows, and I lay down, my ankles crossed, my hands behind my head. Charlotte curled to one side, her hands tucked under her head.

Elysius found all of this nearly impossible, as you can imagine. She was a deeply anxious person. She'd have to break every once in a while to pace around a little or do a few restless yoga poses and then some squats. But she took it seriously. In fact, early on, she handed Abbot her BlackBerry, a great act of sacrifice. She was *trying*, as she'd said in the dress shop earlier that summer. Deep down she knew that quiet observation and contemplation weren't her strong suits, and she was an overachiever, bent on getting things right.

Véronique emerged at some point in the afternoon and asked what we were doing. My mother told her.

"Oh," she said. "Can I sit with you?"

"Of course," my mother said, and they sat side by side. I imagined them as kids again, their childhood selves looking on at the grown-up women they'd become. There were no guests in the house. It was empty. They kept their eyes on the mountains, and sometimes their eyes closed, and they dozed. I couldn't fall asleep. I was committed. I didn't want to miss answers.

The swallows appeared. Together we watched them scatter and swoop against the backdrop of the mountain. Abbot drew pictures in his notebook. This time he drew each and every one of us, and we all had wings and were flying with the swallows—Henry was just another person in the group, flapping among us. That seemed right. He wasn't a ghost. We weren't ghosts. We were all together.

And when the mountain was a dusky, bruised blue, I was struck by how incredibly beautiful it was. I thought of Henry after the miscarriage, how I finally confessed that I felt sorry for him. He told me not to. *I'm only a beggar here.* This mountain, the arched back of the earth risen before us, it made me feel humble, like a beggar, just lucky to be here at all, even briefly. And in light of this mountain, we're all here only briefly. I started to cry, very quietly, because of the ache of missing Henry. A simple ache, and the tears were simple, too. Abbot noticed right away, and he wiggled over and rested his head on my stomach.

Véronique warmed leftovers and Abbot helped her serve. After dinner they disappeared into the house and returned with a tray of candles, red wine, glasses. We set the candles down around us, filled the glasses with wine, and kept on watching the mountain, as the stars began to appear in the night sky.

There we were—Charlotte, my sister, my mother, Véronique, and I—all of us sitting now in a ring of candles, with Abbot falling asleep on my lap. It was strange how loud the world was when you weren't filling it up with your own noise. It was strange how brilliant the colors of the mountain were. Even though I thought I'd been paying attention, I really hadn't. There was the scent of the lavender, still in season, pungent and sharp and sweet, rolling on the wind.

I thought of Henry and, this time, not how much I loved him, but how much he loved me. That was how Julien had put it. *Everyone thinks that it is a gift to have someone love you, but they're wrong. The best gift is that you can love someone—like he loved you.* How had Henry loved me? It was as if he was the world's leading expert on the arcane subject of Heidi Buckley, the *only* expert on the arcane subject of Heidi Buckley. He knew me in exquisite detail, in contradiction, in all of my little vanities and falsehoods and flaws. I would catch him studying me in the kitchen of the Cake Shop, laboring over a cake.

"Stop it," I'd say.

"Stop what?" he'd say back, knowing exactly.

"You look stupid," I'd say, smiling.

"Can't a man show that he's in love? Is that allowed in contemporary society?"

"Yes, but you have a stupid look on your face."

And he did. It was dreamy, almost drunk. "It's weird," he'd say, "it's like I'm having a stroke and all the edges of things fade away and it's just you there and you are the ether and every element in the room gets out of whack, and it's all particles and I'm in the presence of love and I can't believe it, and it's you, and I can't believe I found you, and you found me, and you actually love me back. It's really a wonder I don't fall down and hurt myself when all this washes over me. Yes, I'm love-struck. I'm stricken. I'm a stroke victim and I have a dumb look on my face. I love you."

Henry could go on these little verbal rampages about love. When we were first dating, they were short, like, "I love you and I want to spend the rest of my life with you." But as we grew older, it took him more words to get at love and how he loved me.

And these were my fears. As many versions of Henry that I lost, I was losing his version of me. I loved that version—the one he invented when he watched me while I worked, the one he invented when we first met in the crowded kitchen, the one without her pocketbook, locked out of her house demanding to be kissed, the one who got out of the car in the middle of the intersection to tell him she was pregnant, the one who was so sure she'd die in childbirth, the one who had a miscarriage, whom he lifted from the empty tub and put back in bed.

Where had those versions of Heidi gone? Were they lost forever?

But there, in the presence of the mountain as the sun slipped away and the dark purples emerged and the sky took shape overhead, I realized that every time that I returned to the world at hand—for Abbot, mostly—I grew stronger. And maybe Henry's Heidi wasn't gone but still here, only tougher. What if Julien truly loved me and I loved him? What if there were more versions of myself out there and I had shut them down?

Eventually Charlotte stood up, the candles glowing at her feet, and said, "I'm sorry. I know I didn't get knocked up on purpose or anything, but I'm sorry that I've put everyone through this."

Everyone started talking at once. There was an outpouring. My mother said that she loved Charlotte, that of course she hadn't meant to get pregnant. I said that this was what family offered each other. We were here for her. Even Elysius started to say something, but Charlotte raised her hands and cut us off. "You don't have to tell me everything," she said. "I get it. And I've also realized that I love Adam Briskowitz, but I'm not *interested* in him right now. He's pulling me away from my focus. And I'd rather let him go."

Elysius looked at Charlotte. She stood up, too, and said, "I have a baby already. It might not be something that anyone else really gets, but your father is my baby. I'm protecting and caring for and tending to an artist. And that's why I haven't done a good job of raising you, Charlotte. I'm raising him."

Charlotte nodded. I figured that this made sense to her, although it was hard to hear. It was the truth. It probably put words to a hunch she'd had for years.

"Heidi would do a better job. Her house would be a home. And I'm sorry about what I said earlier, about trying to bring back the dead."

"It's okay," I said.

Elysius looked at my mother. "Is that what's supposed to happen here?" she asked.

My mother looked at Véronique.

"C'est clair?" Véronique said.

My mother translated. "Does it feel clear to you? Really clear?"

Elysius put her hands on her hips and took a deep breath, then let it out. "Yep."

"Then, yes," my mother said. "That's what's supposed to happen."

"So, it's okay with you still, Charlotte?" I asked. "To come live with Abbot and me?"

Charlotte smiled. "I know it's going to be hard. It's a lot to ask of you and Abbot. I mean, it's more than okay with me."

"Me, too," I said.

"Me, too," Elysius said, and then she added, matter-of-factly, "Can I go to bed now? I'm spent."

"Yeah," Charlotte said. "Can I go to bed?"

My mother was staring at the mountain again. Véronique nodded. My mother gave permission with a flick of her hand, once again a matriarch.

"Abbot needs to go to bed, too," I said, pointing to his head on my stomach.

"I'll bring him with me," Charlotte said.

I jiggled Abbot's shoulder and whispered his name. He sat up and rubbed his eyes. Charlotte lent him a hand and I boosted his butt, and he was on his feet, limping sleepily to the house. On the way, I heard Charlotte say, "Uncle Abbot. Do you like that or do you prefer the full proper term, Uncle Absterizer?"

I thought about getting up and following Charlotte and Abbot inside. I'd gotten an answer of some kind. Wasn't I learning to feel, connect, let decisions form? I turned over onto my stomach, propped on my elbows, and looked back at the Dumonteils' house, which was dark. And then I turned and looked at my mother and Véronique. I said, "The box."

My mother looked at Véronique and then bent down and picked up a canvas bag with two hefty straps, which was sitting next to her chair. She put her hand inside and pulled out the box itself. "This box?"

"You found it."

"Yes," she said, "on my bedside table. It was like it had been waiting for me, patiently, all these years. Or was it, perhaps, you?"

"I might have had a hand in it," I said. "Did you look inside?"

"No," she said. "I know what's inside."

"The box is for you, Heidi," Véronique said. "It is your gift. She hid it all these years."

"My gift?"

My mother handed the box to me. "Open it," she said.

I took the box from her, unclasped the small latch, and opened it. Inside, there were papers, folded into thirds, pink papers and also white pieces of notepaper. I picked up a piece of pink paper, unfolded it, and there was my monogram in fancy script on the top—the stationery of my childhood. It was one of the letters that I'd written my mother that lost summer, and beneath that, there was another and another.

"But I never mailed these," I said.

"Your father found them and he sent them all to me in one big envelope."

"These were private," I said.

"He was desperate," my mother said. "He would have tried anything."

"But I thought you told me that the box was filled with love letters," I said to Véronique.

"These are love letters," she said.

I sifted through the box and pulled out one of the white pages. It was a recipe written in French in a messy scrawl. The paper was dotted with oil that made some spots translucent. *Tarte Citron* was written at the top, underlined twice. It wasn't my mother's handwriting.

"Who wrote these?" I asked.

"That is what I was leaving behind. It was hard to leave, and that autumn, I tried to make all of his desserts. But none of them worked. Nothing tasted the same. I gave up."

"He was a pastry chef?" I asked.

She nodded.

"Did you love him?" I asked.

"I loved him with all of my heart," my mother said.

"But you came home."

"Your father would have survived. Perhaps, over time, he'd have thrived. And Elysius didn't need me as much as you did, or not in the ways that I could really recognize at the time. While I was gone, it was like she learned how to take care of herself. She grew up. She came into her own. But you," she said, "you were still so young. You needed me."

"But you really loved him," I said. "Maybe we could have

made it work. Kids are resilient; that's what people say, right?"

"The doors of your heart were open," Véronique said. "Read the letters."

"You would have come home, too, Heidi, if you were me," my mother said. "Your love was stronger than anything in the world."

"It was strong enough to light a mountain on fire!" Véronique said.

"Read the letters," my mother said. "You knew a lot about love."

"It is interesting that this stranger, this man your mother loved, he passed to you the art of baking," Véronique said, "the idea that sweet food is love and love is sweet food, to your mother, and she passed it to you. And that is where it found a home—inside of you."

"Why did you hide the box here?" I asked my mother.

"I filled the box with the love I left behind and the reason why I went home, which was you," she said, "the love I was returning to. That was my love story, the one that the house gave to me. It just seemed like the box belonged here."

"Oh," I said. We were quiet a moment, and then my mind was trying to sort things out. "If you hadn't fallen in love with this man, and if I hadn't written you the letters and if Dad hadn't sent them out of desperation, then you wouldn't have come home and started baking, and I wouldn't have followed you around the kitchen that fall, and I wouldn't have fallen in love with baking, and I wouldn't have gone to culinary school, and I wouldn't have met Henry."

"I never thought of it that way exactly," my mother said. "But that's true."

"But you could have had a life here, a different life," I said.

"I don't regret it, Heidi," my mother said. "Not for a heartbeat."

The small, charred box balanced on my knees, I took a deep breath and looked at the mountain.

"Did watching the mountain give you answers, Heidi?" Véronique asked.

"Yes," I said, "I'm falling in love with your son, the one without the pogo stick."

I read the letters that I wrote my mother that lost summer. Everything I wrote, in my thirteen-year-old's handwriting, was simple, beautiful, honest. *Come home. Come home. Come home,* I wrote. *If you don't, I still won't stop loving you. My love can go on forever and ever.*

When I folded the letters in with the recipes and closed the charred box with its small latch, I thought, *What if the things I've wondered about love all have some truth to them?*

Love is infinite. Grief can lead to love. Love can lead to grief. Grief is a love story told backward just as love is a grief story told backward. Every good love story has *many* loves hiding within it.

Maybe I should put it this way. Imagine a snow globe.

Imagine a tiny snow-struck house inside of it. But this

time the woman stands at the window, and there are no screens. She cranks the window wide open.

And it is not a snow-struck house. The snow isn't snow at all.

It never was.

The snow is really Bath whites—their white wings with black dots—a beautiful storm of them.

And the house isn't a quiet house. It's full of voices, talking, laughing, calling to one another above the sound of the radio. Her lover's voice is there. Her son's voice. Somewhere in an upper bedroom a baby wakes up and gives a cry. A young mother's feet hit the stairs and quickly climb.

This time, the woman isn't alone, not at all.

The snow-that-isn't-snow-but-instead-is-Bath-whites reminds her of her husband as a little boy riding his bike on a country road filled with bounding, massive white Pyrenees, an avalanche of their howling, leaping joy. And the thought of her husband as a boy reminds her of her son and her son reminds her of her husband, and she lets the Bath whites flutter into the house until it fills with the blur of wings.

I decided to circle away and then come back.

I called Julien's cell phone but wasn't surprised when it went straight to voice mail. I'd never seen him answer his phone in my presence. He wasn't the type. Véronique told me that he'd gone to Marseille. I remembered that he'd done the same after his split with Patricia; he'd gone to Marseille, too, to stay with Gerard, the flirtatious bachelor. "Is he at Gerard's?" I asked Véronique.

"I don't know for certain," she said, but she wrote Gerard's address on a piece of paper and gave it to me.

My mother told me that she would watch over Abbot in case he woke up in the night and asked for me. "He'll be fine, though. Don't worry. Just go."

Marseille was only about an hour or so away, and I was soon in my rental car, driving out of the narrow, winding roads lined with shrill cicadas and out on the highway. I didn't listen to the radio. I just drove in silence, hoping to still feel the force of the mountain, holding tight to my answers, hoping for resolve to settle in.

I took an exit for Marseille and, using one of Véronique's old maps, found Gerard's apartment building. I parked in a spot up the street. It was a cool night, a little overcast, with the promise of rain. There was still a good bit of traffic. The city was bustling even though it was late. It was a port town, after all. It was always busy. I slipped into the building's front lobby, and, from a bank of buzzers, I found only one labeled with Gerard as a first name, luckily. I hadn't ever asked for his last name. I buzzed and he buzzed back, without even asking who it was. I took the stairs up to the third floor. The door at the end of the hall was opened a crack.

As I got closer, I said, "Allô? Bonjour?"

The door swung wide and there was a man—gangly and tall with short wet hair, freckled, and naked except for a towel wrapped around his waist. He was talking on a cell phone and digging through a wallet.

"Excusez-moi," I said. "Je cherche pour Julien Dumontiel?"

He looked up, shut his wallet, pulled the phone from his ear and said, "Heidi?"

"Yes. Gerard?"

"I thought you were the man coming with my Chinese food," he said in English. He smiled at me and hung up the phone without a word to the person on the line. Was it a friend? His mother? "Do you want to stay for dinner?"

"I'm really looking for Julien," I said. "Is he here?"

"You have made the man very sad," he said. "He was here, but now he is not."

"Where did he go?" I asked.

He shrugged. "He is a man without reason."

"You don't know where he went?"

"Stay for dinner. I will dress myself," Gerard said with an embarrassed smile. "The Chinese food will arrive. Maybe Julien will return."

"Thanks," I said. "It's a sweet offer, but I'll have to pass." I turned and headed back to the stairs.

"Heidi!" Gerard shouted.

"Yes?"

"I hope you come with goodness. He needs goodness."

I nodded and ran down the stairs quickly. I opened the door to the apartment building and stood, breathless, on the sidewalk. A young woman walked swiftly by with a little dog on a leash in tow. The dog looked at me and pattered on. I looked up at the sky, and in the distance, I saw the shine of a cathedral. Was it Notre-Dame de la Garde, the cathedral that Julien had talked about? It sat on top of a hill; its bell tower, crowned with a golden statue, was nearly lost in the cloudy sky.

I decided to drive toward it, but while I circled winding streets, I lost it for a time, my view blocked by crowded buildings. Finally, I turned a corner and there it was, right above me. I pulled into a parking lot surrounded by blond stone, and there was Julien's father's convertible with its busted lid. I parked next to it, cut the engine. I wondered if he had already decided he was done with me. He'd suffered enough. Maybe it was already too late.

Still, I got out of the car. I walked up a set of stone steps—on and on, dozens of steps. At the top, there was a platform. I looked up at the church, and now I could see the statue on the bell tower—the Madonna and Child in brilliant, almost iridescent gold.

I heard my name. I turned and there he was. Julien, alone, standing by a stone wall. Behind him, there was a packed, sprawling city, a dark, massive port, cranes and freight ships, and then the sea, stretching out endlessly.

I walked to him. The wind ruffled our hair, billowed our shirts. His eyes were wet, shining. "It's a little cloudy," I said. "It might rain."

"Did you come to tell me about the weather?"

"You're driving a convertible with a broken top," I said. "I thought you might want to know."

I was breathless from climbing the stairs, windswept. He walked up close to me, so close, I could feel his warm breath. He wrapped his arms around my waist and kissed me. This was not the soft and tender kiss amid the glowing paper lanterns. I felt this kiss run through my body, swaying my back. He lifted me off the ground and, still kissing, I held his face in my hands. How long did this last? Time no longer existed. Slowly, I slid down his body, my shoes touching back down to earth.

"I bought something for you." He reached into his pocket, hiding something in his fist.

I took his hand, turned it over, and opened his fingers one by one. There, in his palm, there was a little plastic barrette. It was red with a flower. "For me?"

He reached up and lifted a strand of my hair from my face. He clipped the barrette, pinning back a few wisps.

"Do you want to give this a try?" I asked.

"It will be complicated."

"Everything is. I'd prefer to be complicated with you rather than complicated without you," I said.

"We have kids," he said. "We live on two different continents."

"And that isn't even the hardest part."

"What will be the hardest part?" He wrapped his arms around me now. I put my head on his chest, listened to his heart. He rested his chin on top of my head.

I said, "I don't know if it's fair."

"What is fair?"

"You have to know that I will always love Henry."

"But that is what is good about you. You will always love Henry. He's part of you. And I want to love all of you."

"We'll practice joy," I whispered.

"We'll try to live a little."

There is one more small miracle.

It's summer again. Charlotte is giving the baby—a three-month-old named Pearl—a bath in the tub. The baby is beautiful, with Charlotte's eyes. Julien is standing at the back window, looking after Abbot, who's drawing swallows in the fields out by the dig with Frieda, who will be with us all summer. Patricia and Pascal are going through a rough patch. Julien stayed with us off and on throughout the year in Florida, and when Frieda wasn't with her mother, she came, too. It's been more complicated than we could even have imagined—or should I say complex? Why would we want simple?

And I'm baking pastries in the kitchen, which has a shiny new oven but is still unfinished. I'm not sure the renovations will ever be done. I keep the old. I add the new. I don't make decisions. I just listen. It's a slow process—the ox and the patient earth. Right now, the whole house smells like a bakery and that is a renovation of its own.

Soon, Elysius, Daniel, and my mother and father will arrive—my father seeing the place for the first time. My parents will take the fourth bedroom, which I painted ivory just for my mother.

Charlotte, with the baby in a sling, has spent the morning with Véronique in her kitchen, preparing the meal. And I'm in charge of dessert, as it should be. I've used the recipes from the charred box so many times in the Cake Shop this year that I no longer even have to glance at them. The recipes are within me, deeply rooted, and even as I make these tarts, I'm making small changes, little tweaks and variations. I've started making wedding cakes again here and there, but Charlotte tells me I'll never make one for her and Adam. They're parents—good ones—and best friends, but no longer in a relationship. It was too much pressure. "Maybe one day?" I've said to Charlotte, but she only shrugs. Adam will arrive midsummer and stay for a month. For now, though, it is this strange family of the six of us, making this house our own, if only for the summer. And can I simply say that throughout every day, it strikes me that Charlotte is an incredible mother? In fact, she mothers with such patience and grace that she's elegant, timelessly elegant. Ironically enough, one might even say that she has become forever elegant after all.

There's a knock at the front door, three loud sharp raps

of the knuckles—a cop knock, as Henry would have put it. No one ever uses the front door.

"I'll get it," Julien says.

I'm so curious that I have to follow, even though my hands are dusted in confectioners' sugar.

Julien opens the door, and there stands the police officer from the Trets police station the summer before. He's still wearing his sweater vest. He's holding a small suitcase on wheels. "Allô!" he says.

"Bonjour," Julien and I say.

"You two are together," he says, with a wink. "I said that you were and you did not believe. But now you do?"

I look at Julien. "Now we do," I say.

We invite the officer in. He sets the suitcase down on its wheels and pulls it along. It is beaten, faded, worn. But the police officer looks triumphant. "This is yours?" he says.

"I think so," I say.

Charlotte emerges from the bathroom, her face moist, holding the baby, tightly wrapped in a thin blanket. "Who is it?"

"Could you call Abbot and Frieda in from the field?" I ask.

She nods and walks quickly out of the room. I can hear her voice, calling for them out the back door.

"I found this," the officer says. "And I remember you. You are friends with Daryl Hannah, no?"

"No," I tell him. "I never really said that."

He sighs. "Well." He waves away this detail. "This is something stolen from you by the thieves, no?"

Abbot and Frieda run in to the room, see the cop, and freeze.

"Bonjour," the officer says, in a very officious tone.

"Bonjour!" they answer in unison.

Charlotte walks in, patting the baby's back. "What's going on? Is that your suitcase, Absterizer?"

Abbot looks at me. "Is it?"

"I think so," I say.

The officer tips the handle toward me. My hands are covered with sugar, and so Julien takes it and lays it on the floor so that Abbot can have at it. He kneels down, and Frieda plops cross-legged beside him, her frizzy curls bouncing around her head.

"The suitcase was left on the side of the road all year. But it was found and I remember this detail!" the officer says. "You put a star next to this one item on your list. And I did not forget this star!"

Abbot unzips the dirty suitcase and opens it. The clothes smell bad. They're dry but mildewed. Frieda holds her nose and shakes her head, scooting away. But Abbot picks through the clothes until he finds what he's looking for. "Mom," he says, "it's still here." He pulls out the dictionary. The binding is warped, and the cover is deeply rippled. It's dried but a little swollen. Abbot opens it up to the inscription, which is blurred but legible.

"Le dictionaire!" the officer says, beaming. "It's been discov-ered!"

Frieda looks at Abbot, confused.

"It was gone," he tells her. "It's special and it was gone, but it came home to us!" And this was home, just like that. *Home.* The dictionary came home to us, like my mother after the lost summer, like the letters I sent her, like every small sadness that—strangely, and when you least expect it—can return as joy.

Julien puts his arm around me, and I grab the front of his shirt with one fist. "It's a gift," he says. "Take the gift."

"It's all a gift," I tell him. "All of it."

~le fin~

Acknowledgments

I would like to thank the villagers of Puyloubier for their hospitality and incredible patience, especially the beautiful and warmhearted Laurent and Jerome, who were generous beyond measure. I would like to thank the glamorous duo, the mayor and his wife, Frédéric and Beatrice Guinieri, and J.F., for his graciousness. Elizabeth Dumon, thank you for answering all of my questions about your gorgeous home, land, vineyard, and Gallo-Roman dig, as well as your fantastic cuisine. Thank you for being so kind to the multiple generations of my family. Kevin Walsh, I very much appreciate all of the information about the archaeological dig and your important work in the field. Thank you, Melina, for getting us all set up, and Eric for being a man of action. And, after the robbery, we relied on the generosity of Helene Mitchell and her husband, the witty Brit. Thank you. (While I'm at it, I'll thank their dinner guest, Neal, who made a deep and lasting impression on me, giving me a charge that I will spend my life trying to fulfill.) A thankful shout-out to the Trets Police Department! And, yes, Bastien, our occasional extra kid, thank you for the lessons! Jacob Newberry, thank you for the translation help. Frankie Giampietro, how I've come to rely on you and your brilliant mind. Thank you, Florida State University. Margaret Kyle, thank you for your insight into the artistry of pastries—the blur of food and love. Linda Richards, master pastry chef, thank you for allowing me into the world of The Cake Shop, a beautiful place to dream. And I thank those kids in tow, the ones who gave me the child's-eye view—Ph., F., T., O., and Lola. And, as ever, thank you to David. Let me say it again—yes.

Thank you, Nat Sobel. *Il faut d'abord durer!*

And thank you, most of all, Caitlin Alexander, my world-class editor. I am indebted. Thank you for all of the love and care you poured into the making of this book.

If you enjoyed
The Provence Cure for the Brokenhearted,
you won't want to miss any of Bridget Asher's novels.

Read on for excerpts from

The Pretend Wife

"Riveting... charming and insightful." —New York *Post*

"A good choice for a book group... Read *The Pretend Wife* and see
if it doesn't bring back memories of past relationships."
—*The Huntington News*

and

My Husband's Sweethearts

"A gem of a story about love in its various forms... You won't be
able to put it down." —*Newark Star-Ledger*

"An undiluted joy to read... Don't miss this ride."
—JOSHILYN JACKSON, author of *Backseat Saints*

Available now from Bantam Books

The Pretend Wife

CHAPTER ONE

That summer when I first became Elliot Hull's pretend wife,
I understood only vaguely that complicated things often prefer to masquerade as simple things at first. This is why they're
so hard to avoid, or at least brace for. I should have known
this—it was built into my childhood. But I didn't see the
complications of Elliot Hull coming, perhaps because I didn't
want to. So I didn't avoid them or even brace for them, and
as a result, I eventually found myself in winter watching two
grown men—my pretend husband and my real husband—
wrestle on a front lawn amid a spray of golf clubs in the
snow—such a blur of motion in the dim porch light that I
couldn't distinguish one man from the other. This would

become one of the most vaudevillian and poignant moments of my life, when things took the sharpest turn in a long and twisted line of smaller, seemingly simple turns.

Here is the simple beginning: I was standing in line in a crowded ice-cream shop—the whir of a blender, the fogged glass counter, the humidity pouring in from the door with its jangling bell. It was late summer, one of the last hot days of the season. The air-conditioning was rolling down from overhead and I'd paused under one of the cool currents, causing a small hiccup in the line. Peter was off talking to someone from work: Gary, a fellow anesthesiologist—a man in a pink-striped polo shirt, surrounded by his squat children holding ice-cream cones melting into softened napkins. The kids were small enough not to care that they were eating bits of their napkins along with the ice cream. And Gary was too distracted to notice. He was clapping Peter on the back and laughing loudly, which is what people do to Peter. I've never understood why, exactly, except that people genuinely like him. He's disarming, affable. There's something about him, the air of someone who's in the club—what club, I don't know, but he seemed to be the laid-back president of this club, and when you were talking with him, you were in the club too. But my mind was on the kids in that moment— I felt sorry for them, and I decided that one day I'd be the kind of mother not to let her children eat bits of soggy napkin. I don't remember what kind of mother mine was— distracted or hovering or, most likely, both? She died when I was five years old. In some pictures, she's doting on me—

cutting a birthday cake outside, her hair flipping up in the breeze. But in group photos, she's always the one looking off to the side, down in her own lap, or to some distant point beyond the photographer—like an avid bird-watcher. And my father was not a reliable source of information. It pained him, so he rarely talked about her.

I was watching the scene intently—Peter specifically now, because instead of becoming more comfortable with having a husband, after three years I was becoming more surprised by it. Or maybe I was more surprised not that I was his wife but that I was *anybody's* wife, really. The word *wife* was so wifey that it made me squeamish—it made me think of aprons and meat loaf and household cleansers. You'd think the word would have evolved for me by that point—or perhaps it *had* evolved for most people into cell phones and aftercare and therapy, but I was the one who was stuck—like some gilled species unable to breathe up on the mudflats.

Although Peter and I had been together for a total of five years, I felt like I didn't know him at all sometimes. Like at that very moment, as he was being back-clapped and jostled by the guy in the pink-striped polo shirt, I felt as if I'd spotted some rare species called *husband* in its natural habitat. I was wondering what its habits were—eating, chirping, wingspan, mating, life expectancy. It's difficult to explain, but more and more often I'd begun to rear back like this, to witness my life as a *National Geographic* reporter, someone with a British accent who found my life not so much exciting as *curious*.

The ice-cream shop was packed, and the two high school girls on staff were stressed, their faces damp and pinched, bangs sticking to their foreheads, their matching eyeliner gone smeary. I'd finally made my way to the curved counter and placed my order. Soon enough I was holding a cone of pistachio for Peter and waiting for a cup of vanilla frozen yogurt for myself.

That's when the more beleaguered of the two scoopers finished someone else's order and shouted to a customer behind me. "What do you want?"

A man answered. "I'll have two scoops of Gwen Merchant, please."

I spun around, sure I'd misheard, because *I* am Gwen Merchant—or I was before I got married. But there in the line behind me stood a ghost from my past—Elliot Hull. I was instantly overwhelmed by the sight of him—Elliot Hull with his thick dark hair and his beautiful eyebrows, standing there with his hands in his pockets looking tender and boyish. I don't know why, but I felt like I'd been waiting for him, without knowing I'd been waiting for him. And I wasn't so much happy as I was relieved that he'd finally shown up again. Some strange but significant part of me felt like throwing my arms around him, as if he'd come to save me, and saying, *Thank God, you finally showed up! What took you so long? Let's get out of here.*

But I couldn't really have been thinking this. Not way back then. I must be projecting—backward—and there must be a term for this: projecting backward, but I don't know what it is. I couldn't have been thinking that Elliot Hull had come to save me because I didn't even know I needed saving. (And, of course, I'd have to save myself in the end.) The only conclusion I can draw is that maybe he represented some lost part of myself. And I must have realized on some level that it wasn't that I'd been missing only Elliot Hull. I must have been missing the person I'd been when I'd known him—*that* Gwen Merchant—the somewhat goofy, irreverent, seriously un-wifely part—two scoops of *her*.

My Husband's Sweethearts

CHAPTER ONE

Don't Try to Define Love Unless
You Need a Lesson in Futility

Careening past airline counters toward the security check-in,
I'm explaining love and its various forms of failure to Lindsay, my assistant. Amid the hive of travelers—retirees in
Bermuda shorts, cats in carry-on boxes perforated with air
holes, hassled corporate stiffs—I find myself in the middle
of a grand oration on love with a liberal dose of rationaliza-
tions. I've fallen in love with lovable cheats. I've adored the
wrong men for the wrong reasons. I'm culpable. I've suffered
an unruly heart and more than my share of prolonged bouts

of poor judgment. I have lacked some basics in the area of control. For example: I had no control over the fact that I fell in love with Artie Shoreman—a man eighteen years my senior. I had no control over the fact that I am still in love with him even after I found out, in one fell swoop, that he had three affairs during our four-year marriage. Two were lovers he'd had before we got married, but had kept in touch with—held on to, really, like parting gifts from his bachelorhood, living memorabilia. Artie didn't want to call these *affairs* because they were spur-of-the-moment. They weren't *premeditated*. He trotted out terminology like *fling* and *dalliance*. The third affair he called *accidental*.

And I have no control over the fact that I am angry that Artie's gotten so sick—so deathbedish—in the midst of this and that I blame him for his dramatic flair. I have no control over the compulsion I feel to go back home to him right now, bailing out of a speech on convoluted SEC regulations—because my mother has told me in a middle-of-the-night, bad-news phone call that his health is grave. I have no control over the fact that I'm still furious at Artie for being a cheat just when one might, possibly, expect me to soften, at least a little.

I'm telling Lindsay how I left Artie shortly after I found out about the affairs and how that was the right thing to do six months ago. I tell her how all three affairs were revealed at once—like some awful game show.

Lindsay is petite. Her jacket sleeves are always a bit too long for her, as if she's wearing an older sister's hand-medowns that she hasn't quite grown into. She has silky blond hair that swings around like she's trapped in a shampoo commercial, and she wears small glasses that slip down the bridge of a nose so perfect and narrow I'm not sure how she breathes through it. It's as if her nose were designed as an accent piece without regard to function. She knows this whole story, of course. She's nodding along in full agreement. I forge on.

I tell her that this hasn't been so bad, opting for business trip after business trip, a few months hunkered down with one client and then another, every convention opportunity— a life of short-term corporate rentals and hotel rooms. It was supposed to allow me some time and space to get my heart together. The plan was that when I saw Artie again, I'd be ready, but I'm not.

"Love can't be ordered around or even run by a nice-enough democracy," I tell Lindsay. My definition of a democracy consists of polling the only two people I've chosen to confide in—my anxiety-prone office assistant, Lindsay, who at this very moment is clipping along next to me through JFK airport's terminal, and my overwrought mother, who's got me on speed dial.

"Love refuses to barter," I say. "It won't haggle with you like that Turkish man with the fake Gucci bags." My mother insists I get her a fake Gucci bag each time I'm in New York on business; my carry-on is bulging with fake Gucci at this very moment.

"Love isn't logical," I insist. "It's immune to logic." In my case: my husband is a cheater and a liar, therefore I should move on or decide to forgive him, which is an option that I've heard some women actually choose in situations like this.

Lindsay says, "Of course, Lucy. No doubt about it!"

There's something about Lindsay's confident tone that rattles me. She's often overly positive, and sometimes her high-salaried agreement makes me double-think. I try to carry on with the speech. I say, "I have to stick by my mistakes, though, including the ones that I came by naturally through my mother." My mother—the Queen of Poor Judgment in Men. I flash on an image of her in a velour sweat suit, smiling at me with a mix of hopeful pride and pity. "I have to stick by my mistakes because they've made me who I am. And I'm someone that I've come to like—except when I get flustered ordering elaborate side dishes in sushi restaurants, in which case I'm completely overbearing, I know."

"No kidding," Lindsay agrees, a little too quickly.

And now I stop in the middle of the airport—my laptop swinging forward, my little carry-on suitcase wheels coming to a quick halt (I've only packed necessities—Lindsay will ship the rest of my things later). "I'm not ready to see him," I say.

"Artie needs you," my mother had told me during last night's phone call. "He is your husband still, after all. And it's very bad form to leave a dying husband, Lucy."

This was the first time that anyone had said that Artie was going to die—aloud, matter-of-factly. Until that moment it had been serious, surely, but he's still young—only fifty. He comes from a long line of men who died young, but that shouldn't mean anything—not with today's advances in medicine. "He's just being dramatic," I told my mother, trying to return to the old script, the one where we joke about Artie's dire attempts to get me back.

"But what if he isn't just being dramatic?" she said. "You need to be here. Your being away now, well, it's bad karma. You'll come back in your next life as a beetle."

"Since when do you talk about karma?" I asked.

"I'm dating a Buddhist now," my mother said. "Didn't I tell you that?"

Lindsay has grabbed my elbow. "Are you okay?"

"My mother is dating a Buddhist," I tell her, as if explaining how terribly wrong everything is. My eyes have filled with tears. The airport signs overhead go blurry. "Here." I hand her my pocketbook. "I won't be able to find my ID."

She leads me to a set of phones near an elevator and starts digging through my purse. I can't root through it right now. I can't because I know what's stuffed inside—all the little cards that I've pulled from little envelopes stuck in small plastic green forks accompanying the daily deliveries of flowers that Artie's ordered long distance. He's found me no matter what hotel room I'm in or apartment I'm put up in anywhere I happen to be in the continental U.S. (How does he know where I am? Who gives him my itinerary—my mother? I've always suspected her, but have never told her to stop. Secretly, I like Artie to know where I am. Secretly, I need the flowers, even though part of me hates them—and him.)

"I'm glad you kept all of these," Lindsay says. She's been in my hotel rooms. She's seen the flowers that collect until they're all in various stages of wilt. She hands me my license.

"I wish I hadn't kept them. I'm pretty sure it's a sign of weakness," I tell her.

She pulls one out. "I've always wondered," she says, "you know, what he has to say in all of those cards."

Suddenly I don't want to find my way into the line at security with a herd of strangers. The line is long, but still I have plenty of time—too much. In fact, I know I'll be restless on the other side, feel a little caged myself—like one of those cats in the carry-ons. I don't want to be alone. "Go ahead."

"Are you sure?" She raises her thin eyebrows.

I think about it a moment longer. I don't really want to hear Artie's love notes. Part of me is desperate to grab the pocketbook out of her hands, tell her *sorry, changed my mind,* and get in line with everyone else. But another part of me wants her to read these cards, to see if they are as manipulative as I think they are. In fact, I think I need that right now. A little sisterly validation. "Yes," I tell her.

She plucks the note and reads aloud, "Number forty-seven: the way you think every dining room should have a sofa in it for people who want to lie down to digest, but still be part of the witty conversation." She glances at me.

"I like to lie down after I eat—like the Egyptians or something. The dining room sofa just makes good sense."

"Do you have one?"

"Artie bought me one for our first anniversary." I don't want to think of it now, but it's there in my mind—a long antique sofa reupholstered with a fabric of red poppies on a white background and dark wood trim that matches the dining room furniture. We made love on it that first night in the house, the boxy pillows sliding out from under us onto the floor, the aged springs creaking.

She pulls out another one and reads, "Number fifty-two: how the freckles on your chest can be connected to make an approximate constellation of Elvis."

A crew of flight attendants glides by in what seems to be the V formation of migrating geese. A few of Artie's old girlfriends were flight attendants. He made his money opening an Italian restaurant during his late twenties (despite a lack of any real Italian blood in him) and then launching a national chain. He traveled a lot. Flight attendants were plentiful. I watch them swish by in their nylons, the wheels on their suitcases rumbling. My stomach cinches up for a moment. "He actually did that once, connected the freckles, and documented it. We have the photos." I'm waiting for Lindsay's righteous anger to become apparent, but this doesn't seem to be the case. In fact, I notice that she's smiling a little.

She pulls out a third. "Number fifty-five: the way you're afraid that if you forgive your father—once and for all—he might really disappear in some way, even though he's been dead for years."

Lindsay raises her eyebrows at me again.

The Provence Cure for
the Brokenhearted

BRIDGET ASHER

A Reader's Guide

The Provence Cure for the Brokenhearted

Family Dinner

(RECIPES INCLUDED!)

by Bridget Asher

"A poem begins as a lump in the throat; a homesickness or a love-sickness," Robert Frost once wrote. I wanted to explore lovesickness, the kind that's held so dear because it's lost; however, I didn't want to write a novel that felt like an ending. I wanted to write a novel that was about creating a new beginning. That's why *The Provence Cure for the Brokenhearted* is really two love stories told against the backdrop of a house that is famous for its love stories—acts of devotion, miracles of the heart, and cures for brokenness. And because the novel began as a feeling of lovesickness, it was my job to give story to that feeling with language and my own reserve of longing.

One way that I went about this is through the senses—in particular, taste. I wanted to write about food, not solely as food but more as family, culture, history, art, and, perhaps most of all, a measure of vitality. In the novel, Heidi has shut down her senses in order to feel less, to suffer less. When her senses start to return, one of the strongest is her sense of taste. She's in France, after all, where the sense of taste is exalted.

A quick look at the acknowledgments page reveals how much of this novel was inspired by real-life events. (Let me quickly add that my husband is alive and well.) We spent six weeks in France while I researched this novel—with our kids in tow, one of whom was close to Abbot's age and another close to Charlotte's. I saw Paris and then the South of France through their eyes. It was my daughter who coined the phrase "antique graffiti." It was my son who accidentally ran into the Plexiglas in the crypt of Mary Magdalene. There were the small white snails, the warthogs, and the paper globes lit on Bastille Day, bobbing on sticks as the children paraded through the tiny village of Puyloubier. We were also robbed, followed by a torrential downpour, and, yes, there was an injured swallow.

But what's essential to the novel is the pivotal role of food—whether the desserts Heidi made with her mother after her mother's lost summer, or the art of pastries that she can't bring herself to return to, or the meals offered to her by Veronique.

The creation of a meal can begin as one of Frost's poems

and as a novel sometimes does—as *a lump in the throat; a home-sickness or a love-sickness*. And when you turn to a recipe, it's a desire to re-create—a meal, yes, but also a moment, a feeling.

The family house in Provence, so full of lore in the novel, is one that I built in my imagination because I was so enchanted by the house of Elizabeth Dumon. Elizabeth runs a bed and breakfast at Bastide Richeaume, which sits at the base of Monte Sainte Victoire. And it was there, in Elizabeth's dining room, that we were served the meal that becomes pivotal for Heidi in the novel.

After we'd been home from France for a while, I wanted to return to that meal. I emailed Elizabeth, but she couldn't quite bring herself to write down the recipes—the meal exists, I assume, in her head or maybe even as a feeling, something she knows by doing, by heart.

I let it go for a while, convincing myself that it wasn't possible to return to a moment, a feeling, anyway.

But eventually I got restless again. This time, I tracked down Eric Favier, the owner of Chez Pierre, a very well-known French restaurant in Tallahassee, Florida. I'd met Eric a few times and decided to chum up to him while my husband and I were eating at the Cheese and Chocolate Bar inside of Chez Pierre. This entailed eating a lot of cheese and chocolate, which I did (extremely happily) while I cajoled Eric into sharing a few recipes.

A day after my request, the recipes arrived: a tapenade, a Provençal chicken, and russet potatoes. I also decided to try to make something I picked up at Chez Pierre's Cheese and

Chocolate Bar—a balsamic reduction to accompany brie and bread.

Eric is a native French speaker. His English is French-esque. When I received the recipes, there was still some translation work to be done. A *robot coupe*? *Vers* in a bowl? Eric is also a French chef with thirty years in the kitchen, and had left out important details because he expected us to know these things on a gut level. He measures salt by the palm of his hand. He never explains amounts or degrees. Three hundred fifty? That kind of talk is for amateurs. I had to ask Eric for a lot of clarifications.

As the day on which I planned to cook the meal drew near, I mentioned the project to others with nervous anticipation. I told my favorite pastry chef in town, Linda Richards, who owns The Cake Shop, the bakery on which (with Linda's blessing) I based Heidi's shop of the same name. Linda sent in some dessert recipes for me to try.

While picking up my kids, I yammered on about my project with the founder of their school, Betsey Brown. Betsey's mother, it turns out, had a very simple family recipe from her grandmother—chicken in a cream sauce. It seemed appropriate, in honor of the family lore in *The Provence Cure for the Brokenhearted*, to try an easy Provençal recipe with four generations behind it. I added that recipe from her mother, Sara Wilford, to my menu.

I was determined to recapture the atmosphere of our original Provence meal as well. Our house is not equipped with anything close to the Dumon dining room, so I decided we should eat outside. In moments of cooking downtime, my kids helped me haul out a table and chairs, mismatched like those in Heidi's family's house from the novel. My three-year-old filled a vase with flowers. My daughter took pictures.

As we sat to eat, a friend showed up, dropping off one of my sons. She was a caterer who'd had very famous people on her guest lists, including Richard Nixon (who didn't show at the last minute—his daughter went into labor and he and his wife rushed to the hospital instead) and Leona Helmsley (who insisted that my friend tell her how many times she rolled her spanakopita). I asked her to join us. So now we had a small party—my older boys, my daughter, the three-year-old, a good friend, her son, my husband, and our dog, a food-grubbing collie.

The tapenade was just as I remembered it. The truffle oil gave the potatoes a hint of something exotic, one I'd never have been able to put my finger on. The chicken was completely different, but delicious in its own way. Best of all, the tiniest drizzle of Balsamic reduction made the creamy brie pop. The chicken in cream sauce was dreamy. The desserts were amazing. The rosés, so popular in Provence, were cool and lightly fruity. The weather was even Provençal—unusually dry for Florida, breezy and sunny.

Had I re-created the meal that inspired Heidi's pivotal moment in the novel? Not exactly. It was, instead, a strange and wonderful afternoon in my yard with mismatched chairs, the three-year-old feeding his crusts to the collie, the older kids and my friend and Dave and I all talking at once in the dappled shade of our Florida pine.

Still, the act of trying to re-create the moment satisfied something in me. It wasn't the food alone that had created the meal in the first place, and it wasn't the sole thing keeping that moment alive in my mind. Food isn't simply food. It's about slowing down a moment in time, attaching it to smells and tastes, and allowing it to expand. I know that this meal on my lawn—born of longing, lovesickness, homesickness, a lump in the throat—has become a memory that will linger.

In fact what lingers now is the image of all of us in the gloaming, bringing in the dishes, the table, and the mismatched chairs, feeling full and content. The lights came on in the house, and a new kind of commotion kicked in as Dave and the kids started washing dishes. Before locking up for the night, I called in the dog, who'd been nosing lizards in the hurricane flowers, and he came bounding across the lawn.

RECIPES FOR *THE PROVENCE CURE FOR THE BROKENHEARTED* FAMILY DINNER

FROM ERIC GASTON FAVIER, OWNER OF CHEZ PIERRE

OLIVE TAPENADE
Put in your robot coupe (food processor) one bunch of seedless olives from Nice (Picholine). Add pepper, garlic, and a little bit of anchovy paste to your taste. Mix until it becomes a nice spreadable paste.

PROVENÇAL CHICKEN
Cut an organic fresh chicken in eight pieces. (You can also buy these already cut.)

Sauté the pieces in olive oil over medium heat until they are lightly browned all around.

Salt and pepper to taste. Add two diced green peppers and one diced fennel bulb.

Sauté until the vegetables are semi-soft.

Add six whole garlic cloves, fresh thyme, and the zest of two oranges.

Dice ten tomatoes and add them to the pot.

Let simmer on low heat for one hour, until the chicken is cooked through.

At the end, add one glass of red wine. Let it simmer for a few minutes, then cover and let it set until serving.

RUSSET POTATOES WITH TRUFFLE OIL
Dice your potatoes.

Boil them until semi-soft. Drain and sauté in olive oil until light brown.

Add a lot of chopped parsley, a dash of salt, pepper, and a tablespoon of truffle oil, then serve.

BALSAMIC REDUCTION

Quite simply, you first heat up balsamic vinegar until it's boiling, then simmer it until it gets thick, which should happen in an hour. Remember that an 8-ounce bottle of Balsamic vinegar will yield not quite two ounces of reduction. Very little is needed to provide an exquisite counterpoint to the cheese. At Chez Pierre's Cheese and Chocolate Bar, I had the balsamic reduction with a double creamy brie on French bread.

A FOURTH-GENERATION PROVENÇAL RECIPE
FROM SARA WILFORD

PROVENÇAL CHICKEN IN CREAM SAUCE

1½ tablespoons butter
1½ tablespoons olive oil
1 small chicken, cut into eight pieces
16 whole baby onions, peeled
1 cup heavy cream
¼ cup dry white wine
Flour
Salt and pepper
1 teaspoon dried thyme
Chopped fresh parsley

Coat chicken pieces in flour, salt, and pepper.
Heat butter in a heavy, large skillet over medium-high heat, and lightly brown onions. Set onions aside.
Add olive oil to butter.
Add chicken to skillet and cook over medium heat until golden brown on all sides.
Add cream, wine, thyme, and the onions. Cover and simmer until chicken is tender and cooked through, about 30 minutes, turning the pieces once. (Sauce should be slightly thickened by the flour used to coat the chicken.)

Transfer contents of skillet to cocotte or other deep serving dish if desired, sprinkle with parsley and freshly ground pepper, and serve with rice.

DESSERT RECIPES FROM LINDA RICHARDS, OWNER OF THE CAKE SHOP

Linda's Cake Shop cake and icing recipes are top secret, so I couldn't score those. But these are two fantastic dessert recipes that she offered—one very French and one from the heart.

FRENCH APPLE TART WITH CRÈME ANGLAISE
Tart/Pie Dough:
2 cups unbleached flour
1 teaspoon salt
⅔ cup vegetable shortening (cold)
2 tablespoons unsalted butter (cold)
1 tablespoon sugar
4 tablespoons ice water

Mix dry ingredients together, cut the butter and shortening into the dry mixture, add the ice water and stir until the dough just comes together.

On a lightly floured surface, roll the dough to create a 12x14-inch rectangle, transfer the dough to a cookie sheet, arrange the chopped apple mixture in the center of the dough, and fold the edges of the dough over the apples, leaving the center exposed. Bake at 375 degrees for 45–50 minutes.

Apple mixture:
5 lbs. of apples (I use a variety of apples)
1 tablespoon lemon juice plus the zest from 1 lemon
¼ cup light brown sugar
½ cup granulated sugar

1 teaspoon cinnamon
2 tablespoons butter

Peel apples and slice thinly, toss with sugars and lemon juice, zest, and cinnamon. Place the mixture in the dough, dot with butter, and bake.

Crème Anglaise
2 cups milk
5 beaten egg yolks
⅔ cup sugar
⅛ teaspoon salt
1 teaspoon vanilla extract

Scald milk in the top pan of a double boiler, then slowly stir in egg yolks, sugar, and salt. Place the custard on top of the double boiler and stir constantly until the mixture starts to thicken; as the mixture cools, beat to release some steam. Add the vanilla. Serve warm alongside the apple tart.

DESSERT FOR ROMANTICS
This is a favorite that Linda threw in as a romantic. She used it to woo her new beau. I love it because I'm a chocolate fanatic.

Crust:
1½ cups graham cracker crumbs
½ cup toasted pecans
½ cup chocolate chips
6 tablespoons melted butter
¼ cup brown sugar
¼ cup sugar

Combine all ingredients in a food processor and pulse until mixed. Press ingredients into a springform pan and bake at 350 degrees for 15 minutes.

Filling:

8 ounces cream cheese, room temperature
¼ cup sugar
1 teaspoon vanilla
1 cup semi-sweet chocolate chips, melted
¼ cup heavy cream

Combine all ingredients in the food processor and mix until smooth. Add mixture to cooled crust and refrigerate until set.

Optional: Place fresh strawberries or other berries on top and/or drizzle with white chocolate.

To further your *Provence Cure for the Brokenhearted* experience, explore these websites:

Bastide Richeaume
http://www.bastidedericheaume.com

Puyloubier
http://www.puyloubier.com

Pavillon Monceau Palais des Congrès
http://www.pavillon-monceau-etoile.com

The Cake Shop
http://tallycakeshop.com

Chez Pierre
http://www.chezpierre.com

For more recipes, blog posts, and other
odds and ends, visit Bridget at
www.bridgetasher.com

Questions and Topics for Discussion

1. Heidi's mother believes strongly that the house in Provence has magical qualities that help people make decisions and see their lives clearly. Have you ever heard stories about an object or place similar to the love stories that Heidi's mother tells her and Elysius when they're growing up? Do you believe that a place can heal?

2. One of the first lines of the book is, "Every good love story has another love hiding within it." What do you think the author means by that? Do you agree?

3. Discuss Abbot's obsessive compulsiveness. In what ways does he use his tics as a coping mechanism? In what ways do

you think they hold him back? Have you ever experienced similar symptoms brought on by a trauma or loss?

4. During the summer, Charlotte is supposed to be studying SAT vocabulary words, and Abbot is reliant on his father's dictionary. What is significant about language and vocabulary for this family? What do you think it means that their books are stolen at the beginning of the trip?

5. Veronique tells Heidi that it was only because of the fire that the archaeological team was able to set up near the property, saying that tragedy allowed them to dig into the past. In what ways is that true for Heidi? For Julien? For Heidi's mother and Veronique?

6. Heidi and Elysius are sisters, but approach nearly every situation differently. Why do you think that is? Based on their lives as adults, what would you say were the primary repercussions of their father's affair and their mother's lost summer?

7. Why do you think Charlotte is so drawn to Veronique and to her kitchen?

8. Heidi has a complicated relationship with food and cooking—she's a professional baker, yet after Henry's death she can't bring herself to go near a kitchen. Why does it take that side of her so long to reemerge? Discuss some

key food scenes and why they are important to Heidi's summer.

9. Discuss the injured swallow, and the ways in which it serves as a breakthrough in Heidi and Abbot's grieving process. How does Abbot use the bird to think about his father? Why do you think the author chose a swallow to explore this theme?

10. Charlotte tells Heidi that when she prays, she thinks of herself as one of the Flying Wallendas and asks for a good net. What does that come to mean to Heidi? What do you think the concept of a safety net means to other characters in the book?

11. Heidi tells Charlotte that there are many different kinds of love. In what ways does that apply to Heidi's life? How is she able to reconcile her love for Julien with her love for Henry?

12. What do you think the future holds for Charlotte and Adam? What about for their daughter, Pearl?

About the Author

BRIDGET ASHER is the author of *My Husband's Sweethearts* and *The Pretend Wife*. She lives on the Florida panhandle but is always happy to do research in Provence.